Thank you for
your service, dedi-
and sacrifice.
Hope you enjoy
the following pages!
with warm regards,
pejman

THE AGE OF INTOLERANCE
A Story of Power, Struggle, and Human Sacrifice

Peyman Pejman

Raider Publishing International

New York London Johannesburg

First Printing

The views, content and descriptions in this book do not represent the views of Raider Publishing International. Some of the content may be offensive to some readers and they are to be advised. Objections to the content in this book should be directed towards the author and owner of the intellectual property rights as registered with their local government.

All characters portrayed in this book are fictitious and any resemblance to persons living or dead is purely coincidental.

Cover images courtesy of istockphoto.com

ISBN: 978-1-61667-056-6

Published By Raider Publishing International
www.RaiderPublishing.com
New York London Johannesburg
Printed in the United States of America and the United Kingdom

To the memory of Maria

ACKNOWLEDGEMENTS

As a first time "novelist", I am rather queasy about naming people whose only fault has been to lend moral and expertise support for a project that may ultimately receive the approval of only a handful of people. Having said that, I also feel duty bound to name a few people without whom you would not be reading the following pages.

First and foremost I owe an incredible debt of gratitude to David Ignatius of the *Washington Post* and Thomas Friedman of the *New York Times*. I could not bother either one with the arduous task of reading the manuscript for this book so if there is *any* criticism of this book, I am the one to blame. But David and Tom could not have been more generous in offering encouragement and advice. Without their support and encouragement, I would not have dared to pen the following pages.

I am also very grateful to the Institute for Science and International Security in Washington whose experts were invaluable in setting me on the right track when I was desperately looking for the "right plot" for the book.

Bruce and Jennifer McCoy where there when I needed help most. Without their keen and deliberate eyes and sharp minds, there would have been far more mistakes in this book than I care to admit. They have my eternal thanks, not just for their help with this book but also for their valuable friendship. Thank you!

Last but not least, I would not be where I am in life were it not for Elaine Carey and Vincent Schodolski. They know what they mean to me and I doubt there are words adequate enough to express my gratitude.

THE AGE OF INTOLERANCE
A Story of Power, Struggle, and Human Sacrifice

Peyman Pejman

CHAPTER 1

THE year was 2020. It was a cold November day, 2,000 feet up, on a snow-capped mountain in Kurdistan. The sub-zero air was dry and piercing, but refreshing, both for the solitude it offered and for the panoramic view that put matters into perspective.

It was not every day that someone could take refuge in such a place.

Kurdistan had beautiful and notoriously rugged mountains: Ararat, Zagros, Mt. Alvand, Mt. Halgurd, Mt. Munzur – to name a few – some poking the skies at over 10,000 feet. Traversing the elevations could be treacherous, especially with six to seven feet of snow decorating the ranges.

The mountains meant a lot to the Kurds. It was part of their arsenal to fight off one empire and dynasty after another. If it was not the Sumerians, it was the Assyrians. If it was not the Assyrians, it was Persians.

From his vintage point, Charles Shahin appreciated his rare and enviable fortune. In his fifties, his silver-white hair meshed in well with the white snow. The mountain height was a symbolic match for his long experience in this troubled Middle East, and the fire below rivalled the depth of his own inner rage.

The area below was once a pretty part of the

Kurdistan. People farmed what they could. Others used parts of it to graze sheep and cattle. Closer to the mountain base, cafes served as retreats for young, newly-weds, or even entire families escaping the hustle and bustle of city life.

But that was all in the past. In recent years, there had been severe fighting around the mountain ranges for as far as the eye could see. Mortar rounds were fired from nearby peaks. Snipers had set up positions at every height they could. Ammunition storages were carved into the stony hills. Zigzagging roads around the mountains were darted with shells. The closer one got to the bottom of the hills, the more intense the fighting had become. A few miles down the road, farmlands were set on fire, houses demolished, residents forced to evacuate centuries-old, well-trenched family bastions. Chemical warfare was no more a rare novelty in the twenty-first-century armed conflicts.

Hundreds of thousands of Kurds had lost their lives in recent years alone – millions, if you counted back a few decades – testimony to one of the worst ethnic-cleansing atrocities committed in the Middle East. Even by the blood-stained records of the region, the recent years had been brutal and indiscriminate.

However, the Kurds were not an easy bunch to get rid of. They had been down this road far too many times. It was not long ago that the Kurds had finally celebrated their independence. Some seventy million Kurds had jammed the streets of the country, all one hundred-odd thousand square miles of it, the day they became a country of their own.

For far too many years, the Kurds had wanted Kurdish areas of neighbouring Iran, Iraq, Syria, and Turkey to become part of the independent Kurdistan. And for as many years, the neighbours had said 'no'. 'You want your country,' they told the Kurds, 'you fight us for it. Shed

2

some blood, and let us shed much more of yours. Why? Because this is the Middle East; it is a rough neighborhood. And we do it our way.' And the Kurds had dutifully answered that call. They had not regained all the territory they wanted, but had settled for more than half. But then, the Kurds were not dumb, either. They had lived in this neighborhood for as long as anyone else had. They knew how to play the game like everyone else.

The day the Independent Republic of Kurdistan celebrated its formation ten years ago, tears were running down everyone's face, and that included President Hoshyar Kurdawani.

Kurdawani was a true sweetheart. Everyone loved him, Kurd or no Kurd. A bit chubby, he was always clean-shaven, always had a warm smile, and a warmer heart. He knew the lay of the land. He had carried the gun when he had to. He had shot enemies when he had to. Had had fought the wars, but he also played the politics of it well. He was a charmer, and one of the most competent Kurdish politicians.

Kurdawani was a proud nationalist. He had been born in what was formerly Iraqi Kurdistan. His family had been living there for generations. The only time he had not lived in his homeland, was when he and his family had escaped to neighbouring Iran. The past was not pretty. The 'Butcher of Baghdad', as the then-Iraqi ruler was called not so affectionately, had an axe to grind against the Kurds. Whatever number he could not kill, he forced into exile. Or the survivors were wise enough to pack their bags before they ran out of options.

Through the confusing maze of Middle East politics, Kurdawani had led his nation to independence, and easily won the first election, and every one after that, which was a difference in itself. Leaders in the rest of the region

3

just forged ballot numbers, or did not bother holding elections to begin with. Not Kurdawani. He was genuinely popular. People loved him, and he worked hard for them.

However, in the ever-turbulent Middle East, the Kurdish president could only speak for his own people, could only protect his own people from each other, or maybe from smaller and weaker enemies outside, as he and his pre-independence predecessors had done for centuries.

What he could not do – no one could – was foresee, let alone counter, the bulldozing fire that had swept this region away during the past few years. Once again, his nation was paying for the mistakes of others. Many Kurds had started migrating to the very same countries they had come back from years ago: France, UK, and Germany.

Charlie was not alone in reminiscing from the mountaintops of Kurdistan that November day. Kurdawani was sitting next to him. Charlie did not know whether to smile or cry, or – like millions of others – just be baffled by the turn of events.

Not everything had been bad or sad in the Kurds' recent history. They could not be happier about the choice of their controversial capital. They had chosen Kirkuk primarily for its symbolic value. The 'Butcher of Baghdad' had ethnically 'cleansed' Kirkuk from its Kurdish population decades earlier. Families would just wake up one morning and find the tremors of a bulldozer trying to bring down the roof over their head. Some had gone out for daily chores and come back only to discover their homes gone. Maybe they were bulldozed, too. Maybe the structure had just been dynamited. Or maybe – if the occupants had resisted – the secret police had rounded them up and taken them to a maximum-security facility or a torture house, and they were never heard from again. That was the policy in those days. Kick out the Kurds and force

4

some poor Arab family to migrate to a city they didn't know, to a place in which they knew no one. They were just as unhappy being there as the poor Kurdish family leaving it. But, then again, that was the politics of the Middle East. Always was.

However, the 'Butcher' was not what occupied Kurdawani's mind these days. He was gone. Long gone. Today's kids mostly did not even know the 'Butcher's' name. His pictures were torn out of school books, just like Hitler's pictures are hard to come by in a German textbook nowadays. Any memory or mention of the 'Butcher' had been 'purged' from official memory. It was as if he never existed. Only, he had. And people old enough – like Kurdawani – could remember him well, as if it had been just yesterday.

No, the 'Butcher' was not Kurdawani's problem. The neighbours were. And they were not the

same as fifty years ago, or even twenty years ago. Remnants of fires and napalm spots that Charlie and Kurdawani could see from their -20°F mountain retreat were just the latest evidence of brutality in the region.

* * *

Sitting on top of the mountain ranges in Kurdistan, Charlie could not help but notice how the Middle East had moved in a path of destruction in the past decades. The conflict in the Middle East in recent years had emanated from decades of energised and fierce competition between the world's main religions: Christianity, Judaism, and Islam. In each part of the world – east and west – countries had made it their policy not only to propagate their own religion, but also to undermine the others. At times, the leaders were blunt about their desire for religious

5

superiority. They were not ashamed of bragging about their faith, but more often than not, it was a lot more subtle. Influential forces with government connections 'encouraged' and 'lobbied' their government to take the interests of their religion in mind, and to keep in mind that the 'other side' believed in a doctrine that called for 'death' and 'annihilation' of its religious rivals. Each side had plenty of examples to cite by way of condemning the other side. Indeed, there was plenty of blame to go around on all sides. Governments, and even people, did not want to talk about it, but religion had its fingerprints on many of the conflicts in the Middle East.

The Middle East – or the Orient, historically speaking – was never 'really' calm for too long. The best one could hope for was lack of war, not real peace. People had their differences. Countries played power games with each other. They invaded each other's territories. They tried to rob each other of the limited resources left in the region. Wars devastated countries. People died. But life, for the rulers, moved on. They survived, even got stronger. The Middle East has moved on like this for thousands of years. Then, suddenly, the region's political temperature had risen continuously. Inevitably, there were wars. Evangelical Christians and radical Islamists had taken matters into their own hands, because the established religions were perceived as not thinking 'outside the box,' and not realising, and acting upon, the global changes that needed to be acted upon, geopolitical realities to which the leadership of the faithful had to respond. Much of the push for change in the Middle East had come from the West – equivalent to the New Calvinists – and the argument usually went like something like this:

The Middle East was, perhaps, the most troubled part of the world. Ever since the 1970s, when the oil cartel

6

was created, a handful of 'desert shepherds' had catapulted themselves onto the world stage. However, they were inept, and made the 'black gold' their curse, not their blessing. In the course of a few short decades, they had made billions upon billions, but where did the money go? Yes, they had built highways and skyscrapers for their people. Yes, they had imported fancy cars. And, yes, indeed, they had built themselves ostentatious palaces.

But the rulers had also been of massive disservice, both to their own people and the world at large. After all, for years and years, when people heard the name 'Middle East', they – rightly or wrongly – projected a certain image, and some of those perceptions were not far off from reality. Generally speaking, were they not a male-chauvinistic society that had ignored half of their population? Were they not a resources-rich area of the world that had done more to enrich a tiny portion of their society than spread the wealth? Was it not an autocratic part of the world in which the secret service could show up in your bedroom in the middle of the night, and you'd never be heard from again? Was it not a part of the world that made India's cast system and South Africa's former racial segregation system proud? Anyone who has lived in any of the Gulf countries would testify that many people in the Gulf – maybe even the majority – deep down, thought of Asians as the inferior ones: the ones who chauffeured them around, the ones who opened the doors to them at restaurants and shopping malls, the ones who cooked their meals, did their laundry, and washed the dishes at home. They might not speak it, but get under their skin, and there is little of this that would not hold true.

However, there was more than local incompetence that the New Calvinists had objections to. They argued that increasing birth rates in the Muslim world – as opposed to

7

the declining one in the West – and poverty and hopelessness in the region had alienated so many of the local population. Violence had landed on the streets of Washington, New York, Los Angeles, London, Paris, and Madrid, and the gloves were off. Plus, it was not just about politics. Simply put, the New Calvinists argued, their way of life was in danger, and they knew whom to blame.

However, as usual, there were two sides to the coin. The Muslims, too, had got energised. They, too, had grievances. They could point to centuries of being dominated, ruled, invaded, and their resources squandered while their population grew dangerously high, poverty levels rose beyond control, and their once-rich countries' debt to the West skyrocketed. Future generations were just going to grow up poor and in debt. They could – and did – blame their leaders, and had little trust in them. Power corrupts, and much of the Middle East had access to oil, and the security forces ensured the rulers were not going anywhere. The people blamed their leaders, but they blamed the West much more.

Both sides, East and West, toughened their stance. Both sides had arms. Both sides had pride in their way of life and in their beliefs. And, unfortunately, both sides were willing to use their destructive powers to defend themselves.

However, starting a couple of decades ago, salvation had come to the region; in two countries, the forces of 'retribution' were hard at work. In the heart of the Muslim world, in the power houses of Islam's two main factions – Shiites and Sunnis – overt and covert forces were in action to right the wrongs of the past and take revenge on the 'infidels'. They were going to use their money, power, brainpower and access to bring the 'invading crusaders' and 'traitor infidels' to their knees. Both sides, East and West,

8

had managed to create havoc in the world, but now the dust had settled, and Charlie was sitting on the mountain tops witnessing the carnage and death.

CHAPTER 2

IN the best of days, Tehran was a noisy, polluted city – made uglier in recent years by the politics of it. The city had changed drastically over the past half century or so. Once – many, many years ago – it had actually been a fairly liveable place. There were parks; streets were clean; garbage was picked up on time; streets were not packed with cars; the air was clean. Up in the north, you could go mountain climbing, camping, or biking. The city had a cosmopolitan look to it. Whether in the poor section or the affluent parts, you could walk down any street, and walk into bars and restaurants, and order a beer, or a scotch, or whatever. There were nightclubs. Singers and dancers were in hot demand. Boys and girls could hold hands. They could kiss in public. They could listen to music; they could dance. They could be happy – without being afraid. There was diversity, but no group imposed itself on others. Everyone managed to live fairly harmoniously.

Of course, back then, leaders kept their people quiet in other ways. They created cities in various corners of the country, and gave them to different 'ethnicities'. Some were 'Christian' cities; others were 'Kurdish' cities, Arabs, Turks, *etcetera*. That way, they not only kept different groups away from the capital, they also kept them separate from each other. The less they interacted with each other, the less the chance that they could secretly gang up against the central government.

These days, the capital was different. The whole country was different. First off, the city was much bigger than it used to be. The country's population was now a whopping one hundred and twenty million people, and half of them were in the capital. The country's population had boomed much faster than expected. It should have been a hundred million by now, but faulty government policies had practically led to a doubling of the population growth, which had been about one point five percent for many years. However, the geographical cosmetics were not the only issues. Something fundamental had changed, something that had had great impact on the region.

Tehran was no longer the name of the country's capital. The new name was 'Qous' – meaning 'Arc'. The renaming was the beginning of a master political strategy that had divided the region and shaped its politics. For centuries, the Iranians had boasted that they were not 'Arabs,' that they were 'Persians'. Roaming the streets of the capital these days, it was hard to decipher an 'identity' for the place. It did not give an 'aura' of representing one country, one nation, one people.

And the sad part was that it had not happened by accident.

11

CHAPTER 3

THE Iranians and the Kurds understood each other better than the rest of the region understood either one of them. They were both 'ethnic minorities' in a part of the world that prided itself on having one identity based on one religion: Islam. The Middle East was the cradle of Islam, one of the world's primary religions. It was there, tradition had it, that God chose Mohammed to be his messenger, and revealed the Koran, Muslims' holy book, to him. From there, the prophet went on to create a religious empire for his people that, at one point, extended all the way to Spain. However, the empire did not last – in part because of the differences within Islam's two main sects – Shiites and Sunnis. There have been many historical and psychological arguments – some rational, some not – over why it did not last longer. Certainly, the differences between the Sunnis and Shiites, not to mention other sects and branches, had something to do with it, but it has also been argued – much to the chagrin of many Muslims – that the empire collapsed because the Muslim 'greatness' came to an end much, much sooner than the faithful would have liked. Many have claimed that the Muslim world as a whole has still not grappled with the loss of its well-deserved place many millennia ago. It was not just the territory that made the Islamic empire great. It was not just the question of how much land the faithful controlled. It was intellectual. It was arts. It was science. And it lasted a good many years. And then – it was gone!

For the past fifty years or so, many credible thinkers have said the Arab world needs two things, two things it has steadfastly ignored, if not downright refused: reconciliation within the religion, and, much more importantly, the equivalent of a Protestant reformation.

By 2020, there were over three billion Muslims residing in well over a hundred countries around the world. That was a third of the world population. In the land of the world's sole remaining superpower, the United States of America, Islam had become the fastest-growing religion. Just a couple of decades ago, the people of America had voted for the first Muslim member of Congress. It was not a small affair, and did not go unnoticed. At least one member of the legislative body was outspoken – and brazen – enough to come out publicly, warning that if the Muslim power in the government grew, it would pose a national security issue. "Don't let them into the system," he pleaded, "or they will change the Judeo-Christian 'culture' and country's values."

"What Judeo-Christian threat?" yelled some of the Jewish members of Congress. "You cannot zero in on any group! You zero in on the Muslims, and someone will zero in on us. This is not the survival of the fittest. We've been through the Holocaust. We don't need this kind of finger pointing."

Maybe not, but the point was made, anyway!

For centuries, the Muslim world had got itself bogged down in internal fights. Would the Sunnis win this fight, or the Shiites win that battle? Would the Druze triumph with this sect, or would the Wahabis manage to conquer that land? Would the 'moderates' succeed in

13

'neutralising' the 'hardliners'? But they had forgotten the bigger questions: Why had they once been so great, and were now so miserably impotent? What did they lack? Why were they so beholden to the very powers, kings, queens, and presidents who showed so little love for their own people? Was the Middle East so weak because it was so divided?

No one understood that better than the Iranians. Their history had seen good times and bad times. There was a time the Persian Empire's borders had reached close to Rome in one corner and India at another. The empire was known for a vast number of things, from arts and culture to architecture and carpets weaving. The empire brought to the fore leaders such as Cyrus the Great or Darius. The inheritors of the empire, the Iranians, would tell you that their history and civilisation goes back some five to seven thousand years. Then came the seventh century, and the invasion of Muslim crusaders brought the Persian Empire under Islam's reign, and changed its secular character.

The role of religion in ancient and temporary Persian Empire dynasties had been a controversial one. Until recently, there had been much tension and apprehension between Persians and the Arab states of the Mediterranean. The Persians emphasised their secular, non-Arab traditions and values. They did not mind that they were Muslim, but did not want the world to forget that their empire and dynasties had also historically been refuge to all sorts of other religions and sects, from the Jews to the Zoroastrians.

The beginning of the end for the Persians' secularist ambitions came less than a hundred years ago, when a group of Islamist firebrands took over the country. They had not just come to form yet another government. They had a different agenda. This was a purge. This was a massacre of history, tradition, memories, textbooks, and even people.

Every new regime cleans out remnants of the last one, abolishes some of the laws, changes foreign policy, alters economic priorities, and maybe even puts some of the old guard behind bars.

This one was different.

The new owners of the land went far beyond the norm. It was not just that textbooks were rewritten. It was not just that the calendar was now based on Islamic history. These people were smart. These people had not come to power just to change national policies. They wanted to change the national identity, and then go regional. They had international plans, plans that changed the course of history in the most troubled region of the world.

CHAPTER 4

Circa 2010

SADEGHE (Sade) Zaviesaz was an average girl in most ways, extraordinary in a few. She was mid-height, with black hair. She had small, brown eyes, but don't let the size fool you. Look deeper, and you could find them very piercing. There was a sense of curiosity about her that always baffled people. She was born to a middle class family in Tehran. Her mother was just like her: witty, educated, calculating, and philosophical. In fact, many people who knew Sade always believed that she had taken many of her attributes from her mother. When her mother was young, she was forced by forces of nature to become the real bread-winner of the family. Her father was chronically sick. A good man, but physically very weak. He had always worked in the private sector, held odd jobs here and there, but never made it rich, or even well off. The family – as most those days – was traditional. That meant the mother – Sade's grandmother – never worked. She was the homemaker, and happy with it. Sade's mother had a brother, but he was much younger and not of working age. No one in the family would let him work, anyway. They were not economically well off, but they well made up for it in pride and principles.

Sade's mother was everything her grandmother was not. She worked. In fact, she had worked from the age of eighteen, when she entered university. She worked throughout university, and then got a job in a prominent government ministry. Even when she had worked enough years to retire from her day job, she took the retirement package and got a job somewhere else. Also unlike her mother, Sade's mother did not marry someone the family had ordained. She had found the guy himself.

She had gone to a state university, but could only take afternoon and night classes, because she was working during the day. She was a serious student in her own ranks, and enjoyed her field of study: political science. Between work, studies and the worries of life, there was hardly any time left for fun, socialising, or dating.

The day Sade's mother got married, she had one wish and one promise to make to herself: She wished to have a girl, and promised herself that her daughter would have everything she had and did not. You see, Sade's mother knew one thing too well, despite her modesty: She was far more intelligent than people around gave her credit for. She knew − instinctively − that her daughter, too, would possess superb intellectual power, and she had promised herself that she would make sure one of the women in the family would make a noticeable difference in the world.

Sade might have received all the attention she could handle at home, but did not get any preferential treatment in the outside world. She went to a public school, not private school. Her family did not have to worry about her college tuition. She got scholarships year after year. She liked poetry, was into photography, had taught herself how to write software, and knew how to design Internet pages. But most of all, she had become − in defiance of the tradition − a

17

chain-smoking woman in love with politics and philosophy. She would read whatever she could get her hands on, in print or on the Internet. Nothing was a barrier. If she needed to stay up night after night, so be it. If she did not understand the language, she would learn it, or at least buy the best dictionary money could buy, and translate the text word for word. She was often a visitor to Internet political chat rooms. She would pose questions and argue fiercely over issues:

'Who decides the balance of international power?'

'Where do governments really get their power?'

'Is a country's political destiny pre-determined?'

'Is international political power really predetermined by your monetary resources and geopolitical status?'

'Which countries have risen to power despite all odds, and what does that say in terms of the ambition of other nations?'

'What type of strategies did they rely on to get to where they wanted?'

'Which type of might is more important: financial, military, or industrial?'

She would go on and on and on!

However, it was not just politics she was interested in. Science, tourism, liberal arts; you name it. She had studied the geography of most world capitals, their populations, the airports, their public transportation systems, things that a 'normal' person would simply find no reason to do. After all, what high school girl would have collected one of the largest collections of American, French and German movies?

It was not uncommon for her to be skipping days of school, only to have locked herself in her room at home to finish a paper on a topic that no one had assigned her. Her mother might have graduated in political science, but the daughter was the one with the real blood for it.

By the time Sade finished high school, she had a good idea she wanted to leave the country to pursue political studies overseas. It was not that she was not interested in her own country's politics. On the contrary, she was a pure nationalist. However, she knew she could not get the skills she needed by staying. She wanted to go overseas to get the best education and political skills, one could have, not just theoretical but hands on – and then come back and change her country. There was, of course, one problem, a big problem: she was a woman. In a land where theocracy had overturned secularism, and there was no sign that those in power were about to go anywhere. The question remained in the minds of people around her: say you got the best education and skills, and you are the most ambitious and determined person in the world, would anyone take you seriously at the end? She thought so. She defiantly believed so. And that's all that mattered. Nothing or no one was going to stop her. With her family's blessing, she packed her bags – but did not go too far.

CHAPTER 5

THE next stop was the emirate of Dubai, barely a couple of hours of flight time from the hustle and bustle of Tehran.

Dubai was a city like no other in the Middle East. It showed the paradoxes of what life had been like for so many years in the Middle East, and how it had changed over time. The modernity impressed Sade. This was the type of place she wanted to go back and build for her people. Years later, she showed a friend what she had written in her diary when she first arrived in Dubai.

'In many ways, airports and the environment immediately outside say a lot about what you expect from a country. You get to New York's JFK, and you immediately get a sense that it represents the American business mentality: everyone seems to be in a hurry. You get to Frankfurt, and you sense that organisation is the message being exuded. You go to Washington, and it smells government.

'But you come to Dubai, and it is really a mixed message, and it is hard to tell if they mean to send that mixed message, or if it is being sent to you because of a lack of direction. The second the plane taxis off, the overwhelming construction that can be seen from the plane windows speaks of monumental development and modernisation. Yet another leap into the future. Inside, the terminals tell a story of opulence – thank you, petrodollars – and a serious love affair with anything mega-size. Just walking from the terminal entrance to the exit door would suffice as daily exercise. Then the contrast starts. On one hand, there is the local dress – men wearing long, white dresses called *kandoorah*, and women wearing ankle-length black robes known as *abaya*. Verses from the Muslim Holy Book of Koran are prominently displayed on various locations throughout the facility – all signs of respect for tradition and sticking to one's own values. Just a few steps out the terminal, the contrast gets even bigger. There are many more Indian, Pakistani, Sri Lankan, Bangladeshi and other Asians than there are local Emiratis. Is this Asia? Is this the Middle East? Is this a rich-oil country? Is this a poor-man's refuge? What is this? What is it trying to tell me?'

She was right. This was not one country. This was a true amalgam of nationalities, cultures, and religions.

Regardless of what message the city meant to send, its impact on the still-impressionable Sade was irrefutable. Up until her arrival in Dubai, the socio-economic system she knew was one that basically said the following: if you are an average citizen, your destiny is shaped by what your family's status in society is. And your society, generally speaking, rather restricts, you based on norms and traditions dictated to it by its overall form of government. In the long and ongoing debate about whether culture is a static set of norms and values or a revolving door defined by the changing attitudes of the very same individuals who make up the society, most Middle Eastern countries chose the static form – unfortunately.

What had the most impact on Sade was not Dubai's glitz or opulence, or even the mixture of ethnicities and tolerance of others – within limits and certain boundaries. It was the subliminal message that caught her attention, and became her inspiration. It was the message beneath the message. It was the message you only got if you really wanted to read between the lines. Perhaps most importantly, it was a message you got if you thought of strategic geopolitics, something that was very much on the mind of the young female leader-to-be.

Where was Dubai, say, fifty years ago? Where is it today? Where will it be tomorrow? Much, much more importantly, what has it really achieved so far, and what lessons could be learnt for the future? Out of the desert, this cosmopolitan city-state had turned itself into the Hong Kong of the Middle East. In fact, there were several similarities between the Hong Kong of the Asia and Hong Kong of the Middle East. They were both the most developed city-states in their part of the world. They could both boast to be the most free and most liberal in their part of the world. They were both living in a part of the world that could be described as politically unstable or superficially stable. They were both fragile, but had managed to maintain control.

What was it that gave the UAE – of which Dubai was a part – the leverage that almost no other country in the Middle East had? What was the one – if there was only one – trump card that the tiny emirate had over not just other countries in the region, but also over Washington and London?

Sade was determined to get the answers, but did not know how. She was young, and knew no one in a position of power or authority or influence to give her the 'inside scoop' on politics.

One day after school, she went to a nearby mall to kill time. Malls were not just malls for the people in the

22

Gulf. People did not go the malls to just shop. In fact, most of the time, people did not even buy. Going to the malls was not about shopping; it was about escaping the confines of traditional society. Like any other region of the world, there is no such a thing as a monolithic Middle East. No such a thing as 'one' Arab world. As luck has it, there are actually *two* Arab worlds, *two* Middle Easts. First, there are old-civilisation countries like Egypt. Big. Over populated. Poor. The struggling ones, like Lebanon, were tossed around from the Ottoman Empire to the French, to a near-uncertain future of anarchy. Then, there were a few Gulf states that were blessed with oil, the Black Gold. Or, at least, they thought they were blessed. It has been argued many times that oil actually made many of those countries lazier, more incompetent, and more contemptuous of others. However, rich or poor, social traditions did not change much, especially in the Gulf countries where the separation of sexes in public (or at many homes) remained as solid today as it was fifty or a hundred years ago. Okay, people have jobs and can talk to their colleagues of the opposite sex at work, but as soon as work is over, everyone drives home. Maybe that's okay for the older generation, but the younger generation was suffering, and needed a way out before the pressure got to the boiling point and caused real social unrest.

So leaders in those countries adopted a new social policy built around malls. They would not admit that was their intent, but now boys and girls could go to malls to hang out with their friends, go to movies if that struck their fancy, or sit around coffee shops and eyeball potential dates. Simply put, shopping malls offered the opportunity to millions of younger people in the Arab world to escape their otherwise-restricted home-based social life and join the Global Village –while still claiming to adhere to their old values and traditions. They could have their cake and eat it, too!

Sitting at one of the coffee shops one day, Sade marvelled at how different socialising patterns were in the Middle East, compared to the West. She noticed how a bunch of local girls sitting together would only talk to each other – even if there was another girl sitting alone nearby. However, if there was a bunch of local guys talking to each other and they noticed a girl sitting by herself – especially if the girl was not a local – the guys would probably try to strike a conversation, and take their chances.

It was not so much that she needed 'friends' – although, being new to the city, she obviously wanted company. More importantly, she 'needed' to really get to know the locals if she was to succeed in her mission. Exploring her options, she realised she had two. Who would be more useful for her mission to get to really know Dubai's inner political thinking? Who could help turn her stay in Dubai into an extended course in *realpolitik*? Naturally, it would be easier for her to befriend the girls, but women in the Middle East were generally shunned out of politics, or even family business. They still did not fully know what their husbands – or even their sons – did from the time they left home to the time they returned. Men were just supposed to go out and make a nice living for the family. Finding female friends would quickly get her into locals' homes, but would it get her any closer to how the business and politics worked? Probably not, she thought. If she tried to befriend the boys, she would get to know what she wanted faster, but she'd probably have to sleep with them. Men in the Arab world were great at playing the sex double standard. Their sisters and mothers were not allowed to have male friends, but they themselves were free to befriend any Arab or non-Arab woman and have affairs

24

of their own. It was one of those taboo issues that no one talked about, but everyone acknowledged – including the women themselves.

She decided she would take the riskier road. No pain, no gain.

CHAPTER 6

JAMAL 'Johnny' Mohammed never really had to do much to prove himself when he was growing up. Born to a local family, he was the older of the two children. His sister, younger by three years, was always the apple of his parents' eyes. She was also the smarter of the two. She did better at school. She had better friends. She was just a more normal and successful person than her brother. However, that did not matter. Jamal's father was a Bedouin from one of the emirates north of Dubai. He was half literate, at best. His command of his native language was not good enough to even write one page of anything without making numerous grammatical mistakes. What Jamal's father lacked in education, however, he made up for in ambition. When he was growing up, the father was brought up as a gofer-boy in the household of the local emir. As is customary, he was not the only boy running around doing whatever he was told. Emirs in that part of the world always had lots of gofers and assistants. That was both good and bad. On one hand, it offered a lot people the opportunity to prove themselves to their leaders, be noticed, and be given the chance to play much more important roles in their society and country when they grew up. On the other hand, it also encouraged a culture of obedience and cult. Year in and year out, people would run around one single man, do his bidding, adore his personality and contributions – perceived or real – without having a chance to look outside the glass house. Did they ever ask 'is this guy as good as he says he is?' Probably not! They did not know better. The leader was all they knew.

Maybe Jamal's father had not thought about those philosophical points when he was growing up, but he was smart enough to know that he had to distinguish himself to survive and thrive.

He did that in an exemplary fashion. Over time, he showed a knack for making money. He started by taking care of small business matters for the emir. Buy goods here, sell them there. Import a few things, and sell them for profit. Open a small business in town. Things like that. The emir finally noticed, and gave him the biggest chance of his life. He sent Jamal's father to Hong Kong to be his personal 'money manager'. Armed with $100 million, Jamal's father set sail for the uncharted territory. He showed his talent brilliantly. Within a decade, the emir's fortune had grown to just over $1 billion. Jamal's father was handsomely rewarded, and he managed to make plenty of money for himself. Not long after, Jamal's father was worth as much as the emir.

Given that background, it is fair to say that 'Johnny' was born with a silver spoon in his mouth. Instead of a kindergarten close to home and the loving supervision of his mom, the young boy was shipped off to a private and exclusive nursery in Geneva, Switzerland. He would come home once or twice a year, in addition to holidays and summer vacations. His parents would travel to Geneva a couple of times a year to catch up with him. By the time he was eighteen, 'Johnny' had moved to London to go to university, where he would often see his dad in the company of female 'business associates'. He was grown up enough to know what was going on, although, given the strict patriarchal system he had grown up in, he never dared to as much as ask or hint or make a sarcastic remark. He just assumed that's the way life was supposed to be, and that this would be the way he would live in a few years. That did not sound too bad. He was already a mini-womaniser.

When college ended, his father told him he should move back home. That was the last thing on 'Johnny's' mind. He always thought he would stay in Europe, the only place he had really lived. He spoke better English and French than he did Arabic. By the time he had finished high school in Switzerland, his father forced him to join the Sandhurst military academy in the UK. 'Johnny' needed to get some discipline, his father argued. Get off his playboy lifestyle. Learn something meaningful, not the international relations field he was pursuing. What good could come out of that? What kind of job could he get with a degree like that? How much money could he make? However, Sandhurst was too much discipline, and 'Johnny' quit after a year.

Upon returning to Dubai, 'Johnny' received yet another gift from his rich daddy. He was told to open a public relations company that would have exclusive access to the government and emir's palace. He did not have to do much work, except to hire a few people and make sure there remained a solid link between the emir's palace and companies in his domain, on one hand, and his PR firm, on the other. All his company had to do was keep in touch with the companies once a week, find out what they were doing, generate press releases, and field them to international news agencies and local newspapers. It was a good, hassle-free life. It made enough money to pay for office expenses, and that's all he needed, anyway.

He spent some time at the office, but it was hardly a blood-pressure-raising job for him. He would show up around eleven each morning, and would be out by around four each afternoon.

As was his habit, one hot and humid afternoon, where any outside activity would be prohibitive by 110 °F heat and ninety percent humidity, 'Johnny' went to the coffee shop in the mall next to the office, ordered a large Starbucks Macchiato, sat at a table on the outside edge of the store, and pulled out a copy of the *Morning News*, a local paper everyone made fun of because it said nothing of substance about what really was going on in the country, or, for that matter, in neighbouring countries. Lenin and Stalin would have been proud of the newspaper for its unbending commitment to promoting the state and being a 'good soldier' – it was just another tool in the hands of the government. Press development was not an issue that much of the Middle East could be proud of.

As he was sitting there sipping at his coffee, 'Johnny' noticed Sade's presence a few tables away. She was wearing a knee-length white skirt, high-heel shoes, a white tank-top that covered a see-through, light-blue shirt, and almost made her long, shiny brown hair unnoticeable. 'Johnny' noticed that she was reading an article in the *Economist*. He did not care what the article was about. His interest was purely physical. She seemed angry reading the piece. He just thought she was cute. He went over and introduced himself. Not the whole family history, just his name and that he owned a recently-established communications company. She introduced herself as a political science student new to the emirate. Her interest in him, on the other hand, was not physical, only that he was the first guy adventurous enough to make a move.

That day's coffee lasted more than an hour and was

quickly followed by many more, always in public places. From the beginning, it became clear that, while his initial interest in her had started like a high school boy's crush on a prom girl, he soon became mesmerised by her sense of curiosity, by the fact that she was not the average girl next door. She was not interested in fancy clothes or fancy cars or jewellery. There was substance to her. She could have an intelligent conversation about anything from global warming to why Africa needed to clean its own house as a continent before it could count on more world sympathy.

Her interest in him – once the initial admiration for taking risk was gone – was that he was just what she needed: a well-connected boy who could be her ticket into the murky world of Middle East politics.

In was not long before friendship turned to something more serious. What was not clear was who was the more serious of the two in the relations. He had genuinely fallen for her, but there was always something in the back of his mind asking if she really liked him or if she was just using him. She enjoyed the irony of how a chauvinistic Arab man was now in the position of wondering if he was the weaker sex in the relationship, but she did not bring it up. She did not rub it in. Whatever the realities, they both seemed comfortable in the relationship for now, and it continued. His family knew about it; hers did not. That's usually the way it worked in the Middle East, Arab or not.

Sade was also becoming more interested, not only in the politics of the region, but also in the status of women in the Middle East. True, even in her home country of Iran, there were lots of obstacles towards improvement of women. However, there had also been traditional differences in the many women in the non-Arab Iran and the Arab world. The Gulf, for example, was always more conservative than most Arab countries. She was a feminist, deep down, and was ever more so questioning the reality of life for women in the region.

What kind of a system was it that women were still targets of 'honor killing' – in the twenty-first century?

What kind of a system was it that women were still not allowed to vote in many countries in the Middle East?

How about 'arranged marriages'?

Or automatic guardianship of kids to the father?

How about a woman being raped, but the man claims it was consensual sex, and the woman would need three male 'witnesses' to back her up?

Or a battered woman being unable to file for divorce on the basis of abuse, without the testimony of an 'eyewitness'?

The list went on, and on, and on!

However, were those the real issues? When she had first arrived in Dubai as a young, inexperienced girl, first time traveling outside her home country, she would have said 'yes'. As years went by, having graduated from university, having travelled a bit more extensively – east and west – and partly because of her association with 'Johnny', she was reassessing her own views. Living in the Middle East reshaped and jaded her old feministic views. She had started asking herself questions, influenced by her environment: Was life any significantly better for the whole nation, even in countries in which women had more freedom? Was everyone all of a sudden okay because women's situations were 'okay'? Did the GDP rise continuously and considerably? Did the unemployment rate drop? Did men actually, really, show more respect for women? Did women get paid as much as men for the same work, even in countries where they supposedly had a bigger social and economic presence? Or were women's rights in

31

the East a different ballgame than women's rights in the West?

Whatever the answer might have been, the reality was that she now believed in a different political ideology. She convinced herself that women's rights could, perhaps should, take second fiddle to the nation's rights. She had become a believer in a variation of 'might makes right'. She had come to believe that her future role in politics should be in making her country 'great', and that she could do that by making it powerful and feared.

The 'might makes right' part was nothing new in the Middle East. The strong had been butchering the weak for centuries. When they were not strong enough on their own, they made alliances to forge a stronger front – only to change alliances within alliances. It was a power-grabbing, blood-sucking, musical-rotating-chair game that had been going on for some time. The region being what it was, chances were it was going to go on for some time longer. The more she thought about her newly-acquired philosophy, the more sense it made to her. Didn't Muslim and Christian religious crusaders achieve their success, and not through calm, proselytising arguments? Were it not for strong empires or colonial powers, would more people not have died in senseless tribal and ethnic fire fights? Even when the empires collapsed, was it not thanks to dictators that countries did not invade each other?

Name one country in the past fifty – hell, one hundred – years in the Middle East that really worked for the benefit of its own people, built the infrastructure, grew the economy, created jobs, gave democratic freedoms to its people, and held elections.

None.

The question for her now was: What should she do with the newly found conviction and knowledge? How could changes in her political views be put to good use for her long-term, strategic plans?

CHAPTER 7

DUBAI was not a city with thousands of years of history, like Cairo or Beirut, but it was interesting enough in its own right. To understand Dubai, one would have to know two Dubais; the old one and the new one, and a good place to start would be the hot, sweaty, smelly alleyways of Beniyas Square. Dubai is separated by a creek that divides the city into two areas, Bur Dubai and Deira. Historically, Bur Dubai was the newer, more developed part of the city. Streets are wider. Buildings are 'flashier'. Most of the five-star hotels were in Bur Dubai. In fact, the world's only so-called 'seven-star' hotel was on the other side of the creek, away – far away – from Deira. The ruler's main office palace is there, too. It was from Bur Dubai that the new boundaries of the city had stretched farther and farther as the city became bigger and bigger.

Deira, on the other hand, was where you would find the 'old' character of Dubai. That's where the bazaars were, the open markets, the spice market, the gold market, the silver market, and the little import-export loading docks that counted for so much of the sea trade between Dubai and Sade's home country.

There was another type of business that was an important part of Deira, one of those off-the-charts businesses that counted for so much. One of those 'informal' economic sectors. It was called the *hawala*. This business was not just important to Deira. It was one of the unspoken cornerstones of Dubai's economic livelihood for years.

The history of *hawala* is old and complicated. By some counts, it goes back to at least the eighth century. In the old days, merchants used the system to settle payment for transactions or debts. In more recent times, its use had been mostly limited to south-east Asian countries. Millions of people from that part of the world, who either got paid in cash or, for whatever reason, didn't have or didn't want to have bank accounts, looked to *hawaladars* – *hawala* dealers – to send cash around, mostly to family members back home. The system was pretty simple. The person who wanted to send money would go to a *hawala* dealer, give him cash, and the *hawala* dealer would contact – by fax, phone, or email, in more modern times – a fellow *hawala* dealer in the recipient country who, in turn, gave the cash to the recipient.

Hawala operations were perfectly legal until not long ago. In fact, even nowadays, they are mostly legal. After all, no one said everyone should use the banking system. Why should you not opt for an alternate system if it is better? The *hawala* system is faster; the money is usually transferred in a day or two, whereas international banking could take a week. The *hawala* system is cheaper, because banks charge more. Plus, it is not unheard of for banks to 'lose' your money. Those were the legal advantages. In recent times, *hawala* had been used by the 'bad guys', the drug traffickers, criminals and others with lots of illicitly-got cash who needed to 'legitimise' their fortunes. The term for it was simple: money laundering.

Dubai, along with a couple of other countries, had become a centre for *hawala*-based money laundering. Not that it wanted to, at least, not initially. With so many Asians working in the city, it needed to allow a system that would facilitate the transfer of money to various Asian countries. The intentions were good. For a city that needed money, lots of it, allowing *hawaladars* to make some extra – as long they shared it with the government, and as long as the government could control the situation – was not necessarily a bad thing. Yes, Dubai bosses knew about the *hawala* system, appreciated it, and even used it to their own benefit, in part as a bargaining chip in relations with Washington.

CHAPTER 8

ONE of the beneficiaries of the *hawala* system was someone Sade had met a couple of times from a distance, at her boyfriend's family's mansion.

Hajj Mohsen Afghani, was a silver-haired, medium-built man in his seventies. He brandished a long white beard and a balding head that was covered by a white cap. Hajj Mohsen was no stranger to either business or politics. He had lived in Dubai most of his life, starting as a small-time import-export middleman, buying spices from India, and selling them to Europe. He also imported fine carpets from his native Afghanistan and Iran, and either exported them to Europe or sold them to expats in Dubai. That's not the only thing he did. Back in the days of his youth, a young king ruled Afghanistan, one who was secular, a women's advocate, pro-development, and pro-modernisation. Broadminded as he was, he did not have a tight rope over his country's affairs, and state funds kept seeping out of the country, and no one could figure out how or where to or, for that matter, who was sending them out.

Hajj Mohsen happened to be a discreet player in that affair.

Day after day, month after month, and year after year, Hajj Mohsen's tiny office in Baniyas was the meeting place for all types of people wearing Italian-made suits and

Gucci watches. Some held official government positions, but most were not direct employees. They were associates. They were deputies. They were royal family members, or sometimes just business partners. Sometimes they showed up at Hajj Mohsen's office carrying cash, but, more often than not, they would bring in gold and silver. One good thing about the office location – and it was not completely accidental – was that it was also not too far away from the gold and silver market. Shops there, too, were full of Afghanis, Indians, and Pakistanis. Everyone knew everyone. They knew each other's background, history, and family roots.

Every time one of the slick Afghans showed up at Hajj Mohsen's office, he would end up sending one of his junior associates to the gold and silver market. Instructions were always simple: *inra zud ab kon va bargard.* That was Afghani dialect of Dari for: liquidate the goods, and come back quickly.

Once goods were turned into cash, the cash would change hands a few times. It would go from Dubai, say, to Pakistan, from Pakistan to London, from London to Paris, and from Paris to a trusted Afghan in Lake Geneva. A few more transactions like that, and the amount would be respectable enough to be deposited into a numbered Geneva bank account.

State money, illegally acquired, was now 'clean money', deposited safely into someone's personal account.

As months led to years, Hajj Mohsen's clientele changed. Sometimes he liked them; often he did not. The truth was that, when he started his business, it was somewhat personal to him. His clients were all Afghans. His family had roots in the county. His brothers and uncles were all involved in politics. They knew everyone. Everyone knew them. It was not so much a 'business' as

38

much as the continuation of family relations back home. Of course, he knew what was going on. He knew what he was doing, who he was doing it for, and why. But, still, there was a personal aspect to it. With the regime in Kabul long gone, what still kept Hajj Mohsen in Dubai, and why Emiratis let him continue, was the politics of it.

This was a two-way street. Dubai leaders needed people like Hajj Mohsen, and people like Hajj Mohsen needed Dubai. This was a marriage made of necessity, of the need for survival in a rough part of the world. For years, 'insurgents' and 'terrorists' had wreaked havoc around the world, bombed buildings, shot down planes, and kidnapped people for ransom – be that cash or sophisticated arms. The 'bad guys' needed to be able to receive their funds safely, and *hawala* was as safe a method as they could find. Dubai ruler's let their city be used as a conduit, in return for being left alone. Call it hush money, if you'd like. They also used it as a trump card in their relations with the West. 'Give us what we want, treat us the way we want to be treated, and we'll crack down on the terror funding. If not, you might witness more explosions in your cities'. The *hawala* issue had recently become a hot potato topic at some point between Washington and Abu Dhabi, the seat of the government. The *hawala* business had become a headache for Washington. All sorts of money destined for insurgents and terrorists in Iraq, Afghanistan, Indonesia, Palestinian territories, Chechnya and other hotspots of the world was changing hands in Dubai. It did not fit America's strategy of 'promoting democracy' in the four corners of the world. However, Dubai bosses had no intention of stopping it unless the Americans were willing to pay big political points for it. Dubai wanted Washington to give it the world-class respect it felt it deserved. It did not want everything to go through Abu Dhabi, the capital. It wanted the President of the United States to stop in Dubai every time he was in the region, not just go to Abu Dhabi. It wanted the State Department to stop criticising the city-state for its human trafficking record. Stop talking about how billions of dollars of illicitly-got money was pouring in from Afghanistan and Iran, and former Soviet Republic was changing hands in Dubai. 'You wanted us to stop *hawala* money that is financing terror attacks, which are shaking New York and Washington, or you want us to stop import of sophisticated military-use equipment to Iran, you get off our backs', Dubai was telling Washington.

One day, Hajj Mohsen got to witness first-hand the importance of the *hawala* system to Dubai leaders. It was a typical steamy hot and humid summer day in Dubai, and Hajj Mohsen was sitting in his bare-bone Deira office. The Afghan trader was lazing comfortably behind a large desk, air conditioning blowing cold air. The secretary buzzed from downstairs to announce the arrival of a Sheikh Ahmed.

"Do I know him?"

"Don't think so."

"Does he have an appointment?"

"Don't think so."

"Ask him where he is from."

"Union Bank of Emirates."

That was strange. Hajj Mohsen had several accounts with the bank, some of them going back to the days he had first arrived in Dubai. There had never been a problem with any of the accounts. Not even a phone call. Why a visit, all of a sudden? Plus, if there was an issue, why didn't they just call first?

He motioned the secretary to let the man upstairs.

"*As-salamu aleikum.*" It was Arabic for 'peace be upon you'. It was a religious-turned-traditional way of just saying 'hello'.

"*Wa aleikum as-salam.*" And peace be upon you.

The host ordered some tea for both, and then engaged in a few minutes of small talk. It was the Arab way of doing things. They hardly ever just got to the point. The conversation had to be 'sugar-coated' first. The 'message' was not just the 'content'. The ambiance and nuance was a great part of the conversation etiquette.

"Hajj, you have been a good customer for years."

"And you have provided good service for years, for which I am thankful."

"You know, Hajj, when you and I were young, life was different."

"*Al-hamdu-lillah.*" Praise be to God.

"Back when I started working for the bank, if we wanted to see how much money was coming into an account in a month, or how much was going out, we literally had to take out all the receipts, pull out the calculator, and add up all the figures."

"When I started my business, there were not even calculators," Hajj said, to a forced chuckle from his guest.

"But now things have changed!"

Hajj Mohsen was now directly eyeing the bank employee from behind his thick eyeglasses. He had not even bothered asking what exactly he did for the bank. Or, for that matter, no proof showing he did work for the bank.

"Nowadays, we can just feed the information to a computer, and they can tell us everything we need to know."

Indeed, they had done that, and the results were amazing and surprising.

Over the past two years alone, some $20 million had come into and gone out of Hajj Mohsen's business accounts, large chunk for an operation that gave the impression of being not big at all. Plus, there was even more

41

money transacted from his personal accounts than from the official business accounts. Although Sheikh Ahmed did not tell Hajj Mohsen, the analysis showed money coming from many accounts in Afghanistan and Pakistan. Some were a few thousand dollars. Others were hundreds of thousands. Some only came once or twice a year. Others were more regular, almost every month.

"Hajj Mohsen, one issue with the accounts is that, while they come from various sources, they always go to the same sources. Same *names!*"

The Afghan businessman did not really need to ask if they knew who the recipients were. It was obvious; they had him in the bag. What had started as pure *hawala*-style transactions had turned into a mixed bag of *hawala* and traditional banking. Hajj Mohsen was sending out money, both through human mulls and legitimate bank accounts. He had become sloppy, and now he had been caught. The question now was what the Emiratis wanted for not squeezing the bag to the point of a crush.

Thinking this was a normal business transaction, he decided to throw an offer and see if it worked.

"Sheikh Ahmed, this city has been good to me and my family. It has been good to my country when we needed help. Tens of thousands of Afghanis took refuge here when they needed to find a safe place for their families. You and I know business. I know having so many transactions every month is a burden to the bank. If you would like, I would be more than happy to pay additional costs to make it easier for the bank. I can even send the money through some outside banks that you recommend to make it beneficial to everyone."

In other words, he was willing to pay kickbacks or route the money through the personal accounts of intermediaries, so it would not been too obvious that the

Hajj was behind the payments.

"It is not about expenses, Hajj Mohsen. *Al-hamdu-lillah*; God has blessed us. We are doing quite well. It is about people understanding our position and our principles. As you said, our country and our leaders have done what they can for their Afghan brothers. We have been as supportive as we can be. But people should understand that as the Holy Book, the Koran, has said, 'treat people as you would like to be treated by them'. The Arab world has been through wars, devastation, killings, and too much bloodshed. Unlike many other countries in this blessed part of the world, Alhamdulillah, people in Dubai live in peace."

Now it was time to deliver the real message. He paused, took a deep breath, adjusted his white, nicely pressed robe, and thickened his voice.

"People who use our hospitality should know that we are *determined* to keep that peace for everyone. We will *not* allow *anyone* to disturb our society. Our silence should not be confused with either lack of knowledge or lack of will. Our part of the world has recently witnesses an increased level of tension. People in other parts of the region look up to our leaders to set standards, and it is upon all of us now to find ways to calms the waters, and not fish in the muddy ones."

Message delivered! Loud and clear! 'You want to fund the operations of shady characters from our city, go ahead, but you need to cool it off, at least for now! And make sure the operations do not land on our doors, or we will kick you all out'.

As if the verbal message was not enough, there was more to come for Hajj Mohsen. In the coming weeks and months, 'unknown' people constantly followed him everywhere he went. Every move he took was observed. Every phone call was recorded. Ordinarily, he would not have noticed any of it. The Emiratis had one of the best and most professional security forces in the region. Wearing their tradition white robes, they would blend in well within the society. They would not come close enough for you to spot them. They did not wear the typical US military haircut that would identify them from a mile away! They would not wear the intel-style sunglasses. They would simply assign multiple personnel to one person, so they could remain 'un-spot-able'. They would coerce your Indian doorman, Sri Lankan maid, and the bartender of your favourite hangout to give out information about you that you wished no one to know, and they would monitor your Internet connection.

Power, plus professionalism, plus technology made for an unbeatable combination.

Of course, every now and then, they would not mind showing some of the evidence to you, so you would know they were on your tail! Added emphasis never hurts, and Hajj Mohsen was to be made an example of. Not that it was needed. He knew the system well enough, but, for the next few months, he would occasionally receive his own bank statement at his office address, instead of the private post office box he had set up. When he opened the statements, he would see certain shady transactions underlined in red or black. Once he even received pictures of his wife and daughter shopping. To top it off, one day, the secretary rang from downstairs saying there was an envelope from Sheikh Ahmed's office. When Hajj Mohsen opened it, there was a short note.

"Please send a check, every month, to the following address," the message said.

He delivered the first check in person, to show added respect. It was to 'Johnny's' family mansion. Sheikh Ahmed was the young man's uncle. Doing shady business

44

was becoming more and more expensive in the liberal island, but it was still allowed, as long as you played by the rules. As long as core interests were not hurt, you could still count on the hospitality.

CHAPTER 9

Dubai, a few years after Sade's arrival

AS time passed, Sade became more and more involved in politics. She was determined to move back home and get involved, do something for the country. She was one of the increasing number of people who were regaining their sense of historical nationalism. They wanted the 'old glory' back, and they saw an opportunity in the rise of a man Sade knew only too well.

He was one of her old high school classmates in Tehran, someone who was not destined for leadership at all, not someone you would particularly be impressed with the first time you saw him. Not an intellectual marvel by any stretch of imagination. However, they had something in common. Like her, he was a student of the *realpolitik* school of thought. Unlike her, he was devoutly religious, and that was a source of many hot debates.

In the months and years the two were classmates, they spent lots of time together; late-night storming sessions were common. On the surface, they both wanted the same thing: return to the 'national glory', reawakening of the people, undisputed leadership in the region. However, they – like millions of other Muslims – had diametrically opposed views as how to achieve it, and that

– in great part – had to do with how they saw their own religion and its role in the world.

The clash between them had a lot less to do with the classical differences between Muslims. It was not so much about which branch of the religion believed in what and which one was right. It was not about the past. It was about what the role of Islam should be in today's world, in tomorrow's world.

For centuries, the world had basically known Islam by its main two branches, the Shiites and the Sunnis. The Sunnis had the power – and often the money and prestige – and the Shiites felt cheated out of those, and wanted it back.

However, in recent times, the debate had acquired another angle, one that had put leaders on both sides of the fence on the defense. The reality was that, on both sides, many Muslims had become truly disenchanted by their own leaders, their own sense of belonging, their own place in the world, and that sense of dissatisfaction had manifested itself in different ways – and that, too, was a source of consternation for people like Sade, who were trying to capitalise on religion to win back the old times.

Muslims constituted about a third of the world's population, but were increasingly becoming the largest source of immigration into Western Europe and North America. Plus, if you looked closer at who was getting out, it was the more educated, the more affluent, and the more worldly of the Muslims. Why were they getting out? What did they see in the West? What did they *not* see in their homeland?

People like Sade saw this both as a problem and challenge. Clearly, it was a problem that a relatively large part of the Muslim world was constantly trying to get away. It was an even bigger problem that those people were the best and the brightest the region had to offer. This was a very transparent brain drain. If leaders did not see this as a problem and did not do anything to stop it, there was something wrong with their leadership skills.

* * *

After graduation from the university in Dubai, Sade had stayed behind and kept the double role of being 'Johnny's' girlfriend – mingling with the high society – and continuing to be an 'intellectual provocateur'.

The old high school mate, Ahmed, had moved on to bigger and better things. He got into grass-roots politics and, eventually, moved up the political ladder and found himself in the presidential palace. He was now in a position of power, a position of influence. The only problem was that he did not have the intellectual backbone and qualifications to do what he was supposed to: design a cohesive and far-reaching domestic and foreign policy for his nation.

He was on borrowed time. He needed help, and he needed it fast. He had inherited a miserable situation in which more than a third of the country was unemployed, and the economy was stagnating, at best. He needed to gather advisors from various walks of life. Some would be ideological thinkers. Some would be practical politicians. Some should be good at strategic thinking, and others tactical.

From the beginning, Ahmed found the task harder than he had thought. Campaigning was easy. Delivering was much harder. Surely, he was not a very smart person, but he was smart enough to know that if people around him were smart, they would have the vision that could pull the nation up.

His task was made even more difficult by the

performance of his predecessors for the past quarter of a century. For all practical purposes, the previous leaders had locked the doors around the country, and thrown away the keys. They had discouraged all meaningful contacts with the outside world. It was as if people were living in the communist-era Albania. It was no surprise that people lacked in technology, science, latest economic and management skills, and let's not forget political skills and vision.

Ahmed called Sade in Dubai. He wanted her to come back and be part of the administration. He needed two things he sorely lacked. He needed someone he could infinitely trust, and he needed someone who could offer a 'Grand Exodus'. She was hesitant. First, as much as she loved her country, she had not lived in it since high school. That was a long time ago. The country had changed. More importantly, she had changed. Her views had changed. Her aspirations had changed. She had acquired new customs, new habits, and new expectations from people and life around her. Second, it was one thing to talk about politics all the time, or even be addicted to it. It was a totally different thing to become a professional practitioner of it. The former could remain a habit, an idealistic mode of life, but the latter involved responsibility and accountability. Respect and legitimacy rode on it. It was no longer just a vocation. It would become a profession.

And she was not sure she was quite ready for it.

After weeks of back and forth conversation, it came down to one thing:

"What do you ultimately want to achieve if I join you?"

The president had responded, "What can you help with? We need a vision for the economy, infrastructure, education, you name it!"

"You see, that's why I am hesitating to join you. You think too small. You always have. You want to be a leader, but you are thinking just like the other bureaucrats. I will join you, but I will have to have full and free hands in implementing the kind of vision we discussed years ago."

Neither one needed to discuss the details. They both knew what that entailed.

The president finally caved in. He knew she was right. He knew he needed her, and he knew she would be good for him and his political future.

Within months of being on the job, the president – with Sade's pushing and full support – announced he was going to take a full-fledge delegation on the first high-level overseas trip of his presidency. The two of them had spoken about their long-term plan. Now they needed to choose the venue and how to announce their plans.

CHAPTER 10

Almaty, Kazakhstan, circa 2015

FEBRUARY is not a month you'd want to travel to Almaty! Not unless you *really* liked freezing weather. Usually, that time of year, the temperature was well below zero. However, there was also something deeply alluring about the city in the Central Asian republic of Kazakhstan. Most streets in the city were lined up with trees. Pedestrian walkways were wide. Streets were decorated with park benches, so people could sit, talk, or just observe other passersby. Lovers would escape work and school just to enjoy the serenity of the place. In winter, white snow painted the city, and spring and summer days are as pleasant as they are in any European city. Decades of being part of the communist world, perhaps, did not give people lots of material goods to enjoy, but being in Almaty, one could not escape the aura of love the city permeated.

The presidential 'advance team' had already done two things before any of the half a dozen cabinet participants arrived. To avoid possible media attention, they had rented a ski chalet on the slopes of Almaty's Shimboulak mountains, just on the outskirts of the city, where there were only a dozen houses in the area. It was close to the city, yet still secluded enough to satisfy security concerns. The road to Shimboulak was interesting. One would drive on an uphill road for about fifteen to twenty minutes before getting to the bottom of a winding and twisting road that eventually got to the ski slopes. The scenery was beautiful, and the upward-winding road provided a controlled environment for security forces.

The second part of the arrangement was that they informed the host country's president that the meeting was just a governmental retreat for the president and his top advisors. In other words, this was not an official state visit, but they would like to have a meeting with the president on the final day of the journey. That helped them, because then they would not have to announce in advance what they wanted to talk about. It gave them the element of surprise, and kept the issue off limits from media.

Once 4x4 jeeps had transported everyone from the airport up the snowy hills, the president started the meeting.

"Throughout centuries, God Almighty has blessed a certain number of His people. They and their countries are protected inside their national boundaries. They have received the resources that can carry their country for generations. They have received the physical beauty that would make them the envy of all people at all times. But if God pre-ordained some people, why have there been so many turnovers of empires? Why has there been so much bloodshed from one century to another? Why have so many countries seen their boundaries changed by the force of swords and guns? Why is it that some countries have been created? Some existing ones have survived, while some have disappeared. History has shown that it was a mistake to create others to begin with."

Ever since he had come to power, his people had got to know a few things about their president. The first, and perhaps foremost, was that, in the style of former Arab hero, Gamal Abdel Nasser, he was a good orator. He could attend meetings without prepared notes, look into the audience's eyes, feel its mood, take its 'temperature', and just know what the audience members would want to hear.

This meeting was no exception.

The chalet's ground floor had a round table in the dining room, with six chairs around it. Aside from the president and Sade, there was the head of the intelligence, the foreign minister, finance and economy minister, and the army commander.

This was the 'kitchen cabinet', a group of people who had known each other for years, and had spent days and night arguing minutiae of national, regional and international politics with each other. They knew each other so well they could finish each other's sentences.

Except for this time!

He continued with his speech. "In each of those historical instances, what has been missing is the role of a strong leadership. Why are most countries single states, while a few have become empires? Why do some empires last longer than others? Because most lack long term and sustained strategic planning. Our history is different. Our nation is one of the few blessed for grandeur. We brought civilisation to the world before anyone else. Our empire was vast. Our empire was great. And when they defeated us, we fought back. We held our heads high, fought back, and destroyed the aggressors. We have always been destined for leadership. And that's what we are going to offer, again. We are going to use not only what God has given us, but also what we can give ourselves. Our nation has resources others would die for, both natural resources and the power of our people. This nation is stronger than we give it credit. Our people suffered a long war for years;

they lost millions; the country's economy was devastated. And look at it again. It is stronger than it has ever been. But it is also less respected than it has been for a long time. Its outlook is weaker than it has ever been. Our natural resources are running out fast. We have managed to fool the world by making them believe that we have resources for decades and centuries to come. Others might not know this, but we do. We know we only have maybe a decade more. Not only that, but our infrastructure is weak, and needs tens of billions of dollars. We don't have the money, and no one is going to lend it to us – not under current circumstances."

Then he paused. He looked around the table. It was a favourite habit of his. He would stop in mid-speech. It served two purposes. First, he would examine the impact of what he had said so far on his audience. Second, as good as he was, he, too, sometimes needed to sharpen his skills. Come up with new arguments quickly in his mind. Choose the right words. Decide what to emphasise and what not to concentrate on.

This time, he saw nothing but blank faces around the table. He could not tell whether that meant agreement, or total disbelief and disagreement. It was too late to rewind the tape and see what worked and what did not. The only option was to move forward, but, perhaps, he could do it a bit differently.

Let them think about the facts, he told himself. *Let them see things the way I do, and, perhaps, they will come up with the same conclusions.*

He needed them. He needed their support, and he only had one chance to make his point.

This was the make or break point. They might not have known it, but he did.

"Our country's population was sixty-three million

in 2000; it will be over a hundred million by 2050. That's a fifty percent increase in half a century. China's growth in that period is expected to be ten percent. India's about the same. The US population will probably grow from three hundred million in the early 2000s, to about four hundred million by 2050. In our country, in 2000, almost forty-seven percent of our population was at the working age of twenty-five to sixty, while forty-six point five percent were under twenty years of age. In 2050, forty-three percent will be at the working age of twenty-five to sixty, but only twenty percent will be under twenty.

"Compare us to Egypt, which had pretty similar population to us in 2000. Its twenty-five- to sixty-year-old population was about thirty-nine percent of the total population, a bit lower than ours. Its under-twenty population was 35.6 percent, again lower than ours. By 2050, however, its population will balloon to one hundred and twenty-eight million. What does it tell you? A few years ago, an overwhelming portion of our population was either in school or needed work. A few decades from now, the situation will only slightly get better. We have a regional problem. Our country has had the highest population growth in the region. We need to figure out what to do with the people we have. Two thirds of our population will be under sixty years old by 2050. They will need jobs; they will rely on government services. That is a strikingly high percentage."

He paused.

He looked around the table again. He was making headway, but no score yet.

"To feed the people, we need to make some strategic changes. Our economic growth has been much lower than it should have been in the past, partly because of the population growth, and partly because of previous governments' bad management. We don't have the capability to maintain and feed people in the urban areas, because the economic structure in cities either has not been set up right, or is not functioning. We need to force people back to villages, by force if we have to. No more urban-based economy."

"But that's forced migration," the minister of finance and economy objected. "Even if that does not break some international law, it would be against how people have lived for decades, not to mention that is robbing Peter to pay Paul. It won't solve the problem; it might just buy you some time."

Of course, he was right. The minister knew it; everyone around the table knew it, and so did the president. However, he also knew that's what was needed.

How many cities needed to be depopulated, someone asked.

"Overwhelming majority," the president said, without looking at anyone. He just continued to gaze at the oak conference table.

Was he avoiding direct contact because he was ashamed of what he was saying? Was he embarrassed? Was this just his way of showing his pragmatism? It was hard to tell. Plus, it did not matter. He was not asking for a vote. He was dictating policy.

Sadly, that was not the end of the story.

"Bringing people into cities might mitigate the issue for a while, but we cannot take our eyes off the fact that we do have an economic crisis looming, and little solution in sight. We have had oil for decades. And we have been fortunate that the price of oil has been going up. But it is not enough. What we need is a grand strategy, and it will not be found just at home."

He pounded on the message again.

"So, if you look at it objectively, and we have a large population that is growing old, we have an economy that is not keeping pace."

The message had started to sink in. Now people were getting fidgety. They were exchanging worried looks. They were moving in their chairs, clearing their throats, repositioning their chairs. The 'worried' look was hard to miss.

"But you should not worry," the president said, raising his voice. "There is good news here. We are not the only ones with such a problem. By the year 2050, the Arab world will have an influx of thirty million unemployed, semi-skilled men."

So, what's the solution, someone asked.

"The solution is to look for other opportunities," answered the president.

Like what, someone wondered out loud.

"More than any other time in history, perhaps, our nation now has a chance to become great again. I am a firm believer that what makes a nation great is its leadership, and the vision that leadership has for the country."

Then he engaged in historical rambling.

"Max Weber had it right. He said 'the leader has a certain quality of individual personality, by virtue of which he is set apart from ordinary men, and treated as endowed with supernatural, superhuman or, at least, specifically exceptional powers or qualities'. Nowhere is that more true than in the Middle East. What did Ataturk have that made him so special? Why was Arafat who he was? Why did he become more like than Robert Mugabe, and not like Nelson Mandela? Why could Ayatollah Khomeini, may peace be upon him, do things with this nation that the Shah could not? Why did Bin Laden succeed where the Sheikh of Azhar, the appointed leader of Sunni Islam, failed? Why? I have one word for you: appearance of legitimacy! Leadership is a make-or-break business, and the yardstick is the charisma of the office holder. And that's what will make *this* government a success or a failure. Our people are looking to us, and the best reward we can bestow on them is to reinstate the glory of the Old Empire. What we need is to re-create our empire. We need to engage in an aggressive diplomatic and military campaign, if necessary, to re-conquer the territory that once belonged to our ancestors. You are assuming that the strategy requires wars. That is not necessarily the case. In many cases, I would assume, we can achieve our policy by coercing some of our neighbouring countries to simply acquiesce to our demands. Not a drop of blood need be shed!"

The fidgeting was turning into outright mutiny.

"You want to go to war?" exclaimed the foreign minister.

"Sir, you just said our economy is weak and our resources diminishing. How can we afford billions of dollars more to forego another war? Last time we were in war, it took years, and destroyed us. How will you convince the people to sacrifice their lives and economic well-being again? Plus, we don't have any serious disagreements with any of our neighbours. Who are we going to go to war with?" the economy minister asked.

"We have to do this in two stages," the president countered. "First, what you said is incorrect. We have long-standing grievances with many of our neighbours. One has taken islands from us, keeps arresting our fishermen, and confiscates our boats. Others have, for generations, suppressed their Shiite population, the population that has been the pillar of those societies from the day they were created, the day they got their independence from their colonial powers. How is it that the Americans and

Europeans talk about democracy, talk about rule of law, talk about government of the people, for the people and by the people, but, when it comes to the rights of our people, the rules of the game change? And we are supposed to sit back and say nothing?"

His voice had clearly gone up a few decibels.

"We do *have* the *perfect* excuse for extracting justice from our neighbours. That would be our battle cry. That would be our justification for escalation."

Maybe he was not saying it in so many words, but the message was clear: rally the troops – the country – behind a single unified message, and we can sell this. We have done it before. It worked before. It will work again, and it will work better, because we actually have the experience this time.

What would he get for it – if he succeeded?

"Two things. Number one: our neighbors are sitting on top of the world's largest oil reserves. A successful campaign can dramatically boost the resources we lack, not to mention boost our international profile. Second, it will take off the unemployment pressure for a while."

Sensing the uneasiness in the room, the president wanted to come back to the point that, in many cases, no war might be necessary. Wars were dirty, costly, and, often, the outcome was unpredictable. The president's campaign strategy would leave the current rulers in charge. They would be responsible for the good and the bad. They would be blamed for the problems. This was not going to be a military conquest as much as political subjugation.

If the president's people actually took control of other countries, they would easily be blamed for whatever went wrong, and that was the route they would not want to go. No, it would be a lot simpler and cleaner if they just created problems, to the point of destabilising other countries, but without having to offer any solutions. Make them think they would be toppled any day, unless they came to you for help. Play the strength card. Let them come to you, and then you could name your price, and the price was, generally, pretty much known in advance: stay in power, but you will have to make our policy priorities your main goals, especially when it comes to oil and gas production, as well as foreign policy issues.

Before the presidential entourage returned home, there was one more meeting to be had.

President Sheytanbasha Maskharov's palace was no less ostentatious than any occupied by kings. He did not have underground bunkers, but European contractors had gladly collected some twenty million dollars to build him a few residences here and there, and, like many of his counterparts in the Middle East, the chubby seventy-five-year-old was a true relic of the past. The past that included decades of communism rule. Maskharov was no stranger to the system. Truth be told, he was the system. As was the case in much of the former Soviet Union republics, the current head of state was a former local communist party chief, and claimed to have become a 'reformist' after the dismantling of the Soviet Union, and then took over the country. Like others, he had said he would be in office 'temporarily' – until the country had stabilised enough to hold free and fair elections. That had been decades ago, and what had transpired since was a typical example of power corruption.

Over the years, he had consolidated his grip on power. Initially, he had built a semi-real coalition with other political rivals, built a real majority in the parliament and listened to a few voices of dissents here and there. However, as the saying goes, 'power corrupts', and he was corrupted. Bit by bit, cronies around him set up phony companies for him. Large international companies were told – often bluntly – 'you want a large contract in this country? Here is the bank account number'.

After a while, it was not behind the scenes anymore. 'The Family', as they became known, were public owners of dozens of medium and large companies. They ventured into the fast growing energy and telecommunication fields, and owned big stakes in oil, gas, and cell phone companies. They moved into the financial sector, and either bought old banks or opened new ones. The sons and daughters moved into the fray, and purchased rights in the country's already-monopolised gas station business.

However, in that part of the world, business was never far from politics, and politics was never far from media. Maskharov was no exception. He groomed one of his nieces and her son to own and operate a huge media conglomerate that included one f the country's largest television stations, although – again, typical to the business fashion of the region – the station was 'officially' dubbed as being 'independent'.

It is hard to figure out how they thought they would fool people when the first item on the newscast *every night*, without exception, was what the president had done or said that particular day.

However, as in many other parts of the world, globalisation and spread of capitalistic ideas also meant that people became much more preoccupied with making a living than with educating themselves. Because people are so much busier all over the world, television had become much more important to them. It was so much easier to watch ten minutes a day of BBC to find out what was going on in the world than to read one or two newspapers every day.

So, Maskharov's niece and her son slowly built themselves a media empire that either overpowered the weaker ones with less money, or simply threatened and intimidated the rest. Over time, criticism of the regime and Maskharov went down, notch by notch.

Once the president and his family felt politically – and economically – secure, repressing the opposition started. Members of the opposition just vanished. The government cancelled their newspaper licenses. Family members were harassed. Their access to the media decreased. Their passports were cancelled. They would go to the airport to board a plane for a conference somewhere, and would suddenly find themselves on a banned list. Even their personal businesses suffered, because the government used its connections to make sure opposition members suffered personally. Make them hurt where it counts, and they would not create problems politically.

A shady past Maskharov might have had, but discount him, one should not. Not because of any political skills or strategic thinking skills he possessed. He did not! He was not to be discounted because of what he personally possessed. He had something that many countries in the world – most notably the United States and Western countries – needed: oil and gas.

That's why the Iranian president was there. That, and the fact that the Kazakh leader's government policies and the way he ran his country were in sync with how Iran had run its own internal course. So, when the two presidents met, the gloves were off, and Ahmed's message was clear.

"We plan to embark on an ambitious regional plan that will have far-reaching regional consequences. Initially, because of world reaction, we will suffer badly, and for several years. We will need your help to sell us cheap oil and gas. We will need you to help us maintain our import routes by allowing imported goods to cross your country.

Generally, we will need your support – to be our partner, to be our friend."

The Kazakh leader listened intently, but wanted to know what he would get in return.

"There are a lot of American oil and gas companies in your country. So far, they have allowed you to maintain control over your country's resources. Once we embark on our strategic plan, the region will face certain political and economic tension. The Americans will panic and try to exert more control over your oil and gas. They might not do so bluntly, but do that in the disguise of forcing you to embark on political reform. They call it democratisation. You and I would call it interference. Once that happens, you will be in need of stronger political allies. You can either go north or go south. If you go north, you will fall once again in the arms of Moscow, but you have made independence from Moscow a cornerstone of your foreign policy. If you go south, you'd have to choose China as your primary strategic partner. It has money, but going to Peking would alienate the West, because it feels threatened by the Chinese trade imbalance and massive population. And you won't get the technology you need for your infrastructure because of that. But if you help us, we can offer a third option. When our strategic goals are achieved, we will have control of most of the Middle East's oil and gas fields, and all the state-of-the-art American technology that money can buy. The Americans would not sell it to us directly, but there are other Western and Asian countries that would. You, too, will have access to the technology. And since we will control the flow and pricing of much of the energy from the Middle East, you will benefit from guaranteed markets and higher prices."

"And if your strategy does not work, what would be *my* exit strategy?" the Kazakh leader wondered out loud.

"Why should I burn my bridges by allying myself with regional rebel-rousers?"

"Because, right now, much of your oil and gas goes through the Persian Gulf, and we can disrupt it! Sooner or later, you will have to choose between Moscow, Peking or Tehran!"

The implication was clear: do it sooner, on friendly terms, so you won't have to negotiate later, on harsher terms.

The deal was sealed – though both swore to keep it secret, except from ranking and trusted staff.

Now that the broader outlines of an adventurous, potentially destructive, or potentially lucrative, strategy was shaped, the main question was how to achieve it.

CHAPTER 11

THERE was another major point that was the topic of heated conversations between the Iranian leaders: when it was all said and done, would the newly conquered/controlled governments become Islamic states? Was this ultimately going to be a religious conquest? Ahmed and Sade decided to hash it out one day, once for all. It was too important a topic to be left undecided.

"Look, what is it that we are to achieve? What's the end game?" asked Sade.

"Bring back the glory of our ancestors, of course!" replied the president, with an annoyed tone.

"So this is about power, and not religion?"

"It is about power principled by religion, as its base."

"Now that is just nonsense!" She was losing her temper even before a meaningful conversation had started. "Name one system that has worked like that and succeeded."

"Our prophet, peace be upon him."

"That was *fourteen* centuries ago! Name a more recent one."

"Our Supreme Leader."

"Who left the country in near bankruptcy."

"He did not. Bad policies perpetrated by unwise advisors did."

"Advisors and ministers who would not lift a glass of water without his permission."

"It is a historical distortion to say he was responsible for failure of his governments."

"It is hypocrisy to say he did not know or could not correct the course."

"What is the point of this conversation? The entire Middle East is *officially* ruled as Muslim states with *sharia* as source of law and constitution."

"First of all, that is a legal distinction, not a political or economic distinction. Second of all, there is no other country that has tried to put religion as a base of economic development. And when the Islamic Republic did, it failed, too."

"Sade, how can we possibly rally millions of our people toward a path that could involve war, destruction, and loss of life, and say we are all of a sudden deviating from path of religion and policies we have so sternly defended?"

"What you say in public does not have to be what you follow in private. That's part of diplomacy. You want to rally people in the name of religion? Go ahead! How you rally your base has little to do with what you will do with the fruit of that mobilisation. That is part of leadership!"

"But isn't that lying?"

Sade could see the president had very little practical knowledge of communication skills and capabilities. Over time, she convinced the executive branch to hire some consultants to work with him. Over time, it was money well spent. In a few years' time, a naïve-sounding religious fanatic had turned into a conniving media monger who devoured publicity and international media.

"What I am saying," added Sade, this time speaking slowly, and counting her words as if talking to a child, "is that we can rally people in this country and elsewhere behind a cause – call it whatever you want – we can tell the world it is based on certain principles, but, when in power, or when in charge of a territory, run it on pragmatic basis." She did not repeat the 'not the dogmatic religious one' part. She figured she had hammered the point hard enough.

CHAPTER 12

QUIETLY, but persistently, the Iranian regime spent hundreds of millions of dollars over the years, infiltrating neighbouring regimes. It used whatever methods it could think of. Following up on the Shimboulak meeting in Kazakhstan, the Iranians had formed an aggressive two-front foreign policy. One part was so secretive – and certainly not discussed in Shimboulak – that less than a handful of the top leaders knew about it. It was the subject of internal debate when the team had returned to Tehran. It was not debated in the sense of whether it should be adopted or not. That much was already decided on. The debate was on how to achieve it. The president, Sade, and the handful of others who were privy to the detailed, more secretive aspects of the plan, were worried that their country would be invaded once the world – particularly the United States, the 'Great Satan,' they called it – became aware of Tehran's devious and destructive intentions. They had seen how Washington used its military bases in the region as forward-base platforms to invade countries like Iraq and Afghanistan. It had seen how the Pentagon and the State Department had used their leverage with some countries to gain air space and refuelling rights.

If there was going to be an invasion of Iran, Tehran wanted to make sure it would be next to impossible for American ground forces to use 'friendly' countries in the region. Tehran was not so worried about its neighbours to the north – Turkmenistan and Azerbaijan. They had long had their own eccentric foreign policy. It was neither here nor there. The Russians could never trust them, but Washington sure could not rely on them, either. Iraq and Afghanistan were once satellite nations of Washington, but they, too, had kicked out the Americans, and would, most likely, not let Washington use their soil to attack Iran. Turkey and Pakistan were a different ballgame. Each considered itself a superpower of kind in the region, but was realistic enough to know that it, too, was vulnerable to superpower pressure. Both were very nationalistic, and had long history with colonial/imperial powers. Both – but Turkey in particular – had such entangled and diverse relations with Iran that it would think twice before so blatantly siding with an 'outside' power against a 'regional' power.

So, while the Iranians did not have to worry so much about the 'first line of defense', they worried about somewhere else. They worried about the 'second line of defense'. Those were the Persian Gulf countries. Those were the countries that had a lot more incentive being Iran's enemies and American's toy boys. They were ruled by Sunnis, even though they mostly had a large – and loud – Shiite community. There were countries in which a lot of local families had originally migrated from Iran to begin with. They might have left many, many years ago, but they still maintained ties to the homeland. There was a part of them that still 'felt' Iranian. Generally speaking, the Gulf countries were also cash-rich, thanks to their oil and gas resources. They needed to 'feel' they were joining the First World. They needed to feel they were no longer 'desert shepherds'. However, at the same time, those regimes were very conscious of the kind of trouble Iran could generate in

69

the region. The Americans could exert pressure. They could be annoying. The Iranians, however, could be lethal.

If push came to shove, they Gulf rulers were more afraid of Iran than they were of America. The Iranians knew that, and they used – or should we say, abused – that societal weakness. The Shiites in those countries got it. They started asking why they were not given more political rights in their adopted homelands. Why were they kept on the fringes of the society? Why were they considered second-class citizens, even though they were born in those countries? Even fathers, and sometimes grandfathers, had been born there. Was it really about their ancestry going back several generations, or was this the continuation of a centuries-old argument about who should have succeeded Prophet Mohammed? Or was it about geopolitical games in the region? Or were the reasons so badly entangled that no one knew what the reasons were anymore, let alone know how to untie the knot?

It did not matter what the reasons were. The reality was that there existed a set of circumstances that could successfully be taken advantage of, and that's what separated the Iranian regime from many of the Arab regimes. With the exception of one or two, the Arabs were stuck in the past, while the Iranians regime was willing to be provocatively proactive and take advantage of whatever conditions existed that could help advance its 'cause'.

They needed to change the *status quo*!

As part of the covert effort to 'reach out' to sympathetic co-religionists in neighbouring Gulf countries, Sade was put in charge of trying to find ways to finance 'friendly' movements in the region. She had lobbied hard for reaching out to these groups. If her country was serious about changing the dynamics of the politics in the region, it would have to do more than just pay lip service to the

70

people who were on the ground, and were really trying to make changes to the *status quo* of their countries. In the beginning, all that was needed was a few known characters who would be willing to receive large sums of cash into their bank accounts. Then another local – and loyal – supporter would take the cash and distribute it to various operatives, who would spend the money as needed. It could be anything, and it did not even need to be 'subversive' or anti-government at all. It could be something totally unrelated to politics. Organising a poetry session, in which all poets were from the same sect. After that, there would be a 'give-and-take' session about the lives of the poets, about 'their struggle' to publish their work – struggle because of the 'oppressive conditions' in which they lived, conditions that would not allow publication of their work. Then there would be a comparison between the 'hardship' they went through under their regime versus the 'good' times their compatriots had in the 'Shiite heartland'.

The message was clear to anyone who listened: 'you are having a hard time because you are oppressed, and the situation would not be like this if you would help us turn the tables on your regime'.

Of course, if anyone wanted to know more, they could ask more 'discreet' questions after such sessions. Then, they could be told how more 'pro-active' steps could be taken to 'avenge the blood of *Imam* Hussein' – Prophet Mohammed's grandson, and Shiites' first *imam* – who had died in a bloody battle, and whose legacy was still associated with righting the wrong and fighting for the oppressed. If the initial, seemingly benign sessions ignited anyone enough, then they could be told how they could boycott certain goods and commodities that were imported by families with close ties to the ruling regime. How sympathetic neighbours and family should be encouraged to

71

participate in religious ceremonies, and in between all other placards, and raise slogans that could present their point of view – albeit discreetly.

Sustaining this kind of operation was not easy, in the long term. It was expensive, risked too many lives, and the outcome could be limited. The programme was Sade's brainchild, and she had to find a way of sustaining it, improving it, and maximising the result. She had promised that much to some of the 'activist' friends in recent meetings when they had shown up in Dubai on transit to other places. The question was: how?

She had sent out 'feelers' to some contacts, asking how best large fund transfers could be made outside the formal banking system. In business, opportunity is as often made as it just presents itself by luck. The trick is to be on the look-out for it when it does. That's how Hajj Mohsen got his break. In the months and years following the meeting in his Dubai office with the bank official, what Hajj Mohsen needed most was a way to lower the boiling temperature on himself, his business, and his family. In the parlance of economics, he needed to diversify, not the field of business, as much as sources and clients. Once when Sade was in Dubai, he decided to call her and introduce himself. To break the ice, she told him about herself and 'Johnny', and that she had seen him in his house – without saying that she knew what he was doing there. Hajj Mohsen needed a few details. How much money was going to be sent, to whom, and how often?

"Do you also need to know why?"

"Only if I need it to get myself out of jail," he joked.

The operation ran smoothly in the beginning. Each month, Sade would receive a list from her contacts in the Gulf, with their full names, addresses, bank account information, and how much they were supposed to receive.

The money would get there disguised as part of a normal business transaction from Hajj Mohsen's 'import-export' office in Dubai. Authorities in recipient countries would have little to be suspicious about. It was business money, coming from the business hub of the region, going to legitimate businessmen who had established businesses in Dubai. What was there to be suspicious about?

However, the whole scheme ran into trouble after a while, when the original recipients got cold feet, and there were not that many other legitimate businessmen willing to be part of the covert operation to keep up the funding. The money had to be sent to various businessmen on a rotating basis. Do that a few times, and too many and red flags would go up in various government buildings in the region.

There were only two options left, and, in time – given that the amount of money was increasing exponentially – they had to use them both. Some money continued to enter the neighbouring countries as business transaction, but, increasingly, the complicated *hawala* schemes were used, often involving several North American and European cities.

It was *déjà vu* time for Hajj Mohsen. All the things he had done for his homeland decades ago, he was now doing again for a cause he had no sympathy for, and for people he did not know. He did not feel comfortable with it, but economic necessities were forcing his hand. Back in the days when he had started the business, it had been easy to rent office space. Deira was a relatively inexpensive place. The cost of labor was much lower, and there were a lot more workers from the Asian sub-continent who were in the country, if not illegally, at least semi-legally. A sponsor had brought them in to work for someone, somewhere on the dockyard cargo loading docks. The work permit would have been for a short period of time, but the permit would run out, and they would either stay illegally or cut a deal with the employer to let them stay in the country, and they would pay the employer a tiny amount. They could then work for someone else, who would pay more. They would make more money, the original employer would take a cut, and Hajj Mohsen would get 'trainees' who would work for him part time and learn more skills while working at their second job.

However, the situation was changing, partly by accident, and partly by design.

As Dubai had gained fame – you can call it notoriety – for being Heaven for illegal workers from India, Pakistan, Afghanistan, Sri Lanka, Singapore, and many more nations, the population base had increased dramatically. Ordinarily, in a normal economy, if supply goes up, prices would go down, but Dubai had its own logic. Plus, there were other costs: living costs, rent, school fees, grocery bills, *etcetera*. Whereas, years ago, Hajj Mohsen could run his business with a couple of thousand dollars a month, nowadays, the rent on his office was a few times that. If there was one thing he seriously regretted, it was not purchasing a place for his family. Actually, in Dubai, as in most Gulf countries, foreigners, for years, could not buy a place under their own name, anyway. It was not an economic issue, or a matter of supply and demand. It was a pure segregation issue, although you would not dare call it that, and officials would strenuously deny it if you brought it up.

You know, it is one thing to allow our brothers – they would never say 'sisters', or even gender-neutral 'people' *– from the Gulf purchase property here. But the Asians are different from us. They have their own culture, their own habits, and their own way of life. If you allowed them to own property here, it would dramatically change the demographics and nature of our society.* That was a common answer one would get.

Although that was the official policy, Hajj Mohsen probably could have got around it if he had tried hard. He knew enough people in the business circle that one local businessman probably would have allowed him to 'lease' a place for life. Many Asian white collar workers and professionals had managed that. In exchange for years of 'service' to the country, some – a tiny number – of them were allowed certain 'privileges'. They would not ever get the passport or citizenship that would entitle them to massive advantages: free land, lower rates for water and electricity, low interest loans, or being able to open your own business without having to have a local partner – and, therefore, pay a cut of the profits, and many other benefits. However, Hajj Mohsen had not used his connections. He had continued to rent a modest, two-bedroom apartment in the crowded and not-hip Deira for himself, his wife and six kids – four daughters and two sons. As they grew older, the place was much too inadequate, although it was not unusual in the Asian community, not just in Dubai, but the entire Gulf region, for many family members to live in a tiny place.

Now, his kids were growing up. They needed more space, and part of his problem was the 'status thing'. Many of the people who had come to Dubai about the same time he had, had ended up doing quite well for themselves financially, and Hajj Mohsen was under pressure at home.

"Other kids at school already have the latest iPhone. I am still using the first model," one son would complain.

"I have been wearing this dress to school for three weeks. All other girls come with a new one every day," one teenage girl would complain.

"Mr. Vajpaee bought a brand new Jaguar for his

wife last month. When are you going to buy me even another second-hand car?" his wife would ask.

There was always something. Over time, the pressure just became too much.

To ease off some of the pressure, Hajj Mohsen had catapulted himself into the dangerous and shady world of Middle East politics. Thanks to Sade, the Iranians were successfully using Hajj Mohsen to 'facilitate' an elaborate money laundering scheme to finance a regional underground political agitation movement. That put the Emiratis sitting on top of highly classified, highly actionable, and highly 'blackmail-able' information.

CHAPTER 13

ONCE Sade's money routine was in motion, it was time to make it bear some political fruit.

Having recently been given the mouth-filling, Communist-style title of 'Presidential Advisor for International Brotherhood', she was now much more involved in 'coordinating' these regional activities. There were many discussion as to how much to push these movements, and how much to expect of them, and how quickly. There were serious risks to consider.

For now, Sade decided to limit the activity to building up the groups and working with them. Typically, she would fly in from Europe under a pseudo name, sometimes on different passports, wearing different types of clothes and makeup. In each country, she and her contacts would meet in someone's house. Meetings would be limited to a handful of people, so as to not attract attention. The meeting time and place would not become known until only a few hours before. Every meeting would be spent briefly talking about what the latest round of money transactions had achieved. Pockets were deep, but the benefactors were not blind. Surely, everyone realised this was not a philanthropic exercise. There was a lot of diverse opinion on how to proceed. What would make the most sense? What was possible? What would be optimal?

What was the minimum they could count on? Some people wanted to try the political route. Try to modify and moderate the system from the within. There was this idea that if you pressured the regimes long enough and hard enough, they would cave in, eventually. It was not without precedent. One of the Gulf countries had allowed elections not long ago, and the Shiite party had succeeded. Sade did not let up that they, too, had been receiving her cash for a long time. If it worked in one place, wouldn't it work *everywhere*? That was usually the question. *Look what they have done there. They have practically brought the government to a standstill. They have blocked all government reform projects.* Why could it not work somewhere else?

Others wanted to start an armed rebellion against the government, a military coup. Their argument was straight forward: many leaders in the region might *look* strong, but they looked strong to the outside world, not to their own people. They looked strong because they had allied themselves with the 'big powers'. They had borrowed heavily from the outside, bought lots of sophisticated arms, and appeared to have expanded the economy. However, if anything, they were actually weak in the eyes of their people. They were susceptible to pressure. If the underground movement played its cards right, it might be able to get rid of an unpopular regime, and replace it with a government that people wanted and cared about. If anything, Sade and her people should understand that. After all, hadn't they once overthrown the unpopular regime of the Shah and replaced it with one that had now become a serious power broker in the region? If she was serious about 'empowering' people in other countries, shouldn't she wish the same for them? Shouldn't she allow them to reach their own potential? Or was it that she did

78

not trust they could do it?

Sade took the arguments back home, and asked for direction. There were as many divisions inside as there were outside, and the arguments inside the country were accentuated by various interest groups. The Revolutionary Guards; Intelligence; Armed Forces; the Foreign Ministry; *etcetera*. In the end, a decision was made. They would not go for regime change for now, but would target hurting the neighboring countries' local economies by sponsoring selective attacks on some of the oil refineries. Risky, but potentially highly rewarding. Weaken the economies, make the regimes more vulnerable, then tell the governments more would come unless they succumbed to Iranian demands.

The first target was going to be a tiny Arab sheikhdom less than a thousand miles from Tehran. The two countries had disputes over a few islands between their borders, disputes that ran more than a century. However, the Iranians did not choose the sheikhdom to settle old scores. In fact, they did not choose it in order to control its oil fields, either. The country had been the first Arab country to develop its oil fields in the 1930s, but there was not that much oil to begin with, and whatever there was had been excavated, refined and sold. The choice of the country was not for what it had. It was a symbolic choice, because the country also happened to be one of the largest US bases in the region. Hit one of the oil fields, and the panic button would go off throughout the region rather fast.

To have more control over the situation, Sade decided to oversee the initial recruitment process. Getting it right the first time meant all the difference between busting up the whole plan and moving on smoothly from step one to steps two, three, and onwards. When she told her contacts she would arrive in the country, they had offered for her to stay at the house of some local operatives. It was

Middle East hospitality. Someone coming to see you – especially a single woman – should not stay alone in a hotel. At least, that was the conservative thinking, but she was not an ordinary, local woman, and this was a risky business. If she was seen by the local intelligence agents staying with anyone, it could have seriously jeopardised the chances of successfully carrying out the operation. She could find her way out of the country if trouble broke out, but the local operatives and activists could be seriously affected. Neither was it a great idea for her to stay in a fancy, five-star hotel. Those were always watched by the security apparatus. So she stayed in a low-profile place in one of the suburbs. No need to deal with the hustle and bustle of the commercial downtown. Just drive a car, and try to stay out of people's eye range.

On the morning after her arrival, she drove to the house of a local contact, Hashem. People called him 'Arab Hashimoto' because he looked quite Asian. Friends often joked that he got his genes from his Chinese mother, and not his local father, who had studied and lived in China for many years. He had been sent there, working at a local government lab while finishing research on his chemistry PhD. There, he had met his would-be wife. She came from an influential family – the only way a Chinese woman could get permission to marry a foreigner. 'Hashimoto' had always wanted to follow in his dad's path and get into the field of chemistry, somehow. He had been an 'A' student all the way throughout school. Whereas other kids wanted to go to movies or watch TV during grade school, he would stay home and read books. In college, when teenage boys and girls would run away from the scorching heat of their country to more pleasant locales in Europe, he would stay behind, and work on projects at the university's vacant lab.

In time, all of that paid off, and soon after

graduation, he got a job at the National Oil and Gas Company. It was 'national' only in name, for the overwhelming majority of workers were either European or American. There just were not enough qualified locals to fill the vacancies, and the company needed to fill out the jobs fast, because oil and gas revenues were everything to the country. Develop the resources now, or you'd be left behind, since the neighboring countries were all doing the same. The situation was even direr because the sheikhdom did not have that much proven oil and gas reserves to begin with. They were not sitting on top of the world's largest proven oil and gas reserves.

When 'Hashimoto' graduated from college, joining the oil and gas company was an obvious choice, both for him and the company. He started working as an engineer, and was sent immediately to Platform I, the main drilling and refinery facility just off the capital's shores. Workers would be ferried back and forth to work every day. The whole country was so small that everyone practically knew everyone else. They knew each other's families. They knew each other's father and grandfathers, and their background. They knew who was a Shiite, and who was a Sunni. They knew who was educated and ambitious, and who was content doing the job just to get some money at the end of the day.

'Hashimoto' might have been one of the brightest workers at the facility, but you would not have known that, either by his pay check or the way he was treated. Although his academic degree was one of the most relevant compared to others, for the work he was performing, his salary was lower than his friends' with lesser qualifications, and he was always bitter about the fact that he had been passed over a few times for promotion. Every time there was a possibility, they would play with him, treat him well for a few weeks, show him personal and professional respect, get his hopes up, and then, *boom, crash*. Someone else got the promotion. Someone much less qualified.

At first, he had not thought much about it, but he had been hanging around this other engineer a bit lately, and the association was radicalising him. He was asking many more questions.

'Why is it that only Sunnis get promoted?'

'Why is it that they get more money than we do for comparable work?'

'Why is it that the professional staff inside are Shiites, but the security outside are Sunnis?'

'Why is it that the Shiites are doing bulk of the work, but the Sunnis hold top managerial posts?'

'Why...?'

'Why...?'

'Why...?'

The whole time that 'Hashimoto' was becoming more inquisitive and probing in his own thinking, the engineer associate was staying out of the picture when it came time for actually discussing the issues. He would only nudge 'Hashimoto' enough so he would simmer in his own questions, his own uncertainties, and his own unresolved and brewing anger. It went on week after week, month after month.

One day, the engineer invited 'Hashimoto' for dinner after work. He said he and a number of friends were going to someone's house in the suburbs, and asked if he would he like to 'come and shoot the breeze'. *Why not*, he thought. 'Hashimoto' always bemoaned the fact that he did not have enough friends, that he was not hanging out enough, and that the few friends he had were not from work, so he was not really 'in the loop' when it came to work gossip. So, the fact that he was now getting a possible entry into 'work socialisation' actually sounded a welcomed relief to him. When he got to the engineer's house on the appointed night, he noticed that he was one of the only six men sitting in a large living room – *majlis*, in Arabic – filled with ugly, motel-7-style sofas cluttering the room from one corner to another. Then he saw a woman.

Yes, much to his surprise, there was a woman sitting on a single seat sofa at the far end of the room. It was not that he was necessarily a conservative Muslim. His mother, after all, was Chinese. However, society can often condition you in ways that might surprise even yourself. Having lived in the sheikhdom all his life, 'Hashimoto' was always somewhat confused about his own ideas and beliefs. On one hand, he was an Arab and a Muslim. So, naturally, he was exposed to the usual, rhetorical Arab cries of 'America is evil, because it dominates us and supports Israel' that came from certain quarters, but he was also exposed to an increasing number of foreigners – mainly Westerners – who were coming to – practically – run the country. However, still, seeing foreigners was one thing, and seeing a female one in an all-male meeting in the house of a local colleague was something else. It was not hypothetical anymore. This was practical. This was touch-the-flesh nearby. He introduced himself, and sat down. Everyone started their own small talk for a few minutes. It was obvious from the interaction that the members knew each other, that this was not their first meeting. He asked someone next to him how long they had known each other, and the man said a couple of months. Then it was Sade's turn to speak.

She started talking. She just thanked the host for inviting her over. She said she was a 'friend', but did not give her name or nationality, or elaborate on how she knew the host. She went through a bit of a small talk about how

83

there was a serious problem with the power structure in the region. She did not really mention Shiites, Sunnis, and ruling families versus ordinary people, but the message was understood.

"How can we correct the situation?" someone asked, trying to cut to the heart of the meeting.

Sade said she had some ideas, but then joked, "These things can kill you. Or at least put you in jail!"

That was the cue for the group leader, who had attended the Dubai meeting a couple of weeks earlier.

"Brothers, we are all interested in the same things. We all have the same ideas. Or, at least, we are thinking about the same issues. But we also live in a dangerous time, and in a dangerous part of the world. If we are to be able to talk freely with each other, and perhaps find a solution to our common problems, it is quite important that we be able to trust each other. I think, over a period of time, as these meeting continue, *Inshallah,* we can learn to understand each other better. But for now, unless anyone has any objections, I think it would help if we take an oath, *qasm b'illah,* that what is said between these four walls stays in these four walls. Once you have taken the oath, if you still do not want to participate, you are free to leave. No strings attached. No pressure applied. But the important thing is that you don't put other people's lives in jeopardy," he said, eyeing each member for added emphasis.

"'Hashimoto' was a bit uncomfortable. He had thought he was going out to have a beer with a bunch of guys and talk trash. He did not think he was going to be recruited as a member of the 'International Brotherhood' right off the bat, right from the first meeting. He waited to see what everyone else would say. They all said they would be willing to take the oath. So did he, although he was still uncomfortable, and felt quite coerced.

Sade was the first to stand up. She put her hand on her heart. Everyone followed her lead. To an outsider, the whole scene would have looked like one of those underground, secretive, freemasonic ceremonies.

She then uttered the words that everyone repeated.

"I, a member of this small but sacred group, swear to Allah, the most compassionate, the most merciful, that I will hold the proceedings of this meeting secret, and anything said in it, and will take this secret to my grave, and that I will act as a member of a holy group to better the lives of all – myself, my family, my countrymen and women, and my fellow Muslim brethren."

With the ritual put behind, she went through the plan. "We need to get a detailed map of the country's oil facilities. When time comes, an operation would cause limited damage to the facility. You and your colleagues will be notified in advance, so you can be absent that day. We will help you find legitimate excuses, so the government will not become suspicious of you."

"Is this really necessary?" one man asked.

Is there no better way to grab the authorities' attention, wondered 'Hashimoto'. He found it funny that he had started thinking like a member of the group, even thought minutes ago, he had not wanted to be there at all.

They might have been anxious and socially unhappy, but the crowd was clearly unsure if violence was the answer.

"Look," Sade intervened. "No one is trying to cripple the economy of your country. The operation will have limited scope, only to damage the administrative wing of the building, and it will be done after almost everyone has gone home. The purpose of the operation is to do several things. First, we want to put the government on notice that people's patience is running out." She pronounced the words slowly, and with added emphasis. "How many months, years, has it been since you first demanded simple changes to the electoral law? How long has it been since the government dissolved the last elected parliament? How long has it been since the last promise to hold new elections? How many times have they promised that?"

The two men were still not convinced.

"Yes, but oil facilities do not belong to Shiites or Sunnis. They belong to everyone. Plus, my grandfather is a Shiite, and my grandmother is a Sunni. My aunt is married to an Iranian. My uncle is married to a Saudi. You cannot paint such a black and white picture," said 'Hashimoto'.

"Yes, they did not hold elections for the longest time, but when they did, they even invited women to be candidates. Aren't you happy with that? Look around you! How many countries have you seen that have let women run things?" asked the other man.

It was time she toughened her own message.

"Yes, there have been advances here. But that's not because the government wanted to allow them. There have been advances because the United States has been pressuring the royal family to implement these changes. But these are all meaningless, cosmetic changes – and they happened decades after they should have happened. Again, they did *not* happen because you, the people, asked for it. They happened because an outside power pressured your weak government to enforce them. And since you brought up the question of elections and women, just look around you. Look at the family names of the people who got elected. All from rich, business class families that will ultimately support the government. Do you see any worker types in this parliament? As for women: they were not elected to begin with. They were appointed, by the king!

And how many? *One!*"

She paused to regain her own composure. She was becoming too hot around the collar. She could hear her voice going up several notches. She took a deep breath.

"The changes that are happening are not happening for the benefit of the people. If anything, they are happening because the United States is forcing them upon you. Because they are happening for the interest of the United States and the royal family, they are not going to benefit you. If you want to regain control of the government, and have your words and demands heard, you have to find a way to increase your power within the society. Without power, *no one* will listen to you!"

She was ready for the concluding punch.

"Yes, there have been changes, but not the type of changes that will ultimately benefit you. An operation against the oil platform will send a loud message to all the American military anchored here that military might is not everything, and that they are not as strong as they claim to be. You shock the American military, and you'll shock the ruling family."

There was nothing else to say. It was time to decide who was going to be in, and who was going to be out.

The second man, the engineer who worked with 'Hashimoto' on the platform, graciously apologised and bowed out.

'Hashimoto' was left to carry the torch. He was asked to provide a full and detailed map of the facilities in a few weeks, which he duly did, and did not hear anything afterward. Three days before the attack was to be carried out, he and two others working on the platform were sent a message to their homes, through private messengers, saying not to show up at work on the appointed day. When the time had come, the explosion had indeed been a lofty firework. The equivalent of a few thousand pounds of TNT had been placed strategically on various corners of the platform, some placed underneath the structure above water, all wired for detonation by remote control through a cell phone. The administrative wing of the oil platform was mightily destroyed, and while the adjacent facilities had seen some damage, there was no damage to the pipelines. In a small country like the sheikhdom, the reaction was nothing short of shock and utter disbelief. The government immediately enforced a *de facto* martial law, although they never called it that. Police and army patrols were fanned out throughout the city, checkpoints were erected in various parts of the city to check drivers' ID cards, and city exit roads were closed to cut off access in and out. The incident had happened too late in the day for the government to think of stopping the next morning's press, plus, it did not matter; all radio and television stations had gone live with the story soon after the blasts. The US had immediately put its military servicemen and women on full alert. All leaves were canceled, and all off-duty personnel were ordered back to barracks.

If the aim of the attack was to create havoc and chaos, they had achieved their goal.

The Iranians chose the rest of their targets carefully in the months and years to come. Having chosen the sheikhdom as the 'warning shot', they went about establishing their Crescent Empire, similar networks in other countries, from northwest of Turkey down to Kurdish parts of Iraq, to Kuwait and Qatar in the west, stretching to eastern parts of Pakistan, Afghanistan, Turkmenistan, and Uzbekistan in the east. The Persian-speaking Tajikistan's government was already a puppet government of Tehran.

When it was all said and done, the u-shaped half

moon of terror was in place, thanks to numerous sleeper cells that had carried out their operations as ordered. In each case, the reaction was the same: shock, horror, condemnation, and promise of retribution. The pattern in the aftermath of each attack was the same. Shady and shadowy local groups would claim responsibility, the government would round up dozen, maybe hundreds, of people, only to find out they were not really behind the attack. Sometimes directly, but more often indirectly, the Iranian regime would communicate to local governments that it 'could help' identify and even 'calm down' the people behind the attacks. If the local regime felt insecure enough to accept the Iranian help, Tehran leaders would jump in with their political demands. If they did not, there would be more 'incidents' until Iranian demands were met.

The Crescent Empire was not just an offensive tool. It also was a clever attempt to shield the territory from any possible outside attack. If any foreign power was going to invade Iran, sooner or later, it would need a ground force invasion. Iran now established a physical buffer zone against any such invasion.

CHAPTER 14

AS Sade continued coordinating efforts of secret bombing cells in various Gulf countries, she got to spend more time in the sheikhdom, and got to see more of 'Hashimoto'. He was fascinated by the concept of a woman who was smart, tough, and could be enough of a manager to boss people around and get the job done. It was not that she was beautiful or sexy, or things like that. It was the idea that, in a male-dominated society, he was seeing a woman rule, or, at least, dominate.

For her, on the other hand, it was the idea that a man in the traditional Arab world was kind, caring toward women, accepting of them, and allowing himself to feel equal to her. It was refreshing to her that he would read poetry and try to keep up with his Chinese, if only to please his mother, but it was also refreshing to see that, the more they talked, the more he was coming across as a politically motivated scientist type who was more interested in gaining control of any given situation than a person who would sit down and just believe in faith and pre-ordainment. He was a pragmatist, just like her.

Their conversations were usually over dinner, after he would get off work, and more often than not, it would continue for hours. It usually started with discussion of a general topic – what was going on in the region, latest news, exotic places she had been to since the last time they had met, and whatever else might have been going on in his life, *etcetera*. Things not too simplistic, but maybe not too deep, either. However, somehow, inevitably, the topic would always relate back to the socio-economic situation of the region. As an engineer, he made decent money. He was single, so he did not have to worry about family expenses. He lived with his old mother, who received the pension of her deceased husband. 'Hashimoto' contributed some of his salary to help his mother, but only a small percentage. Despite all that, he did not see any bright future for himself.

"You know, I am not a big spender," he told her one night over dinner. "Maybe once a month or something I would go out with my friends from work. Alcohol sales are forbidden here, so if we want to have a beer or something, we have to go to a five-star hotel. A couple of drinks or dinner would automatically cost a good portion of the weekly allowance I set for myself. And I am supposed to be part of the educated class. My father was educated. My mother is a descendant of the Chinese nationalist leader. My grandfather was a rich man, but he fell out of favor with the ruling family."

It was not an unusual story; she had heard similar tales from many others, but, coming from him, with the sincerity and tenderness with which he relayed the story, added more believability to the story.

"A few weeks ago, the government announced an increase in the price of gas and tuition in private schools. This – gas increase – in a country that produces gas! A country that refines gas for other people! We sell our gas at a discounted price to the American military for their people here, but we increase the price for our own people! What kind of people have we turned out to be? And then the education issue." He said the last part with a deep sense of anger in his voice. "There was a time many countries in this part of the world could pride themselves in offering quality public education. All free throughout the primary and secondary education. But lately, a lot of parents are changing to private schools. First, because the quality at public schools has gone down, and parents want to make sure their kids get a good education. Second, because there are so many foreigners flooding the country, and it has become a 'class' issue. Parents want their kids 'seen' with kids from 'high class' families. They prefer their kids to learn their subjects in English, or maybe French or German, rather than in Arabic, their mother tongue. Who is controlling the curriculum? They say the government is still in charge and has to okay all textbooks, but we all know it does not happen. The ministry neither has the resources nor, frankly speaking, the inclination to dictate what private schools do. So, in the end, instead of teaching kids history from an Eastern, Arab, Islamic perspective, we end up teaching them about the Marshall Plan, creation of the World Bank and the IMF, and how that has been good for the poor in Africa!

"And, of course, they don't want to interfere in the tuition fees of the schools. First, because if they did, people would say the government is interfering in how the private sector should run, and how the government is trying to control the economy, whereas the real issue should be: can the parents of *local* kids afford the schools? And the second thing is that they think the more money these schools make, the more money would be invested in the overall economy of the country, and, as long as foreigners are willing to pay for the bulk of the tuition fees, why not? What's worse is that these types of issues are not limited to this country. Yes, we have our issues, but name any country in this part of the world, and there are similar issues."

Sade found it interesting that none of what 'Hashimoto' said had a religious tone to it. He was not arguing that an Islamic government should be set up, or that the government had distanced itself from the principles of Islam. He was not even repeating what was on everybody else's tongues: that their ruler was such a playboy that he barely spent any time in the country, preferring to lust around in his Marrakech mansion.

"What would you do if you could?" she asked him.

"Root out the system completely!" he said with a straight face. "Find a way to fundamentally change regimes in this part of the world."

Then came the kicker. "But don't just change it here. You cannot just get these people to change without scaring the masters. We need to go to America, London, Paris!"

It was not long before Sade and her masters realised they might have found their willing accomplice for the real part of their strategy. Destabilising the region and creating the Crescent Empire were just Acts 1 and 2. There was a deeper, meaner, more sinister strategy into the Iranian game. However, before they could fully trust their new-found asset with the project, they had to test him.

*   *   *

One night, over dinner, she – with blessing from the headquarters back home – threw in an idea that she hoped would open new avenues.

"Don't you miss your family back in China?" she asked, without much warm up into the conversation.

He did not seem surprised or taken aback. He just kept on eating for a few seconds. Then, he put the spoon down, picked up the half empty wine glass, had a sip, but not his usual small sip, then put the glass down, almost empty, and looked her in the eyes.

"I heard, years ago, that when Dad wanted to bring Mom back to the Middle East, there was a huge scandal. Mom was from the fairly high-class family, rooted in the system, the communist system. In those days, it was not like today. People could not just pick up their suitcase and travel. Money was not the only obstacle. The system did not look kindly to free, foreign travel, especially for someone who had Mom's status. My grandparents were the ones most against it. They were old. Mom was the only daughter. And no one from the family had ever travelled before. All of those things kind of freaked them out. They begged my father to stay and not take her out. They promised him a long-lasting and well-paid job in any university he wanted. They said, 'we have the connections. You name your price. We will deliver. And you can live happily with our daughter'. They used every trick in the book to convince her not to go. But, in the end, he decided to come back, and she decided to leave with him.

"My grandparents died a few years after my parents left, and it was left to my uncle to break the news. My mom and her brother had not talked in all those years. They could not. The government did not look favourably at it. Not so much because of her, as for him. He had just become an army colonel when she left, and it took a long time before the regime trusted him enough to promote him to the rank of a general. They naturally did not want him to be associated with anyone outside the country. I am not sure what his motives were for not calling. I am sure he did not want to jeopardise his promotion chances, but I am pretty sure a part of him was just happy to have an excuse not to call. He hated the fact that my mother kind of

94

deserted the family and the country for a foreign, Arab, man.

"That was the first and last time they spoke in all these years."

Sade knew some of the story, having checked out his background. She knew the overall story of his mother and her family. The Communist Party. The brother. However, she did not know everything. Although she knew what she was going to offer before she walked into the meeting, the fact that she was touched by his story made her expression somewhat more genuine.

"Don't you think it would be a great idea if the two of them could meet?" she asked him.

He uttered a quiet, "yes." Then he added, "In the Gulf, when the regime likes you, it is easy for them to throw money at you. They would buy you a house, a car, whatever they can do to keep you on their side. The communist countries have changed, but they have not changed that much. My uncle still makes less than half of what a normal, skilled, mid-level professional makes in the Gulf. He does not have the money to travel, and we – my mom and I – we get by okay, but cannot bring him over and pay for his expenses."

After a few minutes of conversation, Sade made the offer she had come to make.

"Look, you have been great to us. In addition to the platform maps, you have provided info on people. You have been kind enough to give us names and phone numbers of other people we could call. You've worked hard for us. You've worked hard in life. And I like you. If you and you mother want, if your uncle can leave the country for a couple of weeks of vacation, I can arrange to pay your expenses. Perhaps you can all have a vacation somewhere, and your mom and her brother can get to know each other again."

*   *   *

When 'Hashimoto' brought up the subject with his mom, he got less than what he expected.

"Don't you want to see your brother?"

"Of course, I do!"

"But you don't look excited."

"I am excited deep down, but…"

"But what?"

"It is not easy. We have not seen each other in years. I left with so many issues unresolved. Your uncle, in his eyes, I did not just leave to get married, I *left*! I left our parents. I left him."

"But that was years ago."

"Yes, but we never talked about it. We never *resolved* the issues. And years of separation has just made it tougher to now pick up the conversation where it was left off. He stayed behind. That means he is still operating on the old traditional and cultural values of China. They have not changed much, just as your father's father's ideas were not that different when he died. He still did not forgive your father for marrying a non-Muslim, non-Arab. The only reason he finally died in peace was that your father gave him the apology he wanted. I never gave that apology to my family. They have been waiting for it for decades. I suppose your uncle is still waiting for it."

"And now?"

"I am still not prepared to apologise. I don't regret having done what I did. I just wish I had more to show for it than just you and this house!"

She really did not need to say more. She might have been born a Chinese communist, but years of living in the opulent Arab world had made its capitalistic marks on her.

"Do you want to do this or not?"

She asked for a few days to think about. It was not an outright 'no', but it was not a heart-felt 'yes', either. When 'Hashimoto' relayed the conversation to Sade, it made her think harder about how to pull out the stops. The Iranians needed this meeting more than anything else, and Sade was determined to make it happen. What Sade did not tell her new protégé was that they already knew quite a lot about his uncle. In fact, they knew more about the uncle than he did, or his mother, for that matter, and they wanted something from him. Something quite big. Something that could give the Iranians unprecedented leverage in their international strategic game.

CHAPTER 15

FOR the past couple of decades, the uncle, General Jian Min Shang, had been the head of the military industrial production section of the massive Chinese army. He was not just the head of it. He was considered the 'father' of it. He was the one who had convinced the Chinese leaders there was a need for it.

Sade and her colleagues had been very interested in China. They were watching the country rather carefully. On one hand, the country had, by 2020, over two billion people, and the number was rising. However, it was also doing well for itself economically. The gross domestic product rate had been rather high for the past several years. The growth rate had surpassed that of the United States the past several years. Every industry and economic sector you looked at, you could find 'made in China' tags – from your underpants to your computer equipments and cars. The Chinese were always looking for more markets, too. Wherever you looked, there were Chinese business delegations and Chinese Chambers of Commerce.

One area that was working hard – but not much talked about – was the military.

The Chinese military had been caught between a rock and a hard place for decades. On one hand, it considered itself competitor to both Moscow and

Washington. Decades earlier, they had bought some military goods from both the Soviet Union and the United States, but often – not always – you could not call them 'high tech' armaments. Neither Washington nor Moscow trusted China enough to sell its 'best and brightest' military technology.

That meant the Chinese had to scrounge wherever they could. They had to train their own people in science and maths. They had to raise a generation of people smarter than not only their own fathers and mothers, but also smarter than people in their generation in Moscow, Washington, London, and Paris. They improved their education system to the degree they could, but they also half opened their borders so the smart kids could go to the United States and elsewhere to get the education they needed – as long as they came back!

After a decade or two, the Chinese had raised their know-how to the level they needed, but they still had not reformed their bureaucracy enough. The red tape was stifling the country, and the more 'national security' a sector was considered, the worse the red tape got. The military was pretty much at the top of the apex.

Needless to say, General Jian had an unenviable job. He was not a particularly smart or educated man. He was average, and had gone to high school and university inside the Chinese system. Back then, there was no private sector education. It was all government-sponsored schools or nothing. However, what Jian lacked in education quality, he made up for in nationalism and political savvy. He knew he had to break the cycle, somehow, and do it all pretty much by himself, without much help from the establishment.

Some years ago, General Jian had used his position and prestige to argue before the Communist Party leaders to allow the semi-privatization of the army, as long the country was on the economic privatisation course.

"Our army is one of the biggest in the world. We have a historical reputation. Our army has had a role in forming the world's civilization for centuries and millennia. But the world of our ancestors is not the world in which we live. If we want to maintain our name and fame, we have to find a way to improve our army, both the personnel and the equipment. The former is easy. We have the know-how, we can access international literature. We can cooperate with countries that have access to better training. The equipment part is difficult, because we are unlikely to get the kind of massive funding we need from the government. But the funding issue also presents an opportunity. The only way we can advance our military to a first-class technological military is to fund it through the same type of the privatization program that the economy has enjoyed. We need to 'outsource' and allow some military technology for use in civilian purposes. Let the private sector make money for itself. It can help us by 'marketing' some of our excess military production, without getting the government involved directly. There are countries that might not want to openly buy from the Chinese government. But the other side of the story is that there are certain technologies we would like to have that other government might not sell us, but might be willing to sell to a private company, to somehow bypass international sanctions."

Over time, General Jian's ideas had found a home with certain military and political leaders. General Jian had, basically, found a way for China to acquire what is known to the rest of the world as 'dual use' technology.

By the time Mao died in 1976, China's People's Liberation Army had gone into business for its own, owning thousands of companies worldwide, and just making money for itself. It owned anything from real and pseudo import-export companies, to hotels, factories, and technology companies.

The number of the companies was indeed massive, although few people knew the exact number, even within the Chinese military. Even worse, no one had even an estimate of how much those companies were contributing annually to the budget of the Chinese army.

However, until General Jian came to power, these companies were just a commercial arm of the army. They were just making money for one of the largest armies in the world, but they did not play any role in advancing China's military ambitions. When the general came to power, with the blessing of the party Central Committee, they decided to use these companies in a more centralized and organized fashion.

*   *   *

The areas of particular interest to General Jian were missile delivery systems and advanced fighter jets. For years, the Chinese were interested in improving the range and ballistic capability of their missile delivery systems. History had taught them that their deadliest enemies were not necessarily the ones closest to them. They needed improvements in both areas to feel safer. The problem with the high-tech fighter jets technology was that – in a nutshell – no one trusted the Chinese. The Russians sold them some basic planes, as did the Americans. However, when it came to high tech, the Chinese were more or less left on their own to either steal what they could through industrial espionage, or buy through intermediaries. Sometimes, the original sellers knew where the parts were destined for, and sometimes they did not.

One of the missile technologies that the Chinese were active in was an area only a handful of governments around the world had expertise in. It was better known by its abbreviation, MIRV: Multiple Independently Targetable Re-entry Vehicle. MIRVs were a new brand of missiles that upped the ante in the global arms race. In the old days of the arms race, countries had missiles –fitted with nuclear warheads – that could attack the enemy. However, the old system had a few disadvantages. A number of things could go wrong. The missile could malfunction; the nuclear warhead might not deliver the damage expected; the missile could be intercepted before penetrating the target, *etcetera*. So the major military powers had embarked on a new plan: in effect, fit more than one missile on a missile system, kind of like cluster bombs. So you would shoot up a missile, and it would splinter into a number of separate missiles, each with its own nuclear warhead and pre-programmed target coordinates. That would increase, multi-fold, the chances of penetrating behind enemy lines. If one missile did not work, the other surely would. If one missile was shut down by an anti-missile defense system, the other would not be. If one target was buried too deep down in a bunker, others would manage to find their target.

The Chinese always had a big motive for pursuing the arms race. Aside from the commercial side of it, the Chinese felt real and perceived threats from multiple fronts: North Korea, the United States, and Taiwan-related threats, to name a few.

When China entered the 'MIRV world' in the early 1980s, the main delivery vehicles for the missiles were either stationed silos or mobile launchers. Lately, however, the Chinese had embarked on a new road, one the Iranians had got the wind of, and in which Tehran was quite interested.

CHAPTER 16

SADE called on 'Hashimoto' a few days after their last conversation.

"Have you decided whether to meet your uncle or not?"

"No, my mother is still undecided."

"Since your mom wants to make a good impression on him after such a long time, maybe it is best if you all met in some vacation spot. Maybe that would be better for him, and it would be better for your mom, since she would not have to invite him to your small apartment."

That was one of the things he always appreciated about Sade, her 'female touch', knowing how to see the real sense of the things, and make the best of them.

"I told you, we don't have that kind of money."

"And I told you not to worry about that. I will take care of the expenses. Just let me know where you want to go, and when."

In the end, 'Hashimoto' and his mother decided to break away from the Middle East altogether. If they were going to go on vacation, they really wanted to go on vacation. They wanted to explore other parts of the world. The Middle East was out of the question. Asia was old news to them. Africa was too poor. Australia and New Zealand just did not cut mustard for the mother, and the

Americans had made it too difficult to get a tourist visa. That left Europe. It was summer, so the family decided on the Black Sea coast of Bulgaria. The Bulgarians had recently launched an aggressive real estate campaign in the Middle East, and the mother and son thought it would be a good place to visit. It was relatively inexpensive – although Sade told them repeatedly not to worry about money – and it was easy to get visas.

CHAPTER 17

BULGARIA was not exactly the 'jewel' of Europe, or even Eastern Europe, not long ago. For decades, people around the world looked at Bulgaria as a yet another satellite Soviet country, a poor, backward country with little first-world infrastructure. Yes, there was the Black Sea. Maybe it was good enough for the downtrodden third world vacationers, but no self-respecting French, Italian, or German was going to set foot there.

Of course, the Bulgarians looked at it differently. For them, their history goes back to the earliest times in civilization. Archaeologists, not long ago, had found ruins in Kozarnika Cave in north-western Bulgaria that showed remnants of culture going back more than a million years. Before the slaves had settled down in the land, the Thracian Diaspora had ruled the country for close to a thousand years. Many Bulgarians, still to this day, vehemently believe that the Cyrillic alphabet was founded on their land, under the patronage and sponsorship of one of their rulers, Prince Boris I.

In more recent times, it was Bulgaria that became a member of the European Union, much faster than many other former satellite countries.

Communism or no communism, socialism or no socialism, Western monetary standards or not, Bulgarians were a proud people, and no one was going to put them down. And if, with the change of times, they could capitalize on the deep pockets of other Europeans, Americans, or Scandinavians, well, so be it. They had built up the Black Sea area to fit the tourism rush they wanted, and now they were relishing in the hard currency it was bringing them.

* * *

The flight to Varna was a rather pleasant one for the 'Hashimoto' family, although filled with anxiety. They had decided that it would be best to meet at the Varna airport. To make sure things went smoothly, Sade had recruited the services of a nice Bulgarian woman she knew. Desi was a slim, medium-height young woman with inviting green eyes and a charming smile. She and her family had worked in the real estate market for years, and she had mastered the art of staying calm, even when faced with the most demanding and obnoxious of clients. She had learnt the lesson well. The client was always right, even when he was dead wrong!

Sade had arranged that 'Hashimoto' and his mother would arrive first, spend the night, and then go back to the airport and greet the uncle. Desi was expecting the mother and the son at the airport when they arrived. She had their names written in English on cardboards to make it easier for them to recognize her. Sade had faxed her copies of their pictures, just in case. The encounter went without a hitch. The ride from the airport reminded the mother a lot about the old days of socialism and communism, mixed with a bit of *nouveau riche*. Cars were generally 70s and 80s models, but, every now and then, a Mercedes C class or a BMW 700 series would take over. Driving down the main streets in the central part of the city or the residential districts, you could see the standard socialism-style, bland apartment

106

blocks. Many of them had broken windows. The paint had come off most buildings, and the rust on the steel pillars was all too visible. In some parts of the city, the garbage was piling up on street corners.

However, there were also new villas, some with swimming pools, overlooking the Black Sea, raising their heads in testimony to the new economic advances of some individuals. The farther you got from the city centre or the old residential districts, the better the outlook got.

Desi had booked a superior room for each of the mother and son team at Varna's opulent Great Varna Hotel. The hotel was in a touristy suburb of St. Constantine. Looking at it from the outside, it was not anything out of the ordinary. It was grey, ten-storey building. The lobby and the ground floor did not look particularly posh. There was no designer-brand Italian furniture. Not even Ikea. There was an Italian restaurant in the complex, but not much to write home about, and the rooms were normal. You could even argue they were not worth the five-stars the hotel was brandishing. In fact, the interesting part of the hotel was not even inside it. It was outside, in the pool and bar area. The pool and garden were fairly large, separated from the Black Sea by another hotel, less than a hundred feet away. There were two pools, one for the adults and one for the kids. Next to the adult pool was a row of oak, futon-style double beds, with white Sutton curtains on each of the four bed legs that could provide privacy or keep out the sun. The row behind that was a mix of single and bigger wooden chairs, some with umbrellas, some not.

The hotel had built a nice bar by the pool. Every night, there was a different genre of music. One night it was disco. One night it was rap. One night it was jazz. Another, just mellow music. You could just sit around, chill, have a drink, or enjoy the music and talk, if you wanted. Or think,

Or read. Or whatever. They called it the Beach Party.

Plus, if you really wanted to be by the sea, all you had to do was walk a bit, pass another hotel, and you'd enjoy the serenity of the Black Sea.

After checking into their respective rooms, they first wanted to go around and see the area. That was the first instinct of any person arriving in a new area, but hours of being cooped up on an airplane and then having had to wait in Sofia, the capital, to change planes to Varna, had made both of them rather tired.

They decided, instead, that they would have a relaxing time by the pool, and call it a night. The mother had fish and chips, and ordered a Coke. 'Hashimoto' had a salad, and decided to have a glass of wine with it. His mother knew he occasionally drank, and did not mind, but this was the first time he was drinking in front of her. She noticed, but did not say anything. He, too, realized the meaning of the moment, but let it go without saying anything. They just looked into each other's eyes for a few seconds, and continued with the night.

The next morning, Desi was on hand again at around noon to take the two to the airport, this time for the uncle's momentous arrival from China.

Since Sade and her paymasters had decided to pull out all the stops, the uncle was travelling business class all the way. Lufthansa had given him the option of spending a night in Frankfurt, but the general had decided he wanted to fly all the way. Of course, the uncle thought this was all thanks to his sister and nephew's generosity.

Varna airport was not exactly an international airport, even though its official name did include the word, but that did not diminish the importance of this family ending its long separation.

* * *

The mother and her brother found each other as soon as he walked out of the customs area.

He was slim. That was military life. His hair was silvery. She could tell he was slowly balding. He looked much older than his age, she thought. His face and wrinkles betrayed that there was more to his life than his age. He was wearing his dark greenish military pants, but, thankfully, not the jacket, with all the stars and medals. She appreciated that he was not trying to send a signal that this was a 'formal' meeting. After all these years of separation, the last thing they needed was something that would freeze the moment. They needed icebreakers, not added tension.

He was carrying a small suitcase. He put it down, straightened his shoulders and the sports jacket he was wearing, and the brother and sister just stared into each other's eyes for what seemed to be eternity, although it could not have been more than a minute.

It was as if time had frozen for the two of them, as if each was trying to resurrect years of separation through magnetic eye contact. Each was trying to discern as much about who the other person had become in the few seconds they had, trying to remember exactly where they were, what they thought, and what they had done when they last saw each other.

After the long wait, he and she each moved a few steps closer, and, without saying a word, hugged each other tightly. Neither one wanted to let go of the other. She shed a few tears, but tried to hide it. He choked, but controlled himself. Finally, he noticed his nephew. They first shook hands, and then they, too, hugged, although it was not as long or as intense as the encounter between the brother and sister.

Desi, looking from a few feet away, was somewhat perplexed by the meeting. The three of them obviously had a lot of pent up emotions for each other, but Desi found it weird that none of them really had any words to exchange. Not even knowing anything about the relationship, she could tell a thunderstorm was needed in that relationship before calmer skies could prevail.

* * *

Back at the hotel, the uncle settled into his junior suite. It was the kind of posh place he had heard and read about, but never personally experienced. It was not the Ritz. It was not a glitzy place, but it was plenty for a Chinese army officer, even at his rank. He took a long shower, put on his bathroom robe, went back to the hotel mini-bar, and fixed himself a Black Label Scotch. He then sat on the room balcony, and watched the manicured green lawns, the pool, and the sun bathers, with a good number of the female ones parading themselves topless.

He thought about how this was the first time in a *long* time in his life that he really was enjoying himself, how hard he had worked in his life, and how little he had relaxed and enjoyed life. He wondered if, or how, life would have been different if he had got out of service to his country years ago – as many of his colleagues had – and made some money for himself. It would have been an easy thing to do. All he would have had to do was appoint himself as the head of one of the front companies the army had established, one of those private sector companies that made money for themselves while doing the government's bidding.

For years, he had seen how his friends had travelled the world, stayed in fancy hotels, and bought luxury items

110

for themselves and their family. Clothes. Jewellery. Cars. Even houses. Why was it that he was never able to bring himself to do some of that? It did not mean he had to be disloyal to his country, or betray his oath of service to the army.

Before he could answer any of his own questions, the hotel phone rang. It was his sister, asking if he wanted to go for a walk around the neighborhood. He said yes.

As the three started walking the shopping lanes of St. Constantine and Helena, it was obvious each one was trying to find ways to start a dialogue. They all knew that was needed, but no one could figure out how to get around doing it right.

"It is really good to see you, uncle," said 'Hashimoto'.

"Yes, it is an honour to have your company. With your busy job, it's really nice of you to take time off for us," said his mother, trying to be both welcoming and show the kind of obedience and deference expected of a younger sister in a traditional culture such as Chinese.

General Jian had mixed feelings on how to behave. He wanted to be a simple brother and uncle, but he had not played the role in so many years that he almost did not know how to.

"Yes, it is good to see you both," he said.

However, his tone was so formal and cold that anyone could tell he did not really mean it. Or he meant it, but was rather uncomfortable feeling it deep inside. Even he realised it, and was determined to do better next time.

"We have not seen each other in years. It is a nice opportunity to catch up, hopefully." It sounded better this time. He decided to try more. "How is life in the sheikhdom? It must have changed a lot since you moved there."

111

This was obviously a cue for his sister to enter the conversation.

"Yes, when we moved there, it was more or less a desert."

She intentionally used the word 'we', and left out the word 'my husband', or even his name. Given how much agony the whole marriage issue had caused, she decided not to aggravate things. Just a passing reference would be enough. No need to get her brother upset the first day he was there.

"The place has changed in many ways. It is a lot more developed. There are a lot of nice, new buildings, new shops, new offices, new schools, and newly paved streets. They are building a new airport, and they say that when it is done, it will be the largest airport in the world. There are also a lot of foreigners working there, from different countries."

"Yes, they have contacted us, too. They wanted us to send them some of our workers to help."

"Yes, there are a lot of Chinese coming. Every day, I can see more on the streets," confirmed the sister. She wanted to say 'perhaps you might be interested in moving there' but decided it was too soon, and too intrusive to bring up the subject. *Maybe later*, she told herself.

"How is China?" inquired the nephew.

His mother would have preferred him to use the word 'motherland' in front of the general. She was *so* desperate for the visit to go well. However, it was too late, and it turned out that the uncle did not mind it, or, at least, did not show any sign of disapproval.

"It is well. It, too, has developed. It is not the same country it used to be. Some things have developed, while others have stayed frozen in time. We, too, have new building and new roads. We have some people getting rich

112

in a few years, but most people just work harder and harder in life, and grow older and older, hoping their government will appreciate their service, but they just end up retiring poor and not knowing what will happen to them."

There was a moment of silence. Everyone was kind of surprised and taken aback by the statement; even the uncle was surprised at what he had said.

The general was always known for his patriotic feelings, for believing in service to the nation, to China's great, historical role in building, maintaining, and even correcting the direction of the world's civilisation. He had gone into the army believing in those principles. For decades, he had not waived from those positions. And now? What did those words mean? Was he now questioning the wisdom of his own service? Did he think the country had let him down? Let down all but a few of its billion-plus people? Was this the general's jetlag speaking? Was he going through a temporary depression? Or did he mean what he said?

As they continued their tour of the shopping area, no one spoke anymore. Enough had been said. They just did the tourism thing. Looked at the shops, looked at the prices, inspected the 'Made in China' tags on a lot of the goods, looked at each other, shook their heads, and continued walking.

As the holiday moved into the second and third day, the mother decided it was time to embark on a serious conversation with her brother. After all, the main purpose of this trip was to iron out years-old family disputes and bad blood. She was not moving back. He would not throw his life away in China to come and live with them – although his comments a few days earlier showed he might not have been as happy as the family thought he was. One day, when the three of them were sitting at the beach under an umbrella, she decided to get to the point.

"For years, I have lived with this sense of guilt that I have let the family down. When I left, I left not out of malice toward it. I have always loved our parents. When you kindly called to tell me they had passed away, my heart broke into many pieces. I am not sure I have recovered from it."

"I don't think you should be too hard on yourself."

"When I left, I left because I fell in love with someone. I wanted to spend the rest of my life with that person. But it was not meant against my family. It was not meant against my country. And, to be honest with you, I am tired of feeling guilty. Our parents are gone now. My husband is gone, too. The only people left in my life now are you and my son."

She was obviously eliciting some reaction, but, as she waited, she wondered if he was about to give any. It was a good couple of minutes before he spoke.

"When you were a young school girl, our grandfather used to joke that the family had been out of aristocracy long enough, that we had not tasted being royalty in a long time, and that you would elevate the family again. He and grandmother used to joke that you would marry a handsome prince, and you would be the key to the family regaining its lost position."

"Every family says that about their young girl!!"

"Yes, but every family does not truly believe it. With you, it was a different story. To understand the reason behind the depth of the disappointment when you left, you'd have to understand that that statement was not just empty talk. They actually meant it. Your academic record in high school and university proved that. You were an extremely beautiful girl. You were a professional basketball player on the national team. You could have gone

114

where no one else in the family had. So, if you want to understand the disappointment, you have to look at it from two perspectives. One is that an obviously talented girl decided not to capitalize on her abilities, not just for her own sake, but also for the sake of the overall good of her family. Remember, this was China decades ago, when families had little, because there was little available in the whole country. Remember our neighbor, with whose son you went to grade school? When he joined the national Olympics team, all of a sudden, the family had a new car, they had money to renovate their house, they had a new fridge, and they had a summer house in the countryside."

"We had all those!" she interjected.

"Yes, but only because of our ancestry. But our privileges were far fewer when you and I were growing up, compared to the times of our parents. Everyone in the family firmly believed that you would make it to the national Olympics team."

Although she had brought up the whole topic so she could feel less guilty by the end of it, she was actually feeling guiltier now.

"Of course, the other side of the story is that you married a foreigner. You knew back then, and we all made it clear, that it had nothing to do with the fact that he was an Arab. Or a Middle Eastern. Or a Muslim. It had to do with the fact that our culture never did, and does not now, approve of marrying outsiders. That is not unique to us. Look at their culture. They do not approve of it any more than we do."

So far, he had just spoken about the past and the logic of what had happened. What she really wanted to hear was what the future would be like.

"But that is all the history of last couple of decades. Our country has evolved into something few expected. We have all come a long way. You have gone your way. Our parents are dead. I am, well, I am where I am!!"

It was not quite the 'yes, you are forgiven, and I love you now, as I did when you left' type of remark she was hoping for, but it sounded as reconciliatory as he could come up with. She allowed herself deep breath, a sigh of relief, and then she simply broke down and cried, and cried, and cried. Now, he could not – or chose not to – control himself, either. He, too, cried, reached out for her hand, and held it tightly. The brother and sister were finally reunited.

*　*　*

Sade called in to talk to check up on 'Hashimoto', and see how the trip was going. He filled her in on everything, from the time he and his mother had arrived, to the reconciliation a day before.

"I am glad this is happening for you and your family. If you and your mother want, we can arrange for a second meeting. It is now summer, so maybe it is not a good time to invite him to the Middle East. But come February, right around the Chinese New Year, perhaps, if he can come, it might be a good follow up."

He said he would run it by his mother and uncle.

116

CHAPTER 18

THE next time the family met in Dubai, which was something the uncle had suggested. Like many others in world, the general had wondered about the city that had outshined others in the region. Dubai had recently adopted a new approach toward China. Whereas the city had, for decades, relied on unskilled and semi-skilled workers from the Indian sub-continent countries, the city was now turning toward China. Dubai wanted many things from Beijing, from cheap construction laborers to engineers to run the newly established metro system. However, they also wanted arms, different types of it. Most of their arsenal was decidedly Western, mainly American and British, but leaders in Dubai also wanted to make sure they were not tied to one particular system. They had always believed in diversity, whether it was economy or anything else.

The Emiratis were not only interested in imports. They also wanted to talk exports. A couple of the government-run construction companies were desperately looking to expand their operations internationally, and wanted to know if the Chinese would agree to let them run operations there. The Chinese were, at first, hesitant. Why would they need the people in Dubai to teach them how to construct buildings? However, the Emiratis actually had a

117

different idea. What they really wanted was to buy material, and hire subcontractors for their construction projects in other Arab countries. The Chinese were still cheaper than the labor in many Arab countries, and more skilled than those in many African states. Plus, it was a contracting gimmick. Any time you could sign a contract that included your own crew, you could claim you were paying them a few times more than you actually were. It was a technique American companies were well versed in. They had executed that with perfection in countries like Iran and Afghanistan.

The Chinese had come around. They would make money by sending some of their citizens overseas on well-paying salaries, some of which would undoubtedly be remitted back to the homeland. Whatever was not sent back home would, at least, make some Chinese life happier, even if that life was in another country.

Like the trip in Varna, 'Hashimoto' and his mother stayed in a 'superior' room at Dubai's Jumeira Beach Hotel, while the general stayed in a suite.

Jumeira Beach Hotel was one of the nicest hotels in the city, right on the beach, classy, and far enough out of the city centre to allow for relaxation. It belonged – as many other things did – to the ruling family. The hotel was next door to Burj Al Arab, the world's only so-called 'seven-star' hotel. Officially, there was no such category, but the all-suites hotel had 'earned' the reputation because of the luxury rooms and services it provided. Room accessories and bathrooms were gold plated. Bentley and Rolls Royce cars gave hotel guests complimentary rides to the city or elsewhere, and a helicopter pad was available on the roof to accommodate guests who did not want to bother with traffic.

Jumeira Beach did not offer a helicopter ride, but it

118

was not any less comfortable. In fact, one could argue that it was a much nicer hotel, at least, to average guests.

Aside from the usual sightseeing, the trip to Dubai included one more meeting – this time with Sade. 'Hashimoto' had simply suggested that he had a friend from the sheikhdom who happened to be in Dubai, and asked if the general would mind if she joined them for coffee or dinner one day. Based on the little he was told, the general had no reason to object.

The night they were going to meet, Sade booked a table for four at one of the hotel's fancy restaurants that featured oriental food and a belly dancer. She had also requested a table with a beach view, just to add to the ambiance.

The conversation was routine. She had decided she would not push too hard. They would leave that for later. For now, all she wanted was to get to know the uncle better, get a read on him. At the table, she asked him a few questions about who he was and what he did, what he wanted to do, and what his ambitions were. He was not too talkative. Part if it was his nature. He was not much of a talker. Not that he did not want to be, but years of army career in a country like China had conditioned him not to talk. The other part of it was that he had been kind of drawn into his own world since the vacation at the Black Sea. He felt he had lost his motivation, not just for work, but for everything else. It seemed he was in a constant 'blah' spirit. In fact, he so lacked motivation that he did not ask too many questions of her, either. He just asked about her name, nationality, what she did for a living – she lied about that – and where she lived – she lied about that, too.

However, it was not a game she planned to play for long. She had not set out to lie to him. It was just that the dinner was not a good time to get to the point.

The next day, she arranged to 'accidentally' run into him at the hotel lobby.

"General!"

"Miss Sade!"

"General, I was wondering if I could have a word with you, please."

He was rather taken aback. It was a bit too abrupt for him, and he did not quite know how to react.

"Is this about my sister or my nephew? Are they okay?"

"No, General. They're perfectly fine. It's not about them at all."

Then she started to explain what she wanted. "General, my name is Sade, as I mentioned last night. But the rest of the information was incorrect. I am sorry about that."

"Once again, Miss, who are you, and what do you want?" Now he sounded rather agitated.

She calmly introduced herself as an advisor to the President of Iran, and said that she had known about the Dubai visit from his nephew, and wanted to discuss some business that her government had decided would be best handled through informal channels. She said she had sensed that he would not mind being approached, or at least was not about to have a violent negative reaction. She had to gain his interest and confidence quickly, before he had time to rebel against the intrusion of the morning.

"General, we have been following the success of the Chinese army with interest. We know you personally have had a lot to do with the improvement of the quality of what's being produced. We're also aware that your country is trying to capitalize on the armament industry by gaining new markets. You have had some remarkable success, but you're still able to absorb larger orders."

There was a tiny smirk on his face that he was trying hard not to show. She had his attention, at least, for now.

"As you know, General, my country is not only one of the largest arms purchasers in the region, but it also has its own R&D programs. We're also about to embark on certain programs and policies that I am currently not at liberty to discuss. The reason we're interested in talking with you personally is that I believe we can be of mutual help to each other."

"I am listening," he said rather coldly as he sipped at his coffee.

"We can buy all of your surplus arms and ..."

The general cut her off. "Well, you don't need me for that. I am not the minister of defense. Why don't you take your proposal directly to the government? I am sure they would be happy to hear from you!"

"For two reasons. First, we'd rather not be identified as the buyer of some of the material. Second, we also want something that your government would not agree to sell us. We have tried. Several times. Directly and indirectly."

"And you want me to steal it for you? I am not sure what you're asking."

"No, we're not asking you to steal anything. You have made it your life's ambition to improve the quality of the Chinese arms and to increase their sale around the world. But you are also in a powerful position, and your discreet and not-so-discreet lobbying for or against an issue counts a lot. What we are asking you is to lobby the government to sell us some of the arms we are looking for. And there is something in your arsenal that is not for sale, and we would like your help in getting it!"

"And what would that be?"

She paused for a bit before answering, all the while staring him down.

"MIRV."

"MIRV?"

"Submarine-based MIRV."

"And why would you want that?"

"I don't know, and if I did, I presume I could not tell you, anyway."

"I presume not. But would you care to give an educated guess?"

"Not really. As I said, I really do not know."

She was becoming good at lying, and, deep down, she was becoming proud of herself.

"Your country already has a very active missile advancement system. Probably the best thing that happened for your country in that sense was the eight-year war with Iraq. I know you have purchased systems from other countries, not all our friends." He did not mention North Korea by name. "But MIRV is a different ballgame altogether. Why should I try to help with this?"

She was not sure if she interpreted the question correctly or not, but took the unused napkin that had come with her coffee cup, pulled out a pen from her purse, jotted down a figure, and turned the napkin around so he could see the figure. In bright, black, clear hand writing, she had written: $5, 000, 000.

Just for emphasis, she added: "United States dollars. Any bank, anywhere in the world."

He was not sure what to say or do. He had come to Dubai to visit his sister and nephew, and now he was being ambushed by a multi-million dollar bribery proposal to become part of the world's illegal arms trade. Actually, this was not even arms trade. He looked at the napkin and the figure for a few minutes, and she looked at him. He finally

122

broke the silence.

"Are you expecting an answer right away?"

"No. Sometime before you leave Dubai would be just fine. And by the way, we don't want the actual system. We want the blueprint for making them ourselves!"

That is insane, the general thought, then asked, "Why?"

"It is actually simple. With all respect to you, your government would not agree to sell us the full system. Second, it would be a point of national pride to build the system ourselves if we had the technical knowledge. Third, it would probably be cheaper for us to build it ourselves than to buy it on the international market. Last, but probably the most important, buying it from your country might not escape international eyes. Much of what we have done internally, we have managed to keep away from international intelligence services. We want to do it on our terms."

There was another reason why the Iranians wanted this to have a total 'Made in Iran' brand on it, but she did not share that with the general.

She stood up, handed him another piece of paper, this time with a local phone number on it, thanked him for his time, and left.

After she left, the general left for his room, locked the door behind him, and did some serious thinking. What did the Iranians really want to do with this highly sophisticated system? Why had they come to China? A bunch of scenarios crossed his mind, but he could not put his finger on any particular one. In many ways, the Iranians had better relations with Russia – which also had MIRV systems. Military cooperation between China and Iran was not new. The Chinese were a major source of military equipment and technology to their Asian ally. They had sold anything from tanks and aircraft to missile technology. In fact, the Chinese had even helped with the Iranians in indirect ways. The Iranians had long wanted access to some of the top-line equipment that the Israelis had, but neither the Iranians nor the Israelis wanted to be seen dealing with each other directly. Israel, meanwhile, had sold military equipment and, when time came, simply turned a blind eye to the Chinese, re-selling them to the Iranians.

He left the idea, and decided not to think about it. He just spent the rest of the day sightseeing with his relatives.

Although he knew that Sade was expecting a call, he decided to ignore it. Not just one day, or two or three. In fact, he decided he would leave the country without giving her an answer. He just needed to know more. He did not know anything about her, her claims, or her plans. He did not even know if she was who she said she was. He was not going to agree to bribery and treason based on a cup of coffee and a promise on a piece of napkin.

CHAPTER 19

BACK in China, the general ran Sade's name through the military intelligence database and files, but did not find any dirt on her. Her name did show up as who she said she was, along with her studying years in Dubai, and past association with the president. When it came to more recent stuff, it only showed her as the president's advisor, not even a portfolio mentioned. At least legitimacy was established, he told himself. In the weeks that followed, Jian spent quite a bit of time agonising over what to do. It was clear that they were offering him the money, not for approving the arms sales, but for agreeing to sell the MIRV technical details. They did not need him for the arms sales part. China would have been happy to sell them the arms. That's what they had been trying to do for several years. However, the MIRV part bothered him. It was a dangerous system. He did not know how it would be used, and against whom.

On one hand, he was not happy with the notion of becoming a traitor after decades of service. That's all he had done all his life. He was proud of his service. Every morning when he put on his uniform, he stood in front of the mirror for a few minutes, and admired his medals. He had earned them with hard work and honesty. He was not necessarily an ambitious person, but he had worked hard every time he was given a new post. If he agreed to do this, he would be throwing away all of that, even if no one ever found out.

On the other hand, getting access to the blueprint for a sophisticated guided missile system like MIRV was no easy task. It was not like the technical drawings were in a book on a shelf somewhere that he could go steal, or that it was sitting in a safe in some office. Some of the components did not even have technical drawings available for them. He would literally have to knock on door after door to collect the blueprint. If the authorities got wind of it, he would either be sent to jail for a very long time, or simply be handed over to the firing squad. Neither one was a pleasant thought. He knew several people who had ended up in high security jail for alleged and perceived espionage. He just did not think he would have it in him to survive such an experience. Surviving those jails was not just a matter of physical stamina. In fact, it had a lot more to do with mental stamina than physical power.

However, there was another thing he had to think about. As much as he wanted to deny it, his outlook on life and the country had changed recently. He was not the same dedicated army officer of ten or fifteen years ago. He had seen how the country had changed, how the world had changed, and how his country's role in the world had changed. He could not say, in good conscience, that he was happy with what he was seeing. He had grown up in a system that put premium on offering its citizens some basic rights. The right to be born into a classless society, a society that guaranteed your kids would receive free, top-class education all the way up to graduate school if they wanted, a society that said if you work hard until the age of retirement, you would not have to worry about dying of poverty in old age.

When he looked at his country nowadays, this was not the same country he had come to love and wanted to serve.

Just looking around his own small circle, he could point to at least half a dozen close and distant family members and acquaintances who had dedicated their life to serving the country, and now had to take second and third jobs just to pay the bills. Just the other week, he had some business in a city a couple of hours away from the capital. As he drove past the main street, he had thought he recognized an old man begging for money on a side street. He told his driver to slow down and go back. Sure enough, he recognized the man. It was his uncle's old neighbor. In his heyday, the man had been a celebrated university professor. He hadn't saved enough money. He had not made enough money to save. Now, in old age, he was left with no option but to beg, and not even in his own neighborhood. He was too proud to do that. So, every morning before dawn, he used the free bus to move to another city, beg for money, then returned home at night. All in the cover of darkness, darkness that he hoped would spare him serious embarrassment.

Sure, the system recognized some of these disparities, especially in the army. More senior officers received special benefits that 'ordinary' people did not. People of his rank had their private car, with a driver at their service day and night. They did not have to pay for gas. They received free housing, and they could pass it on to their sons and daughters after a certain number of years of service. If they needed to get a bank loan, the interest rate would be half of what other people paid. Whereas 'average' citizens could travel out of the country unless they received special permission from the government, the upper class could move in and out as they pleased.

127

There were still too many inequalities in the system. He could see that, even amongst his own army friends. Some had managed to accumulate a lot more wealth than an army salary could justify. He could not prove it, but he had heard enough justifiable stories about corruption and under-the-table deals between army officers and businessmen that he was willing to believe there was a massive kickback system in the army. One of his close friends had become rich overnight a few years ago. Rumor had it that a top businessman had deposited a massive amount of money in a bank for him overseas, in return for the army officer using his connections to let the businessman buy a piece of land that officially belonged to the army. Stories of that kind were abundant, and the two trips he had taken outside the country recently made him much more wanting of material comfort and a freer lifestyle than he had. He had seen how his sister, while not materially rich by any stretch of imagination, was a happier person than he was – even though he had a much higher position in his society than she and her son had in their newly adopted land.

The agony kept him awake for weeks. He debated with himself day and night. Many times, he would wake up in the middle of the night, pull out the napkin Sade had given him in Dubai, and just stare at it.

$5,000,000
$5,000,000
$5,000,000

The more he stared at the napkin, the more he liked the prospects.

There was something else that occupied his mind, something that made the decision making easier. If the Iranians had asked for the Chinese-made missile system – whatever they wanted to do with it – it could be traced back to Beijing. However, the Iranians had made the decision a bit easier, since they only wanted the blueprint. There would be no Chinese insignia on the missiles when they landed somewhere. Maybe the Iranians were going to mix the Chinese knowhow with that they had picked up from North Korea, Russia, and other places. Maybe the final product would have no resemblance to any of the country-specific systems, and the international community would not be able to point a blaming finger at anyone in particular.

After weeks of arguing with himself and weighing the pros and cons, he decided on what he wanted to do. Now, he had to figure out how to inform Sade. He was also curious as to where the story would go from there.

The simplest way was to pass on a message through his nephew, but the more he thought about it, the more he decided against it. For one thing, he did not know what, if anything, the nephew knew about this whole thing. If he knew nothing, there would be no need to get him involved. Also, if the nephew did not know, admitting to what he was willing to do might shatter any positive image the young man might have had of the uncle. Last, but certainly not least, if he and his mother did not know anything about any of this, they could legitimately deny knowledge or involvement later.

It would be much better if he handled it on his own, he thought. How, though? He did not even know how to reach Sade. He had a number for her in Dubai, but that was weeks ago, when she was expecting an answer from him in days. She was probably gone by now. The number was probably a hotel number. Surely she would not be at that number anymore, but he had no other clues, and decided to try it. To be on the safe side, he decided he would not make the call from his home or office. He went to a pay phone nowhere close to either one. Chances that a previously unarranged call from a pay phone would be monitored were not that high, he convinced himself.

"Hello?"

"Hello!"

"Is this 971-4-567-1234?"

The voice on the other side betrayed some hesitance, maybe suspicion. "Yes, how can I help you?"

"I am looking for..." He paused before he finished his sentence. "Ms. Sade."

The voice was now decidedly more relaxed. "Ah, yes, but she is not here right now. Can I take a message?"

The general was not so sure if it was a good idea to convey his answer this way.

"No, I need to speak with her. When will she return today?"

"Well, actually, she won't! This is her secretarial service."

"So she is not in Dubai?"

"I am really not sure. The past few days, she's just been calling in for her messages."

He was not sure what to do now. On one hand, that was the only number he had for her. On the other, he was not comfortable leaving such an important message with a secretary.

"Can you give me a forwarding number for her?"

"Sorry."

"Okay, then. Please tell her the person she had coffee with the other day called. He would like to meet with her. Two weeks from today. Same place. I will need a hotel reservation for two nights."

"That's it?"

"That's it!"

"Can I give her a name?"

"She will know." He hung up.

130

Figuring out how to get back to Dubai was not going to be easy. He had just been there a month ago. Arranging for an official visit would take too long. Plus, he neither had the excuse for it nor would it be advisable to travel under the glare of other Chinese army and intelligence officials. He decided to keep it simple. He fabricated a story that his sister was in poor health and needed specialist care in Dubai, and he just needed to a leave for a few days. It was easy to arrange, and would not raise any eyebrows, since the headquarters knew about his sister living in the nearby sheikhdom.

At the appointed day, he checked into the same hotel they had met at the first time, and confidently walked to the reception desk to announce his arrival. Sure enough, again, a junior suite was reserved under his name for two nights, and there was a note waiting for him.

'9 p.m.; 360 bar'.

That was just three hours away.

The bar was called 360 for a reason. A few hundred feet away from the Jumeira Beach Hotel, tucked into the sea, was a two-level infrastructure. The lower level was a restaurant, and the upper deck was a circular, open-air bar with a penthouse view of the surrounding, thus the name 360. When it opened years ago, it was one of the hot places to go to and to be seen in. It had lost much of its charisma since then, but it was still a popular place and, given the heat and humidity of Dubai, it offered a nice cool place to enjoy a few drinks and the sea breeze.

He dutifully showed up at the bar at nine, without giving much importance to the choice of location. He was not curious enough, and Sade, on purpose, had not given him much time. It was a Thursday night, the beginning of the weekend in the Arab world, so the place was kind of crowded, although Sade had reserved a couple of seats

131

looking out toward the sea. It was a semi-calm night, with a tiny breeze that made it just about bearable to sit outside. There were a couple of small ships anchored a few hundred feet away. The rainbow colors kept showing off to the left, part of the decoration of the Burj Al Arab Hotel next door.

He showed up dressed in an open-neck, loose, beige shirt and matching color pants, but still wearing his military-issued shiny black shoes. She was wearing a black top that covered from the top of her chest to her midriff, a jacket over it, and pair of jeans. She was carrying a tiny black purse. Although Jian could not see it, there was a sensitive microphone inside transmitting the conversation to one of the ships anchored a short distance away. On board, a photographer, using a professional long-range night lens, was shooting pictures, while another crew member was tape recording the conversation. The general might have been close to striking a deal that would make him richer than he could have ever imagined, but he was not getting it for free. Buyers needed their own insurance policy.

"General, good to see you again."

Silence.

"I was hoping to hear from you last time."

Again, silence. She was not sure if he had suspected the surveillance or not, but it was important for her to get it all on tape and picture.

"General, as I mentioned last time, we are interested in purchasing a multitude of arms from China. You are in a position to help us push the paperwork forward. We want anything from bullets to tanks, artillery RPGs, and airplane parts. But we are also interested in paying top dollars for the submarine-based MIRV system. As a token of appreciation, we are willing to provide you with five million US dollars. We can deposit the money anywhere you'd like."

"I looked into your country's military projects. What are you going to do with these? You already have long-range missiles that can reach any target in the Middle East, even some in Europe."

"General, you asked me the exact same question a month ago, and I am afraid I have to give you the exact same answer. I don't know what it will be used for, and even if I did, I could not tell you. Plus, it is probably best for you not to know, just as it is probably best your sister and nephew did not know about this conversation, not to mention officials in your country."

If it sounded like a threat, it was because she meant it as one. She knew how to play politics when she needed to.

"General, we need to know whether you are on board or not, and we need to know now. This is not something we can postpone for another meeting!"

He did not say anything, but just shook his head. Although they had a deal, she needed to make sure it was recorded on tape correctly, and that there were pictures to back it up.

"I see you are nodding your head, General. Is that a 'yes'?"

"Yes."

Then she extended her hand for a handshake, and he offered his.

She just hoped the photographer snapped the right picture.

In the weeks and months to come, General Jian worked his way through the secretive and meandering bureaucracy of his communist country to get the blueprints needed. It was risky. In some instances, he could just use his title and the power of his office to get what he wanted. In some cases, he could order research done on some

133

components. However, there were times his back was against the wall. He had to ask Sade for a down payment on his $5 million, only so he could dole out bundles to lower-ranking cooperating army officers and politicians.

Even once General Jian had pieced together the documents, getting them to the Iranians was a challenge. Tehran did not have active agents in China, and it was too late in the game to start running live agents. In the end, the Iranians cooked up a deal under which Tehran would send 'technical military cooperation' teams to 'exchange ideas' with military experts in Jian's department every other month, for six months. In between each visit, Jian would collect whatever documents he could get his hands on, and try to time their delivery to his office as close as possible to the Iranian delegation's arrival time. Using their diplomatic passports, the Iranians would bring in a small portable scanner. The Iranian team was to work off an office near the General's. Jian had secretly made them an office key and a member of the Iranian delegation could sneak into the General's office at pre-determined times and days to scan the documents. The General would not be in his office. That would create a deniability leeway. The general could always argue the documents were stolen from his office without his knowledge. Once the team was gone, the General could return the original copies intact.

CHAPTER 20

Los Angeles, circa 2020

IT was a warm Sunday afternoon in Los Angeles, and the beach was packed with people. It was not really surprising. It was mid-May, and the weather had just warmed up enough for people to flock to the water. So Charles Shahin did what Charles Shahin always did when he wanted to immerse in his distraction, take time, burn the mental energy, think about things, and get a grip on himself. He did not think much of the practice. *We all get that way*, he would tell himself. Some people go jogging; some people turn into couch potatoes and lose themselves in front of the box. Charlie hopped into his convertible Corvette, pushed on the gas peddle, and pretended he was on some highway in Germany, where he could go as fast as the car would go, and not have to worry about speed limits or patrol cops.

Fast driving was usually a self-administered psychological test for him. The harder he pushed the gas pedal, the more frustrated he was, and the routine was always the same. He would get out of his Bel-Air mansion, drive south, and then bingo. The CD player would be on; most probably, a fast tune or a dance beat would blare out of the speakers, especially installed inside the driver's seat headrest. He would roll down the windows, put down the top, and the imaginary one-car race would begin.

That Sunday afternoon, the sun was blazing into the car, but the heat was not uncomfortable. Maybe it was the accompanying gentle May breeze that actually made it pleasant. He did not really plan it, but the music was rather opportune this time, matching his mood and his thoughts. It was Nicki French, signing one of the many jazzed up versions of *Total Eclipse of the Heart.*

Charlie looked at the speedometer. It was only 60 MPH. He knew that was not right. He pressed harder, and started thinking. He knew this would be one the most important rides he had taken in his life. Sarah's picture started flashing in his mind. She was smiling, but sort of a smile that he knew there was something wrong with it, sort of a 'Gotch you, honey!' type of smile. Given the circumstances, it was rather disturbing to see that kind of smile flash in front of his face. There were many women in Charlie's life, but none mattered as much as Sarah. She had been the dream of his life from the minute he had laid eyes on her when she was a student and he was university teacher in Egypt, that polluted and chaotic city eight thousand miles away from the beaches of Los Angeles. He was reminiscing, and could feel his blood pumping harder as the black Corvette roared the two-lane beachfront road. He was so engulfed in his thoughts that he was totally oblivious to his surroundings. He was not paying attention to the music, either. It was sort of there, but Charlie was not listening to it anymore. Every once in a while, he would hear the lyrics that conveniently went with his thoughts. They would divert his attention for a while, and then he would find himself submerged in his thoughts again.

The speedometer was now showing one hundred. He changed gears, slowed down, and swerved left into the beach sands, kicking off a huge dust ball. He got out of the car, and walked towards the water. It was wavy, but crystal blue. He went closer, purposely letting the water wet his Brono Magli shoes. He stared at the water as far out as he could, as if he was not going to see it ever again, and got lost deep in his thoughts again. He started thinking about his life. About Sarah. About many years of service to his country, and about how it was all coming to an end. How it all had to come to an end, for everyone's sake. He was having flashbacks of the years past, of events past, of friends who mattered most to him, and of all those places he had been to in his life: Europe; Africa; Middle East; Asia. Cities he adored: Paris; Rome; Cairo; Beirut. They all came with great memories. Some marked great moments of professional stride. Some evoked irreplaceable personal memories.

Charlie started thinking about the fact that he had had a tough life. It was not easy covering wars, watching occupying tanks roam the streets, with artillery fire blasting fifty feet away from you, and the sound of grenades and rocket launchers shattering your windows day in and day out. Neither was roaming the streets of shady places like Beirut, hoping to find out where militant fundamentalists were hiding the Western hostages they had kept month after month, trying to help save their lives. Collecting information on Egyptian intelligence apparatus was not any less risky. Working in Cairo was like working in Vienna during Cold War years. The place was swarming with spies from just about any country you could think of. It was sort of comical: not only the Israelis were spying on the Arabs, but the Arabs were spying on each other, the French and Italians were keeping taps on the Arabs and the Israelis, and, in the middle of it all, were the American spies trying to shop around for information in what looked more like a bazaar than an undercover world of danger and intrigue.

Nevertheless, Charlie had tried to go about his business without paying much attention to his surroundings. After all, technically, he did not even exist. However, he knew more about military and political secrets and high rollers than some of the on-the-book agents, and that sense of self-gratification kept him going more than anything else. For the most part, he did what he did because he enjoyed it. That's what made him effective. He enjoyed the game. For him, collecting information was not a 'job' as much as an exercise in perfection, an exercise that could only be carried out to its fullest if viewed as a sort of entertainment. Like the days he had roamed around Cyprus streets tracking Palestinian and Israeli operatives. As were his many trips to southern Egypt to uncover the secrets of fundamentalists bent on overthrowing the Egyptian government. The times he had snuck into Libya to find out more about a secretive nation about which few people outside knew much. Those were really more about his own sense of curiosity and beating the odds than about trying to satisfy his professional masters.

Charlie was almost sorry that he had decided to put an end to things. He knew he was an unusual person, and, for years, had made that work in his favor. However, it was all getting out of hand, and he had lost the will to fight anymore.

By all counts, Charlie was a complicated man. Like Sade, Charlie was born in Iran to a middle class family. His parent had met each other soon after they had each finished college. Back then, in the traditional society of the Middle East, there was no dating or pre-marriage courting. Nevertheless, they had learnt to love each other, and Charlie had been born, followed by a girl a couple of years later. Like Sade, he had been born stubborn. He was not a person noticeable for any particular qualities. He was not someone who would stand out in a social gathering. He was not terribly educated. He was not rich. He was not handsome. He was not funny. He tried to be humble and self-effacing. Like Sade, he was massively interested in politics. He had been a political animal from an early age. With the same intensity that Sade believed in the Eastern World's grievance against the West, personified by the United States, Charlie had believed in the justness of the Western political, social and economic ideology, and its superiority over the East's. He had such strong convictions that he had packed his bags at an early age, left his birth place, emigrated to the United States, called it home, and promised himself to serve it the best he could.

Over the years, his main complaint was that the new wave of immigrants was not showing enough loyalty to this country. He had not come to the States for the US passport, he would say, even though everyone else seemed to. He thought immigrating into a new culture should be a two-way street. Maybe he was being naïve, but he thought that was the whole problem with America these days. Most immigrants had come here just to have a better life, but were not willingly to pay back the favor and serve their new homeland. They wanted to hang on to their old customs, habits, and traditions much more than they cared about being true Americans. Of course, the native-born Americans were not making things easier, either. The majority, the whites were still having a hard time *really* accepting any other minority, be it the blacks, the Hispanics, the Asians, Arab-Americans, or anyone other non-white, non-US-born Americans. There was an underlying prejudice by many that really was unconscionable to him.

Standing on the banks of the California coast, Charlie realised he had made his life more difficult than it ever had to be. He was also the kind of person who always struggled with something. It was as if he had this kind of mission to constantly create new challenges for himself, to set the bar higher, to make his life more stressful. That's how he had achieved just about everything he had achieved in his life – and, even though they might have been too many for most people, they were far too little for him. He had put himself through college, then graduate school, and then earned a PhD. He had worked several part-time jobs to make ends meet, entered journalism, followed life where it took him next, defied common sense more often than not, and took extraordinary risks in the line of duty, and in support of his personal beliefs. Now, he was giving it all up. He had told tell Sarah that it was over, not because he did not love her anymore. Nothing could have been farther from the truth.

By the time Charlie got back home, it was his favorite time of the day, the sunset. The crisp, penetrating sun rays filtered deep inside the palm tree-ridden entrance of his mansion. That house meant so much to him. Sarah had overseen its building, and had personally spent a year, and over a million dollars, importing everything it needed – from Italian leather to Arabian palm trees – to make the mansion a true mixture of the Western and Eastern cultures she and her husband felt so much loyalty to – he to the West, and she to the East.

Sarah was waiting for him in the downstairs living room of the duplex. She looked unusually beautiful that day. Her long black hair was let loose from the back of her head. She was wearing a see-through white nightgown, from under which her firm breasts and creamy nipples were begging for his mouth.

"Hi, handsome," she said, in her usual warm tone.

"Hello, my love."

"That was a long drive. I thought those gorgeous California girls kidnapped you," she said as she moved closer to him. She knew of his habits, but always left him free, as he had done with her.

"No one dares do that when you are around."

Now he was playing her game.

She was a couple of steps away from him, and was intentionally moving slowly to raise his anticipation. She grabbed him by the sides of his windbreaker jacket, and forcefully mounted a wet kiss on his expectant lips, but, before he could do anything, she had detached herself and moved a few steps back.

"How about a drink?" she inquired.

"Sure."

Without asking what he wanted, she opened the mini fridge in the corner of the bar area, and pulled out two just-made cold martinis.

"Olives?" she asked

Again, she did not wait for an answer. She put one in one glass, two in the other, and handed him the second glass.

Sarah took a long sip of hers, and then moved to the other side of the room, where a huge, multi-part stereo system and a large-screen TV were mounted on the beige wall. She picked up one of the many remote controls piling on a Gucci glass table, next to a couch almost in the middle of the room, between the TV screen and the bar. She clicked on it, and a soft tune started playing through the speakers placed inside the wooden ceiling.

"Care to dance?"

It all sounded a bit odd. She rarely drank martinis. Her favorite was the chocolate liquors that he used to pick up from the Geneva airport's duty free shop. Yes, she did love dancing. So did he, but never in the middle of the first

141

drink, and it never started with a slow song. In fact, they rarely danced at home when it was just the two of them. They often had large and loud parties, inviting everyone who was anyone, and, at some point, the crowd would break loose. Today's scene was different. He went along anyway. Anything that would keep him close to her was a blessing he would welcome under the worst of conditions.

They danced and drank more martinis, and danced more and drank still more martinis. Both seemed to have lost track of time and everything else around them. She was calling the shots, as she often had, and that was just fine by him. Eventually, they sat down on the Arabian-style sofa that Sarah's brother had given them for their wedding. It was large, made of heavy wood, and the mattress and the cushions were covered with beautiful, hand-woven Indian silk. He sat straight on one side, while she put her head on his lap and stretched her bare legs the other side. They had both fallen silent, and were lost in their own thoughts, and both seemed happy with the arrangement.

After what seemed like eternity, he lowered his head and looked at her. She was looking at him, too, and smiled. They moved to the bedroom upstairs. The sexual tension that had started building up when he had entered the living room hours before had reached its climax. He held her hands firmly as they entered the bedroom. He turned her around, and brought her close to him. She was expecting a kiss, but, instead he put his right hand on her buttocks and pressed it real hard. She voluntarily opened up her dress, and let if fall to the ground.

The scene was reminiscing of their first sexual encounter in his Cairo home. She had gone there for one of his regular dancing parties. It had been early in the evening. She, a young man she was dating at the time, her cousin, and his girlfriend had shown up. Everyone was having a good time, happily half drunk, except for Sarah and her company. Being Muslims, drinking alcohol was forbidden to them. Of course, they drank, but only when they were not in the company of other Muslims. It was one of the hypocrisies of the Arab world. Too often, people did things because they looked good to others, or did not do them because it would make them look bad – not because their religion said it should or should not be done. At one point during the party, he had lured her into the bedroom. She had first resisted, but he knew that she had been waiting for it as much as he had.

Upstairs, in their Hollywood mansion, Charlie and Sarah made love for what seemed to be the longest time ever. Soon after, Charlie was sound sleep.

CHAPTER 21

CAPTAIN Robert Haggerty was a thirty-year veteran of the Los Angeles police department, and had just about seen it all. You name the crime, and he had covered it. You name a location in the whole metropolitan area, and he had been there. So his colleagues were not exactly surprised when, every once in a while, the fifty-five-year-old, snowy-haired Captain Bob, as his friends called him, sounded less than enthusiastic when a 911 call would come in. That morning just happened to be one of those mornings. It was 8:55. The captain had started work less than an hour ago, but he was already way into his third cup of coffee, which was surprising, given the quality of coffee in that office. Everyone was always complaining about that, but no one wanted to replace the kettle boiler with a decent, automatic coffee maker. Part of the problem was that the office was so 'office-like' that no one cared to do anything to make it more 'homey'. Most of the furniture was as old as another hometown California boy who had gone all the way to the White House.

Just as he was settling down with his coffee, the 911 operator dispatched an emergency call.

"We need an ambulance. We need an ambulance. He is dead. He is dead," screamed a woman from the other side of the line.

The operator was trying to calm her. "Ma'am, what is your name?"

"He is dead. He is dead. Send an ambulance right now." The woman was not calming down.

"We are sending one right now, but I need your name and address first. What is your name?"

"What difference does it make? Send the goddamned ambulance. It is 3423 Sunset Blvd Street."

Haggerty's eyebrows went up a few notches. He was not quite sure, but he thought he recognised the address. He got onto the secure phone with the operator. He knew who was taking the call.

"Janet, is that you? It's Bob at the South Central station."

"What's up?"

"Do you have a name on that address?"

"Well, let's see what we have here. How about this: Princess Sarah Al-Hodeibi of Saudi Arabia, and Charles Shahin. Got a celebrity here or what, Bob?"

"Roger that. Keep that name to yourself. You don't want no headlines in tomorrow's papers."

"10-4," said a half baffled, half jovial operator, using the police scanner code for 'understood'.

Haggerty recognised Charlie's last name, but did not remember much more, only that he was 'important'. He had come across that name about a year ago, on an early Sunday morning when he had stopped Charlie speeding on I-405. Charlie had been driving so fast that the captain could have revoked his license on the spot, but when he had radioed in for background information, he got a no-touch instruction from headquarters, based on orders from Washington. He did not know anything more than the fact that Charlie had some kind of federal government protection.

"Come on, Jesse," the chief told his junior partner,

145

Jesse Johnson. "This could be a long, unpleasant day."

Johnson's problem was not that he wanted to know *where* they were going. He wanted to know what business they had going there in the first place. Blair was not their jurisdiction, and the same way he would have hated it if someone else had shown up in his territory, he knew too well what the Bel-Air station people would think when South Central people showed up. Haggerty just told him he knew the dead man. Once they got there, they were both excited, though for different reasons. Johnson was thrilled by the excessiveness of the place, even by the decedent style of the L.A.'s affluent minority. The swimming pool had a side Jacuzzi, and a ten-foot high automatic cover that could turn the pool into an indoor one. A hard surface and a grass tennis court were nearby, and the central sound system in the living room, the amazing framed pictures on the walls, and the color-coordinated decor inside.

More than anything else, he was dazzled by the lady of the house.

Haggerty, on the other hand, was interested in learning more about who the mysterious man and his wife were. He knew next to nothing about Charlie's wife. He had just been able to glance at her picture once, the day Haggerty had stopped Charlie's car. The picture had been next to Charlie's driver's license in his wallet. Haggerty was trying to get a quiet moment with Sarah, but she was already surrounded by cops from the Bel-Air station. So he had opted for the second best, the chief maid in the house. She was middle aged, but not Hispanic, although Haggerty did not have a clue where she was from. Then there was a young, tall, handsome man, with blue eyes, and sort of Californian looking. There were also a couple of young Filipina women, who acted more like babysitters, even though the couple did not have children. He finally set his

146

mind on chatting with the chef, but that was a waste of time. She just stared at him and walked away.

Haggerty was still at a loss as to who this mysterious person was. He knew he might never find out, but he was luckier than he might have thought. On his way out, one of the Filipina women he had not bothered to talk to gingerly walked toward him while constantly eyeing the room to make sure no one was looking at her. She quickly handed Haggerty a yellow manila envelope and walked away. Haggerty folded the envelope and put it in his pocket, so no one could see it.

Back at the office, he pulled out his newly found treasure: it was a hand-written letter – probably from Charlie – to no one specific.

Life is about fighting the battles you can win, not just every battle that can be fought. For years, I have worked hard to make something out of myself and serve my nation. It has not been easy. I have tried to help my country in ways that I could. Now, I have reached the crossroads. Terrible things are happening to this country. I have tried to warn people, but no one takes my warnings seriously. I will not sit down and be an accomplice. Politics is a dirty business. Whenever I have been involved in it, I always made sure it was on my terms. To use an old quote, old soldiers never die; they just fade away. It is time for me to fade away. When the documents are found and publicised, history will side with me and prove me right.

Haggerty was confused. He did not know what the paper was trying to say. Was this a suicide note? What did Charlie mean by fading away?

CHAPTER 22

THE memorial service at St. John's Cathedral in downtown Los Angeles resembled a Sunday afternoon gathering of the nation's celebrities and top government officials. Former Defense Secretary, Harold Zimmerman, was there, as was former Joint Chiefs of Staff, General Sherman Ikerson. Both were dressed in civilian clothes. There was also someone sitting to the right of Zimmerman who was guarded by four tall, big men with walkie-talkies. A couple of former US ambassadors were there, as were State Department's diplomatic and intelligence staff. A few of Charlie's journalist buddies and former bosses were also sitting in the back rows, surely wondering why those government officials were there. They probably thought they had come out of respect for Sarah's uncle, the Saudi Defense Minister.

It must have been a coincidence, but the church rows were, somehow, divided. Government officials and journalists sat on the right. Those were Charlie's connections. Hollywood celebrities sat on the left. They were Sarah's friends.

Sarah was not there; she had already told everyone that she would be mourning at home. Instead, she had given the primary job of giving the main speech to Charlie's best friend, Frank Shell, a former Canadian diplomat who had met Charlie when they were both serving in Cairo, a place that had left impregnable fingerprints on both of them. Sarah had called Frank the morning after Charlie's death and asked him to come south for a day. Of course, he had accepted, mostly because of Charlie, but also because of Sarah. If there was one thing Charlie and Frank had in common, it was their love for women. It was not a surprise to either Charlie or Sarah that Frank had a crush on – if not just a lust for – Charlie's wife.

Frank walked to the podium rather slowly. He was sombrely dressed in a dark blue suit, a black shirt, and a dark tie. He looked at the audience, as if to examine their mood, and then started his speech.

"Thank you all for coming. I appreciate it, as, I am sure, do Sarah and Charlie. I have decided that this is going to be an unusual tribute, because Charlie was an unusual person. I first met him, inadvertently, in my own apartment in Cairo. I was new to the post, and my outgoing predecessor had thrown a party at her place, and invited everyone she knew who she thought I should know. I met Charlie there, and I kept seeing him at many other diplomatic occasions."

Then he went on speaking about Charlie's qualities. "If there was one thing he was proud of himself for, it was that he cared for people and much more so for his friends."

Looking at the back rows, he could see tears welling in the eyes of a few male and female friends. "He would have appreciated seeing you now," Frank told those people, to add a personal touch, as he gazed into their eyes, as if he was delivering a personal message.

"Our gone friend was not a sad man. And if he was here today, he would have dismissed this whole ceremony and asked us, instead, to gather in a bar or somewhere and drink to his health."

Mourners now wore unexpected smiles. Some even chuckled.

"So, ladies and gentlemen, without belaboring the ceremony, on behalf of the family, I would like to ask you to simply pray for him, but not be sad for him. He made us happy, and I think it is time we returned the favor."

When it was all over, the man with bodyguards and Zimmerman walked toward Frank, and sort of directed him toward the far corner of the cathedral, where a large pillar went all the way up to the memorial hall's painted glass ceiling.

"Mr. Shell, my name is Andrew Franklin, former director of CIA's covert operations," said the man with bodyguards.

"Yes, sir. I know who you are," Shell said, without betraying his surprise. He was a trained diplomat, and knew how to play his role.

"We were hoping we could have a conversation with Princess Al-Hodeibi. But since she is not here, I would like you and Charlie's family to know how sorry we are. We obviously do not know what happened, but I can assure you we will investigate to the fullest the possibility of foul play in his premature death."

"Thank you, sir. I will pass it on to Sarah."

Driving back, Frank wondered about Charlie's death and what Franklin had said. *Investigate his death to the fullest.* What was he talking about? Was he implying that Charlie's death was not from natural causes? Was he implying that Charlie was killed? By whom, though, and why? Then again, Charlie had been a healthy person. Sure, he drank, but nothing excessively, not anything unusual for people in his line of profession. *Why did he die so suddenly,* he wondered.

He decided he would just report the conversation to
150

Sarah and leave his thoughts to himself.

CHAPTER 23

Saudi Arabia, a few years earlier

EVEN on the best of days, the Saudi capital, Riyadh, was not a 'pleasant' place to live. It was not a 'fun' place. It was not somewhere you would choose to be if you did not have to. The city was full of contradictions. The streets were clean, highways were modern, and there were probably more Mercedes Benz 500 SLCs and Rolls Royces than in any other capital. There were also more foreigners in the kingdom than natives. The most invisible of the foreigners were the Filipinos and Asian maids, servants and baby-sitters who worked for next to nothing. The female ones were known, at times, to have become rape victims, thanks to their domineering male bosses whose culture officially looked down on sex, and certainly banned it with anyone other than their legally wedded wives. They were allowed four wives, under certain circumstances, but many of them were known for their bigger appetite. The visible Western foreigners – mostly Americans – were the ones hired by Saudi companies, mostly in the oil and military businesses. They usually came for one- or two-year contracts, and made bundles of money. Since their contract, more often than not, paid for accommodation, they ended up banking a good chunk of their pay-checks. However, short of making money, there really was no other incentive for living in Saudi Arabia if you were a Westerner. Every other home had a satellite dish, and Saudis knew more about the shows on MTV than people in the United States or Europe. Alcohol was forbidden, but you could always find some – if you paid a higher premium for it and didn't drink it in public. The only thing you would be hard pressed to find in public was a local woman.

However, there was one thing you could say about the monarchy. It had come a long way from the days it had been looked down at as nothing but a bunch of illiterate, uninformed Bedouin Arabs. The Saudi government long ago decided that it wanted to play a bigger role in international politics. It wanted to be heard and be counted on. It wanted to be taken into consideration when world leaders in Paris, Berlin, and Washington sat around a table and discussed issues that affected the Saudis and the Arabs in general. What the Saudis really wanted to become was a second Israel in the eyes of Washington. They had watched Israel for years and, though they would never say so publicly, deep down, they had marvelled at how Israel had its way with Washington. They envied how Israel got anything it wanted, spoilt any US foreign policy initiative by unleashing the Jewish lobby domestically, and, most of all, they were frustrated by how much Israel knew in minute detail about what was going on deep inside the Arab world, even before Arab leaders got around telling one another. So, if the Saudis could not be on the par with their Jewish rival, a close runner-up would do just fine, as long as the distance was not too wide. However, they also knew that they would not achieve that status *gratis*. No one was going to come over and hand it to them just because they were unashamedly rich, and had half of the world's proven oil reserves. They had matured enough over the years to know that respect was like rights. It was not given; it was earned,

153

and, to earn it, the Saudis had decided they would, somehow, have to get inside the mind of America's decision-making apparatus, to understand how it functioned and what it thought. To do that, the Saudis had to find a way to have access to the information America used to make its decisions. What was it that American policymakers read and heard about the Middle East, this most turbulent part of the world? Based on what information did they make the decisions that affected the Arab world? In short, the Saudis needed a diplomatic virtual reality game.

Within forty-eight hours of Charlie's death, rulers in Riyadh were privy to the news. They had not heard it from official channels in Washington, or even from their own embassy in Washington, or the consulate in L.A. Certainly, they were not expecting a phone call from Sarah, either. She had lately turned her back on her family, who happened to be the country's rulers. The Saudis had learnt of the news through their mole in Cyprus. He had also told them that Washington was watching for a reaction.

For the Saudis, the choice of Cyprus was not accidental. It had come after long research.

*   *   *

To an untrained eye, the two towering antennas on top of the Cypriot beach town of Aya Napa did not mean anything. They were about fifty feet high, and seemed to be connected to nowhere. With a country of less than a million, those antennas were far too powerful to be for radio or television transmission. In fact, those cables ran underground all the way to the island's capital, Nicosia, where the US government ran the Foreign Information Service Centre, better known by its acronym, FISC.

Although it was not run out of the embassy compound, and did not officially hold diplomatic status, FISC bosses, all US citizens with Top Secret clearance, had extremely close contacts with the embassy staff. For a good reason, too.

FISC was a branch of the Central Intelligence Agency, with help from the National Security Agency's sophisticated worldwide eavesdropping equipment. The CIA had created FISC to be the coordinator of raw intelligence. All sorts of electronic HUMINT – human intelligence – would pour into relevant FISC centres. Each part of the world had a FICS centre. While the FISCs themselves were not new, the way they were being run these days was the fruit of recent intelligence overhaul in the United States, in recognition of multiple, and serious, intelligence failures of the past. In the old days, 'analysts' - - CIA employees with expertise in a certain part of the world -- would sit in CIA headquarters in Langley, Virginia, and analyze the data they were receiving. However, for the past couple of decades, the process of analyzing data and making recommendations to the civilian leadership had become very politicized. It had actually become scandalous after the Iraq debacle. So, the CIA decided to ship these analysts overseas, where they would be immune from political pressure. They would receive whatever information they needed, analyze it, and then make recommendations to headquarters. Another reason they were moved overseas, and received help from the NSA was in response to a more biting criticism that the analysts had become too tied to Washington, and had lost their 'touch' with the reality of the outside world. It was not just enough to have good agents to collect the information from the field, the argument went. The analysts, too, had to have a better sense of the environment in which they were supposed to be experts.

Cyprus was the US intelligence-gathering headquarter for the Middle East, which covered Israel, the Arab world, plus Iran and Turkey. Inside the two-storey town house in Nicosia, some two dozen strong receivers could get just about any local radio or television station in the region, and printers were constantly trashing out copies of local newspaper and magazine articles. Encrypted telephone lines would connect to agents on the ground. NSA had redirected some of its satellites through Cyprus, too.

The townhouse was divided into two sections. The ground floor was for the dozen employees whose job was just to monitor foreign radio stations and translate important news items in newspapers and magazines.

The basement was a separate story. It had its own entrance and a separate set of employees. The ones upstairs were not allowed downstairs, and the one downstairs did not do much mingling with the ones upstairs.

The employees downstairs were at their desk by six in the morning, and did not leave until very late at night. The downstairs entrance was divided into two, six-inch, solid metal doors. To prevent unauthorised entry, two sets of security systems were installed. The first one was voice activated. Once the computer matched the voice of the person with a pre-stored voice taped in the computer memory, the first door would open and close behind the person, in effect, locking him into a bulletproof, soundproof cubicle. Inside the cubicle, the person would stand underneath an infra-red X-ray system that would match the person's biometrics against those stored on a second set of computers.

The basement was twice as big as the upper floor, because the CIA had excavated much of the underground area around the property. The walls and the ceilings were

156

thoroughly sound-proofed with two layers of special material, to hide the noise from air conditioners that ran day and night in order to keep cool the two supercomputers and a collection of mainframes and laptops installed in the room. The buffering also kept out the range of eavesdropping equipment.

Entering those mainframes, twenty-four hours a day, were two sets of data. The first was the HUMINTEL, and reports by the analysts in Cyprus and case officers throughout the region. The second set was the intel picked up by the NSA and electronic eavesdropping equipment aboard the AWACKS spy planes stationed, of all places, in Saudi Arabia. Although the planes were transmitting the information directly to Washington, a backup copy was also sent to Cyprus.

However, just knowing that the Americans were collecting information in that house did little for the royal family in Saudi Arabia. They wanted to have access to it the same time Washington did. Finding the right person for the job fell on an unlikely candidate.

* * *

Lieutenant Colonel Karim Islambouli was a handsome, tall fellow in his late twenties. Intelligence was never his cup of tea. He had gone to Harvard, spoke English with an American accent, and, if he could have his way, he would have never returned to Saudi Arabia. Born in Lebanon, where his father was the Saudi defense attaché, Karim had met his wife, Dana, one of the most intelligent women around. She was a far cry from the dumb blondes he used to pick up on the streets of America. Being of royal blood, Karim hardly worried about money. He spent money as if it was growing on trees. He was not much into

157

politics, either. He basically had the attitude that the Arabs were defeatist in spirit, and deserved what they got. However, marriage could create odd habits and ideas, and Dana's ideology was rubbing off on her husband very quickly, and, whereas she was not in a position to change things, he was. Why Dana had grown up to harbor such firm pro-Arab political ideologies was beyond anyone's guess. She surely had not picked Karim for his position in the royal family, but, as their marriage settled down after a year or so, she saw no reason why she should not take advantage of her husband's influence. As more 'aggressions' were committed by 'forces of imperialism and Zionism' against the Arabs and Muslims, Dana was determined to make her mark. She encouraged him to give up the good life in America, go back to Saudi Arabia, and get a job that would ensure his career success. Within months, Karim was offered a job as the number two in the Saudi Ministry of Interior's foreign intelligence division. Soon, he had shown his superior sense of analytical thinking, something the average Saudi officer could not be counted on for. Between deserving promotion and having the right family ties, he soon received more and more responsibilities.

The royal family had decided to discretely recruit people who could find out what information was passing through FISC in Cyprus that could help the Saudis in their relations with Washington. They needed someone who could recruit and handle the person or persons. There was no doubt as to who the recruiter should be. Before he knew it, and with no opposition from Dana, they were being shipped on an indefinite tour of duty to Cyprus. Having lived in the social seclusion of Saudi Arabia, Cyprus was a nice break for both of them. Since Karim was supposed to be posing as a businessman, they settled in Aya Napa, which, over the years, had become an important commercial center on the tiny island. They figured that, as long as they were going to be stationed in Cyprus, they might as well try to enjoy the quiet and serene beach scene. They rented a nice townhouse next to the beach, with swimming pool and big reception and dining rooms, so they could have large gatherings. Aya Napa was everything the Arab, Muslim, conservative, Middle East was not supposed to be. The place was a haven for Italian, German and French – and recently rich Russian – tourists. The beach was useable until October, long after many beaches in other European countries were closed for the year. There was also something about being able to enjoy the Mediterranean weather, enjoy the sun, be carefree with what you wear in the middle of the Muslim world, and have a nice vacation for a fraction of what it would cost in Europe. Plus, purely accidentally, it was there that Saudi Arabia's foreign intelligence star had bumped into his first, and best, recruit. Lying on the beach one hot August day was Hassan Marzouk, a Lebanese businessman. Hassan and Karim had started talking. They both said they were businessmen. Karim had rehearsed his cover story well enough, just in case he needed to use it on the spur of the moment. The only things he did not lie about were his nationality and where he had gone to school. He said that, after graduating from business school, he and his uncle had started an import-export business. In the beginning, it was all exporting from the United States to Saudi Arabia and neighbouring Kuwait. Anything the two countries wanted, from chewing gums and Nike shoes to gold and diamonds. He said that, lately, they had started exporting some stuff from Saudi Arabia to the States.

Hassan, too, said he was dealing with the United States. "We buy Egyptian cotton and leather, and Lebanese embroidery, and sell it to the States, mainly to Arab-

159

American shops. But, unfortunately, we, don't sell nearly enough to the Americans."

It was then that Karim decided to check out Hassan's background and explore the possibility of recruiting him. He had not quite thought out how he would or could use his new prey. It was just an idea that crossed his mind.

"Do you have business here, or are you just living here?"

"Both. My partner is American, and he does not feel comfortable living in Lebanon. You know, kidnappings and hostages and all that. But he has been living here for a long time, and has lots of contacts, so we use this as a base. I go to Lebanon and everywhere else, we split the travelling."

"Do you go to States often?"

"Sort of. About once every six weeks. Going to the States takes a long time, and my partner has a young son, and does not like to be away from his wife and son much. So I go to the States more than he does. Someone has to go there often to do the accounts and keep track of the inventory. You know how it is."

The two men kept in touch, and, the more they saw each other, the more Karim started to think seriously about recruiting Hassan. The pressure from home was building up to get the network started. Karim had told his minister about Hassan, and they had checked out his background, and now wanted to bring him in. However, they decided Karim would be the wrong person to use for that leg of the operation. They wanted to keep his identity absolutely under cover, so he could continue to function in Cyprus. Approaching Hassan could have spelt the end of his mission in Cyprus, and it was too early for that. So they decided they would trap Hassan during one of his trips to

160

Washington. That way, once Hassan was back in Cyprus, Karim could actually watch him and make sure he was not blowing off the deal.

CHAPTER 24

THE party at Prince Khaled's home in Washington was an occasion not to be missed. The Saudi ambassador had his parties rather sparingly, but, when it was time for one, it was an honor to be on the invitation list. Hassan was not sure why he had been invited. All he knew was that an embassy dispatcher had left the official invitation envelope at the reception desk of his Mayflower Hotel in Washington. When he showed up at the door of the Virginia mansion three nights later, he was greeted at the door by the prince and his wife, who were standing at the reception line to greet the guests. The host greeted Hassan in Arabic, and held Hassan's right hand with both his hands, a sign of extra welcome, a rather excessively extravagant gesture from a prince toward an 'ordinary' citizen.

"I am very pleased you could make time for us," Prince Khaled said politely.

"I am honored by the unexpected invitation."

"Please, help yourself. I am looking forward to having a more relaxed conversation with you later."

There was no question in Hassan's mind that the ambassador wanted something. This was not just normal, Arabic-style socializing. As he roamed the rooms, the Persian silk carpets, Venetian crystals, French paintings and Italian sofas showed no limit to what money could buy.

Hassan was not greedy or overly materialistic, in part because he had grown up poor, and in part because he could not fathom the concept that so many of his Arab brethren were not far from hunger, while rulers and influential people in his part of the world were living in blatant extravaganza. He was totally lost in his thoughts an hour later when a voice from behind broke up his train of thought.

"Are you into French painting?" It was the ambassador, having found his guest in a room in the far corner of the mansion, which opened onto a balcony overlooking umpteen acres of green garden.

"No, not really. I was just admiring the nice blend of the colors." Half embarrassed, he quickly walked away from the gold-framed painting. "I don't really know much about these things."

"Why don't we walk to the balcony? It is a nice night."

Hassan was relieved that he would not have to show his artistic ignorance much longer. "I am very pleased by your invitation." He was trying to get to the bottom of the story.

"It was long overdue. I have long thought that there should be closer contacts between Arab businessmen in Washington, and we have certainly noticed your activities in the States."

"It is rather modest."

"It always is in the beginning. I understand you have been dealing in the States for only about five, six years, right?" He did not need to ask. He knew not only what Hassan's business was, but also what he was selling to whom, and for how much.

Hassan was lost and confused. On one hand, he wanted to be polite. On the other, he was losing his patience. He wanted to know why he was there and get it over with. "Mr. Ambassador," he said in Arabic. "One of the things I have always admired about you is that you always know how to make the right balance between our Arab tradition of complimenting and the Western tradition of forthrightness. Perhaps you would excuse me for being out of bounds, and allow me to ask to what exactly I owe this generous invitation. After all, we hardly run in the same circles!"

"Very well. Why don't we walk through the garden, and I shall explain?" It was time for the curtains to go up.

"Mr. Marzouk, we in the Arab world live in two different worlds. Our people, the average, ordinary people, may not realize this, but those of us in the policy making circles feel it every day. No matter whether we are talking about, Lebanon, Egypt, Saudi Arabia, Yemen, Somalia, and Arab governments have two big challenges in front of them. The first one is to provide for the welfare of our people. It is not an easy task in most of our countries. The population is growing much faster than we have resources for. But the second task is far bigger and more complex. The days of the Cold War are over. The days when many of us could count on Moscow to get what we wanted, and use the Soviets as a blackmail chip in our negotiations with the West are over. You look around the world, and you see how the south-east Asians have tied together. You see how Canada, the US and Mexico have formed one bloc. You even see how southern African countries are trying to forge closer relations. The only ones left are us, the Middle Easterners. And, of course, there we have the Arabs and the Israelis. Mr. Marzouk, I don't have to recite history for you and tell you how badly we have been beaten so far by the Israelis. To be a player in the international game, we have to learn the game."

Hassan was not going to be lectured. He wanted his

164

two cents' worth in the conversation. "Of course, we must do that. But the reason the Asians and the Africans and the rest have succeeded is that they first agreed to stop killing and discrediting each other. We all saw what happened when Syria and Egypt formed a union, decades ago. And we saw how people in my country kept butchering each other. We also saw what happened when the Iranians and the Iraqis killed each other. It was, I believe, your kingdom that helped the Iraqis kill the Iranians and, when the Iraqis finally invaded Kuwait, who did your country run to? Not to the rest of us – the Arabs. You ran to Washington for help, Mr. Ambassador. Am I incorrect?"

Hassan was not going to be an easy sell, but the ambassador was not known for giving up, either. "Historical revisionism will get us nowhere. We have to learn to live together and forget the past. We have all made mistakes. But we have to start correcting things. Our voice has to be heard in Washington, and we are asking that you play your part and help us."

By the time the ambassador was done explaining the FISC set up and how the Saudis wanted to find a mole inside the station to tell them what the Americans knew, thought, and were interested in, Hassan was sweating. He realized the full implication of what was being asked of him.

"We are asking for every bit of information that goes to Washington. We are interested in topics and trends. Things that would help us understand what Washington is thinking about, so we can use our other resources to influence their decisions."

Hassan was in utter shock, but his interlocutor was not giving him a chance.

"This will not endanger you in any way. You can either do it yourself or help us find someone else who would do it. And when it is done, all you have to do is put

165

the person in touch with us, and then we will handle the rest."

This whole conversation was going too fast for Hassan. Then the ambassador fired the last salvo to make sure Hassan did not think he had the option of refusing to cooperate.

"By the way, we understand your father has been working on various development deals in Beirut. Unfortunately, to get those deals, he will have to deal with a certain cabinet minister who has a personal interest in those projects. I think you can see that your cooperation would make it easier for us to have a word with the minister, who, as you know, is a good friend of Saudi Arabia. I am sure we could arrange something. It would be a shame to see your father lose everything he has invested, which, I understand, is a considerable amount of the family account."

This was sheer blackmail, but it was not totally unheard of in the shadowy world of politics, Middle East or elsewhere.

Having said everything he had to say, the ambassador excused himself and joined his other guests, but asked Hassan to stay as long as he wished.

"I trust you will think about our conversation and let me know your answer before you leave Washington?"

There was not much he could think about. He could not bear the idea of hurting the family, and the ambassador's threat was all too clear.

CHAPTER 25

BACK in Cyprus, Hassan was still half jetlagged and half in shock over his meeting with Prince Khaled. However, he had decided he would go ahead with it, at least for a while. A few nights later, one of Hassan's friends insisted he go to a party at the house of an American reporter. "It should be fun; come," he was told.

There would be a lot of girls, and there would be a lot of drinks, though Hassan was not much of a drinker anyway. "Who else is going to be there?" Hassan had inquired.

"Well, since the party is given by an American, you can assume that there will be a lot of Americans," the friend had replied. "But he is a reporter, so there should be people of different backgrounds."

Hassan was still unconvinced, but now he had started thinking about the conversation with the ambassador. He wasn't thinking whether an outing would be fun or not. He was thinking whether or not he could meet the right person to recruit. He finally agreed to go.

The reporter was none other than Charles Shahin, whom Hassan had not met before. The room was dimly lit, and it looked like there were more candles than people. Charlie was sitting in one corner with two girls and one other guy. In another corner, there were a few marine-looking guys: tall, military haircut, and all muscles. A few girls were clearly lusting over them. There was an extremely beautiful and sexy woman whom Charlie called The Queen. Her nice husband was never too far away, much to every guy's annoyance. The kitchen looked like it had been rummaged through by the Salvation Army. There were beer cans all over. Someone kept throwing balloons into the living room, only so Costas, the goofy Cypriot dancing by himself in the middle of the room, could burst them with his cigarette.

Hassan decided he should join Charlie's group out of politeness, at least to introduce himself. However, the crowd was too involved in its heated argument, whatever the topic was. Actually, in the Middle East, it did not matter what the topic was, because any simple and mundane topic lent itself to some heated political discussion. Anything from democracy, religion or sex to precise topics like refugees or land ownership, or even such a benign thing as water.

Charlie and Hassan started chit-chatting, telling each other how long they had been in Cyprus, how they had ended up there, who they knew, and where they hung out. Hassan did not mention anything about his recent contact with the Saudis, but he did say that he had been to Washington very recently, and threw in a few questions about whether or not Charlie knew any American diplomats. No mention of FISC. After a while, they both realized that it was becoming a little bit too apparent that they were quizzing each other, and decided to cut the conversation short and mingle with other people. The party lasted many more hours and, as parties usually went in Cyprus, by the time it was over, only a handful of people were not totally drunk or out of control. Hassan did have a few drinks, but managed to stay sober and strike

168

conversations with a few other people. He tried to chat up the 'marines', but they were fully consumed by cheap, undemanding flesh that had come their way.

Before he left, Hassan had a second, but short, conversation with Charlie, this time just to agree that they should meet sometime soon for lunch or dinner.

Over the next few weeks, the two met twice, and, each time, Hassan had asked more pointed questions about how the American diplomats worked and who Charlie knew in each branch. It was obvious that Hassan was after something, but he was being too coy about asking more direct questions. To resolve the issue and cool Hassan, Charlie said he was leaving town on assignment for a couple of weeks, but he would throw a party when he came back. There would be a lot of people, a lot of Americans, and a lot of diplomats from different nationalities. He said he needed to throw the party to keep up with his contacts, and asked Hassan if he wanted to come. The knot was untied.

Charlie decided to help his Lebanese contact, because there was something in him that reminded Charlie of his own past. He, too, had been a hustler at a younger age, poked his nose into everything, and tried to network people for information. He obviously did not know that Hassan was trying to spy for the Saudis, but it was obvious his questions were not for business reasons, either. He was trying to collect information on the American operations and workings in Cyprus. What he was trying to do with that information – for now – was, in a way, less interesting to Charlie than the way Hassan was beating at every door.

During his party a few weeks later, Charlie kept a very close eye on Hassan to see who at the party he was trying to befriend. The answer was found quickly when Charlie introduced his Lebanese friend to Gerry Smith.

"If you want to know what is going on in the Middle East, this is the man. He works at something called FISC. They monitor foreign radio and television broadcasts throughout the region. Gerry knows everything about everyone."

Bingo. Hassan's eyes lit up. His heart was thumping six times faster – and it did not go unnoticed by Charlie.

The conversation between Gerry and Hassan lasted only a few minutes, as Charlie had expected. Gerry had simply said that much of what he did was confidential, and he could not talk about it, and did not see a reason why Hassan should be interested, in the first place. That was the end of that. Hassan looked like he had taken an ice cold shower, which is where Charlie wanted things to be. He wanted to help Hassan, but only if he could be in control of the situation. The ensuing weeks seemed like a game of Russian roulette. Everyone was under intense pressure to find out what the other side was up to. Karim was being harassed by Riyahd to find out what Hassan was doing. Had he agreed to be recruited? Was he actually working? Was he still looking for someone inside the CIA station? Hassan was acting as any immature and inexperienced spy-wannabe – just trying everyone and everything, hoping he would find someone to spy on his behalf. He was not having much success, and was getting antsy, worrying about what might happen to him and to his father's business. No one was particularly knocking down at Charlie's door, but his sense of curiosity was killing him. He knew that Hassan – a guy he had come to like – was after something, but could not figure out what that was.

Over the course of the next months, the two of them saw each other a few more times, and Charlie could see that his newly found Lebanese friend was becoming increasingly

170

tense.

*　*　*

In the following week, Hassan's mood got worse. He was impatient, snappy, and drinking more than usual. One day, Charlie decided to confront him.

"What's going on with you these days? You are not yourself!"

"I'm okay. Just a bit under pressure."

"About?"

"This and that."

"What does that mean?"

"Just what I said!"

"Look, it's obvious there's something wrong. Let me help you."

"You cannot!"

"Well, we won't know unless you let me try!"

"You cannot help because it's not my problem. It's my father. He's having a lot of business problems."

That was true, but was not the entire truth. Hassan's father lately had business problems. He had invested in some projects that were not going well. However, after his meeting with the Saudi ambassador in Washington, Hassan had hoped things would improve for his father. If anything, they had got worse, and Hassan was not sure if this was the Saudi's way of bringing more pressure on him, or if his father's luck had genuinely turned south.

One day, Charlie heard from his connections at the American embassy in Nicosia that FISC was looking for a part-time, on-call staff member who could speak Arabic fluently. He asked Hassan if he would interested. Considering that it was not a full-time job and he could still carry on with his business activities, Hassan thought maybe this would be a great opportunity to take the Saudi bait, help his father, and keep his own business going.

Working at FISC was, at first, a very exciting for Hassan. Every time he worked there, he would arrive in the morning, pass through various layers of security check, and then enter his cubicle. Everyone had a specific assignment for the day. They were assigned a certain country to monitor, and the country list changed each day. That way, everyone was an expert in the entire region, and not just one country. If someone left tomorrow, the expertise and the institutional knowledge of the monitoring agency would not suffer.

At the beginning of his shift, in addition to the name of the country he was supposed to monitor, he would receive a sheet of paper on which some 'keywords' and 'concepts' were listed. These were the things he was supposed to watch out for. He did not really know where the list came from. He asked a couple of times, and his boss basically said, "Washington. Now do your job!"

Sometimes, the words and phrases were repeated over a period of time. Sometimes, there were new ones on the sheet. Some of the repeating words dealt with the activities of a president, king, prime minister, some of the specific ministers, and the cabinet. Budget and the military were always items of interest. Apparently, Washington was always interested in how much other countries were spending on various programmes, and how much of that was going to their armed forces. 'National security' issues were hot. Anything that had to do with terrorism and weapons of mass destruction was always on the list.

A lot of the job became rather monotonous after a while. Much of the press in the Middle East was so predictable and uninformative.

Sheikh X of country A received His Majesty, the Royal King of country B.

Leaders of countries A and B renew their pledge to brotherly Arab relations.

President C receives letters of support from labor syndicates.

People at FISC had learnt to rarely pay attention to the front pages or the first few minutes of broadcast news bulletins. However, if you delved deep enough into the news, sometimes you found newsworthy stuff. Nevertheless, the practice gave Hassan a pretty clear idea of how Washington saw – or wanted to see – the Middle East. Now he could see the region through the lens Washington was using to monitor events. Hassan also noticed that Washington hardly ever asked about some countries. They were too 'strategically insignificant'. When it came to some close allies, some of the more delicate questions, such as number of political prisoners, torture, and financial corruption amongst top leaders, were hardly ever asked.

For a while, it seemed like Hassan's mood had improved. He thought he was doing a good job at FISC. He was there three days a week, on average, and had managed to keep working on his business.

However, as days passed, so did Hassan's good mood. He started to behave the way he had before he had got the FISC job. He would show up for work, but not very enthusiastically. The days he was not there, he would claim to be working at home, but he would let the answering machine run. Charlie left him several messages, but Hassan did not return any of them. One night, around 2 a.m., there was a loud knock on Charlie's door. It was Hassan, completely drunk.

"Hassan, come in! Are you okay?"

"No!"

173

"Yeah, I can see that! Where were you?"

"Was out at the club house for a few drinks, and then went to the strip club."

"Wow, not your usual hangouts! What's going on?"

"Things have not been good, Charlie. Life isn't good. I thought life should be good."

"But I thought things were working out for you. I thought you were making more money now that you work at FISC."

"It was never about money."

"So, what was it about?"

"Selling your soul. Spying!"

Then he broke down and cried, under the watchful and somewhat confused eyes of Charlie, who, by now, had completely woken up.

Bit by bit, Hassan spilled his guts about his father's financial problems, his trip to Washington, his unexpected meeting with the ambassador at his mansion, and the diplomat's proposal, or rather, his not-so-subtle demand.

"You see, I used you to get the FISC job. I am sorry. I feel bad about it."

"I don't get it. If you wanted to get the job to help your father and you got it, then why are upset?"

"Because the bastards lied to me."

"How?"

"They have not helped my father at all. Every week, I ask them if they are helping my father, and, every week, they say 'yes', but, when I ask them for specifics, I can tell they are lying. And obviously, talking to my father, I can tell that nothing is being done, too."

After many cups of coffee, Hassan finally left, but the conversation had such an impact on Charlie that he could not sleep. His thoughts were rather confused. On one hand, he was surprised that he had been taken advantage of

174

by Hassan. He was surprised, but not upset. He figured out that one of the reasons he actually liked Hassan was because he was a survivor and street smart. He would do what was necessary to land on his own two feet. He was, however, also intrigued by the new information he had received. He had just accidentally landed on a major piece of information that said one of Washington's closest allies was spying on it. He was very mindful of the national security implications of what he had been told. This was serious stuff. He needed to notify his bosses.

Only if Hassan knew that he was not the only one doing the using. Charlie was now using him. Unknown to everyone in Cyprus, Charlie was not a journalist. He was a spy using journalism as cover, and now, after looking at a sobering-up Hassan, he started to recognize why he wanted to help him, what he saw in him.

CHAPTER 26

CHARLIE realized both he and Hassan were fighters in life. In fact, Charlie had started fighting from the minute he was born. He was born so weak that the family doctor kept telling his parents not to expect their son to survive, and kept saying that for week after week, and month after month. However, Charlie had not died; he had just stayed weak. To make things worse, he had not spoken a word, not until he was four years old. He always vividly remembered the first day he spoke. The whole family had gathered at a relative's house. People were talking. The room was very big, but so was the family. There must have been at least twenty to thirty people in living room. Then someone asked someone something, and there was a whispered answer from the far corner of the room. At first, no one could figure out who had answered. Surely, no one expected it would be Charlie. So someone finally asked, "Who said that?"

Charlie had answered again. Needless to say, there was chaos in the room. At first, people had not known what to say or expect. They were sort of numb and in shock, but shock had soon given way to celebrations and talk of a miracle.

Charlie's first career love was journalism. He got into it in an early age. First television, then radio, then print. However, journalism had gone through changes. It had become very commercial. It had become all about money. Newsrooms were cutting jobs. In short, he was growing tired of journalism.

About the same, time there were also changes in the way America was hiring its spies. For decades, two basic principles governed who America hired to work in its diverse array of spy agencies: CIA, DIA, NSA, *etcetera*. The first was that America did not hire journalists as spies. There was always this rule in America that the government would keep its hands off newsrooms when it came to recruitment. There was a good reason for that. Journalists were supposed to be the honest brokers between government and society. It was their job to collect truthful information to the best of their capability about how government worked, and relay that information to people so they could make up their minds about how effective their politicians were. It was important that journalists be, and be perceived to be, neutral in their job as mind-framers. If the government recruited journalists as spies, then how could people trust the media?

The second principle was that American spy agencies preferred to hire their staff from the ranks of young, mostly white, mostly male, born in America, and born in smaller states. For every one New Yorker there were probably ten from Ohio, Kansas and the Dakotas, places where people had 'real' American values. At least, that was the thinking. Better yet, for every hundred whites, you'd be lucky if you found one African American. Forget about trying to find a Chinese American or an Arab America, or whatever-hyphenated-American in the spy agencies.

But then, if there was one thing good about America, it was that it was willing to be flexible in its

177

attitudes. Yes, it took a long time sometimes, but it did happen. It was like what Churchill – incidentally, a former journalist – said: "You can count on the Americans to do the right thing, after they've tried everything else!" Recruitment policies among America's top spy agencies went through that process, too. Part of it was that, for all those decades, America was really swimming against the tide. Keeping people out was not really improving the country's espionage capabilities, and they knew it, too. After the September 11 terrorist attacks in America decades earlier, the Federal Bureau of Investigation and the Central Intelligence Agency received tens of thousands of applications from hyphenated-Americans, but the system just was not functioning well enough to clear these people. The bureaucracy just could not process them fast enough.

So, after years of internal debate, the government had decided it was time to modify both policies. Loosening the policy on giving preference to US-born whites was easier to handle. America genuinely needed help from all sectors, and was finally ready to acknowledge it. The policy on hiring journalists was still tricky. That was a trust issue. It was a bond issue, a bond between a government and its people. The government could not just willy-nilly hire from the ranks of journalists in established espionage organizations. What if one of them was kidnapped in a hostile environment and confessed under torture that he, indeed, was a spy? That would endanger the lives of thousands of reporters, photographers, cameramen and women, sound persons, *etcetera*, all over the world. Even if they were not in a conflict zone, so what? In this day and age of proliferation and decentralization of terrorism and terrorist ranks, any tiny, previously unheard of radical group could target a journalist in the middle of Paris and London, and freak out everyone.

Then again, the reality remained that journalists could go places and do things that an official spy could not or would not. So the government had adopted a half-way policy. It would not hire journalists from real news organisations. It would create its own tiny, mostly online and 'media consulting' companies, and give them press credentials. There were not that many of them. Maybe half a dozen altogether. They had real offices, even though there might only be two people working there. Or there were real online sites that dabbled in news operation. The agents could legitimately claim they were journalists working for such small organizations that practically no one would know anything about.

Thus was Charlie's introduction to the world of espionage.

One day, a couple of years earlier, just as Charlie had been ending a few days of vacation in Washington and getting ready to report back to work at his Chicago newspaper, he got a mysterious call. The man had simply introduced himself as Richard, said he was a government employee, and had some more information about one of Charlie's recent trips to the Middle East, but could not really talk on the phone. Would he like to get together for a drink one night this week, he asked. They agreed to meet at the 1789 Bar and Restaurant in Georgetown. As he hung up the phone, Charlie had thought more about the venue selection. The more he had thought about it, the more Richard's identity became clear, even before the two had a chance to meet.

Tucked in a corner of Georgetown, 1789 had been famous in decades past as a late-night gathering place for the in-the-know within the Washington intelligence community. Overt and covert operators liked having drinks by the corner bar near the entrance, or squeezed at a corner table upstairs in the restaurant. The fact that Richard had suggested 1789 said something to Charlie about the guy's identity.

Charlie decided to arrive a bit earlier than the agreed hour so he could somewhat scout the place. It was 10 p.m., kind of in between the time the regular dinner crowd would leave and the late-night drinkers would arrive. The valet boys at the door were busy joggling the cars in and out. Next door, Georgetown students were revelling at a late-night party at the basement bar next door. It was two generations of Washingtonians living side by side. Both places were frequented by members of well-to-do or well-connected, or both. If you were older, you would go to one, if younger, to the other.

"Charlie?"

"Mr. Richard?"

"Just Richard, please. No need for formalities."

They each ordered a drink, and waited for the other one to start the conversation.

"Okay, Richard. Who are you, and why are we here?"

"Getting to the point, huh?"

"Why waste time?"

"Okay, I work for the government, and we heard about your incident in Beirut, and wanted to see if we could talk about it."

Charlie had just escaped a kidnapping attempt in Beirut.

"Well, if you work for the government, then surely you know all the details. Come to think of it, what do you exactly mean by the government? Which agency?"

"I cannot quite tell you which agency I work for, at least, not yet. Perhaps later. And, as for your story, yeah, we know a little."

180

"Which is more than what I know about you!"

"Which is kind of why I called you. I didn't have to call you. Someone else could have, but I volunteered. You see, Charlie, you and I have some things in common."

Whatever he was about to say must have been deeply hurtful and personal. He tried several times to open his mouth and say something, but it was obvious he just could not get the words out. Charlie ordered two double whiskeys and, before he knew it, Richard had bottomed up his.

"My father was an all-American boy. Ivy League school; Vietnam. When he came back home, the CIA was in need of battle-hardened people who could work in intel. People who would be different from the normal 'paper pushers,' people who had been outside their own state, not to mention the country, people who could show some appreciation for what the real world was like. So, anyway, they proposed to my father, and he readily accepted.

"You see, back in those days, the days of my father, and, perhaps, yours, intelligence was not such a bad thing. It didn't have the connotations it has today. People actually respected the profession. Anyway, by the time I left college, I, too, wanted to follow in my father's footsteps. Except, this time, it was quite different. People like my father had joined out of conviction. People like me joined out of emulation."

There was silence. Both needed to digest what had been said, and the more they thought about it, the more they realised what a profound and huge statement that was.

"For decades, there has been this debate in our nation – and beyond – about the role of the intelligence community, how we behave as Rambos, how much disregard we have for other nations' independence, how we violate some people's human rights, blah, blah, blah. A few

181

years ago, maybe ten to fifteen, when the Lebanese Civil War started, my father was sent to Beirut. His mission was to sow discord between a couple of the Muslim groups, and try to separate them so the more moderate Muslim ones could become allies with some of the moderate Christian groups. The idea was that, if the United States could redraw the political map of Lebanon from Muslims versus Christian to Moderates versus Hardliners, it would become easier to end the conflict by convincing the regional allies to isolate the hardliners, whether Muslims or Christians, and end their supply lines. It was a theory that, politically, it would be easier to defeat radicalism if it was not based on ethnic or religious grounds. A couple of weeks into his mission, my father was abducted, and has not been heard from since. I have followed the case for years, and I have strong reasons to believe that the group that abducted him is the same group that tried to kidnap you."

"Why are you telling me all this?" Charlie asked.

"I was wondering if you wanted to help us – help me – get more information on these people. I want to know what happened to my father. I want you to know who was messing with your life, and why."

Charlie cut him off before he could go any further. "You want me to become a spy?"

He said 'yes', and went on explaining how the intelligence community had changed its policy and now believed well-rounded people with international experience and the ability to speak foreign languages could serve the country even better than home-grown, ivy-league, young boys with blond hair and blue eyes.

"Look, for as long as I can remember, the government and the media have had a ceasefire on this issue: no journalists spying for the government…"

"The government has thought of the arguments, and

182

found ways to isolate the problems. We can explain it later. Plus, we just saved your sorry ass! A tiny bit of gratitude would not be out of order."

He then slammed down his empty whiskey glass, pulled out a business card, and handed it to Charlie.

"Here; think about it tonight. This is my number."

On that note, he just left the bar. When Charlie looked at it, there was only Richard's name and a phone number; no agency name, no logo, no address, nothing official.

* * *

Charlie left the bar that night confident that he had no intention of becoming a stooge in the hands of the government. And stooge was the right word, in his mind. He had been brought up in a circle of hard-nosed journalists who drew a solid curtain between journalism and espionage. The two should not mix. It was as simple as that. No ifs, no buts.

However, as days went by, that night's conversation kept creeping up in Charlie's mind.

"I want to know what happened to my father."

"I want you to know who was messing with your life and why."

"The government just saved your sorry ass!"

The sentences kept coming back at him like hammer on nail. In his mind, he rehearsed the number of times that diplomatic and intelligence friends all over the world had bailed him out, whether by giving him information for his articles or by safety tips and information that had actually saved his life.

He called Richard again in a few days, and said he would agree to cooperate in principle, but wanted to know more.

Charlie was about to set conditions for how he wanted to work, but Richard cut him off. He would continue to work as a journalist for an independent Internet news provider – one set up by the CIA. He would claim to be the owner and operator of the site; that would lower the need for a fancy office and lots of employees. He would go the Middle East, as needed, to work on whatever projects were necessary. He would pass on the information to handlers back home. There would be no need to contact the embassy, though; as usual, ambassadors and regional security officers in each country would be privy to his identity in case it was needed.

That was another change from the old days. In the past, too often, the intelligence agencies ran their spies without saying a word to the embassy or the State Department. The bureaucracy in Washington had been streamlined, and there was much better cooperation between the State Department and the intelligence communities.

Charlie would be based in Cyprus.

CHAPTER 27

CYPRUS was not a new territory for Charlie. He had moved there a few years ago when he had been a genuine journalist. He could not say much about the city, but he loved the country. The capital, Nicosia, was kind of a sleepy place.

Being an island, the whole country relied on tourism for revenue. It did not produce much on its own. It did not have major industries. It did not have any famous agricultural products to be proud of. It was mainly tourism, but there was not much tourism in the capital, because Nicosia was not on the shore. It was not far from it. You could drive a couple of hours and be at the sea, but why drive when there were cities at the seaside? It was also the capital, which meant it was forced to be a bureaucratic and somewhat stuffy city by nature.

When he had first got there, he only knew a few people. Fortunately, journalists are outgoing people by nature, and everyone found everybody in no time, and a circle of friendship was built. As is the case in most such environments, journalists and diplomats started hanging out with each other. That was kind of common in most places. Sources of entertainment, inevitably, were going to be bars and restaurants, or maybe occasionally attending some sports events, or shooting pool.

So, by the time Charlie went back to Cyprus, he still had some friends, some of the people he used to be friends with, but had not seen in a few years. In the beginning, it was fun; people threw welcome parties for him at their home; they invited him out in groups. He liked it, at first. After a while, it was sort of uncomfortable, because he felt this deep obligation to tell them the truth about who he had become. At the very least, he did not want to lie to them, and, when you hang out with the same people day in and day out, that's kind of difficult. He was tempted to make a drastic move and move out of Nicosia and go somewhere else, most probably somewhere by the sea. That's why he loved the country, anyway. He loved the sea. He loved being close to the sea. He loved being able to just walk to the beach. It was just something about being in that kind of environment that attracted him very much.

The Cyprus of today was very different from the Cyprus of decades ago. In the old days, Cyprus was more of a refuge than a five-star vacation spot. Given its location, it had first become known to the Middle Eastern countries as a place Lebanese had escaped to during their civil war in 1975. Tens of thousands of Christian Lebanese and some well-connected Muslim families took the overnight boat trip from Lebanon to the Cypriot city of Limassol. Some stayed for a few weeks. Some stayed for months. Some just flew away to other countries. Either way, the tiny Cyprus was attracting not just people, but also whatever money rich families wanted to send out. With no customs or restrictions, some people would literally bring in suitcases full of cash. Money would be deposited into Cypriot banks – for a fee, for not asking too many questions – and then leave the bank for some European financial destination. A few years later, Palestinians and Israelis started using the island. For the Palestinians, the island offered a mix of an

186

occasional 'sun and surf' retreat for the movement's 'freedom fighters', not to mention the opportunity to meet secretive and shadowy European arms dealers. On a couple of occasions, some of the more radical Palestinian groups even used the island for land and sea hijacking operations. That was good enough an excuse for the Israeli intelligence service, Mossad, to move some of its assets to the island. They set up an embassy in a quiet street, set up road blocks on all adjacent streets, and rented a few extra houses in the neighborhood for observation and to house 'quick reaction' teams. It was, at times, funny going around the city, seeing clean-shaven, tall, lean, men with military-style haircuts sitting in cafés for hours at a time pretending to be reading newspapers when, in fact, they were observing the movements of Palestinians in some nearby house or office. Either they did not realize the city was so small that a keen eye – maybe even Palestinians themselves – could catch them, or maybe the Israelis did it on purpose just to send a message: We are watching you. Be aware!

As years rolled on, Cyprus's fame – or infamy – was becoming known to others outside the Middle East. Balkan wheeler-dealers were shipping their money to Cyprus. A whole new generation of Russian millionaires and billionaires were investing their cash buying up property.

In the end, Charlie did not have to think too much about whether to stay in Nicosia or not. He was now officially Hassan's handler, so they both had to live in Nicosia. Their last conversation about how the Saudis wanted to hire a mole inside America's listening post in Cyprus, coupled with the conversation Hassan had had with the Saudi ambassador in Washington, had made the issue a priority for Washington.

When Charlie informed Washington about Hassan's

revelation, the initial reaction was less than warm. The bureaucracy in Washington just was not used to thinking about Saudi Arabia in those terms. Saudis were supposed to be friends. This was a country with which the United States had had cordial relations ever since the Arab country's founder invited US oil companies to explore his territory's underground sands for the Black Gold. The relations rocketed into stratospheres over the decades. As the oil production and oil revenues went up, so did Saudi Arabia's fortunes.

As the country made more money, it needed to spend more money, and the US-Saudi relations took a decidedly more strategic turn. After all, the Middle East had always been somewhat of an unstable part of the world, and Washington convinced Riyadh that it needed protection. It needed not just arms, but sophisticated armaments. It needed not just faster and better machine guns to replace single-shot hunting guns. It didn't just need better 4x4 desert jeeps for desert border posts, but also armored vehicles and armored personnel carriers. The list went on and on. Soon, the Saudis were ordering high-end fighter jets and tanks. Since they did not know how to operate them, Washington had to send trainers, for whom the Saudis had to build special barracks and lodging quarters.

The whole cycle had left a bad taste in the mouth of several quarters in the most important country in the Muslim world. However, the ruling family always had the last word, and things continued, as usual. It was not all one sided. After all, Saudi Arabia was the only country in the world whose ambassador to Washington had developed such close relations with sitting presidents that he did not need an appointment to see some of them. He could just call, say he was coming, and then marshal his way into the

Oval Office.

As far was Washington was concerned, everything was on the right track in the bilateral relations. As far as the Saudis were concerned, they were just frustrated by things they could see, and Washington did not, or would not.

The best Charlie could get out of Washington was orders to keep an eye on Hassan and see what exactly he was trying to do. What type of information was he looking for? Was he acting alone? If not, who else was involved? How were they coordinating? Where were they meeting? How long? How often? How did they plan to transmit their information, and to whom?

Washington also arranged, through the embassy, for Hassan to be watched at work – carefully. That was a problem, too. On one hand, Washington wanted to keep an eye on him. On the other hand, whoever was going to do it, or however it was going to be done, it had to be a very delicate operation, because if Hassan got a whiff of it, he would have a good reason to believe it came from Charlie. Not only would that blow away the relations between the two of them, but it would also, most likely, be the end of Charlie's stay in Cyprus. In a small place like Cyprus, word would travel fast. Especially since there were so many people of various Middle Eastern countries in Cyprus, Charlie would be no good as an agent anywhere in the Arab world. For that matter, he would not be any good as a journalist, either.

After much back and forth between Washington and Charlie, they decided it would be best if someone from the office just kept an eye on Hassan to see what he was doing, and left the rest to Charlie. The two had already established a good relationship. It would be much easier for him to get information out of Hassan than someone who did not know him well and just followed him around like some shadowy figure chasing a ghost in some dark alley.

*   *   *

Charlie spent more time with Hassan as time went by. Hassan would pass by his place a couple of times of week, and they would go out for a beer or wine. They would talk about work. Charlie would quiz Hassan about what he had been told to monitor, or what else he had been hearing. It was mostly routine stuff, but, every now and then, Hassan would talk about other stuff he had seen or thought about while working there. At first, Charlie and his bosses had trouble figuring out how Hassan was working. Usually, the value of intelligence was in its timeliness. You found out about a piece of information that somebody had that somebody else wanted – now. Once you got it, you had to transmit it fast. It was kind of like interrogating terrorists or criminals about when and where the next job would go down, but the problem with Hassan was that he was not sending anything to anyone. The only unusual thing about his behavior was that he was meeting Karim more, but, as far as Washington could determine, Hassan was not handing over any documents to Karim, either. It took some time, but, eventually, the CIA put two and two together, and linked Hassan and Karim to Riyadh, but they still did not know what Hassan was telling Karim. Charlie had tried hard to put surveillance on Hassan. It could have easily been arranged. All it took was a couple of guys with sensitive microphones and a long-shot lens to take pictures, but Washington being Washington, the bureaucracy made a mess out of it, and the order was never signed.

Meanwhile, there was news every few months about explosions here and there in the Persian Gulf area. First, there was something about the oil facility in a

190

sheikhdom blowing up. Then there were unconfirmed reports that a police general in one of the Gulf countries was taken hostage. The kidnappers had demanded the release of a hundred 'brothers in dungeons of the oppressors'. Later, members of the parliament in another neighboring country staged a mini *coup d'etat*, deposed the cabinet through a resounding vote of no-confidence, and told the king he would have to either abdicate or give up most of his powers to a prime minister of the parliament's choosing. This was all happening at slow speed. It was not like there was something today and the next thing would happen tomorrow. This was like something would happen today, everyone would get hyped up about it, nerves would cool down over the coming months, and then, bang, something else happened six months down the road. Whoever was doing this did not want to rattle the region or the world too quickly. They were patient.

What Washington could not find on its own about Hassan's intentions was becoming clearer after each 'incident' in the region. A pattern was developing, based on Hassan's conversations with Charlie. Every time there was an explosion, uprising, assassination, or something like that, Hassan would receive instructions to do two things: get more information about that incident, and register whether Washington was interested in it or not. The second thing Saudis were interested in was whether or not there was any connection between those incidents and Iran. At first, it was baffling to Charlie and Langley's bosses why the Saudis would be interested in Iran. Hassan had told them about the ambassador's rants on Israel. But then Charlie started hearing titbits from his sources about Iranian meddling in the region. Travelling around the Gulf, Charlie could tell that the atmosphere had decidedly changed for the worse. Some governments were already gone. Others were

191

visibly weakened. Still others were losing control fast. In an area where political freedom was not welcomed or appreciated by self-appointed governments, political opposition groups were gaining ground. Workers were organising into unofficial unions. Local mosques in each country were hoisting the green flag of Shiite Islam. Half the governments in the region had either been toppled or lost their influence. The local governments knew where the hit was coming from, even if Charlie and his bosses did not.

The parallel information Charlie got on Saudi's interest was both good and bad. On one hand, it showed the US government had been late in preventing the bloodshed, arrests, tortures, explosions, and the rest of the mayhem that had already happened in the region, quietly but systematically. It gave them no insight into what might be coming. It was also bad because, with all its might, the US intelligence was playing catch-up to the Saudis, even though the information Saudis were using had originally come from US sources. The good news was that if there was a possibility that there was still more to come, maybe Charlie and Langley's other assets could solve the puzzle before it was too late.

CHAPTER 28

NOT long after the first couple of explosions and assassinations in the region, Charlie was in Baghdad. If there was one country in the Middle East that had its share political turbulence and violence, it was Iraq. This was a country whose history and civilization went back millennia, a country that was on the forefront of literature and education, a country that, at some point, could pride itself in having the most well-read people in the Middle East and the Arab world. It was also a country that could not say much for itself after the latter part of the twentieth century. Dictatorship. Bloodshed. Military coups. Poverty. Malnutrition. Caught in the Cold War. Invaded other countries, and was invaded by others. Yes, Iraq had more misfortunes than most other countries in the region.

The latest round of invasions had toppled the country's notoriously ruthless dictator, but the new masters just destroyed much of the country, and failed to restore what was broken. They spent billions upon billions, but no one could see much tangible benefit on the ground. Poverty was worse than it had been. Agriculture went down the drain. Education did not improve. After the invaders left, the country went through a period of calm. For a few years, much to the surprise of the outside world, Iraq was quiet. You could even call it somewhat functional.

There was no fighting. Unity governments came, people participated in the elections, and voted for one government after another. Different groups maintained their age-old differences, but they aired them publicly to the people. Governments gave political factions fair and equal access to radio and television, and they legitimately bought newspaper advertisements to publicise their case. People listened and voted. It all sounded very civil and civilized. It was kind of ironic. These were all the things that the latest invaders wanted to achieve, but did not succeed in. Now that they were gone, the people had seen the merits on their own, it seemed. They just did not want to heed the advice while their country was under invasion. Then things unravelled again. Instead of one group dominating and killing all opponents, like in the dictator's time, opposing factions killed each other, not just by dozens or hundreds, but by thousands and tens of thousands. The politics of Iraq had boiled down to Shiites, Sunnis and Kurds – who were both Muslim and Christian – killing each other. Lots of pundits had talked about the place falling apart, but events proved them wrong, at least for a while.

From dictatorship, Iraq had gone through years of civil war. In the end, the Sunnis – previously the dominant faction – lost the battle, because the neighboring Shiite giant came to the rescue of its own people, and the Kurds were just too smart and too battle hardened. In the Middle East, the proverbial political kitchen was never big enough for two cooks. The Shiites and the Kurds were both in the kitchen, and they knew one had to go, sooner rather than later.

Charlie had passed on the on-again, off-again information he had received about possible Iranian connections to the events in various countries in the Middle East, but spy bosses in Washington were not convinced. It

194

was not that they thought it was not plausible. There was no love lost for Tehran in Langley, but the Americans needed 'proof', or, at least, something more concrete than 'our agent in the field says…'

Washington had asked Charlie to go to Baghdad, because there had been consistent reports over the previous months about Iraq having become the centre for smuggling of sophisticated arms: rocket propelled grenades; air-to-air and ground-to-air missiles; nuclear material. All the Americans knew was that the material was being shipped into Iraq from Iran, but they did not know who was receiving them in Iraq and what they were doing with it.

Baghdad International Airport revived a host of memories in Charlie's mind. The last time he was in Baghdad had been at the beginning of the invasion that ousted 'the butcher of Baghdad'. Actually, there had been no airport when the invasion started. The American occupying powers had closed the airport for months. Of course, the military and some humanitarian organizations were allowed to use the runways, but that was about it. It was months into the military operations before the first passenger plane was allowed on the runways. Charlie was one of the first ones to take one of those passenger planes. The alternative was to drive about twelve hours from the neighboring Jordan to Baghdad, and that was pretty dangerous, too. It was common for armed gangs to stop cars on highways and rob everyone clean. They had learnt that journalists who mostly frequented the road carried loads of cash on their way to Baghdad, because cash was the only means of transaction in Iraq after the invasion. Plus, if you were going to stay there for a few weeks or maybe a month, you needed massive amounts of money. So armed gangs had a good time for a while.

Not that taking the plane in those beginning days of

195

the invasion was any easier, either. The 'resistance movements'- which consisted of anything from the previous regime's loyalists to bandits with guns - were constantly firing rockets at the planes on take-off and landing. Fortunately, with the exception of a few cases, their missiles were not 'heat seeking', meaning the shooters had to have a pretty good aim in order to hit the plane. The missiles did not have a guided system that would help them veer their way into the plane. As Charlie's plane was now landing at Baghdad International Airport, he remembered how close he had been to dying a few times while taking those flights in and out of Iraq. He wished he had taken the names and emails of some of the pilots. It occurred to him he had never thanked any of them.

Everything at the airport was brand new now. The Iraqis had rebuilt everything, from the façade and windows of the reception hall to the visa control boots and the baggage collection area. Outside, there was a semi-orderly taxi service. Charlie started grinning to himself, thinking, *this is too orderly for Baghdad!*

The road to the city still gave him shivers. Back in the invasion days, that road had been one of the scariest ones possible. Snipers would hide behind the tall, old palm trees on both sides of the road, and shoot at anyone they chose, for whatever reason, or no reason at all. Some of their targets were American military personnel, but journalists and aid workers were also fair game.

He remembered how a friend of his, Marla, had been killed on that very same road, a few years ago. Marla had been one of the sweetest girls one could find. Born in California, she had been in her early twenties, and was as slim as a skeleton. She would not eat much. Never had been a big eater. How she ever survived was anyone's guess. She was high wired like hell inside; the only reason she did not show it more often outside was her twice-daily swimming exercises that took the frustration out of her. A few years earlier, she had found her mission in life, one for which she ended up sacrificing her life. Marla had been working for a non-governmental organisation that would go from one war zone to another to document information about civilians killed for no fault of their own. Armies and partisans rarely care about how many civilians they kill along the way. They say that if they do, they might be held accountable, or that the military's job should not be prevented by concerns over how many 'collaterals' might fall, or that the other side always uses civilians as shield, so there are inevitably more civilian casualties than there should be. Well, those excuses never sat well with Marla. She – and her organization – lived on next to no money. They would go knocking on door after door, trying to raise money, trying to get grants from whatever organization would listen to them. Five thousand dollars here; ten thousand there; even a few hundred here, and a few hundred there.

Work had been Marla's life. She would hire a local interpreter-helper, go to every village in the conflict zone, and document the life and death of every casualty, every man, woman, and child who had lost his or her life in the conflict zone. She was very non-partisan about it, too. It was not that she hated the military. Not at all. She had respect for them. She worked with them. You would think the military would hate her, considering that she was trying to document the result of their intended and unintended aggression, but they did not. There were times the military even offered her protection. They would give her rides in their tanks and armoured personnel carriers. Every now and then, they would even give her some information that was useful for her work. Over time, everyone had started respecting Marla. People would try to help her any way they could. Charlie had helped her, too. During the war, he had lived in a two-bedroom hotel suite for months. Marla had had no money and nowhere to stay, so Charlie had given her the second bedroom.

Driving on the airport road that day, Charlie remembered the day he had heard Marla had died. Her car had hit an explosive device, and exploded. She had not been wearing her bullet-proof jacket, and had died instantly. Charlie had cried his eyes dry that night, and was choking up again now.

The city had changed quite a bit, too. Some things were better. Most were not. In the period after the invasion party's departure, the Iraqis had spent quite a bit of money rebuilding some of the places destroyed by the war. Baghdad was not a 'rich' or 'fancy' city the way Dubai was, even during the 'Butcher's' time, but things had obviously got worse. Looking at it now, Charlie could see there were lots of new buildings around. The old ones had patched over the bullet marks. Some had just put new coats of paint on the building, and purposefully kept the marks as memorabilia. The government had also repaired a lot of the bridges that had been bombed during the military operations and afterwards. There were not any 'palaces' like in the times of the dictator, but there were certainly a lot more mansion-size houses in some of the new suburbs that had recently sprung up just outside the old city perimeters. Aside from the material aspects, however, there was another kind of change in the city. In the old days, Baghdad was very much a secular city. Yes, Iraqis were Muslim; Islam was the official religion of the country, and – when it suited him – the dictator very much used religion to his own benefit. Average Iraqi people, too, were very religious inside the four walls of their homes, but the city, *per se*, did not 'advertise' Islam.

198

Now, the city had a different look. Decades earlier, Baghdad was primarily a Sunni Muslim city. There were always Shiite neighborhoods in Baghdad, but, nowadays, their population had grown quite a bit. They had expanded to other neighborhoods, and their parts of the city had a distinctly different look than the Sunni parts. The religious look was inescapable. Verses from the Koran were carved onto the façade of almost all buildings. 'Cheerful' or 'objectionable' colors were either officially banned or just not used. There was no lipstick, red or pink or purple. The architecture of the Shiite neighborhoods was pretty much black and white, plus green – the Shiites' favourite color. Aside from the semantics, the whole city was more religiously observant than it ever used to be.

Shiite schools had issued standard uniforms for boys and girls. No shorts or short sleeves for boys. Girls had to don the neck-to-toe black garment better known as *chador* in Iran. Morning classes started with prayer sessions. Classes were canceled for noon prayer. So were shops and all government offices. Calls to prayer were broadcast on speakers in all streets. There were few women on the streets, and they were clad in black from head to toe. The contrast between the Shiite and Sunni neighborhoods surpassed that of the former East and West Berlin. You would have thought these neighborhoods were in two different countries.

Charlie's task was to find out more about the new arms smuggling ring in Iraq, but that's all he had to go by. Other than that the arms were sophisticated, he knew nothing else. Worse, he did not know where to start. It was time he put his journalism hat on once again. He needed to do some basic research. He decided to pay a visit to an old acquaintance he used to know from his journalism days. She was not from Iraq. She was an American. Lilly was one of those unique characters. She was young, pretty and very intelligent. Only in her late twenties, she had already achieved a high-level position with an oil company. Her father was an American diplomat, so she had been in the region before, spoke some Arabic, and had a feel for the place. Her company had been in Iraq almost from the beginning of the invasion. They had got themselves a contract with the military at an early stage to review the status of oil facilities in Iraq. Before they could even start doing serious and systemic surveys of the facilities, anti-invasion partisans had started blowing up oil pipelines here and there. For the next three years, almost all company resources had been spent on putting out the pipeline fires. Maybe it was a good thing for them. The Iraqis had seen what a good job they did with the pipeline, and the government had signed a multi-year contract with the company after the invading armies left. Most of the oil facilities in Iraq were either in Shiite or Kurdish areas, and Charlie thought maybe Lilly could ask around and see if her security people had seen or heard anything suspicious that would help him. Even though Kurdistan was now a separate and independent country, the government in Baghdad had maintained its 'paternalistic' feelings toward the areas to the north, and was keeping a close eye on what was going on in those areas.

To Charlie's surprise and dismay, Lilly reported that she could not find anything. In fact, she said, some of the Shiites were also complaining about an influx of arms in the market in recent months, but it was not ending up in the hands of anyone in particular, and her company did not know who the suppliers were.

Charlie decided it was time to pay a visit to his old friend, Kurdish President Kurdawani. Instead of meeting him in his headquarters in Kirkuk, the president had insisted that Charlie come to lunch at his residence in Erbil. Before independence, Erbil had been the regional headquarters of one of the two main Iraqi Kurdish factions. Charlie had always liked Erbil, partly because the ride to the city passed through a pretty amazing, mountainous road, zigzagging uphill for hours, passing through lush green areas with beautifully fresh air. Of all the people in the Middle East Charlie had dealt with over the years, Kurds and Afghans were his favorites. By the time Charlie got to the president's residence, it was about 2 p.m., just in time for lunch. Kurdawani warmly greeted his old pal at the door. They shook hands for a brief second, and then hugged each other for a while, then shook hands again.

"You look exactly the same," said Charlie.

It was true. Kurdawani had not changed a bit. If anything, he had lost some weight and looked younger. He was also still wearing the warm smile he had become known for over the years.

"I am okay; I am okay. Life goes on. We finally established our own country. It took a while, but we did it." He now wore an even bigger smile on his face.

A servant came in asking what they wanted to drink. "Tea? Coffee? Soda?"

"No, no," protested the president. "He's our old friend. Bring some Arak, with some ice and water on the side. Tell people in the kitchen to quickly prepare some *mezza;* we'll be ready for lunch soon."

This was not going to be a quick interview. He was going to be there for a while, and it was just fine with him.

The servants set a table on the balcony as the two took their places on comfortable sofa chairs. The view was just astounding. The cool mountain breeze was welcome company compared to the warmth that Arak had brought to Charlie's face. It had been quite a while since he last drank in the middle of the day. The surrounding mountains, some of them still with snow at their peaks, looked foreboding, strong, invincible and uncompromising, just like the Kurds.

After a little chit-chat, Charlie got to the point and asked the Kurdish leader if he had recently heard of any arms smuggling rings in his country.

"Iraq has always been awash in arms," said Kurdawani.

"Yes, but groups bought them for their own use, not to sell them."

"But the war is over; well, almost over. We still have groups fighting each other." Kurdawani was pointing his finger toward the other side of the mountain, meaning Shiites and Sunnis in Iraq. "And, occasionally, we still have cross-border attacks by groups trying to come to our country."

"So you're saying people do not need arms here anymore?"

"No, I'm not saying that. I'm saying it is inevitable that some of the extra guns may be making their way into the market."

"So, who's selling and who's buying? Are you selling your stuff?"

"I don't think the amount is much. I think we are, at most, talking about some guns and RPGs."

"Okay, but again, who's selling and who's buying?"

"I'm not sure exactly who's buying, because the market is never a straight line. You usually don't sell directly to the buyer. You sell to trusted middlemen, and they will do their work. We're not selling much. In fact, I don't think we have sold anything in the past eighteen months."

"Why is that? Why are you not selling more?"

"Well, we are still a new country. We are not as

established as we want to be. We don't feel as secure as we want to be. As I said, we are still having cross-border attacks from Iraq, and the Iranians. In fact, they've been attacking us a lot more than the Iraqis. The Iraqis are settling down in their own affairs. The crazy Iranians are always trying to expand and stir trouble. I don't have facts and figures, but I would guess if anyone is selling more than the usual, it must be groups allied with Iran."

"Why is that?"

"Because world politics has changed. Big countries in the West or China are less reluctant to sell arms to their former protégés. So, if you have guns, you'd rather keep them for rainy days, unless you are absolutely sure you can buy more when you need them. In this region, only Iran is willing to sell you arms. They're one of the few 'ideological' states left in this part of the world."

"And who's buying them?"

"I told you, we often do not know who the ultimate buyer is, especially if the buyer and the middlemen are smart. It is like money laundering. The stuff changes hands a couple of times, or passes through a couple of countries, before it settles down somewhere. They do it on purpose to make tracking it harder."

It was clear the Kurds did not have their finger on the pulse of this issue, although Kurdawani's analysis did help Charlie to narrow the field a bit. He decided to pay a visit to someone he knew in one of the Shiite groups allied with Iran.

Charlie's acquaintance with Ali had started years earlier, thanks to Marla. Marla had been trying to determine the number of casualties in one of the earlier rounds of fighting when the Americans and the British were still in Iraq. The victims had been from a Shiite village a few hundred miles south of Baghdad. Even in those days, the area was particularly nasty, and it was not safe for a foreigner – let alone a young, western woman – to go knocking on doors without someone with good connections in the region. Marla's inquiries had led her to Ali in Baghdad. Years earlier, he and a few of his colleagues had started their own non-governmental organisation to document the Iraqi dictator's Shiite killings when he was in power. It had been a secret task, and they had done their work very much below the radars, and had collected complete biographical information of more than a hundred thousand people. Names, addresses, date they were killed, circumstances as best as could be found, if the name of arresting authorities or torturers were available, which jail or interrogation centre the victims were taken to, and anything else they could find, neatly arranged in excel sheets backed up and stored on a few computers, in case one was found by the authorities.

So, when Marla had sought Ali's help, he and his people were all too happy to help. After a while, Ali was a regular at the hotel Charlie and Marla were staying, and that's how Ali and Charlie had come to know each other.

In the years since Ali and Charlie had met, the Iraqi had become somewhat of an 'important personality'. He had risen in the ranks of his group, and had become much closer to the sheikh, who was the supreme commander of the group – and was a major politician –thus, by association, Ali had acquired personal bodyguards, a fancy office, and small house in one of the secluded areas of Baghdad, overlooking the river.

Fortunately for Charlie, Ali had not changed his old mobile number. When he rang, Ali was more than welcoming. Charlie suggested lunch somewhere. Ali said security precautions did not allow him too much of an outing. Iraq was never that peaceful. People still assassinated their rivals. Instead, they decided to have lunch at one of Ali's more private offices.

Charlie told Ali what he was working on and, to save time, he had repeated the information he already had, based on the conversation with Kurdawani, without revealing his source.

Ali's first reaction was a chuckle, followed by a serious face that froze for a minute or two. "You know, I'm telling up upfront, you can get killed if you follow this too far."

"Why is that?"

"Because this story is much bigger than you think."

"How is that?"

"You've heard of war by proxy, right?"

"Yes, when someone uses someone else to fight a war on their behalf."

"Right. That's how Iraq was many years ago after, the fall of the dictator. Several countries interfered in Iraq, not because they cared about Iraq, but because they wanted to settle score with each other, in Iraq. It was kind of Lebanon of the old days. Or World War Two. But then, most of us here cleaned our act. We made it clear that we appreciated the help of our old friends, but were not going to do their dirty work for them here anymore. That did not sit well with some people. So, yes, there is arms smuggling in Iraq, but your previous source was right. The arms are not staying here, and are not meant to stay here. This has become a bigger issue than Iraq."

"So, you're saying they are brought to Iraq, but *no one* wants to cooperate, or just *your* group does not?"

"We are the biggest and the most moderate Shiite group here. So, when people start talking about Shiites, they automatically think about us. However, the reality is, there are many other Shiite groups here. Also, it is wrong to
205

automatically assume that the Iranians would *necessarily* want to deal only with Shiite groups."

"Well, surely the Sunnis would not cooperate with a Shiite country with which they fought a war for years."

"That's where you are wrong. The nature of the region's geopolitics has changed. It is not run based on ethnicity anymore. If the Iranians think other groups might be more beneficial to them than us, of course they will strike a deal with them."

"Are you telling me that it is the Sunnis and not the Shiites who are helping them smuggle arms to other countries?"

"I am not telling you anything. I am just telling you the possibility exists."

All of a sudden, a flashlight blinked in Charlie's mind. He remembered the conversation he had with Richard the first night they had drank at 1789. He remembered Richard's words about the US having *tried* to shift the alliance by dealing with the *moderates* versus *radicals,* instead of dealing with a group based on their religious proclivity.

Once again, while the Americans were thinking of doing something, the Iranians had actually implemented it, he thought.

"Just one last thing, Ali, before I leave; you are not playing with me here, are you? Are you being a politician talking to a journalist, or is this Ali talking to Charlie?"

"I am not being coy with you. We're tired of this issue ourselves. We know this is going on, and we know everyone is automatically blaming us. We don't want this, but we cannot openly talk about it because, at the end of the day, we are still Iraqis, and we have to live with these people. We don't want to stir the pot."

With that in mind, Charlie's task was to figure out

on whom to zoom now. He had – somewhat instinctively, and maybe incorrectly – ruled out the Kurds, and now he was being led to believe it was not the Shiites, either. He needed to figure which one of the several hardcore Sunni groups to pick on. He decided maybe the old mantra, 'divide and conquer', could help him. He decided to pick a group that *most probably* was not involved, claim he had information pointing the finger at them, and then let them point the finger at the real culprits. Of course, it was possible they would *inaccurately* blame someone else, but it was a shot worth taking. Plus, he figured that he knew the Iraqi politics well enough, and had enough sources who would set him on the right course if that happened.

It was not a bad strategy. He went to Sheikh Aqwa. Aqwa – meaning 'the strongest' in Arabic – was not his real name. It was a nickname he had given himself years ago. Now in his fifties, the sheikh was an old-time Iraqi general. When the regime collapsed, he had gone underground, and even joined the insurgents in fighting the Americans and the British, but he had soon had an *awakening,* and decided he could do better working in the open. He had the prestige, the money, and the family name, was disciplined, and had leadership skills. So, he joined politics, which was a first for him. Because he did not have any political affiliation, he decided to join someone else's bandwagon, at first, instead of opening his own party. Charlie had interviewed him a couple of times as a journalist when the sheikh had first joined the Homeland Party. He had left them after a while in a public row. He found them 'extremists bent on destroying the country'. Since Charlie had not seen the general for the past few years, he decided the former air force commander could be a good place to start.

The sheikh was decidedly in a foul mood the day Charlie dropped in to see him, but in the end that worked out to Charlie's advantage. The general was grouchy because the national parliament had passed over his political party for a more radical Sunni group when allocating 'development funds'. The Iraqi political system had just about perfected the American tradition of pork-barrel politics by dishing out millions of dollars each year to various political parties so they could spend it on developing their own communities. Unfortunately, the reality was that half the money – if not most – always ended up in the politicians' pockets, and never made it to the real people who could have used the help. Charlie asked the sheikh about his new political party and why he had left Homeland.

"When you study in the military, they teach you a few things. You learn to love your country first. You learn discipline. You learn strategizing. When I joined Homeland, it was because I thought they had the same priorities. I knew many of the leaders. A couple of them had served under me in the military. Several were from prominent business families in the previous regime. I thought I could work with them. But the more I worked with them, the more I realized they were a true definition of sour grapes. It was not so much the loss of the previous regime they were mourning, as much as the loss of their own status under the previous regime. For them, it was not a national issue. It was a personal issue. I could not work with that. Unfortunately, they are still the same. What they are interested in, first and foremost, is not even the status or prestige of the Sunni community. Maybe they really cared about that in the beginning, but that's because our collective status in society was linked to our brand of Islam. Times have changed. The country has moved on. We are not judged by that anymore, not even by members of our own community. That much they have understood, which is why, for them, the most important thing is making money. Actually, let me correct myself. The most important thing for them is not letting others make money, so they can pick up the business. We have become vengeful, as well as incompetent, both as social leaders and as human beings."

Wow, Charlie thought. He had not heard such damnation of the Iraqi society in a long, long time, whether from Iraqis or foreigners. He decided no introduction was needed in asking about the arms smuggling.

"Are they the ones keeping up the arms smuggling in and out of Iraq?"

"Not into Iraq. That is done by a radical Shiite group. They bring it mainly through the Shat Al Arab waterway across from Iran. Sometimes, they smuggle them through the mountains of Kurdistan. That group, in turn, has a strategic alliance with Homeland, which takes it out of the country."

"Where to?"

"I don't know that. It is such a sensitive and secretive issue that only a couple of people at the top know the details."

Charlie thought quite a bit about what his next step should be, to whom he could go to get more information, and which group he should press. He went over what he had learnt so far.

"We believed country should come first."

"We believed in unifying the country."

"They haggled over lost status."

"For them, it is about money."

"They were from prominent business families."

"They had good connections."

The more he went over these concepts in his head, the more he believed that this was not about politics anymore, at least not for the Iraqis. If there was a serious

209

arms smuggling network operating in the country now, it was all about business and surpassed factional alliances or ethnic differences. He decided his next contact should not be either a politician or a religious character. It should be someone with strong business ties and cross-factional relations.

CHAPTER 29

IBRAHIM Kassdim was a unique and well-known character in Iraq. Tall, silver hair pushed back on the sides of his ears protecting his otherwise bald head, he was one of the richest men in Iraq and one of the best connected businessmen, not just in Iraq, but in the entire Middle East. The only thing that was different about him was that he was Jewish. Like many countries in the Middle East, Iraq at one point, had a large Jewish population, accounting for about fifteen percent of the total population. However, over the years, they were either killed by the regimes or voluntarily emigrated in the face of mounting hardships imposed by governments and uncompromising societies.

Born into an Iraq-American family, he had gone to school in New York before his father, a respected trader, settled in Iraq. One of the first things he had done was to officially change the spelling of his son's name from 'Abraham' to 'Ibrahim'. He figured most people these days would not recognize the Jewish origin of 'Kassdim', but the first name had to go. Although the family was very proud of its Jewish heritage, they knew they lived in a part of the world that too often cracked down on their ethnic minority community in reprisal for the policies of the State of Israel. The less Jewish you looked and sounded, the better your chances of success in the society.

211

By the time Ibrahim had reached his late twenties, he was ready, if not eager, to capitalize on his father's connections, knowledge and success, in order to build a business of his own. Those were the days of the Cold War, the days Arab leaders did not trust each other just as pro-American and pro-Soviet camps did not trust each other. Everyone was suspicious of everyone else, even the ones who were supposedly friends. Every leader was watching his back and, for that, needed information, raw and reliable information about the 'others'. Ibrahim would collect, and even buy, information and intelligence that Arab leaders wanted about each other, and offer it to government heads, only so they would leave him and his family alone to do more business and make more money. It was a revolving door relationship that benefited him and his clients. In the year or two before the 'Butcher of Baghdad' fell from power, Ibrahim had sensed things were to go wrong. He had quietly and discreetly moved much of his assets overseas. He sent one son to Switzerland to study, and his daughter to London to open a branch office. Then he claimed his wife was tired of him working all the time, and spread stories that she had decided to go live in the company of relatives in the United States. Long before the actual invasion, he had sent out feelers through friends and contacts – including Charlie, whom he had known for years – that he was willing to supply information about the 'Butcher' in return for personal and asset safety guarantees once there was a regime change.

By all counts, he was left alone quite nicely after the war. When an extremely small number of people had electricity after the war, chandeliers in his house in one of Baghdad's upscale neighborhoods were always on. He even had extra electricity to clean the engine in his swimming pool. Of course, the electricity was not coming from the city. It was from his personal generator, but, at least he had a steady supply of gas to run it day in and day out. That was more than ninety-nine percent of the country could brag about.

Getting to Ibrahim's house was not easy. In an effort to cripple the previous regime and most of its infrastructure, the Americans had bombed much of Ibrahim's well-to-do neighborhood. It was meant to be a message to supporters of the previous regime. Whatever the invasion had not destroyed, years of civil war between Iraqi warring factions had. By the time it was all over, bridges had collapsed, there were foot-deep and foot-wide holes in the roads, and sewage was piling up. Getting into the driveway of Ibrahim's house, Charlie could hardly believe this was in the same neighborhood he had just passed. *Privilege has its privileges, indeed,* he thought.

Ibrahim entered the courtyard of his large house to greet Charlie. There were three cars in the driveway, a black Hummer with tinted windows, a silver Mercedes sedan, and the one parked farthest was a custom-made, bullet-proof yellow Corvette. Ibrahim noticed that Charlie was staring at it, somewhat suspiciously.

"It's a beauty, isn't it?" Ibrahim volunteered, with a hint of arrogance.

"Sure is!" He was about to ask something stupid like 'why the hell would you want this in Baghdad', but decided to hold his breath.

"I stole it!"

"Excuse me?"

"I stole it!"

"From whom?"

He did not really need to ask. There was only one person in the whole of Iraq who could have had such a car for Ibrahim to 'steal'. They both said it in unison. "The

213

ruler's son!"

The son, the more ruthless of the two, had an insatiable appetite for fast, custom-made sports cars, but that was not his only 'hobby'. Alcohol, drugs, pornography and raping whatever poor woman crossed his way were his other bad habits. Charlie had seen some of the evidence first hand. After the 'Butcher of Baghdad' had been overthrown, Charlie had a unique opportunity to visit the son's 'porn palace' on the banks of the river in Baghdad. The place was as cheesy as one could imagine. There were badly-drawn paintings of naked women on the walls of the entry hall, lurid, cheap, cloth, red sofas in one room, and a couple of completely dark rooms in other parts of the mansion. One room was filled with expensive imported alcohol that filled the room from the floor to the ceiling: gin, vodka, whiskey, and cases after cases of various types of champagne. It was hard to tell what some of the rooms had been used for because aerial bombings during the war had destroyed much of the building.

As he was reminiscing and telling Ibrahim his thoughts, he noticed how dapperly his host had dressed up for a Friday morning, Muslim weekend. Standing at six point two inches, with his silver hair, salty, thick eyebrows, and a long forehead, Ibrahim was an impressive character by any yardstick. The fact that he was wearing a matching beige suede suite and light brown shirt with the top buttons open, just added to his stature. Charlie, standing at five feet and five inches, and wearing dirty jeans and a totally un-matching shirt, felt out of place, but tried not to show his inferiority. He just kept his eye on the surroundings, the house, the cars, the pool in the back, the nicely cut green grass. Anything he could do to avoid looking at Ibrahim. Not that his host minded it, or even cared. He had always used his stature and attire as a tool to outgun his adversaries, business rivals, or any other type of interlocutor. The more they felt intimidated by him, for whatever reason, the better off he was in his dealings with them.

As they entered the house, the chic mix of light-colored silk sofa, Italian glass coffee table, abstractionist style paintings on the wall, and a few large Iranian silk carpets gave the place a much bigger aura than any ordinary house would convey. An Iraqi servant, dressed in perfectly ironed black pants, matching shiny shoes, and tuxedo white shirt with open collars, promptly made his entrance into the living room to take drink orders. Ibrahim asked for a cappuccino, and Charlie asked if he could have a cold diet coke with no ice. Tap water in Iraq was not safe, and Charlie was not sure what type of water the staff was using to make ice. It just was not worth the risk.

"So, it's been a while since I last saw you," Ibrahim started the conversation.

"Yes, it was three years ago. You were in Washington, and you had a fabulous luncheon at your even more fabulous McLean house."

"Oh, yeah."

It was obvious he had been about to say something, but cut himself short. For a good reason, too. There were a couple of young Russian beauties in their mid-twenties who decided to undress and swim in the pool in their skimpy bikinis. That did not go down too well with some of the older and conservative Washingtonians. Washington is a conservative, government-type city, anyway. Charlie hated the capital city. Too stuffy for him. He told Ibrahim he was working on a story about arms smuggling in the region, and had some information that maybe some of it was going through Baghdad, and wanted to know if Ibrahim could help him. He was studying Ibrahim's reaction as he was talking,

215

and noticed what he thought was a certain discomfort on his face and in the way he carried himself. He first kind of closed his eyes. With his thick eyebrows, it became ever more noticeable as the eyelids moved down. Then he opened his eyes wide, causing the eyebrows to go up a few notches. He took a deep breath, and then repositioned himself in the chair, moving his right leg over his left one.

"Well, arms trade has been around from time immemorial. It has been going on long before I was born and, I promise, it will go one for centuries after you and I are gone. Is it a good thing? Is it a bad thing? It is hard to be moralistic about it."

Charlie wondered why Ibrahim had started off that way. He sensed something was not right, but could not put his finger on it.

Ibrahim continued, "I know you like hard-core investigative journalism, but the thing or two I *heard* about arms trading tells me it would be really hard to *really* pin down the details: who is involved, how much money, what types of guns, or even the final destination, sometimes."

"Well, let's take Iraq, for example," Charlie pressed on. "If someone wanted to buy arms here, any of the factions, not the government, how would it work? Who are the likely suspects one could contact to initiate the process?"

"Well, that depends. In Iraq, it is different, because most militia groups belong to political parties, and they have traditionally had their alliances with other countries, and those were the sources for arms."

Now Charlie could tell that Ibrahim was not telling him the truth. Maybe that was the case decades ago, but at least a few militia groups had sprung up lately, which did not have any allegiance to a particular party, and they had no troubles arming themselves.

216

"What if you'd just wanted to use Iraq as a passage point to somewhere else?"

"There is no reason for–" Before Ibrahim could finish his sentence, the servant walked in to say there was a call for him from a Mr. Akram.

"He says it is urgent, sir," the servant informed his master.

Ibrahim excused himself for a couple of minutes to take the call from his office. As he walked out, Charlie could not help but see the number on the caller ID screen of the living room phone, which sat next to his coffee table. Ordinarily, he would have paid no attention to it, but, given the way he felt about Ibrahim's reaction to his questions and the sensitive topic of the arms trade, he decided to look at the number. It was a mobile number from Cairo, the Egyptian capital. He wrote it down in his notebook: 00-20-12-555-4444. He could hear Ibrahim's muted voice and, by this time, curiosity had taken the better part of him. He was trying to eavesdrop, but did not want to get caught. He observed the geography of the room for a few second, to see how much closer he could get to the office door so he could hear better. He saw that the sofa he was sitting on was in one corner of the room, but, if he moved across to the other side, he could get closer to a large window that opened to the back side of the garden, with a view of the swimming pool. However, it was also closer to a door that led to the private part of the floor that included the kitchen on one side, and Ibrahim's office on the other. He pondered for a few seconds if it was worth it. What were the chances of being caught? What would he say if he got caught? He rehashed those quickly in his mind, and decided to make a move for it. Even as he was getting closer, he could hear Ibrahim's voice more clearly.

"Akram, I know–"

"Akram, Sorry–"

"Listen, I know there has been a delay–"

"Yes, yes, the guns and the bullets are fine…"

"No, we cannot send those right now. It is too dangerous. Basra is not the best option–"

"I don't think we should discuss this now. It might not be safe…"

Charlie did not really like what he heard. Clearly, Ibrahim was up to some sort of arms deal, and the fact that Basra was mentioned made it pretty clear that there was some Iranian involvement. Basra was the closest border down to Iran, except for some of Kurdish areas. Its population were mostly Shiites, and many families and tribes there had close personal and professional ties across the border. If Ibrahim was talking about guns and bullets and Basra, Charlie could pretty much take it to the bank that there was some arms deal going down involving Iran. Charlie moved quickly back to his chair, and pretended he had been waiting all that time Ibrahim was on the phone. He watched Ibrahim as he re-entered the room, and compared his demeanour to when had shown up in the garden to greet him about forty-five minutes earlier. It was obvious he was bothered by something. He looked distracted, even a bit mentally tired. It was not until he was a few steps away from the sofa that he even tried to regain his composure, but, even then, it was apparent that his mind was not quite back on the conversation. Charlie thought about jumping back into the conversation where they had left off, and asking a bit more about arms trade and Ibrahim's possible involvement. Maybe he could get Ibrahim to divulge something about the conversation he had just had. He decided against it, however. Ibrahim was too smart to let up something like that. Plus, Charlie had pretty much got what he wanted. Yes, most probably, there was an arms

218

smuggling ring in Iraq; yes, the Iranians were most probably involved; and yes, Ibrahim most probably had something to do with it. He decided to bid his friend farewell and move on.

CHAPTER 30

CHARLIE returned to Cyprus. He decided he needed to do some research on things he had found out, and he also had to report back to Washington. His laptop had the latest encryption technology, but he still could not trust the connection. The agency had installed a secure line for him through one of its dedicated satellite connections in Cyprus. Of course, they never spoke in detail about anything on the phone. Anyone could be listened to, especially in a place like Cyprus, where almost everyone was running some sort of intelligence operation. In the comfort of his apartment, he reported on the meeting with Ibrahim and a few other things he had learnt. He wrote a long report, and sounded an alarm bell at the end of it.

Given the recent explosions, assassinations and political disruptions in the region, the fact that we know from Hassan that Saudi officials are concerned about an Iranian link, and information we now have from Ibrahim, it is my firm belief that there is a concerted Iranian effort to reshape the political map of the Middle East. I believe we need to take this very seriously, pursue it quickly, and prevent any future plans they might have at the earliest time possible.

He figured that, with a tone like that, someone would take him seriously, take the issue seriously. However, to his surprise, nothing happened. He waited a couple of days, a week, a couple of weeks. Nothing. Not a word. He sent another email, asking if anyone had seen his previous memo and if a response would be forthcoming. The only thing he got back was, 'Received. Thanks'. That's it? That's all they could say? He had poured out his heart and soul in the memo. He was peeved. He was offended. He took it as lack of professional respect for his efforts. He told himself, *to hell with it; I am going to take a few days off and fly back to LA.*

He missed Sarah badly. He longed for her. When he accepted being based in Cyprus, the deal with the agency was that he would fly home once a month for a few days, on his own dime, but that he needed to maintain a healthy relationship with his wife. Sarah had promised she would fly to Cyprus frequently, although she had not defined 'frequently'. She obviously did not *need* to be in LA. It was not like she had a job there or anything. She did not need to work, being a Saudi princess. However, she was not at all that keen on flying off to Cyprus. In LA, she lived in a mansion, and had maids and a cook. Charlie was living in a two-bedroom apartment in Nicosia and, even if they wanted to spend their money to live in a spacious house, something more suitable for a princess, the agency would not have agreed to it. He was supposed to be low profile, a simple journalist working for a small start-up Internet site. Living in a mansion and splashing money would have raised too many questions.

Charlie picked up the phone, called his boss on his regular cell phone, and told him point blank he was flying to see Sarah for a few days. "Call me when you guys have decided on my memo."

He was not asking for permission. He was just telling his boss what he was going to do. That was the advantage of being rich, or at least, being married to a rich woman. You could tell your boss to go to hell, and not worry about the consequences. He booked himself a business class ticket direct to LA. When he traveled on business and on the company's dime, he had to fly economy, and he had to fly an American airline, to the degree possible. Obviously, when he traveled in the region, he would travel on whatever airline he could, but still economy class. Actually, he could not fly just any airline. Certain countries were still on the 'aiding and abetting international disorder' list. You could not fly Iranian or Sudanese airlines. Washington had even recently added Lebanon's flagship carrier, because an anti-American Shiite factions had taken control of the government, and there were concerns for the safety and well being of American citizens if they flew on that airline.

However, he was now flying home on his own dime, and he could do as he damn well pleased. He and Sarah had talked quite a bit before Charlie took the job with the agency. They were both worried that the job might have severe adverse affects on their marriage and their life. Up until the issue had come up, they had had a very open relationship. They talked about everything. The told each other everything. They asked each other's advice on almost everything. The new job could have potentially changed that. He was going to be a spy. Spies were required to hide the nature of their work and details of their assignments from their spouses. Also, not only Sarah was a foreigner – she had never cared to become an American citizen – but she was also a Saudi, an Arab, and a Muslim – the last one, only in name.

Still, Charlie's work was going to be in the Middle

222

East, maybe even in Saudi Arabia itself. What if he had to spy on members of the ruling family? That would be Sarah's uncles and cousins, and maybe father and brother. Could he, would he, come back and discuss those with Sarah? After days of long conversations and many sleepless nights, they had made a promise that they would not let the job affect their life and their relationship. They would still tell each other everything, including discussing Charlie's missions, even if it involved Saudi Arabia. They also agreed that the only time Charlie would hold back any information was if telling Sarah something might endanger her life.

They had duly informed the agency about the agreement. The message was clear: if you want me, you'd have to trust my wife, too. It was an unusual, if not unprecedented, request, but given the changing principles and ideologies at CIA, and the fact that Sarah was a princess from a country that was considered one of America's closest allies in the region, the agency had succumbed. Now that Charlie was back from this round of overseas assignments, it was time to put the theory to practice, to see if he could tell her everything and not feel bad about it, or feel he might be compromising his mission, and also see if she would remain as open with him about things she had come to learn. After all, she had her own network of people, most just Hollywood socialites, but also many well-informed Saudi and non-Saudi contacts. She was not on terribly good terms with her family back home. Her family considered her a rebel, not a good enough Saudi, not too adherent to the country's social and religious edicts, too Western, and too independent minded. There had always been tension in the relationship, but both sides had decided to maintain at least the pretence of a relationship.

As it turned out, things went well. Charlie told Sarah about the trip to Baghdad, the meeting with Ibrahim, and his angry memo to Langley.

"People have just gone crazy," she told him. "I am telling you, that whole region has gone crazy. I heard something totally weird while you were gone. Back in school at home, I used to have this assistant principal. She was also teaching religious studies. I did not know it or understand it at the time, but I remember older people around saying she was a fanatic. They called her a *wahabi*."

She was referring to the centuries-old sect of Islam known for its strict interpretation of the religion.

"We always kind of ignored what she said. She talked about things that made no sense to me. I remember her saying we should avoid any encounters with non-Muslims, especially Westerners. My grandfather, the ruler of the country, the founder of the nation, had good American friends, Christian friends. My most favorite place in the world was Paris, not Riyadh or Jeddah. And this woman was telling *me* – granddaughter of the custodian of the Holy Shrines – how to behave. Anyway, I heard the other week that the government is about to open this special school, not far away from Washington, to 'offer better Islamic education' to kids living around the capital. Better Islamic education? Compared to what? Compared to where? What's wrong with the religious schools we already have? All they care about is doing it *their* way. That's all it is about. And this is not the only thing. I hear they are doing all sorts of things here. I am telling you, Charlie, something is going on. Just look at how many times my uncle has been here lately. He used to come, what, once every couple of years! Now, he is here once almost every other month. He is a ranking minister in Saudi Arabia. What could he be doing here so often?"

Charlie listened, but did not make much of it. His mind was still on Iran, not Saudi Arabia. He did not really understand the significance of what she was saying, and neither did she. Frankly, at that stage, neither one had a reason to think there was any significance. He asked her for more information; was her uncle the source? Was any other family member the source? What else had she heard? Sarah said it was no one in the family, but told him a few more details she had heard.

When Charlie woke up the next morning, for some odd reason, Sarah's words of the previous day were on his mind, and they just would not go away. He tried to brush them aside or divert his attention to something else, but it just did not work. He decided that he needed to ease his curiosity, and find some answers. There were some interesting stories on the Internet about Saudi Arabians in the United States, and also in a secure government database he had access to, but no smoking gun, so to speak. If the Saudis were doing something inside the country, they were not leaving too many fingerprints or making their moves public. There were a couple of articles in local newspapers across the country on the Saudi government opening Islamic schools here and there. There were some other articles on disputes in various corners of the country – Alaska; Texas; Washington; Louisiana; North Dakota – about ownership of companies and non-governmental organizations, or activities of non-profit organizations. Charlie looked at the article from North Dakota a bit closer. It was a short news agency report from *The Associated Press*:

[BISMARCK, N.D. (AP) – The tiny Muslim community leaders of the state Friday cried foul over what they see as 'foreign invasion' of their ranks, and asked state attorney general to probe into whether or not state laws are broken.

The controversy began during local elections for

leadership positions of the estimated five hundred-strong Muslim Association of North Dakota. At the last minute, two hundred voters previously unknown to the organization entered the election hall, nominated their own candidates and, in effect, hijacked the process.

The association's current leader, Hajj Ahmed Knutson, an American Muslim of Norwegian heritage, said a 'foreign country' had bussed in the new members to take over the association and its budget of ten million US dollars. The North Dakota chapter of the Muslim Association of America does not require proof of residency as a pre-requisite for voting. As long as a member claims he is a state resident and five others vouch for his claim, he can vote, and be elected.

"We are Muslims, but we are also Americans and, for God's sake, we have Norwegian heritage. How much mellower can we be? We are being invaded by a foreign country, because they want to force us to adopt more confrontational policies and attitudes," says Hajj Knutson.

He would not name the 'foreign country', but others accused Saudi Arabia of interference.

Charlie looked at another story, this one from El Paso, Texas.

[EL PASO, TX (AP) – Every month, the state corporate registry, by law, publishes the list of acquisitions and mergers in Texas companies.

Every month – almost – the list goes unnoticed.

This month, however, was different, as prominent Muslim businessmen of the state pointed to the hostile take over of Lahoud General Contractors, LLC, one of Texas's oldest and largest companies.

Established in 1947 by a family that had just

226

immigrated to the United States from Lebanon, the company had started by winning small state construction companies. Over the coming decades, the scope and dollar amount of its contracts got bigger, as did its penetration into state bureaucracy.

By the time the company was fifty years old, its revenue had ballooned to a hundred million US dollars annually. It was now winning just about every state and local contract.

The story went on to detail how a few weeks ago a 'rich foreigner with suitcases full of hundred dollar bills had shown up on the CEO's door and said, in no uncertain terms, 'sell me your company, or I'll go straight to the shareholders'.

The 'rich foreigner' was a distant cousin of Charlie's wife, Sarah.

By now, Charlie was gasping. He put the story aside to show it to his wife when she woke up, but decided to look into one more. This one was about the Islamic centre in Washington, DC – the nation's capital.

[WASHINGTON, DC (AP) – In an unprecedented move, the board of governors of the Islamic Center in Washington has barred female worshippers to enter the mosque, fired all female employees, and ordered male employees to grow full-length beards.

"For years, this institution was associated with what they claimed to be the 'more moderate' and 'liberal' factions of Islam. There is no 'moderate' or 'liberal' faction of Islam. There is only one Islam," says the center's director, Mohammed Abdul Wahab, in a statement released to the press.

"It is of utmost importance that an Islamic centre

227

situated in such a strategically important city of the world adheres to the strictest interpretation of the world's fastest growing religion. We invite all Muslims to return to the religion of Allah, as he introduced to us nearly one thousand five hundred years ago," he adds.

Charlie realized these might be individual and unrelated events. He figured that, if they amounted to any 'grand, Saudi design', big national newspapers like the *Washington Post* or *The New York Times* would cover them, but he could not see anything. He decided it was time he took a trip to the places where the wire service stories had occurred, and do some reporting of his own. Sarah had planned a trip with a friend to Paris long ago, and he had not heard anything back from the agency since his Baghdad trip. Why sit in LA by himself when he could satisfy his curiosity and get some answers?

The trip to Bismarck was long. There was no direct flight from LA to Bismarck, or to any other city in North Dakota. The nearest airline hub was Minneapolis, Minnesota. So he took a Northwest Airlines flight to Minneapolis, and then took a connecting flight to Bismarck. Even compared to some of the small-town international cities he had been to, the Bismarck airport looked and felt small. The airport building only had one gate. It did not need more. There were only three flights a day to Bismarck: two from Minneapolis, one in the morning and one late afternoon, and the third one was from neighbouring Montana. Bismarck – or the whole North Dakota, for that matter – was one of those cities in the States that people rarely volunteered to go to if they were not from the state. It was considered the 'outback' of the country. The whole state was just one giant flat land, one great farmland. It was one of those misfortunes of the state that people not from

228

the Midwest always made fun of them.

But that was just the stereotype. Charlie knew better. Years earlier, he had actually lived in Bismarck as a reporter and loved the place and the people. He had covered state capitol and its legislature. North Dakota legislature was a bit of an oddity. The state did not have a full-time legislature. Lawmakers met once every two years for a month or so. They would drive from all over the state to Bismarck, and either stay with relatives or at a hotel, take care of business, pass laws, debate the state budget as proposed by the governor, and then go back to wherever they had come from. Some of them were big farm owners; some were big businessmen.

As Charlie thought about the good old days, he kind of remembered how there were very, very few female lawmakers. In fact, come to think of it, he could not think of any! Okay, the state was conservative and *very* republican, but not in a prejudicial way against women. Actually, there were a couple of saber-rattler female politicians in the state. One was an attorney general. Another was state tax commissioner. Several worked for the State Historical Society. North Dakota had a large Native American community, and there were always bruising battles between some of the community leaders and state archaeologists. The former wanted the Indian artefacts buried without examination. They considered any examination to be 'disturbing' to the soul. The archaeologists wanted detailed forensic studies done. It was one of those times when people were just culturally talking past each other. They talked apples and oranges, and it was hard to think how there could be a fair resolution.

Charlie had booked himself a room at the new Sheraton hotel in the city centre. The hotel was a sensation. It was the first time a brand chain had opened a hotel in

Bismarck, and it had done marvels to the ego of the city residents, who saw this as a vindication that they did not live in a 'loser state'! Finding Hajj Amhed was not a difficult task. North Dakota had a fairly large Nordic and Scandinavian population, but almost everyone knew everyone in the city. With a population of one hundred thousand, it was hard to remain anonymous in Bismarck, not that anyone really wanted to. Even the politics of the state was far more open compared to the rest of the country. There was little of the Washington-style cloak and dagger politics in the city.

The state government and the legislature pretty much abided by the concept of 'open-politics'. No secrets; no hidden games. They even extended the concept to reporters and the media. If a reporter wanted some document, he or she could have it. It was a rare occasion that even a threat of Freedom of Information Act had to be made. If you genuinely told state officials that a document you wanted was a matter of public record, a simple phone call to the state agency lawyer would either confirm or deny it, and that was the end of that story. No one could remember a single FOIA case making it to the court. If the lawyer said the record was a public record, they official conceded. If the lawyer said it could be confidential, the news organization accepted the lawyer's word.

Hajj Ahmed's office was in a villa in a northern suburb of Bismarck. It was in a quiet corner of a mostly residential neighborhood. In addition to the Muslim Association of North Dakota, there were a few other businesses with villas as offices. They seemed like quiet neighbours in a quiet neighborhood. Charlie did not know what Hajj Ahmed looked like. When the newspaper ran the AP story, there was no picture attached to it. In the absence of a physical description to go by, Charlie had drawn a mental picture of the community Muslim leader as a man in his fifties, a bit overweight, big beer belly, maybe balding, maybe a prayer mark on his forehead – all the characteristics he could expect in a Muslim community leader in the Middle East. He obviously had forgotten that this Muslim had been born and bred in the United States, and had Norwegian blood in him. When he rang the doorbell, he got the surprise of his life.

"You must be Charlie. Please come in. We've been expecting you." Hajj Ahmed had turned out to be a dashing, six feet five inches tall, thin, blond, blue eyed, and was dressed in a three-piece, tailor-made silk suit. Charlie had forgotten the Nordic heritage when imagining Knutson. The host detected the sudden shock in Charlie's eyes, but did not pursue it or comment on it. Charlie opened the conversation by saying he had seen the AP wire story, and was doing a story for his website about the Muslim communities of the States, and was curious about what was happening in North Dakota, and what was behind the recent association election. Despite his calm manner and cool appearance, Hajj Ahmed turned out to be a pressure cooker on the verge of explosion.

"For decades after decades, Muslims in American have faced huge challenges. Challenges on many fronts. First, our numbers were miniscule for a long time. There was a time only half of one percent of Americans were Muslims, and even half of those had come to America, immigrated to America. So the number of people born in this country who had adopted Islam was really, really tiny. But we worked on it; we worked on it hard. We spent a lot of time working with members of Congress in Washington to pass laws that would make immigration from Muslim countries easier. We also worked a lot overseas; in my case, in Scandinavian countries. That was really difficult, and

231

took lots of effort. For decades, Scandinavian countries offered exactly the kind of social security that an immigrant community wanted: help in getting a job; fully paid health insurance; even some upfront money to buy furniture and get set up. Immigrants in the States would have killed for any of those. We could not compete with those things, but there were weaknesses in the Scandinavian system we could explore. First, the political right gained grounds in several countries, and Muslims did not feel comfortable. Second, as parents and family members of the immigrants back home got older and needed financial help, Muslim immigrants in Scandinavian countries realized that economic opportunities in their new homeland were limited. They could make a comfortable life for themselves, but they did not make *that much* money to send some back home."

The phones around were ringing off the hook, but Hajj Ahmed ignored them all. He just waited for someone else to answer them. Charlie wondered if the place was always so abuzz, or if the elections had turned the place upside down.

"What we could sell in order to bring Muslims into the country was the 'American Dream', meaning we could convince people that America was 'open for business', and that a new generation of Muslim immigrants could uphold their religious beliefs, and make money."

Charlie decided to cut him off. He was afraid this might turn into a lecture. "So, is the recent election a bad thing for Muslims in America?" He was trying to ask a question to tie the knot and link the past to the present.

"It is very much a bad thing. Why? This country, the Unite States of America, has traditionally been a Christian country. It is like building a neighborhood. To build a new neighborhood, you need the goodwill and cooperation of old neighbors. For years, we worked hard to convince our Christian and Jewish brothers and sisters that we can be good neighbors, that we are not here to take over anything, but that we want to work with everyone. We just wanted our Muslim brothers and sisters to have an opportunity of their own to grow in their own communities, just as anyone else was. But now, to answer your question, the recent elections, what happened here and what's happening in other parts of the country, show that the country might actually have a good reason not to believe in our moderation anymore. And I am quite concerned that, if things go on the way they are, I and people like me cannot ask for the goodwill of this country we call 'home' anymore."

"How is that? How exactly are these elections going to lead to a breach of trust between the Muslim community and the rest of America?" Charlie asked.

"Muslim history in this country has gone through two major stages. Up until the September 11 attacks, we were trying to introduce ourselves. Since September 11, we've been trying to prove we are *bona fide* Americans. In the past couple of years, we have come under tremendous pressure from overseas. Certain powers are claiming that the reason the Muslims in America have not grown bigger in their political influence is because they have not become political enough, that they are too comfortable pursuing the American life, the dream of a good, materialistic life. They want to teach different things in our schools, to get involved more in politics, to have a say on a national level."

"And what's wrong with that, with getting more involved on the national level, in becoming more involved in politics?" asked Charlie.

"On the surface of it, nothing. But the kinds of things they want us to get involved in will put us on a confrontation course at a national level. It is like the old saying, 'prove your brotherhood, and then ask for inheritance'. All we've been trying to do so far is prove our brotherhood, but we are not quite there yet. We still have an image problem, and pushing us to be more confrontational on a national level – especially if the agenda is set overseas – will really hurt us and our reputation inside the country."

"And is this happening or starting to happen in North Dakota?"

"It is happening in North Dakota, because we are considered a middle-of-nowhere place. If they chose a place like this, kicked out the moderate Muslims – people like me – and replaced us with people who believe in confrontational Islam, it would get no national coverage, but it gives them a regional foothold to start with. That's why they brought in non-Americans from Saudi Arabia and other Muslim countries, paid their tickets, are giving them salaries, and telling them to live here and run the association. All they need is a dozen people committed to their cause."

Before leaving Bismarck, Charlie tried to locate some of the new members who had crashed the association vote not long ago. He was surprised to find out that he could not locate a single one. He even went through the association records, where they had to fill out their addresses. They all had the same Bismarck PO Box number. It was too much of a coincidence. He used an old friend in the city to find out who owned the box or where the mail was being delivered to. It turned out that it belonged to a farm about forty miles outside the city. He jumped into his car and drove there, only to find the place empty. There were no neighbours to talk to, either, and he decided to look for evidence elsewhere.

He then went to Texas, but, this time, decided he

would meet with people around the story, instead of just meeting with the top managers of the Lahoud company, who had become the target of the unending Saudi cash. Talking with Texas businessmen and women, as well as with members of the state chamber of commerce, Charlie found that there was a long history in the acquisition and merger story. Chamber of Commerce sources, backed up by documents Charlie found in the court system, showed that the company had successfully fought off several law suits against it in the past decade. The suits were, more or less, all about the same thing. The company was accused of denying subcontract business to a handful of companies, which were all owned by people whose names appeared to Charlie as being from the Middle East. In a couple of cases, some of the companies had repeatedly been denied access to the multi-million dollar state contracts. The would-be subcontractors had even presented their skill sets to the court. Looking at the documents, even Charlie, with no expertise in the business, could tell that the plaintiffs had a case. Reading deeper into some of the court documents, Charlie found something he thought was odd. One of the plaintiffs had said, during a court session a while back, that "owners and managers of Lahoud Contractors, LLC, routinely discriminate against other companies on ideological grounds". Charlie found the phrase odd, and looked all over the rest of the documents for something that would explain it. There was nothing. He looked at the transcript of that particular court hearing to see if the judge or the lawyers representing Lahoud had asked a follow-up question that might shed light. No one had. His break came when he ran the name of the person who had made the claim, Abdullah Al Omari, in LexisNexis, a large national database search engine. Abdullah Al Omari and his family were better known for their publishing industry and

235

political activities than they were for construction or contracting business. The Omari family had a book publishing company in Florida. To its name were publishing and distribution of millions of Holy Korans in the United States, but the company also had an exclusive contract with the Saudi ministry of education in Riyadh to print textbooks for Saudi-funded schools in the United States. Those schools in American had become ever more controversial in the past couple of decades. When they had started way back when, they were seen as legitimately filling a vacuum. There were tens of thousands of Muslim kids in America, and their parents did not want their kids to go through the normal American academic system. Some objected to the secular nature of the studies in American schools. American textbooks spoke of evolution. Muslims believed in creation. American schools were generally co-ed. Devout Muslims wanted their kids in a segregated school. Mixed company, especially after the age of puberty, could mess with children's minds, they claimed. The students would concentrate on each other, might be tempted to date, hold hands, kiss, and so on. Those were *haram*, forbidden, in Islam. Finally, some parents had only come to America for a few years, and had every intention of returning home after a while. If they kept their kids in Islamic schools, they could easily slide back into their country's school system and not have to worry about missing a grade or having to re-learning subjects. However, over the years, Islamic schools had adopted a different tone, a tone approved and financed by Riyadh. The new-sanctioned books spoke about Jews as pigs, spoke of non-Muslims as *infidels*, made no reference to the existence of Israel, and taught children that it was okay to burn American and Israeli flags and to 'disfigure the face of women who did not adhere to principles of modesty'. The more information had become public about

236

the content of these textbooks, the more average Americans had wondered about what good these schools were doing, and why the government allowed them to continue to operate. Of course, from the public relations point of view and what Hajj Ahmed was talking about in terms of 'making peace' between the Muslim community and the rest of America, these schools added little – if any –value.

Perhaps to make things worse, Abdullah Al Omari was also Mohammed Abdul Wahab's brother-in-law, the new director of the Islamic Center in Washington. The centre was quite an icon in the nation's capital, and had a story of its own. According to the center's own website, the idea for building the compound came in 1944, and it did not have anything to do with the Saudi Arabia, which is traditionally known as the leader of the Muslim world, thanks to its hosting of Mecca and Medina. The idea of building the center came from the Egyptian ambassador at the time.

Some Arab ambassadors to Washington, and members of the Muslim community then formed the Washington Mosque Foundation, and raised enough money to buy the land on Massachusetts Avenue, where the Islamic centre is currently located. According to the center's website, 'Professor Mario Rossi, a noted Italian architect who built several mosques in Egypt, designed the building. Egypt donated a magnificent bronze chandelier, and sent the specialists who wrote the Koranic verses adorning the mosque's walls and ceiling. The tiles came from Turkey, along with the experts to install them. The Persian rugs came from Iran, which are still in the center's mosque. Finally, with its completion, the Islamic Center's dedication ceremony took place on June 28, 1957. Former United States President, Dwight D. Eisenhower, spoke for the American representatives. In his address, he praised the

237

Islamic world's "traditions of learning and rich culture," which have "for centuries, contributed to the building of civilization."

He affirmed America's founding principle of religious freedom, and stated, "America will fight with her whole strength for your right to have here your own church and worship according to your own conscience. This concept is, indeed, a part of America, and without that concept, we would be something other than what we are." Eisenhower concluded, "As I stand beneath these graceful arches, surrounded on every side by friends from far and near, I am convinced that our common goals are both right and promising. Faithful to the demands of justice and of brotherhood, each working according to the lights of his own conscience, our world must advance along the paths of peace."

However, the center's history had not always been calm or peaceful, whether in terms of its clientele or the powers that controlled it. The center was actually registered as a non-profit corporation with a board of directors that included all Arab ambassadors to Washington, although the Saudis paid most of the bills and, thus, the center's director was always 'nominated' by Riyadh. The Middle East's thorny politics soon followed the center to Washington, and the Iranians and the Saudis started competing for power on the pavements of Mass Avenue in front of the center. After the Shah was overthrown, Iran unleashed its 'supporters' – many of whom were paid agents, to try to take over the mosque, by force, if necessary.

The Saudis beefed up their security inside the four walls of the mosque, and hired their own agents to infiltrate the Iranian agents outside, and the Saudis had a weapon the Iranians did not: Washington metropolitan police. With a wink and a nod from the federal government, the Saudis sought help from Washington police to round up and jail the Iranian demonstrators outside the mosque. After a while, the Iranians realized they were no match for the inside powers of Saudi Arabia in the corridors of Washington, and gave up their quest.

For some years, that had been pleasing enough to the rulers of Riyadh, but then came the new Saudi policy of trying to influence Washington, to warn it against what Arabs said Iran was doing to them in the region. It seemed the Saudis woke up one day and said to themselves, *'Oh, wow, we also have this beautiful, convenient tool in the heart of Washington called the Islamic Center, and how little we are using it'.*

CHAPTER 31

HAVING gone to places like North Dakota and Texas, Charlie felt he was onto something, but he needed the 'big picture', and decided a colleague at the CIA could put the dots together and paint the picture. He decided to call James, one of the first people Charlie had taken a liking to when he had joined the agency. He could never quite figure out what he liked about James. On the surface at least, they had little in common. James was close to seventy; Charlie was much younger. Charlie was happily married to Sarah; James had gone through a succession of bad marriages. Charlie was fit, and exercised regularly; James was quite overweight, and probably had not been to a gym in a couple of decades – if ever. Charlie was a democrat; James was as red as a republican could get. The more Charlie had thought about it, the more he had realized that there was one, and only one, reason why he liked the old man: they were both very outspoken and independent minded.

Neither one cared for the bureaucracy, and they did not like how the American intelligence community was performing badly, and how the political system was failing the country. They felt frustrated that America was bragging about being 'great', but was not acting 'great'. They wanted to get the job done, and get it done right. So, when Charlie called James from California to say he was coming to the Washington area, James was only too happy to take time out for a lunch in the city. There was another thing they had in common: they both hated the agency's cafeteria, and hated even more talking about private matters in it. So they dined at a Lebanese restaurant around Dupont Circle in Washington.

"I've been hearing stuff about Saudis that is kind of strange, to say the least."

"Go on," James said in a quiet, hushed voice, while continuing to stir his hot chicken soup with a spoon. He did not even lift his face to look at Charlie.

"On one hand, we have this issue in Cyprus," he said, without explaining the whole matter with Hassan. He had filed everything he knew in his memos, and, as a senior member of the Middle East/North Africa desk, he was sure James was in the know. "Now I hear about things Saudis are doing *inside* the country."

"Like what?" asked James.

He knew the answer to that, too, but needed to establish what and how much Charlie knew before tipping his hand.

"Like opening *Islamic* schools. Like trying to replace management of small companies and organizations here and there. Like bringing people from Riyadh, and putting them in management positions, instead of hiring from the Muslim communities in the States, and like taking control of the Islamic Center."

By now, James had stopped stirring his soup, and was staring directly into Charlie's eyes.

"Is this something you are picking up in the region?" he asked.

"Actually, no. I am hearing it from *my wife!*"

James knew who Sarah was, and knew about her

241

family background.

"Hmm, for someone who does not have security clearance, she knows more than she should," said James, with a touch of sarcasm in his voice. "Maybe she should work for us. Maybe the White House would listen to her."

"So, is it true? What are they doing?"

"When the Saudis recruited Hassan, he was just part of a multi-pronged operation. They hired Hassan because, initially, they wanted to compete with Israel. They wanted to know what we know, the way Israel knows what we know. That way, the Saudis could use their diplomatic channels to counter whatever policies we wanted to adopt, before we actually adopted them or, at least, argue against them with the same facts and figures we had used to reach our decisions. But somewhere along the line, the game changed. Remember the explosions and assassinations in the Middle East you wrote about? Well, the Saudis had the same intelligence we had, that it was the Iranians who were behind it. The countries that were targeted were a stone's throw from Saudi Arabia. They were very worried that they might be the target, too, so they launched a series of quiet initiatives to warn the White House. Ambassador Sultan personally spoke to the president several times, but the president and his administration had other agendas, and the Saudis felt rejected."

"But Saudi Arabia is supposed to be our ally. Why would the White House not listen to threats against them, coming from an adversary like Iran? It sounds like something the White House would *want* to jump on," Charlie said.

"Because the argument never rose to that level. This never became Saudi Arabia versus Iran. It became a victim of a big, bad screw up of the gigantic bureaucracy of the United States of America."

242

There was a blank look on Charlie's face. He was not getting it.

"When the ambassador brought his case to the White House, no one on our side had *proof* of what he was saying. We all had the same gut feeling that the Iranians were up to a discreet and quiet regime-change game in the region, but we could not prove it. It was one thing to say some of the suspects in each incident had ties to Iran. It was a totally differently thing to say there was a master plan in Tehran for this. What the Saudis wanted was for us to take major action against Iran. We couldn't do that, because all we had was circumstantial evidence. Years ago, a president invaded a country based on flimsy evidence, and the nation learnt its lesson. We couldn't do it again. When the Saudis saw they couldn't get what they want by influencing our foreign policy, they turned their focus to our *internal* policy. If they couldn't directly get the administration to change course, perhaps they could do it *indirectly*.

"From time immemorial, every American administration has had to face the music of public opinion. If the Saudis could convince the American *people* that *their* survival – the survival of America's *best* Arab friend – was threatened by Iran, the American people could force the White House's hands. They could shape a new foreign policy course. Remember, gone are the days that white Christians ruled this country. Today, the single largest ethnic and religious minority in this country are the Arabs and the Muslims. If you can find a way to mobilize these people against a single issue, you can bring about policy changes like never before. Look at the way they mobilized their forces in the Bosnia war. For the longest time, they could not get the White House to move, although everyone could see on TV that Bosnian Muslims were being

243

butchered right and left.

"So what did they do? They adopted a two-part policy. On one hand, they helped, *directly and indirectly,* the Bosnians to receive the arms they needed to defend themselves. The Saudis even made a deal with the devil – Iran – so Tehran could send arms to Bosnia, and the Saudis paid for it by giving the cash to the Bosnians. On the other hand, they organized a massive public relations campaign inside America, showing the massacres being committed in Bosnia. They helped major networks get visas and go safely shoot pictures of what was going on. Then they encouraged their friends on Capitol Hill to hold hearings. In the hearings, there were gruesome pictures of death and destruction. They hired some top-notch PR companies to launch campaigns in key states and cities. By the time they were done, it was the American *people* pushing the White House to take action and save Saudi Arabia's fellow Muslim brothers. It was pretty slick. It was nicely executed, and it worked!"

"So, bring about a foreign policy engineered-coup inside the United States?"

"Call it what you want. End justifies means. This is politics."

"Is this just your theory, or is this the agency's opinion?"

"Let's call it the educated guess of a lot of people inside the agency, including the director's!"

"Okay, okay, if the director thinks that way, why can he not bring a case to the president?"

"Well, a lot of things have changed in this country in the past fifty or so years, but turf battle is still the name of the game. On an issue like this, you have at least four major departments involved: the CIA, State Department, NSC, and FBI," he replied, referring to the Federal Bureau of

244

Investigation and the National Security Council by their abbreviations. "Each of those still has its interests. Yes, the director has expressed concerns about the Saudis. And he did it in private. But, in the corridors of power, there is little privacy.

"The FBI heard of it, and interpreted it as the CIA trying to interfere in the FBI's work. After all, despite September 11, the CIA and FBI still have pretty clear-cut mandates. The FBI does not engage in foreign espionage, and the CIA does not get involved in operations inside the country –Homeland Security or no Homeland Security! They can *share* information, but *sharing* does not necessarily mean *accepting*. And then, of course, you have the State Department and its intelligence bureau. Often, they are the most neutral of all, but, in a case like this, their hands are tied."

"And the NSA? Can it not provide any proof?"

"The NSA was the wild card of all. The biggest machinery in the world for conducting electronic eavesdropping, its long hands can reach anywhere in the world, but its powers in the United States are limited by law. Knowing all that, the Saudis have been very careful not to talk about their grand plan on the phone or write emails. Much of the planning and discussions have taken place in person in areas they are fairly sure the NSA would not tap."

Sarah was right. It was not for nothing that his uncle was now coming to the States once every couple of months. He needed to oversee things in person, not ask about them by phone or through videoconferencing, or the Internet from Saudi Arabia. Meeting with the privates in his army in Louisiana was safer than conference calling with his top Generals from Riyadh.

There was still one thing that was bothering Charlie

about the whole Saudi business. If the Saudis wanted to discreetly increase their visibility inside the United States and push America to adopt a certain foreign policy course, then why allow radical groups to dominate its presence in America? The people who were running the Islamic Center, or those who had contracts to publish and distribute offensive textbooks in schools, were anything but 'moderate' Muslims. They were radicals. How would it help the Muslim world's image by letting these people loose on American soil? The answer was: it didn't. The answer also was that rulers in Riyadh had little control over the issue.

"When the Saudi kingdom was formed, there was no such a thing as 'moderate' wings and 'radical' wings of the society," said James. "They were all one, and, by today's standards, they could all be branded as 'hard line' or 'radical'. Those groups and branches have always been an inseparable part of the Saudi society. To this day, the real powers behind the rulers in the country are the old-fashioned, very conservative, older generation, all-male groups. They are the ones driving the power. All the things we hear about this ruler or that ruler trying to bring about change, they are real minority. Why do you think the pace of change in that country has been so slow? Because the minority, which is trying to engineer the change, is really powerless. It is the same thing when it comes to how the Saudis operate here. When there is time to appoint a director for the Islamic Center or give a contract to publish hundreds of thousands of books, those conservative forces sneak their heads out and exert their power. It is not just our country that has multiple interest groups!"

"But then why not pull the plug when you know the policy isn't working, when you know whatever you wanted to do has gone awry?"

"Well, again, there are people in Riyadh pushing for the policies to go ahead. Just because the ruler and his foreign minister might think the policy has been hijacked from the within, it does not mean they actually have the power to stop it! Second, Arabs in general, and Saudis in particular, are a proud bunch. Part of it is that they are the guardians of Islam's holy shrines, and part of it is that the country sits on a quarter of the world's known gas and oil reserves. Between the moral God and the material God, they are a pretty confident – bordering on arrogant – bunch. Somewhere in the back of their heads, the Saudi leadership still believed that, if they really wanted to get something done, they would get it done.

"So, yes, they realised that there were a whole lot of Saudi 'initiatives' in the States that were controlled by the radicals, but they were in denial. They just did not take action. And, of course, they were playing politics with it themselves. They figured they could always go the White House and, in effect, say, 'yes, we know there are a bunch of radical Saudis running around in your country. You can either try running around and finding them – which you won't – or you can pay us the political price we want, and we'd just deliver them to you'. Everyone needs everyone. Everyone is trying to call everyone's bluff."

Charlie's head was kind of spinning. He cared about his country, a country that had gone through so much. The idea simply baffled him that another country was running a network that was, in effect, to the detriment of his country, that senior officials in the country knew about it, or, at least, could have easily found out about it, but did next to nothing to stop it. The idea that the very essence of a democratic political process that was supposed to help Americans be safe in their country had led to an ally running secret networks inside the United States seemed

247

incredibly wrong to him. He decided he would have to do something, go on some kind of a campaign, blow the whistle somehow and take the message to the highest officials.

To whom? He did not know. Do what? He was not sure. He was just a little spy, appreciated and celebrated by a tiny few who knew him. Officially, he did not even exist. He was nobody. He did not exist in CIA staff directory. He did not exist on the agency payroll, and he certainly had not done any serious journalism lately, so had not been able to maintain his network. As he was thinking about this, it dawned on him: he truly was no one, and had no leverage with anyone. *But surely that did not matter,* he told himself. He was a *reporter*. That was all the license he needed to do anything he wanted in this world. That's how all his life had been. That was the only motto he had followed ever since he had known himself. *I am a reporter; therefore, I have the right to pursue anything, ask anything of anyone, or tell anything to anyone.* He decided he needed to think about it more, and come up with a plan, but, either way, he had decided he needed to do something. It just was not his nature to *know* about something really bad, and *not* do something about it.

CHAPTER 32

AT Langley, agency bosses finally had pored over the report Charlie had filed based on his report from Baghdad, and decided he should follow the trail and go to Cairo.

Cairo was a quintessential Arab city. It was so different from places like Beirut or Dubai. Dubai was new and shiny, but small. Cairo was big, polluted, dusty and vast. Beirut was critically divided along diametrically opposite political lines. Cairo was just one big mass of people. Dubai was built by foreigners, Asians and Western. Half of Lebanese identified more with Paris than they did with their own capital. The millions and millions of people who lived in Cairo had next to no affinity for any other capital, in the Arab world or the West. Part of it was that most people in Egypt were poor, and had become poorer over the past decades. However, even the rich ones – and there were more than a handful of super-rich ones in the country – pretty much had their loyalty to their own country. They went on vacation to Europe and the States, and maybe kept their money in foreign banks, but their first love was their own country.

Cairo had changed a lot over the past couple of decades. Whereas it was once limited to three of four known neighborhoods, the city had now ballooned right and left. The population had exploded. Old, traditional buildings were torn down, and one could now see high-rises and skyscrapers on every corner, but real estate was probably one of the few industries that had developed in the country. Egypt used to rely on agriculture and cotton production for most of its exports, but the government used to heavily subsidize the agricultural industry. It could afford to. Every year, the government received billions upon billions of dollars in economic handouts from Washington, a price for former President Anwar Sadat's initiative to travel to Jerusalem and make peace with Israel.

Over the years, the politics of the region had changed, and Egypt no longer wielded the same clout that it used to. Slowly, but surely, Washington had cut its economic aid to Cairo, and the government suffered badly. It could not come up with a substitute source of revenue. Farmers were traditionally poor, and did not hold any political power in the corridors of Cairo. There was no one to champion their cause. With every passing day, more farmers had decided to quit farming. Cotton growers faced the same subsidy cut, but they also suffered from decreasing worldwide prices. Much as they tried to keep up their ancestral profession, one by one, they had to quit cotton farming.

The signs of economic downturn were apparent the second Charlie walked out of the airport. In traditional Middle Eastern fashion, Cairo airport always had a few unsanctioned drivers offering their private taxi services. No sooner had a passenger picked up his or her bags than the person would receive offers from private individuals, even before organized taxi services had a chance to pick the passenger. That was still the practice, but Charlie noticed there were now far more private drivers inside the airport hall. He was literally swamped by offers.

He also noticed that the prices had fallen substantially. He was surprised that five years after his last trip to Cairo, he was now being asked to pay more than a third less than he had paid before. Charlie decided to play it safe. He brushed off the many clearly poor and visibly eager men who were trying to push him toward their private cars and, instead, took one of the official cabs.

His destination was a hotel he always liked in the bourgeois neighborhood of Zamalek. At some point in his life, Charlie had lived in Zamalek. He knew the neighborhood well. Zamalek was an island in the middle the gigantic Cairo. Being surrounded by water very much added to the neighborhood's aura. If you lived in one of the buildings along the Nile River in Zamalek, and had a good view and balcony to the water, you were a sure bet to become a major Cairo socialite. Charlie asked the driver to take him to the Marriott Hotel, one of the historic buildings in Cairo. Its value was that it had once been one of the palaces of Egypt's former King Farouk. Rumour had it that Farouk used the palace to house one of his many mistresses. Others said the king had built the palace just for the inauguration of the Suez Canal.

Although the current-day Marriott included several building complexes, the original building only had one wing. It had then, as it did now, two storeys. The ground floor was divided into several large halls and reception rooms. The upper floor included some rooms, the business center, a café, and a few other function rooms. The buildings surrounded a large swimming pool connected to a gym, not far away from the tennis courts. Charlie had called one of the former king's sons – albeit one of the illegitimate ones – to say he was coming.

Farouk Jr. had been banned from returning to the country until a few years ago. He had just sat in his Geneva

251

apartment, leading the life of a celebrity in exile. However, Farouk Jr. had never really liked Geneva, and always yearned to return to Cairo. One of the first places he had visited when he was allowed back in Cairo was Marriott. He had found the general manager, introduced himself, and told him about his memories of it. Over time, Marriott had become his home away from home. He would go to the hotel almost every day, sit on the outside veranda, order a coffee, sometimes with the hotel manager, and reminisce. So, when Charlie decided to come to Cairo, he called Farouk Jr. and asked if he could help with getting him reservation for a nice hotel room.

By the time Charlie arrived at the Marriott, it was almost sundown. The sun looked a bit pale, probably because of all the dust in the air. He checked into his room, took a cold shower, and opened a beer from the mini-bar. As he sat on the chair next to the bed and stared at the television set, he thought of his first task. He had a number – the mobile number of the person he had seen when he was meeting his arms dealer friend in Baghdad – and he needed to find out more about it.

He could make a cold call, introduce himself, get an appointment, and find out more about the person during the course of the interview, but that was risky. Maybe the person was going to be unreceptive. Maybe he was too clever to fall for the trap. Maybe he would not agree to the interview to begin with. Maybe he would agree to meet, but Charlie could not get everything he needed, and the person would not agree to a follow-up meeting. It was too sensitive a topic to be left to chance. Charlie decided to call upon an old friend, seek his help on the number, and also get a crash course into Egypt's current state of affairs, but the friend he was seeking help from was not Egyptian. He was a former American ambassador who had served in Cairo

252

many years and, after his retirement, had decided to top his State Department pension by becoming a 'resident political advisor' to the Egyptian presidency.

Erik was an all-American boy, Ivy League, Yale, Princeton, Navy Seal, and then State Department. He often joked that he had too much brain to stay in the military, and too little bureaucratic skills to qualify as a diplomat. He was probably right in both. He had trained in the military with the best of the best. It was not just any Joe who could cut it as a Seal, but he had. He had been involved in some daring operations that remained secret up to this day. Every now and then, he would talk about the gist of them, just the outlines, without the specifics. No dates, no names of places or comrades in arms.

By the time he was thirty, he had decided that he was getting too old for Operations. He could have gone into business and made lots of money, but he did not. Not that he did not care about making money, but he did not think it was that important in that juncture in his life. So he joined the Foreign Service, and moved up the ranks until he became the ambassador. He had served in Cairo as a junior political officer years earlier and, when he approached retirement, he asked the department if he could choose Cairo as his last post. He had just served a three-year term as ambassador to Bulgaria, and the department did not mind him moving to another region. The State Department did not mind people moving around the globe; it just did not like people staying in one region all the time. It was part of the strategy to make sure US diplomats were well-rounded employees, familiar with as much of the globe as possible.

As his good luck had it, the Egyptian presidency was also going through reforms. The Egyptians had one of the best Foreign Service machineries in the Arab world. They had recruited younger and more educated male and female diplomats in the past decade or so, and had pretty much moved on with the world and modernized with times, but the presidential machinery was still old and clunky, perhaps in line with the occupant of the place. That had cost them recently.

There had been a number of international incidents in the past couple of years, in which the presidency had not reacted fast enough, not reacted at all, or, if they had reacted, their public relations office had not conveyed the message fast and loud enough. They had finally realized it. They knew they needed advice, but they did not know who to go to. Towards the last months of Erik's tenure in Egypt, some friends had approached him discreetly on behalf of the presidency, to see if he might be interested in working with the government as a political-public affairs consultant after his term was over.

It was a sensitive issue, making overtures to a working ambassador. There were a whole lot of ethical and conflict of interest issues involved, definitely for the US government, if not the Egyptians. Erik decided not to give an answer, one way or the other. His only response was that he would be happy to think about – and talk about – it once he was officially out of the government. Of course, he had made up his mind almost as soon as the issue had been raised. Not only could he cash in his government retirement pension, but he could also rake in massive sums being a consultant to the presidency in Cairo. He would still be under confidentiality agreement on some issues, and it could have affected his Top Secret security clearance, but Washington decided to turn a blind eye this time.

Egypt was an ally, and having a former ambassador on the inside might actually help, rather than hurt. Plus, they knew Erik well, and were confident that he would not jeopardise any US national security issues. So, after Erik's retirement, he and his wife went to the States, went through the retirement process, he officially resigned from the State Department, filled in the forms to receive his pension, checked up on the kids and grandchildren, met with their old-time house renters, and then bought a business class airline ticket – courtesy of the palace – and moved with his wife into their nice large villa in the posh suburb of Maadi.

The two-storey villa, with four bedrooms, a common area upstairs, and a large living room, dining room and kitchen downstairs, had its own swimming pool in the garden area, and the government had provided a BMW-700 series with a driver and two armed security men at the gate outside the house. All the trappings of money and luxury befitting a former US ambassador and an advisor to the republic's president.

Charles and Erik decided to meet at the same place they had first met decades earlier: on the Marriott's tennis court. Charles had been playing tennis with a friend from the US embassy, and Erik, then a political officer, was playing with his brother-in-law while his wife and kids were walking around the courtyard and, otherwise, enjoying the day and the hotel amenities. After the game, Charles' embassy friend had introduced Charlie to Erik. The two stayed in touch, and nurtured a friendship that had lasted until that day again in Cairo.

They played a couple of games of tennis first. As usual, the air in Cairo was polluted, but, fortunately, the temperature was not very high that day, and it was a bit overcast. It all made it a bit more pleasant to play. They walked over to the pool area afterward, and had a cold lemonade. Charlie told Erik what he knew in terms of Iranian arms shipments going through Iraq, his meeting with the arms dealer, and the Egyptian area code number.

"I guess what I am confused by is why the Iranians

would be involved in shipping arms to Egypt, and who their intermediary is," Charlie said.

"Well, finding out to whom the number belongs is easy. But, in terms of why the Iranians would be shipping arms to here, we have known about some of it, but there certainly can be more that we don't know about. Or it just might be that there are certain quarters in the Egyptian government, like the *Mukhaberat* -- the intelligence service-- that know something, but they have not told me. As far as I know, there are some shipments smuggled into Egypt through the Sudan. Of course, the Iranians have close ties with some leading factions there, and it is easy for them to even airlift guns straight to the Khartoum airport in the capital. From there, they just use the vast border with Egypt, and then local smugglers take it for the Palestinians in Gaza."

"If it is all meant for the Palestinians, why not just send it through Lebanon? It is closer, and probably even safer and easier."

"It would be safer and easier, and they probably are doing that, but maybe the Iranians want to diversify or use multiple channels. We also know that the Lebanese government is not too happy about it, and wants to minimize those shipments from Lebanon. They are getting a lot of heat about it from Washington, and Tehran's Shiite allies in Lebanon don't want to appear reckless, so they are trying to cool it themselves."

Erik took the phone number Charlie had, and promised to get back to him the next day. When he called back, Erik's news was something Charlie could not have expected.

"So, have you seen our royal friend since you've been back?" Erik asked, referring to Farouk Jr.

"As a matter of fact, I am having dinner with him

256

tonight. You are welcome to join us. I am sure he would not mind."

"Oh, he probably would, given what I am about to tell you!"

"What's that?"

"The number you gave me belongs to him."

"That's impossible! What makes you say that?"

"Well, first, we ran the phone number through the system. It is registered under his name. Second, the Egyptian intelligence service has tape recorded some of Farouk's conversations with your Iraqi businessman friend, Ibrahim. He might be a royalty, but he is certainly not cautious when it comes to talking on the phone."

That much was true. Farouk was always a loud mouth, happy to brag about his royal blood and how his father owned the country. He had little appreciation for, or understanding of, how easy it was to pick up a mobile phone conversation.

"But it makes no sense. Why would Farouk jeopardise his welcome in Egypt after having been banned for so many years? And also, I heard Ibrahim talking in Baghdad to a guy named Akram, not Farouk!"

"I cannot explain that, but if you find the answer, I would be only too eager to hear it."

"Yeah, I am eager to hear it myself. I will catch up with you. Thanks for the tip."

Charlie was puzzled by the information. He knew Farouk well, or, at least, thought he did. In all the years the two had known each other, Farouk had never expressed any interest in politics. All he cared about was that he was allowed to come back to Cairo so he would not have to live in his tiny one-bedroom apartment in Geneva. All he could talk about was how well he could live in Cairo with his money.

"I am a *pasha* again," he used to say, using the Turkish word for someone with social stature.

So, even the thought that Farouk would be involved in any kind of arms dealing involving Iranians and Iraqis was just mind boggling to Charlie. However, he decided it was something he had to confront Farouk with. That night, he walked the couple of blocks between his hotel and Farouk's luxurious apartment. It was a nice breezy night. Cairo was just adorable when the weather was good. He walked four floors up to Farouk's apartment, and rang the bell. A black Sudanese butler, dressed in a tuxedo-style suit, with black pants and white jacket over a white shirt, buttoned up without a tie or bowtie, opened the door.

"*Masa al kheir, afandam.*" Good evening, sir.

"*Masa an-noor.*" Good evening.

"Ostaz Farouk will be in shortly. He is getting dressed," the butler said, using the honorific word *Ostaz*.

Charlie showed himself into the living room, and admired all the antiques, paintings, furniture and rugs Farouk had collected. The last time Charlie has seen the place was when Farouk had just been moving into it. There were workers in every corner, pounding on the walls, tearing down doors, and mounting new cabinets in the kitchen. He certainly could understand why Farouk did not want to go back to Geneva. His whole apartment back there was not half the size of just his living room here.

Farouk showed up a few minutes later, dressed casually but elegantly in blue jeans, a silk shirt and a light, cashmere jacket. The better-dressed butler soon showed up with a tray, carrying two glasses of whiskey and a side plate full of ice cubes. Farouk loved whiskey, as many rich and/or intellectual Arabs do, and he knew Charlie liked it, too, so he had asked the butler to arrange it.

They raised their glasses to each other, and had a

sip. It was hard for Charlie to bring up the topic for which he had come. They had just started enjoying each other's company. He had not seen Farouk in a while, but he also knew that the longer he waited, the harder it would become to slip into the question. The best he could do was, "So, Ibrahim sends greeting to you!"

Of course, Ibrahim in Baghdad had done no such a thing. He had not even mentioned that he knew Farouk, but it was a bluff he felt he had to make.

"Ibrahim?" Farouk was giving the look of a puzzled man, pulling his eyebrows toward his forehead, and appearing pensive.

"Ibrahim Kassdim, the renowned Iraqi businessman you know from Geneva. I was at his place when you called him from your cell phone." Then he said, with a wink, "He told me about the conversation. Heavy duty stuff, Farouk, or, should I say, Mr. Akram?"

Farouk figured out quickly that his cover had been blown. Plus, he knew Charlie well, and knew that Charlie knew him well. He knew Charlie was smart. There was no point trying to deny it. He decided to come clean.

"Actually, I am not Mr. Akram. But, yes, I was involved in arranging the conversation."

"How? And who is Akram?"

"Are you taping?"

"What? No! I am here for dinner. Come on!"

"What are you planning to do with the information, if I tell you anything? After all, you are a journalist."

"Well, just like you said, I am a journalist, so I will publish it. What else?"

"I am willing to help you, but what is it they say in your profession? On deep background."

'Deep background' basically meant Charlie could use the information for his own reporting purposes. He

259

could not quote any of it, even anonymously. He could not mention Farouk in any identifiable way, and he had to get independent confirmation for whatever he was about to hear before he could publish it. That all worked just fine for Charlie. He could just claim he did not get it confirmed, so he did not have to print any of it, but just report everything back to Langley. He agreed to the condition.

"Akram is Akram Sharafeddin. He is one of the older members of *Ikhwan al Muslemin*," the Muslim Brotherhood.

"So you pretended to be him when talking to Ibrahim?"

"No, no, no! I know both Ibrahim and Akram, and I put them in touch with each other. Akram was using my phone the day he talked to Ibrahim."

"But what did Akram want from Ibrahim?"

"Here is the whole story. About six months ago, I was in Geneva to take care of some stuff. There, I met an Iranian businessman who was introduced to me by an old friend. The Iranian gentleman said he deals in general import-export stuff, and has very close government connections. I told him I was basically living in Egypt these days, and we exchanged numbers. About a month later, I got a call from him saying he was in Cairo, and asking if we could meet. So we did. Over lunch, he said he had some sources in Iran who were trying to locate a guy named Akram Sharafeddin. Did I know him, he asked. I said I did, and he asked if I could make an introduction so he could personally pass on a message he had. I said, well, tell me the message and who it is from, and I will deliver it for you. He said thanks, but no. The message was sensitive, and from an important person in the Iranian ministry of intelligence, and he was told to deliver the message personally. So I invited Akram over one day."

Charlie cut him off. "But who is Akram Sharafeddin, other than from the Brotherhood?"

"Akram is what you Americans would call a 'radical Muslim,'" he said with a chuckle. "He is one of the old hands in the Brotherhood, one of the original members. He spent a number of years in jail under Nasser, and then Sadat. He was initially friends with the people who later became Al Qaeda, but split over ideological issues. For years, he had argued that political struggle did not need to become violent. That was until about six months ago. Come to think of it, just shortly before I went to Geneva and met the Iranian guy. At that time, Akram had a serious row with the Brotherhood's leadership. They were ready to reach a serious compromise with the regime, and Akram saw it as a total sell out. He threatened that he would split from the organization and take his followers with him to set up a more militant branch. When the Iranian businessman met with Akram at my place, the message he was bringing was that Tehran was willing to sell him good and cheap arms, if he wanted."

"How would the Iranians know so fast about the split, and why would they be willing to sell Ibrahim arms at a cheap rate? More importantly, what is Akram planning to do with the arms?"

"Akram does not know what he would do with the arms. He is not the militant type anymore. He is angry and frustrated, but he is not the fighter type. The Iranians are selling him under-priced arms, because they want him to arrange the delivery of some of the arms to Port Said."

Port Said was the northernmost city at the tip of the Suez Canal, and close to the Gaza Strip, bordering Israel.

"What type of arms did they want to deliver to Port Said?"

"They would not say. That was part of the deal.

Akram could ask for anything, from AK-47s and grenades to shoulder-held missiles, but the stuff they wanted to deliver would be under seal, and had to be delivered under seal."

"And where would the arms go? Gaza?"

"I don't think so. If the arms were meant for Gaza, they would send it through Lebanon."

"But I hear the Lebanese are trying to crack down on it."

"Maybe, but it is just too laborious and risky to ship it from here."

"So how did Ibrahim come into the picture?"

"Akram said he had to think about the offer. He came back a week later, and said he would be interested in the arms, but wanted a discount. He said the group was never cash-rich anyway, and, lately it had suffered more. Amazingly, the Iranians agreed to that. They must have really been desperate to get the arms to Port Said, for whatever reason. But Akram didn't want to talk directly to the Iranians. He didn't really like or trust them. The Iranian guy left and, a few days later, I got a call from Ibrahim, who offered me a hefty price if I agreed to act as a go between. I agreed."

"What were you supposed to do?"

"Nothing! That was the beauty of it. I was just supposed to facilitate the two sides talking to each other through Ibrahim and me. I just had to let them use my phone, and occasionally host Akram or the Iranian or the two of them at the same time."

"And aren't you worried the Egyptians would find out and kick you out?"

"Oh, dear boy. Oh, dear boy!" Farouk sighed. "Do I look like the type of person who cares about the Iranians or the Brotherhood? My father was a heavy drinker, and a womanizer! Do I look religious or political? No, dear; I cut my own deal with the intelligence services. I told them I would tell them everything if they let me be. Plus, I greased the wheels a bit, if you know what I mean!"

"Un-fucking-believable!" was all Charlie could utter.

Dinner was served, made more digestible with few more rounds of scotch.

CHAPTER 33

BY the time Charlie reached to Nicosia, he had a pretty bad feeling about what the Iranians were doing, but he still had two problems. First, he did not really know what game the Iranian regime was playing. Second, and perhaps because of the first, he did not know how he could convince his bosses of anything. After all, he was not an analyst. He was just an agent, albeit the only agent with access in the region. He needed to discuss things further with his bosses. He tried to do that on the phone, but, typical to a bureaucracy, they told him to put things in writing and send a cable, beginning with a detailed account of what he had found out in Cairo.

He did so. He drafted what he thought was an impartial but still alarming and to-the-point memo. In it, he chronicled the bombings, assassination attempts, attempts to undermine local governments, setting up *de facto* sleeper cells that were responsible for some of the activities, reports he had heard about money laundering through Dubai, plus now the arms smuggling trail stretching from Iran to Iraq to Egypt.

The events of the past couple of years, random and occasional as they might appear, point in the aggregate to policy. There is no doubt whatsoever in my mind that the regime in Iran is up to a widespread, well-coordinated, and well-planned covert operation that, if triggered, could have extremely significant and catastrophic impacts on the region and, perhaps, the world as a whole. Time for action is now. Tomorrow might be too late, he concluded his report.

It probably was not just because of his memo, or just the Saudis bogging the Americans, or maybe even any one particular incident, but the whole 'Iran issue' was finally getting the attention of the White House, which, in turn, instructed the State Department 'to do something'. However, that was a tall order, since no one even knew for a fact what Iran was really trying to do.

In the weeks after Charlie's memo out of Cairo, the US intelligence had picked up on ocean-faring Iranian merchant ships passing through the Suez Canal, noticing that their 'behaviour' was rather suspicious. Usually, there was a fairly long queue at the canal. It was not unusual to take three or four days for ships to cross it. So, when their turn came, they would usually be anxious to move out fast, but, lately, the Iranian ships would actually slow down once they passed the canal and got to the Port Said area, and it always involved anchoring overnight. The Americans did not know the details, but they had kind of put the two and two together and confirmed what Charlie had said in his cable based on talking with the former ambassador and Farouk.

The State Department's intelligence desk and the CIA figured the Iranians were using their good offices with the Sudanese government factions, and sending arms to Khartoum directly by plane. Then they would cross them by land to southern Egypt, where they would be delivered to radical religious groups fighting the government in Cairo. They, in turn, would smuggle some of the arms through their own underground network to Upper Egypt and Port Said. The arms shipments went on for months, and, every now and then, some of those arms would end up on Iranian ships after they passed through the canal. Mostly, the arms went to support other anti-regime movements in various countries around the world.

The Iranians did not want to risk being caught smuggling arms on their ships passing through the Persian Gulf. The US navy had, for decades, established a large presence in those waters, and was monitoring Iranian ships pretty closely. They would often stop Iranian ships and search them. If the Iranians were trying to smuggle arms out of Egypt – to wherever the final destination was – it was probably safer for the ships to cross the Persian Gulf 'clean', enter the Gulf of Oman, pass through the Arabian Sea, go to Gulf of Aden and the Red Sea, and then pick up the arms past the Suez Canal.

However, up to that point, that's all America's collective intelligence knew: a 'clean' Iranian ship escaping the watchful eyes of the US navy, passing through the Persian Gulf, going all the way to the Suez Canal, invariably taking their time overnight around Port Said, and then moving along on the Mediterranean towards – somewhere. The only semi-suspicious thing the Iranians were doing was that all the recent ships – without exception – were carrying small navy super speedboats, in addition to the regular rescue motor boats. It might have all looked sinister, but no smoking gun!

Not long after the US intelligence had established a regular and increased passage of Iranian merchant ships through the Persian Gulf all the way through the Mediterranean Sea, the President of the United States gave a prime time speech on national television, carried by all channels.

"My fellow Americans, one of the main reasons for the establishment and creation of this great nation of ours was the willingness of our forefathers to stand against oppression. Throughout the history of our nation, the noble conviction that we stand against threats to destroy genuine democracy, be that ours or that of our neighbors and allies, has been a pillar in our righteous struggle against evil and undemocratic practices and regimes in the world. In every nation's history, there are times of upheaval, times of uncertainty, and times of determination to face injustice. The United States of America, by the God-given power and responsibility afforded to it, has, and must, shoulder more responsibility than most other countries. We have strategic interests around the world, interests we have safeguarded for decades, allies we have supported for generations.

"One of the areas of strategic interest for us is the Middle East. That turbulent area of the world is, once again, brewing with uncertainly. For some time now, various United States agencies, as well as our allies in the region, have noticed conspicuous movement of Iranian military gunboats and armed merchant tankers in and out of the Suez Canal. We have strong reasons to believe that these naval operations are part of a systemic arms smuggling network. The recipients of these arms are terrorist groups bent on annihilating the State of Israel, our closest ally in the region, and the region's truest, and only, democracy.

"In cooperation with our allies in the region, we have taken steps to neutralize the enemy and defeat its plans. At the same time, we have been working with our allies in the region to take significant and far-reaching diplomatic steps. If the Iranian regime does not wish to face a thunderous international anger and find itself isolated, it must stop its disruptive and harmful activities now.

"The United States is a peaceful nation. We would like to have cordial relations with all countries in the world, but we will not shrink from our international

267

responsibilities, and that includes protecting our allies.

"Thank you for your attention. God bless you, and God bless the United States of America."

The presidential speech was certainly unusual. Usually, in cases like that, a host of measure would be taken before a presidential speech is scheduled. Task forces are set up, various rounds of meetings for 'deputies' and 'principles' are scheduled, draft recommendations are sought, interagency measures go into effect, international emissaries are sent to deliver 'tough messages', United Nation resolutions are passed, and then – finally – the President of the United States would give a prime time speech to say, 'do this, or else'. The 'else' is usually not elaborated on, but everyone knows that means 'or we will attack you'. This time around, Washington had decided to do it backwards.

For its part, the State Department was putting pressure on the countries in the Middle East to clamp down on Iranian activities and movements. Do anything, they were asked. Close their bank accounts, kick out their diplomats, impose heavy duties on their exports, don't give them entry visas. Anything, absolutely anything. However, it was not easy for those countries to take such unilateral and arbitrary measures. *Show us some proof of what you are saying, and we will help,* leaders in the region shot back, but Washington could not do that. Despite what the president had said, the United States did not really have any proof that the Iranians were running guns for anti-Israeli forces. In fact, Israel had confidentially told Washington that it had no evidence of Iranian guns entering its territory through the waters. The allies knew Washington was acting on a hunch, and they were not willing to be an accomplice.

Meanwhile, the mood in the United States was
268

changing, too. The president's speech was, obviously, on the front page of all major newspapers in the country. The networks, radio, and television stations had broadcast the speech live, and the airwaves were filled, in the next twenty-four hours, with commentary and analysis. Media in the States are creatures of habit, but they also have a life and logic of their own. Sometimes, stories snowball and stay on headlines for days and weeks, and sometimes they just die in no time. The story of threats to the State of Israel had always been big items in American media, but they had also always died down after a few days.

Partly because they had come up so often in the past eighty or so years, everyone was convinced that just ringing the alarm bells would make the threats disappear. It was also partly because the American media, or America, for that matter, was so far removed from the actual scene – Israel – that there was little the media could do in practical terms, other than just talk about it, and, of course, part of it had to do with how much the pro-Israeli lobby and Israel's staunch allies in the country chose to push the story. The more seriously Israel took the story, the more seriously it would push its allies to raise 'public awareness'.

This time, the story stuck for weeks, even though there was no Israeli push for it. It helped that it had been a really slow news season. There was hardly any domestic or foreign policy issue that the press could run with. No sex scandals. No corruption stories. No stock market crash. No natural disasters. It had all been pretty lame, and the press needed to harp on something. Forget about 'shaping public opinion', 'agenda setting', and all those theoretical ideas about the role and responsibilities of the press. The news vacuum was seriously cutting into the networks' and papers' advertising revenue, because there was no 'juicy' story that whipped up programming.

There was not necessarily much of a link between how long television networks ran with a story and how newspapers treated the subject. Usually, it was the networks that gave major coverage to a story, and national newspapers followed up. In this case, it was the reverse, and it had started with the nation's capital. The *Washington Journal* had picked up on an AP story a few weeks earlier about the new leader of the Islamic Center in Washington, telling women they should cover themselves, and insisting male employees should grow beard. The story questioned how the center was being run, why Arab ambassadors to Washington, who comprised the center's board of directors, had acquiesced to such radical demands, and what role Saudi Arabia played in the selection of the new director.

The *New York Herald*, a local but respected paper in New York City, ran an exposé of the city's biggest mosque. The mosque was not just a New York City attraction. People from all over the East Coast and New England area went there. It had gone through massive management changes in the past few months, and the article spoke about how the new management had quietly 'purged' the old staff, and brought in its new loyal friends to work at the mosque. The story went on to enumerate how the management changes were actually affecting the type of clientele that the mosque was attracting. To illustrate its point, the paper ran two full-length, back-to-back middle pages that showed the types of people who had been going in and out of the mosque a year ago, and the type of people frequenting it now.

The picture of a year ago showed clean-cut men, some wearing suits and ties. There were even women with long, uncovered hair, dressed modestly in long skirts. The pictures on the next page had no women in them whatsoever, and the men looked distinctly different. Suits

270

were substituted with religious robes, Afghani and Pakistani *shelwar kemiz,* and Gulf style *dishdashas.* Trimmed haircuts were replaced with long, unkempt hair, and shaven faces were substituted with months' and years' worth of beard. In case the contradiction was not blatantly clear to everyone, the two-page bold and large headline read: "Moderation versus Radicalism". News agencies started running updates for stories they had previously printed out of places like Bismarck and El Paso.

At that point, television networks jumped in. Camera crews were sent in all over the country, wherever the networks thought they could find an angle: Washington, New York, Los Angeles, Detroit, Atlanta, and on and on and on. Plus, of course, you could not have one network jumping on a story without the rest joining the bandwagon. The theme of the stories, whether in the papers or in the networks, was the same. Within just a couple of days after the president's speech, the tone of the 'threat' had changed, but it was not clear how or where along the process that had happened. When the president spoke, it was about Iran threatening Israel. Nowadays, newspaper headlines spoke of 'Muslim Invasion,' 'Islamic Terrorism', or 'Destructive Sleeper Cells'.

Somehow, the whole Iran angle was lost; the message had become more generalized, and more dangerous, but the media stories were not just media stories anymore. They were beginning to have impact. American people were beginning to react to the stories. People were watching out for their neighbors. If they saw a 'Muslim-looking' neighbor, they panicked. If a woman covered her hair, they made assumptions. If Muslims in a community asked that a mosque be built, they assumed they were going to use it to recruit new members and radicalize the society, or worse, plan some kind of terrorist attack.

Tension was building across the nation wherever there was a concentration of Muslims and Arabs. They, too, felt the pressure. They, too, became tense. If the media had intended to gear up the nation to face a threat faced by an ally thousands of miles away, they had, in turn, created an atmosphere of tension and uncertainty inside the country.

It was only weeks before the trigger was pulled. The press started reporting small and not-so-small clashes between the Muslims and the rest of the population. The dividing line was now 'us' versus 'them'. The fact that many Muslims were also Americans – even born in America – had taken a back seat to reality. No one quite knew how the clashes and skirmishes had started, or who had started them. All people knew was that tit-for-tat attacks were going on in various places in the country. It took a couple of weeks before the disturbances stopped, but, by then, there were hundreds of casualties and millions of dollars worth of property losses.

Many wondered why there was no high-level appearance, like that of the president or any of the Cabinet secretaries. It was all left to the governors and mayors, who urged their communities to maintain peace. Washington dispatched agents from the Federal Bureau of Investigation and Department of Homeland Security to determine if there was coordinated crime or terrorism being committed. For the most part, they decided the incidents were spontaneous, people just losing their temper, feeling uncomfortable and being afraid of others, and just over-reacting to perceived threats.

However, that was about the majority of the incidents. In a couple of cases, there were more serious skirmishes – what investigators called 'hate crimes'. These were cases that involved more than simply attacking individual peoples' homes, smashing car windows, or painting graffiti on the walls. These were cases that involved planning and spending money on operations, recruiting people, and causing maximum damage to society and the economy. In one case, a group of masked men with concealed pistols took over a primary school in a quiet mid-western city that had a large Muslim and Jewish population.

People of all faiths in the city had lived peacefully with each other for decades. When the gunmen took over the school, they separated the Muslim children from the Jewish and Christian ones. They kept the kids in separate rooms for a day, and then released the Muslim kids, but only after giving them a copy of the Koran and pamphlets inviting them to 'the path of Allah, the Most Compassionate, the Most Merciful', before you and your families lose what little is left of your faith'. They were keeping the Jews and the Christians, but had not made any demands. The police had brought in hostage negotiators, but the cops eventually ran out of patience, raided the compound, and freed all kids.

The gunmen turned out to be born and bred Americans, with lots of cash in their pockets. When FBI agents analyzed the copies of the Koran and pamphlets that the released kids carried home with them, it turned out they were printed in the same printing houses that printed textbooks for Saudi-financed schools. In another incident, the trouble was not physical violence, but financial. A group of hooded gunmen had ambushed a bank owned by a major Christian family that had been bigoted enough to adopt a *de facto* policy of not giving loans to any Muslim person or family.

By the time the gunmen were done, they simply had burnt all the cash they had stolen, and painted graffiti on the bank walls condemning the owner, saying they – the gunmen – would make sure he never lived in peace. 'Watch your shadow from now on, every day, every hour, every second, and you'll feel how our children and wives feel'. The bank security camera tapes showed the overall physical description and measurements of the men and fingerprints found at various places. The intelligence community had identified one of the men as a Pakistani national who had been indoctrinated in the Middle East by radical groups financed by Saudi Arabia.

The FBI, with help from local and national law enforcement agencies, had reasonably established that there was a domestic network of radical Saudis operating in the country, fanning the flame. The bigger question, to which no one had an answer, was what to do with this network. The law enforcement machinery had the same problem with the internal Saudi threat that Charlie and the CIA had with the Iranian threat in the region: You could arrest individual Saudis running a terror network in the country, but that was a far cry from proving that the Saudi government or its officials were involved.

After days of intra-agency brainstorming, everyone agreed that they had best kick this up to higher levels and land the ball on the doorsteps of the State Department, which, in turn, sent the issue to the White House and the President of the United States. Agencies could arrest and interrogate the individuals involved in incidents across the country, but, if there was a bigger 'Saudi problem' in the country, someone else had better figure it out and call the shots. The law enforcement had figured out who the ringleaders were: seemingly legitimate business people and community leaders.

Ordinarily, the White House would have been happy inviting 'community leaders' to 1600 Pennsylvania

Avenue for 'consultation', but, in this case, it could not be seen getting involved with alleged terror networks or potential criminals. The State Department did not have a mandate, since this was a domestic issue, and the federal law enforcement agencies, even the FBI, felt the issue was too big for their shoes. Days came and days went, and no one quite figured out how to get a handle on the problem, yet everyone felt the pressure and the urgency of having to deal with it, and deal with it fast.

After all, no one knew what else the perpetrators had in mind, what they had planned, and when other incidents were to happen, if any was, indeed, planned. The longer they waited, the more they could be accused of inaction. Lives could be lost. Financial damage could mount. In the end, they decided the meeting would be held at the Department of Homeland Security's headquarters. Law enforcement officials from various agencies would meet with 'Saudi community leaders', all of whom had links to radical groups in Saudi Arabia. It would show that the issue was considered both a national issue and a security issue. They also decided to invite the Saudi ambassador and the vice president to emphasise the diplomatic aspect. So as not to connect the vice president with potential criminals or imply a link between them and the Saudi government, they decided the VP and the ambassador would be sitting in a separate room, and linked through a video connection to the room in which the law enforcement and other Saudis were sitting. The dignitaries could hear the conversation in the other room and participate at will, but they could also hold a private conversation and not be heard by the others.

If someone had to write the scenario and predict how the conversation would go, they might have guessed that the vice president and the ambassador would have a diplomatic conversation while talks between the law enforcement officials and the Saudi 'community leaders' would be heated, maybe even accusations flying around. In reality, it was the other way around. FBI and Homeland Security officials started saying they were sorry for numerous acts of violence around the country lately, some of which were targeted against the Muslim and Arab communities around the nation. They said officials from national and local law enforcement agencies had worked hard, not only to stop the violence but also make sure those responsible were brought to justice.

"If we find any evidence of who was responsible for violence against members of your communities, you can be sure we will bring them to justice. Arabs and Muslims, whether they are US citizens or not, should have the right to peaceful life in their cities and communities as much as others do," said the FBI director, piercing into the eyes of all the invited guests around the table.

His deputy jumped in. "And we sincerely appreciate the cooperation we have received from all of you in ensuring peace and stability around the nation."

They then laid down facts and figures, and even pictures about the more serious criminal acts. Threading gingerly, they made the link between the high school hostage taking and the textbook printing shop, which was owned by one of the people at the table.

The man pre-empted further discussion. "Yes, unfortunately, we just noticed a couple of days ago that a couple of dozen of our Holy Book copies were missing from the inventory. They were stolen by an employee who was terminated a few weeks ago for theft of company equipment, petty things like pens, notebooks, and file folders."

"Did you report the theft?" one of the officials asked.

"No, we did not," the company owner responded firmly. "The man was fired already, and there were only two or three dozen copies of the Koran missing. It was not a huge financial loss."

"But you realize the link to the school," the FBI director said.

"Yes, now. But we had no reason to suspect it back then, and had no knowledge of it till you mentioned it right now," the Saudi man countered.

The law enforcement men asked for the fired man's name and contact information. The Saudis provided it, only to add promptly that the man has already returned to Riyadh. They moved on to another subject. The FBI director took a picture from a folder in front of him, and showed it to one of the Saudis at the table.

"Do you know this man?"

The man studied the picture for a few seconds, and then said, "No."

"But isn't he a cousin of yours?"

"Sir, this is Saudi Arabia. Everyone is someone's distant cousin. You have heard of the land of ten thousand princes and princesses, right?" the man shot back with an ill-hidden grin.

The director pulled out another picture. It was taken by a security camera next to the man's office. A local bank next to his office had multiple cameras. The picture showed the suspect entering the Saudi man's office.

"He was in your office the day before the bank robbery."

"Our office occupies the entire three floors of the building. I have over two hundred employees. If he entered, it does not necessarily mean he came to see me, because he did not."

The law enforcement officials knew they did not

have anything concrete. They had known that from the beginning, but the point of the meeting was not to indict any of the Saudis. The point was to show them that the FBI and others were on their tail, and scare the bejesus out of them. If they were succeeding, the Saudi men were good at concealing their feelings. They just sat there, cool as a cucumber. However, the mood next door, where the Saudi ambassador and the US vice president were sitting was quite different. The VP was frustrated that his agents could not crack the Saudis. "Pressure, pressure, put more pressure," he kept saying to himself. The ambassador, too, looked angry, but for a different reason.

"Your men won't get anything out of them," the ambassador told the vice president towards the end of the conversation next door.

"Why is that? Because they are clean, law-abiding citizens?"

"No, on the contrary, because they are trained criminals!"

The vice president was taken back.

"Martin." The ambassador addressed the vice president by his first name. "Why did you bring me here without telling me these men were going to be here? Why didn't you tell me you had something on these men? Why didn't you ask me what I knew about them?" His voice raised a few decibels every time he asked a new question. "These people are crooks; they are criminals!"

"And yet they are recognized by your embassy. In fact, they win large contracts from your embassy. Some of them have close ties to certain people in your government." It was the vice president's turn to get testy.

"I cannot talk to you about this now, not here. I am willing to help you. But it will be between you, me, the president, and director of the CIA. No one else. Only the people with whom I have a personal relationship and can trust. And nothing I say will be official."

"It is a domestic issue. If you have something to say, you should also say it to the FBI and Homeland Security directors. And what do you mean it won't be official? You are the ambassador of the kingdom, are you not?"

"What I will tell you, not even my government would want me to tell. I am volunteering because I love your country like my own. I have spent more time in your country than in mine. I went to school here. I met my wife here. She gave birth to our first son here. I own more property in your country than I do in mine. I have more money invested in your country than I have in mine. In a weird way, yours *is* my first country." Tears welled in his eyes. "The information I can give you will be on a private basis, from a friend. That's why I can only deal with the people I know."

In a strange way, the vice president was moved by the conversation. He and the ambassador had known each other for more than thirty years. They had attended Georgetown University together in Washington. He had known the ambassador long before the high-flier Saudi had befriended the president. He could tell when the ambassador was bluffing and when he was sincere. This time, he could tell the consummate diplomat was not dealing in diplomacy. He was dealing in humanity. The vice president had a little chat with the president, and they agreed they should accommodate the ambassador. As a sign of reciprocity, the meeting was held at the president's private dining room at the White House residence. They had debated whether or not the First Lady should attend, just to make the atmosphere less formal, but then decided against it. Both the president and the ambassador were whiskey *aficionados*, and the butlers promptly showed up with two glasses. The vice president had a glass of wine, and the CIA director decided to stick to soda. The president invited everyone to join him in the sitting room next door, where comfortable sofas and lazy chairs decorated the room.

"So, I hear you actually have some dirt on some of the guys you met the other day." The president thought it was his place to open the discussion.

"Yes, I do." He was debating whether to end his sentence with 'Mr. President' or just be informal and use his first name. He decided he would be safe, and do neither. "For some time, we have had a problem, a deep-rooted debate in our country. Our country is a deeply religious country, a deeply conservative country. But we don't live under stones, either. We might not be reacting as fast as some other countries, but that does not mean our people are unaware of what's going on around the world. The population is young. The country is rich, so people have increasingly been able to travel to the West. That has moved the social tectonic plates in Saudi Arabia, but the effect has not been an earthquake. It's been a very slow movement. But pressure has been building for some time and – despite the objection of some of us in the country – a decision was ultimately made to let some of the pressure points – people and groups most objecting to social reform in the country – actually leave the country and focus their efforts somewhere else.

"It was not exactly a new policy. We had adopted a similar version after the Soviet occupation of Afghanistan, and it had generally worked. There were some mistakes, but we thought we have learnt from them this time around. While we did not encourage anyone to come to the United States, we were aware that some did. Some came to pursue business. Others came to genuinely spread Islam in this country, and some came just to see what could be done to better the lives of the Muslims and Arabs already living here. There was no conspiracy, no organized network. Many of these people did not even know each other back home. Once they were here, however, they behaved liked any other immigrant community would behave; they tried to find people from their own country, people who spoke the same language, people who shared the same religious convictions.

"I am going through these elaborate details because I need you to understand that we, as government, had nothing to do with what I am about to tell you. Over a period of time, these groups found each other and created a network, which we later on understood was – you might call it – a terrorist or a fanatic network. We put them under surveillance whenever they traveled back home, monitored their movements, and observed whom they were meeting; we even bogged conversations. Throughout the whole process, we did not find anything that concretely pointed to a plan of action. There was no conversation about a specific operation, nothing that we could decipher. When the ugly incidents started happening here, we watched carefully for who might have been involved, but, for the most part, as you and your agencies have concluded, these were just individual disturbances. It was only halfway into the whole thing that we started to recognize names. We used our connections, and realized there is a plan of action in place by the most radical of these groups, to cause whatever damage they could."

"When were you planning on telling us all this? After another 9/11?" The president was visibly angry.

"I wanted to, very much wanted to. But I was ordered not to. The calculation back home was that, given

281

the history of our relations – especially after 9/11 – we could not be linked to headlines saying we have let another fundamentalist group flourish in this country."

This time, the vice president interrupted, "But didn't your government nominate and push for this guy to be the head of the Islamic Center in Washington? Didn't you give lavish business contracts to some of these people who are now linked to terrorism in our country? If you knew them, why did you keep supporting them?"

"Some of the people you are referring to were genuinely moderate Muslims. And, yes, we supported them and gave them incentives to stay here, but our goals were two. First, as I just said, these were people who had just come here to help their Muslim and Arab brothers and sisters. Second, there was a deep sense of frustration with the US at some point, and we thought our outreach programme would not only improve our image in your country – which we badly needed – but also help us achieve some of our agenda-setting goals in a backhanded way. I must say I did, and still do, support that. That is part of democracy, and I see nothing wrong with that. The same way you use your media that are beamed to our countries, and speak of democracy and human rights, the same way your NGOs operate in our countries and encourage our people to think differently, yes, we did encourage some people and groups to play the game of democracy in your country, but we never imagined the outcome could be this. And it is not that we didn't do anything. As soon as we realized some of these groups might have been sidetracked, we lured, or even forced some of them, back to Saudi Arabia, detained them, or simply didn't let them back into your country. We did try to rectify our mistake, quietly, but simply put, we lost control over some of our people."

Everyone sighed, and looked at each other in

bewilderment. The president and vice president gave each other a puzzled look, as if asking 'now what?' The CIA director knew what everyone was thinking: why had his agency not picked this up, and why had the agency not picked up on the background of some of the Saudi operatives in the country? There were just too many questions to be asked, and too many fingers to be pointed, but everyone also knew that this was all water under the bridge now, and they had to figure out what to do next.

The situation could potentially be too dangerous. No one could be sure that the violence had ended for good, and they all remembered full well how the media had had a field day with the events of not too long ago, and how those days could return in a flash. There were long and detailed stories in hometown and national papers about people's homes being attacked. Graphic artists were using any symbol and picture to turn this into a religious hatred of America. When the high school kidnapping occurred, television stations across the country had run the video of Muslim kids walking out of their captivity holding up their Korans, as the hostage takers had instructed them to.

They had only let them out in groups of three or four, and told the children the rest would not be released unless they properly showcased their Holy Books in front of cameras. The hostage takers were not stupid. They knew television cameras were poised across the street and would film every bit of it. When squad teams stormed the school and killed the hostage takers, law enforcement agents took off the masks hostage takers were wearing and showed the long, black beards to the public. The police did not need to say anything about their ethnic or religious background. It was all written on their faces. The backlash was immediate. Members of Congress, House and the Senate, were bombarded with phone calls, emails and letters. People were angry. They were confused. What was happening in their country? Was this the beginning of another September 11? They wanted answers. They wanted action, but no one knew what action to take. They had some facts, but no one could connect the dots. The four men sitting in the White House that night were all too conscious of what could be gripping them in no time again.

CHAPTER 34

IN the midst of all domestic issues, the White House woke up one morning to an ever more confusing turn of events. It was 4 a.m., and the White House switchboard was waking up the president. The VP was on the other side of the line.

"Sorry to disturb you this early, sir, but we have a situation."

"What is it?"

"I think you'd better come down to the Situation Room. We are all here."

There was no reason for the president to ask more. Calls to attend a Situation Room meeting meant only one thing: the most serious of the national security issues that had better not be discussed in an open forum.

The president changed into jeans and a track suit jacket, and went to the White House basement. Someone gave him a cup of warm, fresh-brewed coffee.

The White House Situation Room, or, as it was aptly called, The Nerve Center, or the Communication Center, was called those for a good reason. The size of a small suburban town house, the Situation Room was in one of the basement floors of the White House. Which basement floor? Well, that was classified! The Situation Room was built after the Bay of Pigs *fiasco* during JFK's presidency. Up until that point, the White House really did not really have its own intelligence center. There was no place in 1600 Pennsylvania Avenue where the 'most powerful man on Earth' could receive secure, direct intelligence communication by satellite from sources outside the building.

So the White House built the Situation Room, divided into two operations centers and a conference room. The operations rooms, where senior military and civilian officers were seconded to the National Security Council, was where the staff pored over all sorts of classified and unclassified information, from *Associated Press* wire reports to CIA and NSA intelligence data. The conference room itself, where the principles gathered, was not really big at all, but it did the job. Flat screen LCD television sets connected the president and his top aides to anywhere in the world via a secure and encrypted connection. The NSA could redirect its satellites to give those in the room a bird's eye to any spot on Earth, and, if the president was not in the room, those present could have secure communication to Air Force One. Not only was the room totally soundproof, but no electronic equipment was allowed into the room.

"So, what do we have?" the Commander in Chief addressed a room full of men and women in military uniform or suits.

Attending were the vice president, chairman of the Joint Chiefs of Staff, National Security advisor, Secretary of State, Secretary of Defense, and the CIA chief. This morning, the monitors on the wall were showing aerial satellite pictures of somewhere in the middle of the Atlantic Ocean.

"Mr. President, these pictures were taken less than two hours ago. Although we are still studying various details, we are fairly confident that, based on location, depth of the sea, and shape and nature of the clouds arising, this was a deep sea nuclear test," The Joint Chiefs of Staff said from his position two seats down from the president.

"Nuclear test? By whom?"

"That's the part we don't know, sir."

"Do you have any suspects?"

The CIA chief jumped in. "Sir, to reach that location, they obviously would have needed ocean-faring ships. To conduct such an exercise, they would have needed submarine prototypes to reach the depth they needed, and then explode the device. We have gone over satellite intelligence, and there were only three countries with any kind of movement in that area: Iranians, Israelis, and the Indians."

This was 2025. Nations had better and bigger capabilities than they had fifty years earlier.

"Each of which could have a motive to conduct such a test, and each of which would have a motive to do it, deny it, and blame others," said the president. "Never mind how they got there, can you not tell by the movement of ships in the area *after* the explosion, who it might have been?"

"Unfortunately, no, sir. For one thing, this was obviously exploded by remote control. Also, the ships in the area have been a good distance from the site. We cannot make a reasonable assumption that it was any of them. Given the size of the ships, it is likely that whoever was behind the explosion used small navy speed boats, and traveled the distance from the test area to a ship using the cover of darkness. They probably loaded the semi-submersible or flammable boats on the ship or hid them under the cargo somewhere.

"So, where do we go from here?" The president was getting restless, and wanted answers.

"We are analyzing the data we have. We are also making an inventory of all ships within a hundred-mile radius of the site. We will follow their path, and see where they anchor. We can take it from there. We are also talking to the Israelis and the Indians."

"Okay, then. Looks like I can go back to sleep!" the president said, half joking.

He stood up, and that was a clue for everyone else to do the same. The meeting was over, even though the crisis was far from being settled.

In the following days and weeks, there were other such Atlantic Ocean tests, each from a separate and distant place. Some clearly were nuclear. Others were simply to test missile ranges. The Iranian missile technology was not exactly a secret, although much about it was totally unknown to the world. The Iranians were rather tight lipped and secretive about it. They certainly had made massive strides in the past years, but testing missiles in the middle of the Atlantic Ocean did not make much sense, at least, not on the surface of it. Iran had two 'mortal enemies': Israel and the United States. The distance between Iran and Israel was less than a thousand miles, and Iran already had missiles well over that range. It could have attacked Israel from anywhere in the middle of a desert inside its borders. Attacking the United States was logistically more problematic, but not impossible.

Iran was rumored to have had developed Intercontinental Ballistic Missiles, but previous tests were not all successful. If the Iranian leadership was set on attacking the United States, it would have been foolhardy to rely on missile systems that had less than a hundred percent success rate. Were the Iranians testing the missiles in the middle of the Atlantic Ocean because they wanted to test the lower-range ones to make sure they would hit the

US coasts? Were they testing something so far away from home so they would not be identified as being behind it? Were they just showing their muscle to the United States? Were they fooling the world into thinking the target was the United States, but maybe they had other targets in mind? All of the above? None of the above?

Not long afterwards, the mystery had somewhat been solved. The US intelligence had identified a large Iranian cargo ship – registered in Panama – that had anchored off the coast of Spain. The Spanish navy and American undercover agents had boarded the ship, temporarily detained all the crew, and confiscated semi-submersible, fast North Korean navy boats, sophisticated computers, and some other equipment. The equipment was taken to a lab, and showed proof that the Iranians were testing nuclear warheads.

That threw the entire US government into high alert. It was now pretty reasonable to assume that the Iranian leadership wanted to target the United States, but there were still many questions to be answered before any policy decisions could be made. For one thing, the intelligence community had no idea how close the Iranian were to launching an actual attack, how many other missiles were in the area, if they were to be launched off a submarine, and, if so, where would they would find it. If more than one missile was involved, how would they find them and their carriers?

It was now full-fledged, dizzying speed, politico-espionage mayhem in Washington, the likes of which no one could remember.

Another strange thing about the ship was that, when the Spanish navy boarded it and made a list of the people, there was a woman amongst the many men. That in itself was unusual. The fact that it was an Iranian ship made it even more bizarre. When American intelligence ran the names of everyone in the various databases, her name did not come up at all. It was only when they searched the biometrics database that it turned out she was Sade. She was using a fake passport, had colored her hair, cut it short, trimmed her eyebrows, and was wearing seventies-style eyeglasses. Testing the material on the boat had taken longer than expected – Spaniards are not known for speedy action – and, eventually, the Spanish authorities and the Americans had to let the crew ago, as long as they handed in their passports and agreed to be under 'house arrest' in their hotel room.

Within hours, there was no sign of Sade. No one knew where she had gone. One moment she was in her hotel, and the next she had disappeared. The Spaniards checked the land borders, but could not find anyone by that name driving away. They checked the airports, but that did not turn up anything, either. The one person who could have possibly helped resolve the situation was gone. So the Interpol agents went after a couple of the crew members who seemed like navy divers. After much duress, pressure and even threats, the investigators connected the dots, but only after the divers' lawyers cut a deal with the Spanish government. The divers would tell the government anything it wanted to know, but they could not be jailed, charged with anything in Spain, or handed over to the Americans. In return for full cooperation, they would agree to be expelled from Spain and be put onto a direct flight back to Iran.

The Spaniards – and the Americans – were baffled by how quickly a first class and super-expensive Spanish lawyer with tons of credibility in international legal issues had shown up on the police's doorsteps to represent the men. The only way anyone would have known that the men were arrested was by having staked out their hotel.

Not only that, but they must have had the lawyer on call, waiting for an emergency. This was during one of the many periods of lengthy holidays in Spain. Unless the lawyer was forewarned, he would not be in town at all. This was not a shoddy affair. This was a cold and calculated international military intelligence game. The adversary was far smarter than people wanted to give it credit for.

The navy men said that, while they were not a party to it themselves, they knew that a regular cargo ship had crossed the Persian Gulf, traveled south, and up again into the Gulf of Aden and the Suez Canal. Once they had passed the canal, they had anchored for a night while some cargo was loaded from Port Said. The divers did not know what it was. The crew was flown from Iran directly to Morocco, where another ship had taken them to a submarine in the middle of the North Atlantic Ocean.

They claimed they did not know what the explosion was about. They were not part of the 'scientific team'. They were just there to make sure 'the lady' got out safely. The others left through a different route. Despite tremendous pressure and back and forth questioning, they claimed they did not know who 'the lady' was. Apparently, she was on board under a pseudo name that did not match either her real name or the name under which she was travelling. Investigators asked why the ship that picked up whatever it was from Port Said could not just bring it from Iran.

"The navy was very concerned about US flotilla in the Persian Gulf. They did not want to be subject to random checks. It was safer to send it somewhere else, and then pick it up when it was safe," they responded.

The White House was not losing any sleep over losing Sade. Between the 'evidence' that Iran had just tested at least one underground nuclear device and the crisis with

291

the out-of-control Saudi fanatic network inside the country, the administration felt it had the best chance in a long while to thwart a foreign threat and one in the homeland, at the same time. This was not 'Wag the Dog'. No one was 'creating a situation'. This was not 'selective' intelligence 'analysis'. No one was forging anything or lying about anything. The fact that the President of the United States had given a prime time television speech not long ago claiming that the Iranians were a threat because they were arming groups hell-bent on destroying Israel was now something no one wanted to remember. The question now was how much they could tell the world about the possibility of a nuclear threat. They were mindful of the fact that, this time, as with the time of the president's speech, they did not have proof. They had lots of bits and pieces of truth, but they did not know the full story.

CHAPTER 35

CHARLIE had the proof, or, at least, he thought he did, and he was concerned, angry and confused – professionally and personally. He knew that after he had gone back to Cyprus from Cairo and sent the memo over the secure communication lines to the CIA, the Pentagon was already working on sending major battleships to the Mediterranean. Battleship carriers from the US, Europe and the Pacific were ordered for immediate temporary assignment to the region. The list of the battleships was long: USS Enterprise; Aircraft Carrier Constellation; Eisenhower Strike Group; Expeditionary Strike Group 5.

US airbases in Germany were told to have fighter jets ready for last-minute operations, and the Central Command in the Persian Gulf received personnel and technical reinforcements, and was put on high alert. Ships already in the Persian Gulf area were told to increase their vigilance and watch out for any 'suspicious naval activities' in the area. Charlie had received reports of the movements and alerts from Langley but since he had not received any responses from Langley to his cables, he did not really have a full picture of what was going on. Things did not get better in the coming weeks; they only got worse, and the first indication of it was when Ibrahim showed up at his door in Nicosia, unannounced. It was shortly before midnight when the doorbell rang. A clearly taken aback Charlie saw the guest, with his right arm and left leg in a top-to-bottom heavy plaster cast as white as his face.

"What happened to you? What are you doing here? How did you find me?"

Charlie just threw out question after question. It was a minute or so before he got hold of himself, and stopped.

"Can I come in?"

"Ah, yeah, I guess!"

He fixed Ibrahim a straight doubt shot of scotch, and gave himself a quadruple. They both had a long sip, and took a deep breath before either was ready to say anything.

"So!" This time, Charlie was pacing his questions. "To what do I owe such a midnight honor?" He figured that maybe a bit of humor and sarcasm would melt the ice.

"It's not to 'what', but to 'whom'!"

"I am sure you are about to explain that."

"Remember your visit to Baghdad, many months ago?"

"Yes."

"Remember the phone call I got?"

"Yes."

"Well, that's where it all started. At the other end of the line was an Egyptian friend who had put me in touch with a local contact in Cairo. I was going to sell them arms."

Charlie pretended he was surprised and did not know anything about it.   "Arms?"

"Charlie, you need to publish something, because we are about to have a major war on our hands. Millions of people can die. This could be the end of Earth as we know it!"

"Calm down! Calm down! What are you talking about?"

Ibrahim was clearly anxious and worried. His lips were twitching, his left arm was a bit shaky, and he had a hard time putting sentences together. He finished what little was left of his scotch, and asked for more. Charlie brought the bottle, and let his guest help himself. Ibrahim filled up his glass, took another sip, and started talking again.

"Months ago, I met an Iranian official in Geneva. He said they wanted to sell arms to this Egyptian group, but that some of the shipment would be given back to the Iranians in Egypt to be put on specially designed military ships that looked like normal cargo boats. In return for the 'favor', the Egyptians could ask for whatever arms they needed, and they would get a major, major discount. The deal was that the Iranians would bring the arms by land to the No Man's Land between Iraq and Kurdistan, and then I would arrange for it to be loaded on specially chartered flights to Sudan. My job would be done. From there, the anti-regime groups in southern Egypt would take some of the arms, and deliver the rest to this guy I know in Cairo. His end of the deal was that he would arrange for the boxes to be delivered to Port Said, and then Iranian navy boats would pick them up."

"Why would the Iranians bring the stuff all the way to the border to be flown to Sudan?" Charlie asked. "Why not just fly them from an airport in Tehran?"

"Because they have their own internal battles. You know, moderates versus hardliners," Ibrahim explained. "The president's men thought it would be politically safer not be directly tied to this."

One more sip of the scoth.

"When the material got to the border between Iraq and Kurdistan, we realised that some of boxes were totally locked, and we could not examine them. It was not just one or two. There were many, many boxes. Some of the

295

material had markings on them saying 'nuclear' ".

Another taste of the scotch, and the second glass was gone.

"They were not just shipping arms to Port Said. They were shipping boxes of missiles, a missile system, plus nuclear warheads."

"Was the material delivered all the way?"

"Yes, I have the confirmation that they were picked up in Port Said."

"So, where did they go? What did the Iranians want to do with it? They want to attack Israel?"

"Don't be silly. Israel doesn't have anything to do with it. If they wanted to attack Israel, they would not need to go through this elaborate scheme. They could have just lobbed a missile from somewhere inside the country."

The picture was now becoming clearer to Charlie. He was figuring out what was going on, but he needed to find out what had happened to Ibrahim.

"When the arms showed up along the Iraq-Kurdistan border, we insisted on inspecting the boxes. We had to. I was the middle man. I had to ensure that the merchandise was what they had promised. And I was the one who had to arrange for the stuff to leave the country. Plus, I had the money in an escrow account. There was a lot involved in the process. I didn't want anything to go wrong. So the Iranians agreed to our inspecting the boxes, and I found out about the nuclear stuff. It became tense, but things worked out, and everything was fine. Last week, the same Iranian man in Geneva man called for an urgent meeting in Europe.

"When I got to the hotel, some goons beat me up as badly as they could. There was one guy who was doing the interrogation. He kept asking me to whom I had told the story about the nuclear stuff. I kept telling him no one, but he would not buy it. They kept beating me with a hammer on my knee and elbows, and beat me more with an iron club. They would ask me more of the same questions and, when I kept giving me the same answers, they eventually broke my arm and leg. The interrogator guy kept insisting I must have told someone about the nuclear stuff, because there was some kind of accident, and someone had found out and some people were arrested in Spain. I kept telling them I have no connection to anyone in Spain but they just would not believe me."

Maybe the CIA, FBI and NSA still did not have proof, but Charlie thought he now had it.

Between the information gathered in the interrogation from the men in Spain, information leaked from the president's Situation Room meeting, and now the information Charlie was hearing from Ibrahim, he drew a picture in his head.

The Iranian navy had sent ships into the Mediterranean, loaded with nuclear arms smuggled from Port Said. The ships then entered the Atlantic Ocean, and detonated some of the missiles equipped with nuclear warheads. The question was: why? He did not know the answer, obviously. However, by now, he had known – or thought he knew – enough, and, perhaps for the first time, he was scared as much as he was frustrated. He had been writing cables for months to his superiors in Langley, warning about an Iranian threat. He had picked up bits and pieces. He had warned them, but it seemed either no one was listening, or no one could bring himself or herself to draw the same conclusions he had, connecting the same dots and coming up with the same conclusions.

He kept asking himself what he could do to make it right. He might have been an undercover agent, but, deep down, he was always a journalist. He had the spirit of a journalist, and part of that spirit – a good part of the spirit – was the desire and need to correct the wrong, or at least to give the right information to people, so they could judge the situation for themselves. Now that he was on the other side of the fence, he had a dilemma. How could he – or could he at all – do his job *and* maintain his integrity? How could he prevent the evils he knew were to set loose upon the world?

He was not sitting in Nicosia just to make money. He believed in the justice of the world, that there should be justice, and that he had to have a part in it. As he pondered those thoughts, he realized that those convictions were ever so stronger now, because of the support he had from his wife. Although she was rich and had no need to ever work in her life, Sarah was anything but a rich, spoilt woman. She cared. She listened. She believed in the same justice system he did. When they had first met, he used to tease her that she believed in justice because her religion taught her so. "You learnt it by instinct, but I learnt it from first-hand experience, having seen the injustices of the world," he used to tell her. She would not argue with him, only to promise him that, one day, she, too, would see the world the way he did. Until then, she kept saying, "be glad that we believe in the same things, and that's what makes our marriage happier."

Charlie sent another cable to headquarters, based on his late-night meeting with Ibrahim, and repeated his warning. Then, out of resignation, he booked himself a ticket to LA. It was time to have a serious conversation with Sarah.

CHAPTER 36

Los Angeles, Bel Air

WHEN Charlie got home, Sarah was not home. He had known she would not be. They had talked on the phone from Nicosia, and she had explained that she was still in Paris with friends, and had a hard time getting a ticket back. There were only some economy seats available, which she would never consider. For someone of her economic 'class', it was either first class or nothing. The only time she had even flown business class was when she and Charlie had been coming back from a trip to Germany, and she had to fly back home quickly because her father was flying to LA. That was the days when they still had good relations and it was unacceptable for her not to be in the city when he was coming by. This time around, Sarah said she would have to arrive a couple of days after him. She had suggested they meet in Paris and fly back together, but he was not in the mood to see Sarah's friends. There were times he could not understand why his nicely educated wife would want to be friends with people whose only claim to life was their hefty bank accounts.

"What do you see in those people?" he had asked once.

"Nothing," she had replied. "They are part of the

circle of people I grew up with. I am used to them. I don't have to talk politics or economics or culture with them. I have other friends for that. I have you. I can just talk trash with them for a few hours, or go shopping, or just sit and have a cup of coffee. It is the same as guys going out and having a beer with other guys, or watching a football match in a bar."

He could not much disagree with that, only that *all* of her Saudi female friends were like that. Given the nature of the Saudi society, which pretty much prohibited friendship between men and women, Sarah did not have more than one or two Saudi male friends.

By the time Sarah arrived back in the States and flew from John F Kennedy airport in New York to LA, Charlie had prepared himself for what he wanted to say and how he wanted to say it. He had told the cook to make a nice seafood dish – Sarah loved seafood – and a light salad to go with it. He had chilled a bottle of Dom Perignon for her arrival, and chosen a bottle of old, dry, red wine to go with the dinner. He had told the staff to set a nice dinner table in the garden next to the swimming pool. He had chosen some nice, quiet, romantic music to set the mood. He had filled the master bathroom in the house with candles and red roses, and bought his wife an expensive and very revealing dress that he knew she would love.

True to her reputation for being smart, she picked up that something was up when she entered the house. Not that they did not have a romantic relationship. They very much did! Plus, the fact that, this time around, they had been apart for a few months, had added to the expectations from both sides. As soon as she entered the house and the servants went to the limo cab to bring her suitcases, she threw herself into her husband's arms, who was waiting by the door between the garden and the living area. They

300

kissed each other passionately, their hands starting with each other's head and hair and, ever so gently, moving to the hips. They eventually moved their way up the bedroom, and made love. By the time she was done with her bath, the sun had set and the temperature was down a few degrees. There was even a breeze, and a sweater would not have been out of order.

"Honey, we need to talk about something important."

Just looking in his eyes, Sarah could tell it was serious. He told her a synopsis of what he had learnt in the past few months.

"Remember how you told me about the Saudis opening schools around the country months ago? Well, it turned out that was the tip of the iceberg."

He then told her about the government inquiries into the clashes, and how it had led to some underground Saudi groups. Next, he told her about the meeting between the ambassador and the vice president, and the subsequent meeting with the president.

"Can't say it surprises me," she said. "There's something arrogant and yet naïve about Gulf leaders. They think because they have tons of oil and gas and their bank accounts are loaded, they can control and influence everything."

"Well, it gets worse. While the Saudis have been trying to get the White House to change policies on Iran, the Iranians have been playing their own game, a very dangerous game."

By the time he was done telling her about assassination attempts and explosions in various parts of the Middle East, Baghdad, Cairo, Spanish interrogations, and Ibrahim's late-night visit, she had come to the same conclusion he had: the Iranians were about to carry out a major attack against someone, and that, in turn, would unleash America's might against Iran. The whole region could be up in flames.

"Have you spoken to anyone?" she asked.

"I have told my bosses. The White House, by now, knows about everything. It is just a question of whether they will act or not, whether they will come to the same conclusion or not, and which side will act first."

"Is your life in danger? Is my life in danger?"

"No, I don't think so. I don't think it is a personal matter. Of course, it is possible that whoever broke Ibrahim's arm and leg also followed him to my place and now thinks I am also somehow involved, but I don't think so."

The rest of the evening was spent mostly in silence. Charlie and Sarah simply looked at each other, and drank more wine. Sometimes, they would try to read each other's thoughts. At other times, they would simply be immersed in their own. Either way, they had agreed on one thing: something drastic was about to happen. If they could not save their country, they should, at least, save themselves. They mostly wanted to do both.

The next morning, when they were both a bit more cool headed, they decided to pick up where they had left off. It was something they both wanted to resolve. The importance of the issue could not have been overestimated.

"Why don't you push harder?" Sarah asked. "Surely, there must be someone at headquarters who will eventually get it!"

"Yes, but who knows when *eventually* might be!" he responded. "What if some sort of an attack happens *tomorrow*?"

"Well, if you think it's that urgent, then what's the fastest way to stop it, outside the channels?" She did not wait for Charlie to answer. "It seems to me that you have two options: leak it to the press, or find someone or some way to quietly stop anything that might have been planned."

"I cannot leak it."

"Why not?"

"First, because I don't like the idea. I took an oath to keep the government's secrets. It's the press's job to share information with the society. This is not the kind of information the whole world needs to know. Second, with my background as a journalist, if there's a leak, I'm the first place they would look."

"Honey, there are leaks in the government every day! All you have to do is look at the *Washington Post* and *The New York Times*. *You* are *not* the only person leaking to the media."

"No, I am not. But most of those leaks are *authorised* leaks. That's why they don't get caught. There are occasional leaks that are *unauthorised,* but on an explosive issue like this, they're sure to want to find out. They will find out."

"Okay, let's say they do find out. What would the repercussions be?"

"Put me in jail! Put you in jail! Confiscate our assets!"

"Let's say all of that is true, which I don't think it is. They won't put me in jail. They won't put the daughter of a high-ranking prince in Saudi Arabia – a country they have such reliance on – in jail, and, for the same reason, they won't confiscate our assets, and, even if they did, we won't have to worry about money."

"And me?"

"Yes, they could put you in jail, legally. But let's work backwards. Let's work on a plan that would *not* lead to your going to jail, or me. I am not worried about money, and neither should you be!"

As their days of planning and revising previous day's plans dragged on into weeks, the national political tempo had increased feverishly. Every day, congressional and White House officials, and ranking staff ratcheted up the calls 'to defeat the enemy' or 'to ensure homeland's safety'. "Those who are using our country's hospitality and then burn our houses should feel the anger of our hearts" was the battle cry of a famous and influential senator on Capitol Hill. Network television stations invited 'military experts' to opine on 'how easy' it would be to attack Iran in surgical strikes to ensure it could not attack the United States or its Middle East allies first. The talk and the momentum for surgical attacks just kept building. It was all but inevitable for the talk to turn into action. Of course, absent from all the discussions was the fact that the White House knew about the arms smuggling through the Mediterranean, and the nuclear and conventional arms tests in the Atlantic.

CHAPTER 37

IT was a chilly November evening in Washington. The air felt nearly frozen. It was probably a couple of degrees below zero. The sheet of white snow had carpeted the capital city the night before. Washington was simply majestic in snow, until cars started driving around. As beautiful as the city was in snow, it was a mere mess when traffic started rolling. The city just could not handle more than a couple of inches of snow. It was safer – and more pleasant – to just close the roads and send everyone home.

The weather in the Iranian capital was not much better. It was cold, colder than Washington. There was little snow, but it was also very cloudy. Visibility was quite low. Plus, since there was an eight or nine hour time difference between Iran and the East Coast of the United States, the clock had just turned 2 a.m. in Iran when the President of the United States appeared for a live broadcast on network television. What the president had to say might have been news to the American people, but it was not news to anyone in Tehran. People there could not see the planes buzzing tens of thousands of feet above, but the sound of multiple explosions was unmistakable.

American jets and smart bombs fired from warships in nearby waters were pounding not just positions inside the capital, but select targets in various cities. Many of the targets in the capital were 'leadership' and 'strategic' positions: air defenses, the airport, military headquarters, the presidency, *etcetera*. The bombings had devastating effects on the people and the country. Almost every family had suffered injury or death. Every family had telltales of small or large financial or material losses.

The government, too, was suffering. Roads were bombed, airports were taken out, and runways filled with holes and made inoperable. Outside the capital, military, energy and nuclear reactors were favorite targets. Oil fields were set on fire. In some places, the flames could be seen from miles away. The country's new Chinese-made fighter jet squadrons never got a chance to get off the ground, because the hangers were attacked mercilessly. Even some of the long-range missile silos were destroyed by 'bunker busting' bombs that penetrated deep into underground storage depots.

Ironically, while the country's leadership headquarters were under a ferocious barrage of bombs, some of the top leaders were not even in the country. Days before the American attacks on Iran had started, the top leadership had seen the writing on the wall, and left the country altogether. Most notable among them were the president, the Joint Chiefs of Staff, the intelligence chief and, of course, Sade, the president's top advisor. There had been much discussion in the preceding few months about 'transition of power' and 'government survival'. No one in the inner circles of the government doubted that if there was an attack, it would be massive.

Every site that was hit, they had imagined it would be hit. They had known 'command and control' facilities would come under attack. They had even imagined that the 'enemy' might try to assassinate the leaders. The history of American military incursions and invasions in the past half a century had left no doubts about that. So, this time around, the leadership had taken the safe road and set up 'temporary transitional' headquarters. The small 'leadership team' had moved in a convoy of bullet-proof cars with tinted windows to the city nearest to the No Man's Land between Iran, Iraq and Kurdistan. One of the middle cars was filled with cash. They knew they would have to bribe their way out of the country.

When they decided to leave the capital, the presidency had made no contact with either Iraqi or Kurdish governments. They had informed neither country they would be coming, or who exactly would be coming, and for how long and why. They knew other leaders in the region had been edgy about Iran's policies. They knew tension had built up in the region, a region that had seen its share of political rumbling and military wrangling. They did not want to have anything to do with the hard-line politics of Iran. The presidential team knew that if it gave advance notice about the arrival, the request most likely would be turned down. So, when the convoy arrived in the No Man's Land, the leadership team split into three. The president stayed behind with his bodyguards along the border, the intelligence chief went to Baghdad, while Sade and the head of the army went to see the Kurdish president.

Sending a delegation to Baghdad was risky. There was so much bad blood and cynicism between the two countries. During the reign of the 'Butcher of Baghdad', the two countries had fought a protracted and bloody battle. When the dictator was overthrown, the relations had improved somewhat, but then the Iranians had started meddling in Iraq's affairs, and formed alliances with shady groups, politicians or pure thugs. Alliances had shifted and made a mockery out of the whole political system. No one knew what the Iranian policy was, and no one could trust

307

them.

The meeting at the presidential palace in Baghdad was ceremonious and cold. The president, a Shiite Muslim – just like most of his co-religionists in Iran – had, in fact, been born in Iran, not Iraq. His father belonged to one of the major Shiite religious groups in Iraq, but had been exiled to Iran. His mother was not his father's first wife. Many Shiite men back then opted for the behind-the-scene civil marriage tradition of proposing to a woman for a 'limited period of time' – be that fifteen minutes or fifteen months. The traditions became popular in the Middle East in the early 1980s when Iranian militia, military and intelligence men flocked Lebanon – without their wives – and could not resist other women or be abstinent. They would 'marry' women – more often girls – and 'divorce' them at will.

So, when the Iranian intelligence chief met the Iranian-born Iraqi president, he had hopes for some sort of understanding, if not sympathy.

"Mr. President, we have received intelligence that our country is about to come under heavy attacks. If our information is correct, it will include nuclear attacks against civilian targets. We expect hundreds of thousands, if not millions, of casualties. This will be the worst attack ever in our part of the world, much worse than even the aggressions that your country faced from the Americans. You know our country perhaps better than anyone else, better than many Iranians. Our president and a carful of senior advisors are currently in the No Man's Land. The president, in sending his best wishes, has asked me to seek your permission for the delegation to enter and remain in your protection until the hostilities end. We realise that our presence might cause political and financial distress for your country. You can, naturally, count on our eternal political gratitude once the aggression is over. As for

308

financial gratitude, for now, at least, I can present you with a tiny gift of appreciation."

He then opened the large Samsonite suitcase he had carried with him. The president's eyes were visibly widening. The suitcase was filled to the rim with stacks of hundred dollar bills. Before he could ask the question, he received the answer.

"It is five million dollars, Mr. President."

Granted, that was a huge amount of money, which, no doubt, was going to the president's personal account. There was hardly any leader in that part of the world who was honorable enough to deposit such a sum into the government treasury. Not even his own president would have done that. However, the Iraqi leader had other things in mind. He might have grown up in Iran, but, like most other Iraqi exiles, he hated Iran and the Iranians. The Iranian government had allowed them to live on its soil, but only as refugees in extreme conditions, along the border lines where mountains were cold and summer deserts boiling hot, where the tents they lived in were miles and miles away from any sign of civilisation.

Simply put, they were kept at arm's length. The Iraqi refugees knew the Iranians wanted it that way, and hated the country and its leaders for it. It was one grudge they never forgot or forgave. It was time for the Iraqi president to pay back the old debt. He gently put his hand on the handle of the suitcase, wrapped his fingers around it, and started pulling the suitcase towards him, watching the smile on his guest's face.

"Of course we remember aggression and mistreatment. Our nation has been on the receiving end of it for decades, if not centuries. We know who the enemies are, and who the friends are. We would condemn any aggression against your country as if it was against ours."

By now, the suitcase had completely disappeared from the desk and landed neatly next to the president's feet.

"You and your delegation are more than welcome to stay in our country. You are aware that we have never recognized the status of what others call No Man's Land. That has always been part of our ancestral land. As such, your delegation should remain in that area – in our country – where no one will recognize you. Of course, we will send you whatever facilities are needed to make your say comfortable on the borderlines. We know how difficult it can be. I think that area would be least dangerous for you. In fact, considering the presence of your president, I will order some of the Presidential Protective Forces dispatched to the area immediately."

The Iranian emissary, getting the essence of the message, left the capital to report back that they were on their own, in the desert, and five million dollars shorter in cash. He just wished he had not offered the money before securing the deal. Meanwhile, Sade was having a better time with the Kurdish leadership. The Kurds offered the presidential team whatever it needed, but they told her, honestly, that they did not want the team in, or even near, any of the big cities. People would recognize the president. He was too much of a political liability. It had not been that long ago that the Iranian artillery had shelled Kurdish villages. Memories were fresh. Wounds had not healed.

However, the president was willing to help, not because he loved the Iranians or Iran, but because he was a pragmatist. He did not know whether what they Iranians were telling him was true or not, but he figured if the leadership was escaping, it was either because they were about to attack or be attacked. Either way, the Kurds thought, they could use the presence of the Iranian leaders on their soil as a bargaining chip. If Iran was about to be attacked, the Kurds could bargain with the Americans for more assistance to the Kurds in return for keeping the Iranian leadership under some sort of house arrest or, at least, under close surveillance. Furthermore, if the Iranians were about to attack someone, then the Kurds would be sitting on top of the hottest intelligence asset any espionage organisation would pay top dollars for.

The Iraqi leader was living in the politics of the past. The Kurds were eyeing the future, and it was all evident in the dismal economy of one and the boom in the other.

Within days of the arrival of the Iranian delegation, the Americans had started their bombing. In the beginning, it was unclear what the Iranian leadership was doing in Kurdistan. They president and his top men, and woman, were mostly just talking to each other in their villa just on the outskirts of No Man's Land. Other than that, there was no activity on their part. They were not calling anyone. They were not accessing their emails. They were not moving in and out of the villa. There was no sign that anyone was trying to sneak into the country to meet up with them. For a country that was being bombed day in and day out by an enemy, its leaders were showing surprisingly little care about knowing what was going on. They did not seem interested in knowing what was happening in their country, in receiving the latest information, the latest bombing reports, the latest casualty reports.

Maybe they knew their communication channel was not secure enough. Obviously, they also suspected the villa would be watched, so they did not try to get out, disguised or not. It was spooking the Kurds a bit. They had not told anyone about the Iranians being on their soil, and they did not know the Iranians had approached the Iraqis first, so they had no reason to believe that Baghdad might rat on them either. Still, they were getting a bit uncomfortable not knowing what was going on, or what might be going on. They were about to make a move and ask the delegation for a 'meeting', but it turned out they did not have to. An early morning, almost three weeks after they had arrived, the Kurds monitored an incoming phone call on Sade's mobile satellite connection. The message was some kind of a code, which the Kurds could not decipher, but, the next morning, Kurdish officials received an official request for an Iranian chartered passenger plane to land in a nearby airport to take them out of the country.

Obviously, they were not going back home. They could have easily driven back to the nearest city inside their country and have a military plane take them back to the capital. They were probably moving to another Middle Eastern country or to Europe. The Kurds had understood from their spies bringing supplies into the house and cleaning the villa, that there was probably around twenty million dollars worth of cash stashed in various suitcases around the house. The team was either out on a *long, long* vacation, or about to buy something super expensive that they had to pay cash for, or were about to do something else that required lots of money. The pilot, as required, had filed a flight path out of the country. It showed the plane was heading for Morocco.

Although the Kurdish president had kept the story of the Iranians to himself up until that point, he decided it was time to have a chat with an old CIA friend. Langley had had lots of agents in the Kurdish areas before and after they gained their independence, and the president knew many of them. After he had become president, he had to keep them at a distance. He officially had no contacts with them, but had maintained business-like ties through indirect links. The day the Iranian president was supposed to leave Kurdistan

312

on the private chartered plane, the Kurdish leader had passed on the details of the plane, its destination, its passengers, and the details of the previous negotiations to his Langley friends. They had called Charlie in LA. That was the day after he and Sarah had their romantic dinner at home.

Within days of their departure, the CIA had lost the presidential team. One night they were staying at a hotel, and the next morning they were gone.

CHAPTER 38

Somewhere in the Atlantic Ocean

THE Chinese-made Jin-class submarine was the latest in the Iranian navy's collection. It was their pride and joy. For years, the Iranian navy did not have much to brag about. They were the smallest, least advanced, and least appreciated of the army or 'special forces' branches. When the Shah was toppled, the Americans had cancelled whatever new frigate and submarine orders Tehran had in place. As a result, whatever equipment the new regime had inherited soon became inoperable. In the end, maybe that was not such a bad thing, because the Iranians had ended up being creative and built whatever they needed. However, it was not just about repairing the old equipment and building new ones. In the old days, the Iranian navy had been focussed on operations in the Strait of Hormuz and the Persian Gulf; its job had been mostly defensive. To the degree that it was offensive, it was limited to lying mines underwater.

Submarines had always been a dream 'gadget' for the Iranians, dating back to the Shah's days. The emperor was desperately asking his American backers to sell him a submarine. When the Americans refused, he went about to cut a deal with the Germans, but the Islamic revolution

314

shortened his tenure. The mullahs were no less fervent, but why not? Submarines seem to be a must-have item for the military arsenal of numerous regimes in the Middle East, from Israel and Egypt to Algeria and Pakistan. After Iran was done fighting Iraq, submarines played a more central role in Iran's military strategic thinking. Of course, as with many other aspects of the Iranian politico-military life, there was perhaps more bravado involved than actual reality. They had claimed they had built their own submarines from scratch, but many doubted it. They had also paid cash to buy some others from the North Korean and the Russians, much to the chagrin of Washington.

However, their latest acquisition was a different story in many aspects.

This submarine was simply called, unceremoniously, 094ELKM. It had been in the Chinese arsenal only a couple of years, and much of the time in the submarine hanger in Huludao, in the south-western province of Liaoning. With a length of over 420 feet, it stood –literally – an arm and a leg superior to its old brethren. With a range of about 5,000 miles, it posed serious threats to the enemies of the Chinese motherland, but aside from the semantics, it was most feared because it could accommodate MIRVs, the guided intercontinental ballistic missiles that could aim multiple targets with the firing of each single missile.

MIRVs were what Sade had negotiated for when she had sat at the 365 Bar in Dubai.

For years, the Jin-class submarines had limited themselves to roaming around the vicinity of Chinese waters. Bit by bit, Beijing would send them out to farther waters in the Pacific and the Atlantic. Again, at first, the international military community had watched closely, suspicious of what China might have in mind. The Indians,

315

the Americans, the Russians, they all had their proverbial antennas up, but China had not done anything wrong. It had not attacked anyone or any country. So, over time, people had put down their guard.

The Iranians had watched the movement of MIRV-carrying submarines and, when they thought they had produced enough MIRV missiles – thanks again to General Jian – they had approached the Chinese with an unusual deal: we will pay you cash to purchase one of your submarines. Odd as that was in itself, there was another element in the Iranian proposal that would have rung alarm bells had they become known. It is normal practice that, when you buy a fancy machine like an attack-class submarine home, the seller would deliver it to buyer's waters, and it would be 'inaugurated' within national borders. However, this time, the Iranians did not want the submarine anywhere near Iranian waters. The submarine was already in Atlantic waters, and that's where the Iranians wanted it. They had paid for 094ELKM, which they had renamed *Entegham,* meaning Revenge – but were keen on the world not knowing about the transfer. Of course, the Chinese navy did not know that the Iranians had already purchased the blueprints for MIRVs and built their own system. The submarine had been sold to them without the sophisticated missile system.

Attending the official takeover ceremony in the middle of international waters were Sade, the Iranian president, head of the Iranian navy, and head of the Iranian intelligence. The Chinese side was represented by General Jian – head of the military industrial production sector and uncle of the 'Arab, Hoshimoto', who had played a key part in blowing up oil facilities in a Gulf country – plus the head of the Chinese navy. General Jian was clearly nervous. He was sweating, and his hands were somewhat shaking. He claimed he was not feeling well and was not used to seafaring. Most of all, he was trying his best not to establish eye contact with Sade. Sade sensed the general's uneasiness, and pretended he was not there. He had thought he could continue disguising what he knew but the guilt was too much of a burden on him.

Once the handover was complete and the Chinese had successfully left the area, it was time for business. The next day, the president took over the submarine's public speaker system, some four hundred feet below the surface. He was in the submarine's control cabin, wearing a navy uniform as Commander in Chief of the armed forces, although he had never served in any branch of the armed forces. Next to him stood *Daryadar*, rear admiral, Javad Khodayar. The president called everyone to appear in person in five minutes. The rest of the submarine crew, about fifty of them, hand-picked for the mission, had arrived from different routes over a course of hours, all aboard the same type of international merchant ships used in Sade's previous excursion into the Atlantic. The Iranian-made MIRV missiles were aboard the ship.

The president started his speech. "In the name of God, the most Compassionate, the most Merciful. Brothers, you are here for perhaps the most important mission of your life, the most important mission of *our* life. You have been hand-picked for this mission. So far, you have not been told what your mission is, because secrecy has been the essence of this operation. In a few minutes, you will all know what you are doing many thousands of kilometers away from your home, your family, and your country. Secrecy has been the key, because what you are about to embark on will change the history of mankind as we know it. For decades after decades, our great nation was hostage, beholden to either the forces of imperialism or

317

Zionism. If we were not suppressed by one, we were controlled by the other.

"For years, your leadership has worked hard to regain the respect our country once had, to right the wrongs of the years past. But we want to do more. We want to do more, because we understand the nature of the beast, because we understand how the world works. We, and billions of other oppressed people in the world, from Palestine to Puerto Rico, from Zanzibar to Zaire, have learnt our lessons. Cancer is not curable. You cure it for a couple of years, but it will come back, and, once it does, it will permeate your entire body until it takes over, completely and permanently. No, brothers, you don't cure the cancer; you remove the cancer; you uproot the cancer. You don't negotiate with the enemy; you destroy the enemy; you kill the enemy, and the enemy's father and mother and brothers and sisters. And, when you are done with them, you move on to their neighbors. A solution is not a solution unless it is the final solution.

"This newest addition to our arsenal of warfare, this submarine, is a state of art. But what is most important about this ship and this mission is that the real weapons you are going to use, the missiles we just loaded onto the ship, are, thanks be to the Almighty, the fruit of the sweat and hard work of your own fathers and brothers. The missiles loaded on this ship, the guns you will use to shame the world aggression and imperialism, are one hundred percent homemade. They are truly designed and made in the Islamic Republic. This is our answer to those who said we are incapable of facing the world, that we don't have the knowledge or the guts. Well, in a short few moments, you, the loyal soldiers of the Prophet – may peace be upon him – will prove them wrong."

The president did not tell them the blueprint for the

318

MIRVs was originally Chinese, and that the Iranians had bought them with a five million dollar bribe.

The president continued, "Today, in your capable hands, rests the means to deliver crushing blows to our eternal enemies, the Great Satan, the United States, and the aggressor Zionist, Israel. Today, with your action, the fate of billions of people on Earth will change. This is a new day. This is a sombre day. It was only weeks ago that the Great Satan and its allies attacked our country with all the force they have. They have caused massive damage. Your mothers, your sisters, your fathers and your little brothers have been murdered, murdered for nothing. This is a day of responsibility, and we can only praise God for trusting us with that responsibility."

With that, he led a prayer session deep into the sea waters. He then gave the PA system to the navy commander who, in turn, gave some coordinates as torpedo targets. It was only then that some of the crew realized what was about to happen. They eyed each other in disbelief, but no one dared say a word. The commander repeated the coordinates and asked for confirmation. He got the affirmative response.

The commander gave the PA back to the president, who ordered the launch of the first missile. There was a moment of total silence in the control room. You could hear a pin drop. Not that it mattered much. They could not see anything. Anchored deep in the middle of the ocean, their only 'window' to the outside world was the electronic blips they could see on their radar screens. To ensure maximum damage and increase the ferocity of the attacks, the president had ordered new missiles be fired within two minutes of each other. The MIRVs were like cluster bombs. Each of them had multiple warheads, and each one had a different target registered for it in the computerized control

319

system. The first missile was to hit New York City. The second was pointed at the capital, Washington, DC.

Within minutes, there were cheers all around the vessel as the blips indicated 'target encountered'. Everyone assumed the 'target' was the 'programmed target'. It took everyone a couple of minutes to realize the missiles had landed off course – in fact, way off course. They did now know where. At the exact same time as the president had issued his orders from the submarine, he had ordered a second set of attacks for surface-to-surface missiles to hit Tel Aviv from inside Iran. Jerusalem was not on the target list in case the missiles accidentally hit the Muslim holy places or the Palestinian areas. Again, instead of Israel, the missiles had landed nearby in the mountains of Kurdistan, not too far off the mountain ranges on top of which Charlie had taken refuge.

If the missiles heading toward Israel landed somewhere in the region, the ones whizzing towards New York did not land anywhere. Within minutes of having been fired, the missiles had slammed into incoming and intercepting missiles, and exploded over the Atlantic.

It did not take long before the mood inside the submarine did a one hundred and eighty degree flip. What was supposed to be a momentous day, a historic day, a joyous day, a day that would bring out the pride of the nation and its leadership, had turned to anything but that. It took just minutes before everyone knew the missiles had not hit their targets. The president and the commanders on board had also received immediate reports that Israel was not hit. No one knew why, but everyone knew they probably would not have enough time to find out, either. The president and his top commanders and aides had a split second to decide what to do next. It would not take spy agencies around the world long to perform some mathematical calculations and find out where the missiles had been fired from – and then unleash ferocious and lethal attacks on the submarine.

It was now clear that the game was over. They were found out; their bluff was called. They obviously did not know how, especially not at those early hours and minutes. What was clear was that something had gone awfully wrong. The only thing they needed to ponder now was whether they could get out of the waters and back home safely, or if they would soon die under the cold water. Natural instincts would tell any human being to run to safety, whichever way possible, but these were not 'normal' beings. These were people dedicated to a cause. These were people who – following the path of their Shiite *imams* of centuries past – believed in and valued the principle of martyrdom. These were people who believed in the concept of 'going all the way', the concept that they were there for a mission, a sacred mission, a holy mission, a worthy mission, one for which giving your life was not just an option, but a duty.

The reaction came much later than the Iranians had guessed. If they knew they had hours and hours, they would have deserted the submarine and run to safety somewhere, but they did not. Hours later, underwater torpedoes from nearby US warships and fighter jets taking off from various aircraft carriers rained all sorts of explosives on the Iranian submarine.

Once it started, it was over in minutes.

Although the Iranians had spent years planning for that day, the results were clearly disappointing to the leadership. So much thought, human and material resources had gone into planning for a day that was supposed to bring back the glory of the Islamic Empire, an empire that was kept at bay by kings who prided themselves on secularism.

Kings who believed in military domination. Kings who saw no use for religion. Now, however, the result was the annihilation of perhaps the most determined set of leaders – maybe not the smartest, but certainly the most conniving. The missiles meant for the United States exploded over water, and the ones meant for Israel malfunctioned and landed in almost-deserted mountainous areas of Kurdistan.

CHAPTER 39

SITTING on top of the mountain range, Charlie pondered the events of the past few months. He remembered the last night he and Sarah had had dinner together back home. He remembered the conversation well.

"Let's work backwards. Let's work on a plan that would *not* lead to your going to jail, or me. I am not worried about money, and neither should you be!"

Over the following days, they had done just that. They had worked out the problem. They had shared notes. They had combined their brainpower. Most important of all, they had put *their* interests above anyone else's. Despite their deep desire to do otherwise, they had come to the conclusion that what leaders of their own countries had done was regretful, if not treacherous and treasonous. The kingdom of Saudi Arabia had allowed, even encouraged, the entry of religious fanatics, some with intentions to harm and undermine the social fabric of the very country Saudi rulers called a 'friend' and an 'ally'.

Not only that, but the Saudis had instigated a foreign policy that forced the United States into a serious collision course with a rogue nation that had its own international ambitions and was only too happy to enter a 'forced' confrontation. For its part, the US leadership was not only sleep at the switch, to use a metaphor, but could perhaps be accused of wilful ignorance. This was a bunch of leaders who knowing they were being used, yet not only allowed it to happen, but took the bait and redirected their anger to settle political scores with another foe. This was a game of Russian roulette, with players who had nuclear weapons.

Charlie and Sarah had decided that what they needed to do was to find a way to avert the potentially tit-for-tat attacks. Sarah had insisted on her point: "leak it to the press," she had said several times. Every time, Charlie had insisted he could not do that, because he had taken an oath to protect government secrets, and that leaking it to the press would cause undue social panic and unrest. Then, they both started thinking, what if they leaked it, not to the press, but to a government that could and would take sufficient action to neutralize the outcome? There was only one country in the world that fit all the criteria. It had the capability. It had the determination, and it 'lived in the neighborhood', close enough to be able to take quick action against Iran: Israel. For a Saudi princess and a CIA agent who had spent most of his life dealing with the Arabs, neither Sarah nor Charlie was too keen on Israel, but they were both realistic enough to realize that it was the only solution.

However, Charlie's concern was much more than averting what could have been a nuclear attack, possibly on both the US and Israel. Big as that was in itself, Charlie wanted to do something that would also embarrass his bosses and his bosses' bosses, so that they would take a hard and cold look into intelligence failures of the system. Going to the Israelis would create a maximum shock to the system. If he did that, he would not only be fired, but possibly be put in jail for treason. The United States did not look kindly on unauthorised intelligence cooperation with foreign countries, especially with allies such as Israel. Charlie and Sarah decided it was worth it, but also realized they might have to leave the United States, permanently.

Lately, his memos had got sharper, edgier, and even accusatory, and the bosses had not liked it. They took his official passport away, and told him he needed permission to travel outside the country. It sounded draconian and unprecedented, even resembling the behavior of communist states, but this was an administration that took hasty decisions. Forced to live under a *de facto* house arrest, Charlie needed to find a way to get back abroad so he could blow the whistle on the imminent threat the country was under. That's when Sarah had come up with a solution. At their lavish house in LA, Sarah had taken Charlie to the pool area for fear that the house might be bugged. She had then unravelled her plan for him. What if Charlie could 'die' – temporarily?

"What if we could find a way for you to disappear, and then get you out of the country?"

"What does dying have to do with disappearing? Why would I die if I can just disappear?"

"Because 'dying' will buy us time. Right now, they are hot on your trail. They are probably watching you, and me, everywhere we go and everything we do. Your 'dying' will get them off our back, so we can get you out of the country. It's just a lot more convenient that way."

"How would I get out of the country?"

"You will have to use your connections to get yourself a fake passport. I can use my connections with rich Saudis to arrange for a private plane to take you out of the country. I will send you to Switzerland for the best plastic surgery money can buy. Then you can leave Switzerland and do what you want, and I will join you at some other point, and we can start a new life."

It was a risky plan. There was no guarantee, but, as long as they had considered the idea of passing on the information to Israel, Charlie figured it would be a good idea to run the whole plan by an old Israeli Mossad agent friend, Yaacov, known to friends as Cobie. Charlie and Cobie had known each other for years, back from the time Charlie had been a genuine journalist. They had lost touch for a few years, and then found each other again, quite accidentally. Charlie had been roaming the streets of Dubai one day when he had seen someone who looked exactly like Cobie. At first, it seemed impossible that an Israeli – let alone an Israeli spy – would be found walking freely in the streets of an Arab state with which Israel did not even have a peace treaty.

However, in reality, there were a few Israelis in the country, albeit under the guise of 'businessmen', and they were not there on Israeli passports. They were carrying American or European passports, some of them genuine, some forged. Charlie had been about to yell out Cobie's name, but logic soon prevailed. Instead, he had just walked fast until he caught up with his old friend, and tapped him on the shoulder. The Israeli suddenly jerked back, as if he was going into a self-defense mode and was getting ready to perform martial arts on his would-be hijacker. Cobie quickly recognized Charlie but, he, too, was not sure how to react. Any show of public affection or hugging an old friend could be detrimental to his safety and security if he was being followed. They decided, on the spur of the moment, to greet each other coldly.

"It is good to see you. I am staying at the Fairmont Hotel, room 651. Come by at 8 p.m."

That's all Cobie had said. He had then turned around and continued walking, as if he had just told a passerby that he was not the person the man was looking for. The two met a few hours later in Cobie's hotel room. Charlie did not needed to ask Cobie what he was doing. He would not have got a straight answer, anyway. Cobie had heard about Charlie's new career from mutual connections in Langley. Following the meeting in the hotel room, the two had promised to stay in touch, and had kept their word, more out of friendship than professional courtesy or cooperation.

This time around, sitting in LA, Charlie sent a message through a mutual friend that he was in trouble. Would Cobie consider making a short trip to Washington, to which Charlie could get without restriction? True to their friendship, Cobie sent a positive response. He could leave Tel Aviv within seventy-two hours. The meeting was set for a non-descript restaurant just outside Washington, in one of the Virginia suburban neighborhoods. He wanted to talk to him openly, but did not know how to start. He was uncomfortable telling Cobie about his new life, and his Israeli friend sensed that.

"You don't need to cut corners. I know you work for the agency."

"Phew!! That saves a lot of hassle." He wanted to find a way to express himself and thank him, but was simply unable to. "Sarah and I have been discussing a lot of things in our personal life and in my professional life. We have spent a lot of time going over what we know and what we think we should do. But I did not ask you to come here for personal reasons. As you said, I have been working for the agency for some time. I have come across certain information and, based on that, I have come to certain conclusions. They are more than educated guesses. Some of them are even shared by my bosses, and maybe even by their bosses. Some of the information has either come from Sarah and her connections, or been corroborated by her. I guess what I am trying to say is that this is not something she or I have come to lightly."

He then went through a synopsis of what he knew, and tried to draw as accurate a picture as he could. He had gone through the Iranian dealings years before with China, to get access to the MIRV blueprints, building them in-house, and then getting them out of Iran to Iraq and Sudan, and, finally, shipping the missiles with their nuclear warheads to the submarine in the Atlantic.

"Now, look, I don't know the target or targets. But, if they are moving nuclear warheads on missiles all the way from the Middle East to the Atlantic Ocean, and, if my information is correct, they are also moving more of their missiles inside Iran on mobile launchers to the south and the west; that tells me they are about to attack a target in the West, or a target in the Middle East, or both."

Cobie suddenly seemed pensive. It took him about a minute before he could open his mouth.

"So, you are telling me the United States of America is about to come under nuclear attack?"

"Maybe."

"And you are sitting here, telling me this, because...?"

"I am not just sitting here, telling you this. I am sitting here saying that I think my government thinks it is such a ludicrous idea that it is not taking me seriously. And, by the way, can you guarantee me those missiles pointing south and west are not meant for your country, either?"

"So what do you want from me?"

"I am giving this information to you so you can potentially save my country, and maybe even yours. Go back home and check the things I just said. I am sure you have your means. If you think I am right, push it to the highest level of your government, and have them talk to my government. If it comes from the senior leadership in your country, they will listen to it. But the minute this gets out, the government will find a way to prosecute me."

Technically, what he was doing was not illegal. Intelligence agencies all over the world share information. Agents share information. The kind of life they lead, the isolation of their world, the bubble in which they operate, all of those actually make it next to impossible for them to befriend anyone but each other.

What he was going to say next was going to be a problem.

"I might be saving my country, but I will still be guilty of sharing extremely sensitive intelligence information with another country."

"You still have not told me *how* I can help *you*?"

Charlie told him about Sarah's idea.

"If you are asking me to help you get a fake passport, you are asking *a lot.*"

"I am not asking you for anything now. I am asking you to check out my information and talk to your bosses. If my information is correct and you agree with my conclusions, then I would potentially be *saving* your country. I would think that would be priceless to you! Even if I am saving *my* country by giving you a tip, that tip would give you a trump card that you can hold over Washington for an incredible price!"

Cobie knew Charlie was right. Either way, Israel would gain. He agreed to look into Charlie's information and, if true, lobby for Charlie to get the help he needed.

It did not take Cobie long to verify the information. In fact, he and his bosses were more than ready to jump on the bandwagon of Charlie's conclusions. Israel was always much more gung-ho against Iran than Washington. Charlie could not tell whether Cobie and his bosses had really believed and verified what he had told them, or if Israel was just being opportunistic. Either way, he was convinced that something terrible was about to happen, and had Sarah's concurrence. What Israel's motivations were, he did not care much. Cobie had sent a coded signal that 'a friend would bring the package' to Washington in the coming weeks, and that a Jewish-American friend would bring it to Los Angeles.

True to his word, Cobie had sent a friend over to Charlie's house. One of the maids had opened the door and ushered him into the living room downstairs. He was an overweight man, short, with a bushy white beard. He certainly did not look like a Mossad agent. His face or manners were not easy to read, either, and he was not high on words. There was little pleasantry once he was inside. He did not even introduce himself, short of saying that Cobie had asked him to bring the 'package'. He had then simply left it on the living room table, shook Charlie's hand, and, in a cold and somewhat sarcastic tone, told him 'good luck' before leaving the room.

The plan worked just the way Sarah had planned it. That momentous night five years earlier that Sarah had made the frantic 911 emergency call was the night Charlie had reportedly died. Charlie had written the mysterious suicide note while the two of them sipped at their Dom Perignon champagne. They had saluted themselves, saying 'to ending the Age of Intolerance'. Sarah had administered a certain sedative –provided by the family doctor—that had temporarily decreased Charlie's heartbeat. Almost stopped it. Temporary sleep. Sarah then called the emergency number and the police and ambulance had arrived soon. Sarah's family doctor had been faster. He had arrived before the cops and, supposedly, certified the cause of death as natural. The police wanted to take the corpse, but Sarah and the doctor had prevented them. After Charlie's 'death', there was only one thing on Sarah's mind: whisking him out of the country, quickly.

With Charlie back in her arms, Sarah's next task was to get her husband out of the country, in case there was a sinister attack befalling the country, or if the authorities had figured out the couple's plans. With the fake American passport Charlie had received from Cobie and company –which used a pseudo name for Charlie – Sarah used a friend's private plane to fly them out to Switzerland, a country known as much for its reputed 'numbered' bank accounts as for its reputation for money's ability to buy anything, including good plastic surgeons operating very private clinics.

Sarah had secured the services of a doctor well known to the royal family members back home. In a country where the official count of princes and princesses runs over ten thousand, hardly anyone bothered to check on the facial or body work of other members. It was just one of those things they'd rather not dig into. After all, if you unearthed work done on someone else, others might well be tempted to do the same to you. Everyone just stayed clear of other people's business, and that kept everyone happy. With Charlie recovering fast from his face job, he could move around safely to do whatever was necessary to either prevent a war-like situation or, at least, minimize casualties if one broke out. While he and Sarah had trusted Cobie – and the state of Israel – with their most prized information and speculations, they had turned off future 'radio contact' on purpose. Charlie trusted Cobie on a personal level, but espionage and national security were dirty businesses. The less the Israelis knew about his detailed plans, the less the chances that they could betray him to the US government.

Armed with a new look that turned him into an

incognito man, Charlie boarded a plane for the Middle East, one last time. He and Sarah had talked about what they could do, personally, to minimize the damage. Despite her hatred of her family, and despite having numerous and serious differences with her country's policies, Sarah did want to find a way to save her country if it was going to be the target of any attacks. However, she and Charlie just could not find a way to trust anyone with such a huge and international secret. Any whisper of a possible attack against the United States of America – or Israel, for that matter – could, and probably would, have serious ramifications. Stock markets could crash. Economies could suffer badly. Old enemies might venture into war with each other, thinking there would be no superpower to stop them. The list could go on and on.

There was only one thing Charlie and Sarah could do at this point: sit back and watch the curtains fall, so to speak. Sarah did not particularly care for being a 'witness' to anything, but that was not the case for Charlie. Quite the contrary. His old journalistic feelings, sentiments, and desires were oozing out again. If there was a major event about to unfold, he needed to be there, or as close to it as possible. The problem was that he did not quite know where he needed to be this time. Where was the conflict going to flare up this time, or, for that matter, was it? Was he, or his Israeli co-conspirators, now totally barking up the wrong tree? He did not know the answer. No one knew.

The best he could do was guess. Partly out of sentimental reasons, and partly from of an educated guess, he decided he would go to the mountains of Kurdistan. He figured that Israel must be part of Iran's end-game plan, he knew many of the missiles were stationed in western Iran near the Kurdistan border, and he wanted to be in Kurdistan because he genuinely liked the Kurds, and wanted to be close to his friend, President Kurdawani. When his plane landed in Erbil in Kurdistan, the Kurdish president was on the tarmac waiting for him. Charlie had sent a message from Geneva through an emissary, saying he was coming and would appreciate a quick meeting with the president. He had also said the president might not recognise him, and that he would explain later. He did not expect the head of the state to greet him at the airport, but that was the kind of unassuming and friendly person Kurdawani was.

"Mr. President!" Charlie was really surprised by the red-carpet treatment and the presidential motorcade waiting to take him to the palace.

"Come on, Charlie, not after two decades. You've got to stop calling me 'Mr. President'".

"Okay. I promise to stop when we are in private."

"How is life? I didn't know journalism drives people to have plastic surgery," the president said with a chuckle, basically saying he knew Charlie was in the espionage business now, and that there was something so seriously wrong that he had to disfigure himself.

Charlie just took the verbal blow, got onto the motorcade, and spent the drive time on small talk and past memories. Once they were at the presidential palace, the usual lavish lunch was served, and Arabic Ouzo – the Arak – followed in large quantities. Charlie got to the point.

"I wish I could tell you everything I know, but I cannot. For now, you just have to trust me. You know I love the Kurds, and I particularly love you as a dear friend. I cannot guarantee that it will happen, but I have strong reasons to believe that there might be some, err – what should I call it? – missile activity in the region. I don't really think anyone is trying to attack the Kurdish Republic on purpose, but you know this region better than I do. Things have a way of going awry in this part of the world, and I don't want to see anything happen to you or your people. If I were you, I would send as many people as possible to secure areas, or as far away from towns and cities as possible. Just keep them safe somewhere."

Leaders do not like being told what to do. They become a leader so they can tell the rest of us what to do. They hire advisors and employ ministers to tell them what do to, not the other way around. They certainly do not like being told what to do by foreigners. However, Kurdawani was not an ordinary leader, and Charlie was not a 'foreigner' to the president. After years of knowing each other, and knowing now that Charlie was a spy, Kurdawani did not feel offended by being told he had to do something about something he did not know anything about. It was just one of those moments when trust mattered more than solid information or details, but he, like Charlie, was working on scant information and, therefore, could not really do much. The best he could do was guess. So that's what he did. He could not possibly evacuate all of Kurdistan, so he did the second best thing he could.

He emptied the biggest cities and those smaller ones that were historically controversial. He dispersed the population to remote areas, villages that had no history of conflict, villages that were unlikely to be targets. Kurdistan did not really have underground facilities, although the new republic had built a couple of emergency bunkers. Still, the best refuge from danger for most Kurds, especially the older generation that had grown up fighting neighbors and escaping the 'Butcher', was the mountain ranges. Close to a million people were sent to various locations while the president and a handful of his top aides and bodyguards took to an airbase close the mountains with Charlie. The air base was, naturally, protected by a solid air defense system, so it was safe and offered a newly built bunker of its own. The Kurds had learnt their lessons from the 'Butcher's' reign of terror. They had been attacked before with chemical and poisonous guns and bombs, and one could only imagine what else could happen.

As luck had it, they did not need to wait long. The air defense system siren started sounding just as the presidential team and Charlie were taking off aboard a military helicopter. It was not long before sound of explosions echoed from the valley below. Missiles parts could be seen scattering on the ground. In the early moments, it was more confusion than cohesion. People were running around rather aimlessly. Some were carrying the injured, others to find shelter from expected, or presumed, future attacks. Since the government had already taken precautionary action, there were no reports of too many casualties, but any injury or death was painful, and the president and his entourage were constantly trying to get information. Where were these coming from? What were the perceived targets? Who was trying to attack what? Why were a bunch of missiles landing mostly in empty areas around the mountains? For a while, it even looked like some of the missiles were coming from different directions. For now, Kurdawani had come to believe what Charlie, his old friend of many years, had told him, that something big was about to happen. So, for now, all they could do was wait on top of mountain ranges with military binoculars and stare at the impact sites, burning land, fleeing people and ambulances rushing from site to site.

It took all but hours before it was over. The 'all clear' sirens sounded all across Kurdistan, and the air defense systems were called off. For security reasons, the president and Charlie stayed behind a little bit longer. By the time it was time to come down from safety, it was also time for the Kurdish leader to get more answers from

Charlie. Yes, Charlie had, perhaps, saved many Kurdish lives, maybe even the president's, by giving advance warning, but he had not told them the story. The security services and the armed forces had combed the area and found remnants of Iranian and Israeli missiles. What was that about? Kurdawani was not 'asking' anymore. He was demanding.

By the time Charlie told him everything he knew, the president was fuming. He may have been the leader of a small country, but he was the leader of a sovereign country, nevertheless, and did not appreciate his country being used as a battleground in a proxy war. He did not know who to be mad at: the Iranians for putting the launch pads near the Kurdish border, or the Israelis for downing the missiles so the debris would fall on Kurdish land. However, by then, it was all over anyway. What was done was done, and all the Kurds could do was complain. They knew that would not get anywhere, anyway. Even though the missile remnants clearly had Persian and Hebrew writing on them, forging insignia was not unheard of in the secretive realm of espionage or military blackmail.

If President Kurdawani was confused by what was happening on his land, so were the Americans.

CHAPTER 40

IN the weeks after Charlie's conversation with Cobie and the Israelis' check on Charlie's information, Jerusalem had tried to have discreet conversations with various quarters in Washington. It was certainly a sensitive issue, and the Israelis had to be careful how to approach it to get the results they wanted. Relations between Iran and Israel had been a complicated one, going back all the way to the *shah's* time. The *shah* was known to have had good relations with Israel. His regime bought tons of arms from Israel. The Israelis had trained the dreaded Iranian security agents. While the relations had, on the surface, gone south after the mullahs came to power, that was just the surface of things. In fact, the Israelis had continued to supply arms to the Iranians. The reason was rather simple. It was not that the Israelis liked Iran or the Iranians, even though a massive number of Israelis were Iranian-born-Jews, but Israel never defined its relations that way. For the Israelis, it was strategic.

They liked the *shah* because he offered an opportunity for the Jewish state to gain a foothold in a traditionally hostile region. Israel hoped the clerical regime would offer the same. They were wrong, and the more the clerics stayed in power, the more Israel became aware of its strategic mistakes, but, instead of accepting the reality and dealing with it, Israel tried to discredit the Iranian regime, fanatical and fundamentalist as it was. In the end, Israeli had cried wolf against Iran far too many times. Most people simply did not believe Israeli when it said Iran was on the verge of this or that. Every time the Israelis had done that, it had backfired. It had become clear that the Israelis would just do anything to push Washington into a corner on Iran.

It had also become clear to Washington that Israelis were not always honest with their biggest ally in the world. So, when they had tried to approach the White House and the CIA in the aftermath of the meeting with Charlie, they had received the usual cold shoulder. The Israelis had pretty much told their American counterparts the essence of what Charlie had told them, which was already available in CIA cables, but the Americans had not taken it seriously. For one thing, they assumed – not without justification, it appeared – that the Israelis had a mole inside who was leaking information to them.

The Israelis had tried to tell the US administration that the Iranians were up to the equivalent of a 'total war', and that nuclear missiles were to rain on the United States and its staunchest ally in the Middle East. Fairy tales, the Israelis were told. The Iranians were not that smart. They would not think that far ahead. They would not dare mess with the biggest power in the world. They were not suicidal. That's where they were wrong. The top Iranian leadership had no qualms about being suicidal. For the leadership, committing suicide or launching suicidal operations was not seen in the same light as the people in the West saw these things. For them, suicide was called by another name: martyrdom.

Martyrdom was a centuries-old tradition for the Shiites, dating back to the battles in which *Imam* Hussein, the revered *imam* of Islam, sacrificed his life and the life of others in a battle to fight 'evil'. That momentous battle in Karbala, Iraq, had always been a guide map for the religious Shiites, who saw personal sacrifice nothing short of a duty that would help right historic wrongs. The Americans, obviously, knew the historical context of it, but had not grasped the seriousness of the Iranians' intent. They had not adequately understood what this operation meant to the Shiite psyche, to the fanatic leadership's psyche. All that became clear the morning Charlie and Kurdawani were watching missiles fly over their heads.

Somewhere in the middle of the Atlantic Ocean, the sky had looked like the Fourth of July. The Iranian submarine had fired missiles towards the eastern coast of the United States, but the missiles did not have to travel long. Within minutes of being in the air, loud explosions had rattled the sea waters. Debris had fallen all over the place. Since the radars had obviously picked up the US-bound missiles first, Washington and the Pentagon were already on alert, high alert. Memories of September 11, 2001, were becoming fresh in everyone's mind again. People were trying not to panic, but, in fact, they were. The White House had immediately ordered an inter-agency working group to do nothing else but monitor the situation, and take whatever action or actions were necessary. The air forces and coast guard were activated, and all leaves canceled. In the chaos of the moment, no one knew what would or might come next.

Maybe there was another attack coming. No one could say there was no precedent for it. By the time the reports started coming in about the Atlantic incident, reports from the Middle East were detailing events in Kurdistan, and those reports had a lot more details than those coming from the Atlantic, because remnants of the missiles had landed on the ground. Pictures showed the various parts, the insignia, and the engine numbers, *etcetera*. In the middle of the ocean, debris was hard to come by, though teams were dispatched at once. The Pentagon had contacted the Israelis, and they had, indeed, confirmed that their missiles had intercepted Iranian missiles fired from near Kurdistan. They also confirmed, much to the embarrassment of Washington, that they had just saved millions of American lives in New York and Washington by firing missiles from an undisclosed location to bring down missiles fired from the Atlantic.

By then, the mood in Washington had completely changed. The idea that a foreign country had now saved the United States – any country, even a close ally – was politically untenable, if not morally embarrassing. It wanted to save face, but did not have all the facts; indeed, it had little facts other than that the missiles had been fired from somewhere in the Atlantic. Short of having better coordinates for a fixed target, there was little it could do. Just knowing where the missiles had been fired from did little for the American policymakers because the missiles could have been fired from a point deep down in the sea, and activated by remote. The Americans had no reason to believe that there was any human being at that site from which the missiles were fired. They – up until that point – had no reason to believe that a handful of martyrdom-seeking leaders were about to bring death, not only to themselves, but to about fifty crew members in the submarine.

For that matter, they did not even know that the Iranians had used the MIRVs and, therefore, could not even pressure MIRV-producing countries for more information. It was simply too early in the game to get accurate information, and America just had to trust whatever Israel was giving it.

However, the Israelis knew that the missiles were fired from an actual submarine. They knew where it was and who was in it, and they knew what would happen if they gave its location to Washington, but there was a problem. A big problem. For reasons only Charlie and the Israelis knew, Charlie had preconditioned any help to Israel on the Jewish state not releasing any information to the US government that would identify the location of the Iranian submarine in the Atlantic Ocean. The issue became a serious point of contention between Washington and Jerusalem. The Americans simply could not understand why the Israelis were now withholding the last piece of the puzzle. Washington had come to Israel's rescue virtually every time. Israel had always got everything it wanted from Washington. With such strong allies on Capitol Hill and 1600 Pennsylvania Avenue, there seemed little need for Jerusalem to play hardball on an issue it knew was so important to America.

However, Israel could afford to play hardball now, because it wanted something from Washington, but something that was totally not negotiable in the eyes of the United States govermment. For decades, the United States had kept, in a maximum security jail, a man convicted of spying for Israel. The issue had been sour point in the bilateral relations for decades. Washington was utterly and genuinely disgusted that Israel would run an espionage ring inside the United States. That ran against the time-old tradition that friends do not spy on friends. However, Israel had spied on the US, had been caught red-handed, and was now paying for it. The man doing the spying was going to pay for it for the rest of his life; he was sentenced to remain in a high-security jail, with not even an option for parole or brownie points for good behavior. If there was ever a perfect time for Israel to win the release of its man, this was it. Israeli bosses knew they probably would not find a higher card in the deck than the ace they already possessed. As much as they cared for what Charlie had done for them, the favor had been rendered; it could not be taken back; the nation was safe, and it was time to move ahead.

Ungrateful? Maybe. Practical? Absolutely. Biting the bullet was as hard for Washington. All these years, it had claimed the spy case was totally non-negotiable, that it was completely off the table. It could say so because it held the trump card in the relations. It knew that years of political, moral and financial support carried more leverage than Israel could ever pay back. However, it never foresaw a time when the tables would be turned. Never, until today. In the end, a deal was made. In the middle of the night and under the cover of darkness, a rugged looking man with a slightly bent back, white hair, and white beard emerged from a Midwest jail, resembling nothing like a man dangerous to the national security of the world's remaining superpower.

Once Israel had confirmation from its ambassador on the ground that the spy had walked out a free man, the coordinates of the Iranian submarine hiding deep in the waters of the Atlantic Ocean were transmitted to Washington. Minutes later, the President of the United States, in his capacity as the Commander in Chief of the nation's armed forces entered the Situation Room in the White House, and authorized unlimited unleashing of the conventional weapons on the enemy submarine. While US submarines in the area inched in toward the target and fired their torpedo, air force jetfighters swooped over the area to drop their heavy bombs, while a second squadron zoomed in to confirm first hand that the 'enemy is smoking'.

CHAPTER 41

IT took the international press all but a few days to get hold of the story and flash it on its front pages. The initial reports came from the Middle East. Not only was a missile blowing up in the land-locked Kurdistan hard to suppress, but the Kurds themselves could use some international pity and solidarity. Plus, of course, in the age of 24/7 international satellite broadcasting, it did not take long for the news to reach all across America. One interested reader was Captain Haggerty of the LAPD, the officer who had found – and supposedly kept – a suicide note from Charlie. The shock on his face was evident as he read a news agency wire report printed in one of LA's morning papers.

KIRKUK, Kurdistan (AP) – The scene in the mountainous areas in north Kurdistan today was one of anger and despair, with the people being cognisant that the situation could have been worse.

For the past few days, the government had encouraged citizens to move out of certain cities and neighborhoods in the country to take shelter in government-approved facilities. And they had reason for doing so.

Shortly before 2 p.m., the scene down the mountain valleys looked like a war zone. Just like in a war, the immediate situation was one of chaos and confusing reports. Out of nowhere, skies over the area lit up like it was Christmas, except it was exploding missiles that had lit the skies.

It is still not clear how many people died or were wounded, and how many of those suffered critical injuries. But the reason it was not worse is clear: the president has a good friend; the Kurds have a good friend.

According to several sources, an American undercover agent identified as Charles Shahin flew in on a chartered flight to warn the president of the impending dangers.

Then the story went on about the origin of the missiles and the Israeli involvement, *etcetera*. Officer Bob Haggerty did not have to read any longer. All he had to do was see the picture of Charles Shahin. Haggerty remembered the name well, but the picture did not look anything like the man he remembered. He did not have not to wonder why. The story had already told him that Charlie had come from Geneva, where he had gone from his home in LA. For an experienced officer, he did not need to know more. He figured the suicide note was a fake. All he could do was smirk.

If Haggerty could see a positive ending in the story, 'Hashimoto' and his uncle were less happy about the finale of the submarine story, which also came out within days. Part of the deal between the Israelis and the Americans was that Washington would take the credit for destroying the Iranian submarine. Whatever information the Israelis had given out, including the names of the Iranian leadership, was going to come out from the White House.

For 'Hashimoto', nothing could have been more painful than reading Sade's name in the papers. He could not, did not want to, believe some of the stuff the papers said about her. A revolutionary. A terrorist. Secret operative. Dangerous. *Etcetera, etcetera.* He read what US government sources had said about her and the Iranian leadership's efforts to bomb the United States, how Sade had recruited and trained 'terrorist cells' around the world, and how she had supervised 'subversive activities' around the world. 'Hashimoto' was conflicted. On one hand, he did not want to believe the stories, but how could he deny the fact that he himself had been recruited by Sade to be part of those 'terrorist cells', be one of the 'subversive' elements? After all, he had helped blow up oil facilities that nearly crippled a nation's economy for a while. However, that was not the time for philosophical arguments. He was feeling a personal loss. He was young, and not too refined in international politics. He was still trying to master the ins and outs of personal relations. His focus was not on himself. It was on Sade.

His uncle, General Jian, on the other hand, was not thinking of Sade. He was thinking of himself and his own role in the *fiasco*. He was probably the only one alive who knew how the Iranians had got hold of the missiles fired from that ill-fated submarine in the middle of the Atlantic Ocean. Other Chinese submarines in the Atlantic had registered the explosions on the radars, and General Jian was pretty sure the missiles were MIRVs, albeit Iranian-made ones. The general was not what one might call 'pro-American', but he sure had no reason to wish the superpower and its people ill, either. He had no intention of getting involved in what could turn out to be World War Three. He had had no idea the Iranians had successfully made the MIRVs, let alone being able to smuggle them halfway around the world and load them onto the submarine. As he sat in his office in Beijing, he, too, was immersed in sorrow, and his guilt did not go away. Months later, he committed suicide.

Hajj Mohsen was probably the only one without a sense of guilt or sorrow. He, too, had seen the name of the people on the Iranian submarine and recognized Sade's name. However, for him, unlike 'Hashimoto' and General Jian, there was no person attachment to the story. 'Hashimoto' felt he had a 'personal' relationship with Sade. The general had got involved, in part, because he felt the Chinese system had been corrupted, and could not see a reason why he should not benefit while many of his other friends did. For Hajj Mohsen, it was about money from day one. He had become a conduit for Sade's – or the Iranian government's – money, funding 'opposition' movements in the Gulf, but he was not an Arab or an Iranian. He did not particularly have an attachment to either side of the story. He was just making money by illegally transferring money.

By the time he read Sade's name in Dubai's morning papers, Hajj Mohsen had made millions. He bought himself a nice large apartment in a posh neighborhood of the city, purchased the car his wife had been nagging about for years, and resigned to her children becoming just another bunch of nouveau riche snobs in a city so full of them already. Aside from the fact that he had made millions, he was also politically free. For years, the Emirati leadership had squeezed him for money and information. They had also squeezed Washington for all sorts of financial, political and military advantages, saying they could offer valuable information on Iranian intelligence activities in the region. Every time, they would only offer the equivalent of small proffers, leaving Washington hanging and wanting more. Now the Iran 'file' was closed. No one could harass Hajj Mohsen anymore, and Washington would not remain beholden to Dubai. That chapter was closed, for good.

346

CHAPTER 42

MEANWHILE, Charlie and Sarah had gone ahead with their plan that they had concocted back in Los Angeles, not knowing anything about what the Israelis had done, or what the Americans managed to do. Charlie had said his goodbye to President Kurdawani and other Kurdish friends, and flown off to Amman, then Paris.

Oh, how he loved Paris! Every time he flew into the Charles de Gaulle airport, the first thing he did was sing the famous Ella Fitzgerald song to himself:

> *I love Paris in the spring time*
> *I love Paris in the fall*
> *I love Paris when it sizzles*
> *Or when it drizzles*

The tube ride from CDG to Gare de Nord was always a brute contrast to Ella's portrayal of Paris. Charlie always found it ironic that, within minutes of leaving the airport, when the train was still in the capital's suburbs, it would be filled with blacks and Arabs heading to the center of town. They worked there all day, but always went back to the suburbs, because that was the only place they could afford. No 'foreigner' lived on the Sein, unless you were a rich Arab or had bought your place decades ago. That was for the 'true' Parisians. The second-class citizens lived either on the periphery or places around the train stations, like Gare de Nord, Gare de l'Est or Pigale. Once again, inside, the train terminal looked like it did not belong to the neighborhood. More often than not, it was just full of tourists, mostly Europeans and Americans.

He soon bought himself a ticket from the ground-floor sales office. Destination: Perpignan. The train ride from Paris to Perpignan was always a joy for Charlie. It kind of reminded him of taking the Amtrak from Washington to New York City. The scenery was beautiful. Mile after mile of green – in the summer – or snow-capped flatlands – in the winter. The ride in the summer was particularly pleasant. The closer the train got to the coastal cities, the more cheerful the whole mood of the place and people became. It was just that summery feeling that excited people.

Charlie's favourite pastime when taking the train was to sit in his chair for the first hour or so, and then promptly disappear into the cafeteria wagon. There was something about sitting in the train, sipping at a glass of French wine, reading a good book or typing on his computer, all the while listening to good music on his iPod. So, that day, on the train from Paris to Perpignan, Charlie decided not to break the habit. He took a copy of the latest political best seller he had picked up from a bookstore in the States, and started reading. He had carried the book all the way from LA to Geneva to Kurdistan, but his mind just wasn't into it. He had not even read a page.

Now, however, the espionage intrigue was over. The whole game was over. Sitting on the train and having a drink, he – for the first time in a very long time – felt that a big burden had been lifted off his shoulders, like a new chapter was beginning in his life. He felt relieved. As the

348

train passed through farmlands, vacation homes and beach towns, and, perhaps, in tune with his new light-hearted mood, he also started thinking of all the things he had not done in his life, all the things he always wanted to do, and never had. He remembered how he had always worked full time and gone to school full time, from high school to university to graduate school. He remembered how had never gone to parties, never dated enough girls, never taken enough vacations – not even after knowing Sarah.

This, he thought, was the beginning of the rest of his life. He would now do all the things he had not done before, minus the dating part, of course. For he was now on his way to see the woman of his life. He was a new person, literally. He had a new face, had legally changed his name, and, much to his dislike and consternation, was homeless. Ever since he had poured his heart out to the Israelis, the American government had made it clear that Washington did not want him in the country again. He was, obviously, fired from his job. The government had come to know about his escape and plastic surgery. As far as the government of the United States of America was concerned, he did not exist anymore, and that hurt. The country to which he had given everything was now turning its back on him, because he had tried to right the wrongs of how it was run. He understood that it was politics, but that did not diminish the pain. As the train stopped at Perpignan, Charlie felt a tear falling from each eye.

From the station, he rented a car from one of the car agencies at the corner of the train station. He had called before, and the agency had reserved a convertible Peugeot 307 CC for his arrival. He loved driving a convertible on the road between Perpignan and Couiza, where he had built a villa for himself. It was his pride and joy. Sarah was okay with it, but did not like it as much as he loved it. She was more of a posh, Paris girl, or nice-area person, but Perpignan and a small, typically French village in Couiza were not exactly her type. Nevertheless, over the years, and because of his love for the place, she had warmed up to it. He had bought the land many years ago and built a classy, but small, three-bedroom, two-floor villa with a swimming pool. He had named it Chez Maria, after his good friend, Maria, an American friend he had known for years. They had become good friends.

He had been close to her, and she to him. Then she got cancer, for the second time. At first, everyone thought she would beat the disease the same way she had the first time. She believed it, too, but then she got worse. At five feet two inches, her body was not exactly strong, even though her heart and faith were. Eventually, the doctors had told her it was terminal, but no one knew how much time she had. The doctors said anywhere between months and years. It was too vague to mean anything to anyone. Charlie had spent part of the summer she died in Paris, but never got to see her. He wanted to. In fact, he had arranged the trip in great part so he could see her, but she had told him not to come. The latest round of chemotherapy had taken its toll on her, and she was not up to receiving guests. Neither one of them had thought then that she might pass away so quickly. It was barely four months later that she went away – for good. Her departure had a lasting impact on him. He missed her. He missed her a lot. When the house was built in Couiza, he did not have to think twice before deciding to name it after her.

By the time Charlie arrived, Sarah was already there, had put her suitcases down and fixed herself a drink, and was waiting in the living room. He noticed there was a letter on the kitchen counter. He asked Sarah if she knew anything about it. She said she had found it at the door when she arrived, and had brought it in.

He did not seem to have expected it, and was not in a rush to open it. Kissing his wife and fixing himself a drink were more important. The two of them had a lot to talk about. As he finally made time to pick up the letter, he could hear his heart beating harder.

Dear Charlie,

You probably have not heard this, because it just happened yesterday and your government is going to hold on to the announcement for a couple of days more. While you were on the plane, the government of the United States destroyed the Iranian submarine, Entegham, in the Atlantic Ocean.

Charlie felt a chill go down his spine. All the warmth his martini had given him suddenly disappeared.

I know, at this point, you feel betrayed. I know you are telling yourself 'we had a deal. They were not supposed to give the exact location of the submarine to my government'. The reality is that we did not have too much of a choice. The history of this great Jewish nation of ours, just as the history of your great nation, has been nurtured by the sacrifice of people who have been willing to work hard and take risks. We had to make a choice. You might not like it, but it was a duty we felt we had to render to secure the freedom of someone who has worked hard for us. But we know that this is personal to you. We understand it, and that's why we felt we need to write to you personally. Charlie, we are sorry for your loss. She was not close to you. You had parted ways decades ago, but she was still blood related, and we wanted to express our condolences to you.

As Charlie put down the letter, it dawned on him that the secret he had buried in his heart and from everyone except his wife, and a couple of spies who had made it their business to find out, was finally dead, too, with the sinking of the submarine.

Sade, the ranking advisor to the President of Iran, was Charlie's sister.

As Charlie tried to grapple with the news of his estranged sister, he could not stop thinking about how circumstances had shaped his life and that of his sister, how different they had become as people. He tried to think of a moment or a point in time, or maybe an event that had separated their lives and beliefs so passionately and so irreconcilably, but he could not. He could not find one momentous second or hour or week, or even year. He could do nothing but remain solid in his conviction that they were different from birth, and that circumstances and events had only helped buttress and shape who they already were. For Charlie, it was, perhaps, his early exposure to the American culture, politics and media. Long before he had actually escaped Iran and sought political asylum in the United States, it was the *Voice of America* he listened to. He spent his afternoons mingling with American tourists in town. He had kept up with the Nixon impeachment scandal when he was a tiny kid. He was drawn to the people, the culture and the politics before he had a reason to, or even knew it was happening to him. By the time he had actually moved to the States, he did not need convincing which culture was a better fit for him, or to which he could plead allegiance.

Sade, on the other hand, had grown up not being exposed first hand to any other culture. She had read a lot about other people, languages, politics and culture, but only academically, philosophically – only on the intellectual

352

level. So, her inclination, mentally speaking, was more to critique her Iranian culture, not getting attached to another one that she could call her own, that she could, or would want to, adopt as her own. By the time she was in Dubai, her mental and ideological frame was leaning towards defending the system, not destroying it. In Dubai, she had learnt from the Emiratis how to build from scratch, how to believe in a dream of something that might seem unreachable. She had also believed in the power of determination, regardless of flawed the ultimate goal might be. She saw how the Emiratis built a dreamland out of sand dunes, got arrogant in the process, and fell, but remained proud, defensive, and even more determined. If a country that had been nothing just decades ago could become an international example, why couldn't Iran, with thousands of years of glorious history, regain its place in history?

Dubai did not teach Sade anything, the same way America did not teach Charlie anything fundamentally new. Each person already had his or her convictions. The surroundings just solidified them.

As he played more with such thoughts in his mind, Charlie realised that, more than being a story about en evil leadership bent on dominating perceived historical enemies, this was a story about a brother and a sister, two determined, hard-working individuals who saw their future in serving totally different masters, for different reasons, and in different ways. One paid for that mission with her life; the other suffered for years, but ultimately saved many other lives. They had not spoken a word since Charlie had immigrated to America when he had been a kid. The family had disowned him, and he had disowned them. However, he had always kept a distant eye on his little sister, even if he never called to say 'hi'.

Sarah just took the letter from Charlie's hands, read

it, and then burnt it in the fireplace, and whispered into his ear, "It is now *truly* the end of The Age of Intolerance."

LaVergne, TN USA
04 May 2010
181394LV00002B/3/P